THE LAST
MISSION OF THE LIVING
A FUTURISTIC ZOMBIE NOVEL

RHIANNON FRATER

The Last Mission of the Living
A Futuristic Zombie Novel
By Rhiannon Frater

ISBN-13: 978-1500959357
ISBN-10: 1500959359

Edited by Erin Hayes
Copyedited by Kody Boye
Cover artwork by Claudia McKinney
Interior Formatting by Kody Boye
Cover Typography by Corey Hollins

http://rhiannonfrater.com/

This book is a work of fiction. People, places, events and situation are the product of the author's imagination. Any resemblance to actual persons, living, dead or undead, or historical events, is purely coincidental.

For the fans of *The Last Bastion of the Living*

Dedicated with much affection and gratitude to my husband for encouraging me to be open to another novel set in The Bastion

Special thanks to Tim Kirk, who helped create the Constabulary and the Science Warfare Division. You'll always be my hero!

OTHER NOVELS BY
RHIANNON FRATER

Zombies
As The World Dies Trilogy
The First Days: As The World Dies Book 1 (Tor)
Fighting to Survive: As The World Dies Book 2 (Tor)
Siege: As The World Dies Book 3 (Tor)

Untold Tales Series
As The World Dies Untold Tales Volume 1
As The World Dies Untold Tales Volume 2
As The World Dies Untold Tales Volume 3

Living Dead Boy and the Zombie Hunters

Vampires

Vampire Bride Series
The Tale of the Vampire Bride (Vampire Bride 1)
The Vengeance of the Vampire Bride (Vampire Bride 2)

Pretty When She Dies Trilogy
Pretty When She Dies
Pretty When She Kills
Pretty When She Destroys

Pretty When She... Universe
Pretty When They Collide

Young Adult Supernatural
The Midnight Spell (co-authored with Kody Boye)

Short Story Collections
Blood & Love and Other Vampire Tales
Cthulhu's Daughter and Other Horror Tales
Zombie Tales From Dead Worlds

Apocalyptic Ficiton
The Mesmerized

Supernatural
Dead Spots (Tor, Fabruary 2015)

PART 1

THE END OF THE BATTLE

"Lindsey, I've reached the subway door," Castellan Dwayne Reichardt's voice said.

Specials Sergeant Lindsey Rooney cast a wary look over her shoulder at the arguing officials at the far end of the Constabulary Command Center. The gleaming black and stainless steel austerity of the room was offset by the diffused glow of the vid screens and workstations. Fingers flowing over her console, she replied in a tone that she prayed didn't sound too edgy, "Deactivating the locks now."

Hopefully, if Dwayne detected her nervousness, he'd believe it was associated with his mission. Vanguard Maria Martinez was hiding in the valley that surrounded The Bastion, the last human city on the planet, awaiting rescue along with one of her squad members. Lindsey and Dwayne both had a vested interest in her retrieval. The vanguard was Lindsey's best friend and the woman Dwayne loved.

As the tiltrotors destroyed the last remaining throngs of the undead, a secret battle was taking place in the upper echelons of the government and military for control of the city. Two of the major players in that fight were in a heated argument on the other side of the room.

Commandant Adeleke Pierce stood with her arms folded across her chest, facing Dr. Beverly Curran of the Science Warfare Division. As the officer in charge of the Constabulary, everything happening within and outside The Bastion was of greatest concern to the formidable commandant. Pierce was imposing with her tall, slim build and strong-featured face, but she was also beautiful, with ebony skin and dark eyes. Her black hair was twisted into many braids, then coiled into a tight bun on top of her head, giving her a sterner appearance.

The scientist Commandant Pierce was facing was just as intimidating. Dr. Curran's expression was completely devoid of emotion, and with her blond hair skimmed back from her face, she resembled a statue. Lindsey wished she could hear what they were saying, but she had to concentrate on making sure Dwayne was safe.

Lindsey focused on the vid screens in front of her. She'd hacked into the city security systems to open the blast doors in one of the old subway stations so that Dwayne could enter the valley and find the two surviving soldiers. What she was doing could be considered treason, yet, to save her best friend, it was worth the risk.

After fussing with the tendrils of blond hair threatening to fall into her eyes, Lindsey flipped her long braid over one shoulder. There were much more important things to concentrate on other than her hair unfurling from her military hairdo and being an annoyance while she was trying to perform her duties.

Humanity was on the verge of victory over the Inferi Scourge. For nearly half a century, the undead throngs had kept the survivors of the apocalypse trapped within the high walls of The Bastion. The millions of Inferi Scourge that had once resided in the valley were now reduced to radically low numbers, the end result of the secret mission in which Maria had been involved. Tiltrotors from the city now filled the night sky, obliterating the remains of the living dead. Terrifyingly, the men and women in the aircraft were also seeking to destroy her best friend.

It was very difficult for Lindsey to process what had happened. Maria had volunteered for a top-secret mission nearly a half year before. The objective was to seal the massive gate that was the only entrance to the valley where The Bastion was located and eradicate the Inferi Scourge. It wasn't until after Maria had vanished into the depths of the Science Warfare Division Facility that Lindsey had uncovered that Dr. Curran, an SWD scientist, had altered the virus that made the Inferi Scourge and infected Maria. The mutated virus had made Maria an Inferi Boon, a thinking undead creature able to walk among the Inferi Scourge and kill them without fear or danger.

Now, according to Dr. Curran, the modified virus was returning Maria to life and possibly making her immortal. This information was unknown to the top officials in the SWD. They had ordered the eradication of the Inferi Boon after the mission was a success. Only Maria and one other squad member were alive and on the run. If the SWD found out about the virus restoring life and possibly granting eternal life, Maria would be in even more danger. Lindsey didn't want to see her best friend vanish into the secret laboratories of the SWD.

Dwayne was violating the security protocols with the knowledge of the commandant of the Constabulary to retrieve Maria and bring her back to headquarters. Lindsey hoped they could keep Maria safe from the SWD, but wasn't certain if it was possible. The SWD's grab for power had effectively destabilized the government and robbed the Constabulary of a lot of its power.

The security camera feed revealed the doors creeping open and Dwayne slipping outside. He was a dark, sleek shape in the black armor he'd somehow acquired from the Science Warfare Division. Lindsey suspected Dwayne's assistant, Petra, had secured it for him. There was little love lost between the military officers of the Constabulary and the scientists and security officers of the SWD, but Petra appeared to have some contacts within the SWD.

The tall, almost too-thin woman sat beside Lindsey at a workstation, monitoring transmissions on the battlefield while also typing away on a secured pad. The tension in Petra's jaw and shoulders revealed her anger at Dwayne for leaving without telling her. Lindsey wasn't too sure why Petra was so upset. Dwayne would be returning with Maria shortly. Of course, it was highly irregular for the castellan, one of the highest-ranking officers of the Constabulary and the person charged with the city's security, to be out on the field. It was even more irregular for him to be alone on a mission.

The feed from the cameras was on a loop to The Bastion City Control Center, but Lindsey watched the live footage nervously. It was in night vision, since all the lights were off in the tunnel system below the city to conserve energy.

Beside Lindsey, Petra scowled, then tapped her headset to kill the sound. "They're dispatching a squad near the station Dwayne is exiting," Petra said in a low voice.

"How close?" Lindsey asked, alarmed.

"Within a kilometer. It's the mining facility."

Lindsey pulled up a schematic of the valley resources and several maps. Layering them swiftly on her vid screens, her pulse accelerated. The armor Dwayne was wearing would keep him invisible to the scanners. "They'll have to be right on top of him for visual detection, so he should be fine. The castellan will know to take cover if the tiltrotors get too close."

Petra's thin lips set into a fine line, then she shook her head. "I hate him being out there. He should have taken someone else with him."

"Did you tell him that?"

"Of course! And..." Petra waved her long, gaunt hand irritably. "He wouldn't listen. Which makes me very nervous."

"Well, he is a commanding officer."

"Yes, but he *always* listens to my advice. I think something more is going on." Petra gave the two arguing women on the far side of the room a wary look.

A beep indicated a message coming in from the castellan. Lindsey switched over to his comm feed.

"Lindsey, open the door to the subway."

Struggling to decide if she should tell him about the SWD squad being deployed near him or not, Lindsey obeyed but didn't say anything.

Petra leaned toward her, observing Lindsey's fingers moving over the panels on the workstation. "Is he coming back in?"

Lindsey shrugged, uncertain.

The vid screens revealed the opening subway doors in an eerie inverted image. A man's form stepped through the opening, then abruptly slumped.

Lindsey and Petra exchanged frightened looks.

Another figure pushed the body into the tunnel just before the doors shut again.

"Lindsey," came the castellan's voice.

Lindsey was both relieved and unnerved. "Yes?"

"Denman was an Anomaly. Dr. Curran must tell Commandant Pierce what she told me about the virus she gave everyone, but Maria. His body *must* be destroyed immediately."

Lindsey stared at the corpse in the tunnel. The blood in her veins was thick with ice. Glancing at Petra, she saw the other woman was waiting nervously, her bony fingers clenched into a fist. "Understood." Lindsey muted her headset. "Denman was an Anomaly. The castellan killed him."

Petra's eyes flared with fear. "He's not coming back! Shit! I knew something felt wrong! He's going to go out and deal with Maria personally and then..."

With a sinking heart, Lindsey realized Petra was right, and feared what that might mean. She reopened the comm link. "You're not coming back, are you?"

"No, I'm not." The castellan's voice was firm.

Lindsey shut her eyes, her heart breaking. If Denman turned into an Anomaly, was Maria turning too? What did he mean about a different virus? "What are you going to do?"

"What I have to do."

The feed went dead.

"Oh, shit," Lindsey whispered. "Shit."

"Tell him about the squad," Petra said urgently.

"I can't. He killed the feed." Lindsey took off her headset.

"What are you going to do?" Petra asked, darting a worried look at Dr. Curran.

"I need to talk to Commandant Pierce." Lindsey had no idea what she should do about Dwayne. If Maria was infected and going to turn, then it was a kindness to kill her, but she hated to think of him taking his own life out there. Yet, it was his choice. The city was teetering on the edge of chaos. Life was difficult. Maybe Dwayne didn't want to continue without the woman he loved.

Motioning to Vaja, her tech wizard boyfriend, Lindsey grabbed her cane and slid to her feet.

Vaja hurried over in a cloud of nervous energy. Tall, slender, and sporting a head of dark mussed hair, Vaja was good-looking. It helped that he was brilliant and loved prowling around the hidden depths of The Bastion's computer grid. He was not a soldier, but she'd asked him to assist the Constabulary fight off the SWD coup d'état.

"The worm that will deliver the information we gathered is ready to download to all the wristlets," he said, clearly thinking she wanted an update. Tapping his own wristlet proudly, he waited for her to shower him with praise.

"I need you to help Petra monitor what's going on. I need to take care of something," Lindsey said.

Looking a little deflated, Vaja nodded. "Fine. But once this is done, I'm not doing any more of this." He gave the commandant a dark look. "I refuse to be conscripted."

"You won't be conscripted," Petra sniffed.

"I also don't want to be prosecuted," Vaja continued.

"The commandant already said you don't have to worry about that," Lindsey replied, though she wasn't quite sure how the commandant planned to protect them all from the inquiries that were absolutely going to happen after the planned SWD coup was revealed.

"I better not be," Vaja muttered, taking her chair.

Petra bestowed Vaja with an annoyed look before tapping her headset to turn it back on and returning to her task, worry nestled firmly on her brow.

Lindsey hurried over to Commandant Pierce. Dr. Curran was nowhere to be seen. The woman unsettled Lindsey and she was more than happy to avoid her.

"Sergeant," Commandant Pierce said in her husky, silken voice as Lindsey approached. "What do you have to report?"

Leaning on her cane, Lindsey relayed what she'd witnessed on the vid screens and Dwayne's last command. "I don't understand what he meant about the virus that Curran gave everyone but Maria. Maria's Inferi Boon, too."

Commandant Pierce set her hands on her hips and stared thoughtfully toward the busily working people under her command. Commandant Pierce gestured toward a door that led to a small conference room. "Follow me."

Once inside, the Commandant locked the door and initiated the privacy protocols. No one could hear them. Well, except for Vaja if he decided to spy.

"Dr. Curran just told me that the virus she gave Vanguard Martinez was not the same one given to the Boon," Commandant Pierce said in a lowered voice despite the security in the room.

"What?" Lindsey gawked at the Commandant in shock. "I mean, what do you mean, sir?"

"Dr. Curran gave Martinez a different virus. That's why she's returning to life. Apparently, Dr. Curran asked Castellan Reichardt to kill both Martinez and Denman and return with samples."

"So the immortality thing was bullshit?"

"For the other Boon, but not Martinez. She's the only one who has the virus that could possibly grant immortality. Dr. Curran can't give any assurances of what may happen to Vanguard Martinez and to protect The Bastion, she told the castellan to eliminate both Boons."

"But if he knows Maria isn't like Denman..." Lindsey instantly realized what he'd do. "He's not coming back because he's going to infect himself."

Commandant Pierce's full lips slightly twisted. "Romantic, isn't it?"

The dread that had been filling Lindsey at the thought of Dwayne having to kill Maria dissipated. "They're going into the world."

"Most likely. Dr. Curran is convinced he'll return with the samples. But then again, I don't think she understands how deeply the castellan loves Martinez."

"So what do we do?"

"We protect them if possible. If the SWD realizes they're alive, immune, immortal, and out there in the world, they will exhaust The Bastion's resources trying to find them."

"To stick them in a lab," Lindsey grumbled.

"To experiment on them. For the good of humanity, of course." Commandant Pierce rubbed her temples. "But we know that it would never be administered to the general populace. Imagine an immortal government."

"They can't come back," Lindsey said, the knot in her stomach reforming. "Ever. They're exiles."

"Dr. Curran isn't even certain how the virus in Martinez would affect the general populace. Vanguard Martinez was in exceptional health when infected. The civilian population is not as fortunate. There's a possibility of an adverse reaction."

"Like the Anomalies?"

Commandant Pierce sighed, then bobbed her head once.

"So it's not like Maria could come into the city and kiss everyone and it would be instant utopia," Lindsey joked, but her tone was laced with despair.

"A kissing spree like that could result in an instant outbreak with only a few of the infected becoming Boon. This was the issue with the Anomalies. Dr. Curran doesn't have enough data to extrapolate on the long lasting effects of the virus that Vanguard Martinez has in her veins."

Something in the commandant's tone frightened Lindsey. "You're not thinking of killing Maria, are you?"

"No, no," Commandant Pierce answered. "Let Dwayne and Maria go find a life together if that's what they want. But once the Constabulary is in control of the city's defenses, I will not allow them back into The Bastion. I can't risk humanity. There are too many unknown variables and hazards. Dwayne may be willing to risk all for the woman he loves, but I can't risk The Bastion."

Lindsey grimly agreed with the nod of her head. She was never going to see Maria again. The thought shot a sliver of ice through her heart.

"This situation has created a strange dynamic between us," the commandant continued after a beat. "I would not usually divulge such information to a sergeant, but you're a valuable asset to me and this city."

"You can trust me," Lindsey said, lifting her chin. "I want what's best for The Bastion, too."

Commandant Pierce met her gaze evenly, and then slightly smiled. "I'm glad we understand each other. Now, take care of Denman's body. I don't want Curran getting any samples off Denman."

"But doesn't the SWD already have the virus?"

"Admiral Kirkpatrick ordered all the viruses destroyed after the Inferi Boon were successful as a precaution against further outbreaks, but it was probably a move against Curran. I have a feeling that Kirkpatrick regards her as a wildcard. He also ordered all the Boon bodies to be burned. Dr. Curran presently doesn't have any sway with the SWD, but that could change once the worm goes out tonight."

Commandant Pierce started to reach for the controls next to the door, then hesitated. "Dr. Curran is a temporary ally. Though I do believe she will do everything she can to destroy Mr. Peterson and Admiral Kirkpatrick's designs on taking over the city, she's also going to be maneuvering herself into a position of power."

"And she knows about me, Vaja, Petra..." Lindsey narrowed her eyes on her wristlet. She could instantly make herself invisible to the city sensors, but she had nowhere to really hide.

"We're going to have to be hyper-vigilant."

"You're afraid of what she might do, aren't you?"

"She likes to play with people's lives and viruses."

"Will she tell the SWD about Maria's virus? And that she might still be alive?"

Commandant Pierce lowered her brows, obviously pondering the question. "Once she's in power again, I wouldn't be surprised if she tries to find Maria. But she'll keep it to herself for now."

"Because she wouldn't want anyone else getting the glory."

"Exactly. Vanguard Rooney, this isn't over yet. But we will be victorious." The commandant extended her hand, a small silver star-shaped rank pin in her palm.

Lindsey arched her eyebrows, realizing she'd just been promoted to vanguard. "Yes, sir."

The commandant deftly attached the pip to Lindsey's collar. "Suit up and get things done."

"Yes, sir!" Lindsey saluted, her heart wildly fluttering.

With a satisfied look, the commandant opened the doors and strode out.

In a daze, Lindsey followed, her fingers tight around her cane. Gradually, a smile slid onto her lips as she realized the commandant hadn't even questioned if she could fulfill her assigned task. It was the first time in a very long while that someone hadn't doubted her abilities because of her damaged leg. Lifting a hand, she touched the small star on her collar in awe.

With a straight spine and determination in her stuttering gait, Lindsey rushed to suit up.

CHAPTER 2

The wind sweeping off the mountain range enclosing the vast valley buffeted the tiltrotors as the vehicles circled over the drop zone. The darkness of the night was broken by the bright flashes of the tiltrotors' bombardment against the howling Inferi Scourge. In the distance, near the hydroelectric plant, there were fires, but Master Seeker Torran MacDonald and his squad were being set down near the mines. Firebombs were not allowed in that area due to the underground coal deposits.

The tiltrotors banked and swooped low over the dwindling horde of Inferi Scourge. Instead of fleeing, the rampaging undead creatures raced toward the deadly flying craft. Even when the tiltrotors opened fire, the bullets shredding through the flesh of the undead, the survivors continued to race along the ground, following the flight path of the tiltrotors.

"Fuckin' Scrags," Fortis Plebis Sara Goodwin grunted beside her superior officer. "They act like they can somehow grab us right out of the sky."

"Maybe they think they can," Torran answered. "They do have one track minds."

"Yeah, to bite us." Goodwin's round, pale face was grim behind the facemask of her helmet. A strand of red hair clung to her sweaty brow. "Fuckers are not going to get a chance with me. No way I'll ever be a Scrag."

The Scrags, as the military nicknamed them, had no sense of self-preservation or awareness. The Inferi Scourge Plague Virus not only returned the infected to life, but compelled them to bite and infect the living. The sole purpose of the reanimated dead was to spread the virus

"Keep alert, follow orders, and don't try to be a hero, and you'll do fine," Torran assured her.

Strapped into the tiltrotor, Torran's squad was preparing to disembark once the area was cleared of the immediate threat of the Inferi Scourge horde. The readout on the facemask of his helmet was a fast scroll of updated information from the battlefield. At last, the final campaign for the land and resources surrounding The Bastion was well under way.

In the distance, the massive gate into the valley was closed. Decades before, it had been sabotaged by a group called the Gaia Cult. The cult had been devoted to exterminating humanity in order to save the planet. They'd opened the gate and escorted a massive horde of the Inferi Scourge through the opening. The Scrags had swept into the valley and destroyed the city's resources such as farms, ranches, mines, fuel depots, and settlements, effectively trapping humanity behind the high walls of The Bastion.

Tonight, all that had gone wrong was being set right. The gate was closed, the Inferi Scourge were nearly eradicated from the valley, and Torran MacDonald was leading one of the Science Warfare Divisions search and destroy squads on a mission to clean up the last pockets of the Scrags. He was grateful to the mysterious special ops team that had wiped out nearly all the undead in the valley. They had his utmost respect. Sadly, word was that the last of the special ops team had died earlier in the day near the hydroelectric plant and now it was up to the SWD search and destroy teams to mop up the Inferi Scourge in their honor. The pride that swelled within him at the thought of the successes the mission had garnered so far was tempered by the fact that they weren't done yet. The night stretched long and treacherous before him and his squad.

Shuffling his boots against the metal floor, he swallowed the hard lump in his throat. The last time he had faced the Inferi Scourge, he'd watched his former squad be dragged down and infected by the undead. He'd barely escaped with his own life. His emotions were a mixed bag of excitement, fear, and the thirst for revenge for his fallen comrades in arms.

"Master Seeker MacDonald, we're making another pass," the female pilot's voice said through the comm link. "Prepare to disembark."

"Understood," Torran answered. Flipping his comm to speak to his squad, he said, "Time to kill Scrags and avenge our fallen brothers and sisters." His Scottish brogue was a bit stronger than usual, but his squad was used to it. Torran's family was from the Scottish borough of The Bastion and the distinctive accent of Scotland still lingered on the tongues of the small contingency from the fallen country. "Keep to the mission, no deviations. Remember, the abnormal Inferi Scourge may attempt to speak to you, but you are to kill them on sight. Even if they wear the uniforms of the SWD and Constabulary, they are the enemy. There's no cure other than a bullet to the head."

The nods of black helmets all around the interior of the tiltrotor was what he expected.

"Fucking Abscrags," another soldier grunted, and there were murmurs of agreement. It was Ray Jonas, a lanky young man with dark brown skin and deep red hair. "Can't act like normal Scrags. Have to ruin the flow."

This brought guffaws from several others, but there were enough tense faces to indicate the squad was well aware of the danger of their mission. The group of twenty – twelve women and eight men – were tightly knit and worked well together, but they were also very green when it came to real world interactions with the Scrags. They'd only been involved in one sweep of the subway system that had unearthed some abnormal Inferi Scourge, mockingly nicknamed Abscrags. It had been an intense fight. The Abscrags had created projectile weapons from the scraps of the abandoned settlements outside The Bastion walls. Though the SWD armor had deflected most of the incoming shrapnel, Senior Seeker Rosario Smyth, his right hand, had ended up severely injured when one of the Abscrags had tossed a handmade grenade at her. Though she appeared to have fully recovered, he could tell by the set of her jaw that she was dealing with her own fears. Noticing he was studying her from across the narrow walkway, she forced a smile.

Torran winked at her and the smile turned genuine. Dark eyes focusing, Rosario shook off whatever thoughts had been sifting through her mind and sat up straighter. "Scrag or Abscrag, they'll die tonight."

The squad stomped one foot against the metal floor and grunted in unison. It was something Torran had taught them to do to inspire a sense of unity. When he'd arrived at the SWD, he'd found the squads disorganized and adrift. He'd busted his ass for a year to make them into actual soldiers. Tonight would prove whether he'd succeeded or not.

The tiltrotor banked sharply, then hovered over a clearing. The escorting tiltrotors continued to fire at the remains of the once-large herd of Scrags. The undead numbers were now significantly reduced, much to Torran's relief. The special ops squad had done an impressive amount of killing to clear the valley of so many of the Scrags, but now came the cleanup. In some ways, it would be harder to search every little nook and cranny to ensure none of the Scrags were still alive.

The tiltrotor lowered and the hatch at the rear yawned open.

"Prepare to disembark," he ordered.

Torran unhooked his harness and was instantly on his feet. The vibrations underfoot were a little disorienting at first, but he rapidly found his balance and moved to the head of the squad. Simulations never quite captured the reality of disembarking from a tiltrotor.

Torran narrowed his eyes on the information scrolling across the clear faceplate of his helmet. The scans of the area were incomplete due to equipment in the area malfunctioning after years of neglect. Hopefully the projected number of Scrags wasn't wrong. It was unnerving to see how many were rushing into the spotlights of the tiltrotors. The aircraft hovered fifteen feet above the ground, but that wasn't keeping the Scrags from attempting to charge and leap toward the extended ramp. The gunner in the rear managed to keep the scattered raving undead at bay.

"We're clear to set down," the pilot's voice said through the feed.

The sensation of Torran's insides dropping as the tiltrotor descended was an unnerving reminder of the last time he'd faced the Inferi Scourge on a mass scale. Gripping one of the overhead straps and setting his feet apart, Torran fought to keep his balance. A flash of memory from the fateful day he'd rushed across bloody, sodden ground as the Scrags chased down the soldiers attempting to erect a new perimeter outside The Bastion's walls filled him with unease. Inwardly shuddering, he reminded himself that this was not the same sort of situation. The valley was nearly cleared. The advantage had finally shifted to the humans.

The tiltrotor lowered until it was almost touching the ground, but close enough to allow the squad to exit. Barreling across the slanted ramp and leaping down, Torran aimed into the darkness dwelling beyond the pools of luminosity cast by the lights on the underside of the aircraft. As he moved out of the sanctuary of the spotlights, the helmet night vision flicked on, revealing shapes moving through the murk toward their location.

The mining facility area loomed straight ahead. The mine had been instantly sealed off when the gate had been compromised, so at least they didn't have to venture down into the endless tunnels to clear them out. The main building sat to one side of the weed-lined road and across from thick woods.

"Keep alert," Rosario's voice ordered.

She was right behind him and her presence was reassuring.

Rushing into the darkness toward the facility, the squad kept together in a tight formation as the tiltrotors soared into the starry sky. The finality of their departure uncurled a ribbon of dread within Torran. Swallowing hard, he kept focused on the task the squad needed to perform. Securing the area was of vital importance.

The Scrags erupted out of the trees lining the fissured asphalt that had once been a parking area. Torran aimed and pulled the trigger of his weapon. The slight jolt as it discharged was almost as reassuring as the Scrags tumbled to the ground.

The search and destroy squad hit the downed fence line and Torran glanced toward the rundown building looming before them. It had been built to last a century, so the foundation and walls were still upright, though covered in dense vines. The reinforced windows in the front had deep gouges burrowed into the thick glass. The openings, surrounded by a latticework of cracks and edged with greenery, were large enough for a human to crawl through. The Abscrags must have used their makeshift weapons to punch through.

"They're inside," Rosario said in a grim tone.

"We should have known this wasn't going to be easy. Check the guard posts outside the mine," he instructed Rosario. "Then make sure the mine doors are still secure."

"Yes, sir," she answered. "At least the mine doesn't have windows." She gave him a brief smile behind her faceplate before switching her comm to speak only to those in her party. It was disconcerting to see the life signs of half his people wink out of his display, but they were Rosario's responsibility now until the squad reformed.

Immediately, Rosario and half of the squad peeled off to race toward the small building near the massive steel doors. They'd performed this mission maybe a hundred times in the training rooms, but this was far different from the holographic images projected in the safety of the SWD Facility.

The Scrags continued to appear out of the murk, hurtling toward the force with only one intention: to infect. The harsh bark of weapons firing overpowered the screech of the Scrags. Torran kept his focus on their objective, moving swiftly to the entrance of the building with his people at his back while thinning out the undead. The Scrags were drawn to the humans like bugs to lights, so it was easy to decrease their numbers with short bursts of gunfire.

The Inferi Scourge looked just as Torran remembered: like frightfully wounded human beings. So many people had died in the initial outbreaks when they'd perceived the Scrags to be victims of violence, not actual monsters, and they paid a terrible price when they'd rushed to offer assistance. The virus froze the bodies at the moment of death, and only milky, vacant eyes gave away to their undead nature. The virus could simulate life, but not the soul.

"Open it," he ordered when he reached the heavy metal door.

Jonas darted forward, a key-hacker in his hand. Pressing the device over the locking mechanism, he swiftly activated it. The key-hacker fed just enough electricity into the lock to allow Jonas to enter the access code. There was a loud, audible click as the tumblers inside the door sluggishly whirled into motion after years of disuse. Jonas disengaged the key-hacker and dodged around Torran while stuffing it in his pack.

The door retracted, revealing a long corridor. Weapons at the ready, the squad advanced at Torran's signal. The night vision created an eerie environment for them to traverse. The Inferi Scourge were room temperature, so they were very difficult to spot if they remained still. Torran was very uneasy about the whole scenario. He'd worked diligently to shape the SWD security forces into actual soldiers, but experienced Constabulary soldiers would've been better for the job. If only the SWD had allowed the Constabulary to participate in the clearing of the valley. Torran worried that the SWD's small security force didn't contain the personnel needed to do the job. He wasn't privy to what exactly was going on between the SWD and Constabulary hierarchies, but he sure as hell wished they'd found a way to collaborate on the strangely named Operation Cleansing Waves.

Probably Admiral Kirkpatrick had come up with the name. The elderly soldier was so well respected, he'd been allowed to keep his rank from his pre-Bastion days. He'd been in a navy and led one of the last human armadas before it had to be abandoned due the difficulties of maintaining a healthy community on the sea.

The first room the group encountered was in the front of the building near the broken windows. Years of exposure to the elements had rotted the broken office furniture and allowed nature to creep inside. The walls were covered in thick vines and a carpet of mildew made the floor slick beneath the soles of their boots. The squad warily sidled into the room, cautious of the many hiding places. The sensors were struggling to pick up readings, and the information scrolling on

Torran's helmet screen didn't inspire confidence. There were blanks in many of the entries.

"Trust your eyes more than your feed," he instructed.

Torran approached the far wall, the muzzle of his large weapon aimed at the tangle of vines. This would be a great place for the Abscrags to attack. Goodwin edged forward and dragged a huge swatch of the leafy curtain to one side with one rapid tug while Torran prepared to fire. There was nothing hiding behind the vines except a wall covered in mold. Around the room, the rest of the squad followed the same procedure. Each time the vines were drawn to one side, Torran's heart beat a little harsher.

"Clear," voices said over the comm, one by one.

The layout of the building loomed in the upper right-hand corner of Torran's visor. There were only three other rooms the Scrags could have entered. The rest of the building was protected by blast doors at the end of the long, winding corridor. Torran knew for a fact that on the other side of those doors, only the truly dead remained.

When the gate to the valley had been compromised and the Inferi Scourge rushed through, killing everything in sight, the mine personnel had shut down the facility and retreated behind the safety of the blast doors. An underground train ran from the mining facility to The Bastion. There was a loading station inside the mine and an employee station beneath the building. It would have been a perfect way to escape into the city, but all the subway stations and tunnels had been cut off immediately when the gate had been compromised. Twenty people had starved to death waiting for a rescue that never happened because it had been deemed it too risky. Images of their mummified corpses had been part of Torran's debriefing. He couldn't imagine the terror and hopelessness they'd experienced. It was obvious from the way the Abscrags had burrowed through the safety glass that they had hoped to reach the train tunnels.

The shots from outside diminished to a few short bursts, and then were silent. The two squad members he'd left guarding the front entrance gave him the clear signal, and he nodded.

"Move on," he ordered.

With deft motions, Torran ordered the squad to split into groups. Goodwin, Jonas, and two other soldiers followed him while the other teams moved deeper into the building through the long hallway. The vid screens that once displayed work schedules, the latest information on the amount of coal extracted, and city news were now white squares in the inverted realm the soldiers inhabited via their helmet night vision. Torran wondered what this building had been like before the gate failure. It'd probably been filled with people just like him that were happy to exist in a safe haven far from the ravaged world.

Then it had all fallen apart.

Torran hoped that the people within The Bastion would never suffer such a dreadful event again.

As the other two parties moved on, Torran pointed to his group's destination. Two of the fortis plebis, the lower ranking members of the squad, Anya Helmich and Sydney Marshal, moved into position to watch the hallway. Both were new to the SWD, but competent. They'd enlisted when the gate closure by the special ops team had been reported on the news. Like many of The Bastion's young people, they wanted to be a part of the restoration of their city and the valley. Torran had enlisted in the Constabulary and later with the SWD for the exact same reasons. Though he was terrified with each step he took further into the darkened building, he was also proud and thrilled to be part of the final destruction of the Inferi Scourge in the valley.

Torran preceded Goodwin and Jonas over the threshold into the next area. It was a conference room flanked with windows along one wall. The frosted glass revealed the darkness of the night. Since the windows were intact, the room had not been exposed the elements, but it had obviously been used recently and in a most gruesome way.

"What the fuck?" Jonas exclaimed.

Flashes of memory from the failed battle outside the wall assaulted Torran's mind and his stomach clenched into a painful ball of dread, but he shoved those thoughts aside and concentrated on the horrific scene before him. He'd witnessed terrible things the day of the battle outside the wall, but this was far worse.

There were human skeletal remains on the table with only bits of stringy meat hanging from the bones. A Constabulary uniform was tossed into a corner along with a shattered helmet.

Goodwin inched over to the discarded garment and squatted to check the nametag. "Cormier," she said, her voice hushed with reverence.

"How does this make sense? What did the Abscrags do?" Jonas asked creeping toward the grisly scene.

"Ate her." His words were gruff with grief.

Torran knew exactly who Cormier was and her apparent fate was far too gruesome to accept. She'd been a brave, highly decorated pilot who'd sacrificed her fuel-drained tiltrotor during the failed push against the Inferi Scourge in order to save countless soldiers boarding another aircraft. She'd barely escaped with her life that day. For her to die at the hands and teeth of the Scrags was a cruel fate. She must have been part of the special ops clearing the valley.

"They don't eat us," Goodwin said tersely. "That's an old myth."

"Abscrags do," Torran answered. "There were rumors, but this is evidence." He pointed to a femur that had visible gnaw marks on it. "They're eating us now."

"No fuckin' way," Jonas uttered in disbelief.

Torran wondered what the higher ups at the SWD would have to say about the images being collected by their helmets. When he'd confronted them about the cannibal rumors he'd heard after the failed final push, they'd denied it.

Goodwin covered the body on the table with a plastic body bag she tugged out of her pack. "This can't be real."

"It is. Now let's finish this," Torran said, and started toward the doorway.

Helmich and Marshal were gone.

"Helmich and Marshal report," he said, stopping short of the exit out of the room.

There was silence. The readout on his helmet flashed that they were alive, but why weren't they answering? Their location indicated they were right outside the door.

"What the hell?" Jonas breathed.

"Sir?" Goodwin said in a fearful voice, falling in beside Torran.

Torran switched frequencies. "Englert and Argento, report in." These were the names of the two leaders of the smaller groups he'd sent off.

Again, no answer.

But the readout continued to register them as alive.

"Sir, why aren't they answering?" Jonas asked, his voice raspy.

Beside Torran, Goodwin switched to full auto on her weapon. Torran and Jonas followed suit.

A second later, all the readouts altered to read KIA on all his missing people.

CHAPTER 3

It had been a long time since Lindsey had worn Constabulary body armor. After the failed final push against the Inferi Scourge and her injury, she'd been trapped at a communications console. It felt strangely good to be back in the old, bulky suit. Securing her helmet, she watched the display light up on the facemask.

"Testing comm," she said.

"I hear you," Petra's voice answered.

"Squad sound off," Lindsey ordered, glancing toward the three Constabulary soldiers suiting up with her in the prep room.

"Hobbes reporting, Vanguard Rooney," the big man with the blond hair and ice blue eyes said.

"Giacomi reporting, Vanguard Rooney," came the husky voice of the woman with the black eyes, raven hair, and burn scars along the side of her face and neck.

"Franklin reporting, Vanguard Rooney," was the call out from the tall, powerfully built black woman with gold-flecked brown eyes and a shaved head.

Lindsey cut the comm long enough to say, "Bitches."

The three laughed.

"You're the one who went and got herself promoted," Hobbes teased, then winked.

"Always an overachiever," Franklin agreed.

Giacomi blew Lindsey a kiss.

"I'm your commanding officer now, so I'd like to see a little respect," she said, but knew she would have to endure a certain amount of ribbing.

All three saluted.

She wasn't certain if the action was mocking or not.

Though she wasn't a part of their squad anymore, Lindsey knew the trio well enough to occasionally have drinks with them. They were all survivors of the failed push against the Inferi Scourge. They were war hero veterans, but their wounds hadn't sidelined them like Lindsey's had. Giacomi's scars weren't even from battle, but from a pot of boiling water she'd pulled off the stove when she'd been an inquisitive toddler.

Reopening the comm, Lindsey said, "Command, we're on our way to the subway station."

"We're standing by to open them," Petra replied.

Lindsey picked up her weapon, and then moved to pull out a flamethrower from the weapons locker. She already had the biohazard collapsible container in her backpack to bring back Denman's remains.

Hobbes finished loading his bulky firearm and looked up. "Any chance of action down there?"

"Probably not," Lindsey answered.

"Why do the squids get all the fun?" Giacomi asked while grabbing a flamethrower and hooking the strap to her armor.

At some point in time, the Constabulary had started calling the SWD security forces the squids. Lindsey supposed it was because Admiral Kirkpatrick, the man in charge of the SWD, had belonged to one of the old world navies. It had stuck through the years. Meanwhile, the Constabulary soldiers were called grunts.

Lindsey realized she couldn't answer. The three soldiers in front of her had no idea of the internal struggle for power that was going on within The Bastion. "That's just how the cards played out," she said at last.

"So no chance in hell we'll get to shoot something," Franklin groused.

The thought of the Scrags or another smarter variation getting into the subway tunnels was something Lindsey didn't even want to consider. "Probably not. I know you're a bloodthirsty lot, but we're basically just a clean-up crew."

"It fuckin' sucks that the squids get to take care of the Scrags and not us," Hobbes muttered. "It was our people we lost out there."

"I couldn't agree more," Franklin said, bobbing her head so the helmet caught the overhead light and the faceplate gleamed, obscuring her face.

For a second, Lindsey saw Maria, not Franklin, and her heart hurt. Dwayne would take care of her friend, one way or another.

"Let's move out."

It was embarrassing to have to use her cane while in her battle armor, but at least no one said anything as they departed the prep room and headed up the corridor to the elevator that would carry them down into the bowels of the Constabulary headquarters.

A private message popped up in the corner of Lindsey's screen from Petra. She read it quickly:

There may be a problem. The SWD squad at the mining facility is taking heavy casualties.

Lindsey entered the elevator and pressed the screen for the lowest level. She also toggled the comm over to Petra. "Talk to me."

"The squad is pinned down and it sounds like they're in dire straits. The SWD is insisting they hold their position."

"Dwayne could be in that area."

"If he tries to return with Maria..."

"He won't. I don't think. We'll...maybe..." Lindsey wished she could rub her suddenly pounding temples. "Keep me posted."

The eyes of the three soldiers around her were watching her hold her private conversation. The worry in their faces probably reflected hers. She switched the comm over.

"So...do we get to shoot stuff?" Hobbes asked hopefully.

"Sir!" Goodwin breathed.

"I see the readout." It was impossible to conceive that the others were gone. Opening the comm to the soldiers in the building, Torran said briskly, "Everyone report. Respond now!"

Strange guttural noises were his only answer.

Torran hit his wristlet, again switching the comm to contact Rosario's group. "Smyth, report."

As the other half of the squad was added to his helmet visual, he sucked in a deep breath. They were also reported as Killed In Action. Stunned, he swallowed the hard lump forming in his throat. What was going on?

"Sir?" Jonas queried his voice unsteady.

"Watch that door! Smyth, if you can hear me, respond now!"

Through the static came the sound of someone choking.

The line hissed and buzzed for a long second, then a woman's voice that was not Rosario's said, "Don't worry. She'll come for you."

A wave of horror washed over Torran and plunged him into the blackest depths of despair. They were all dead. Just like before outside the wall when the expanding perimeter fence had failed and the Inferi Scourge had swarmed the soldiers.

"Sir?"

The sound of Goodwin's voice tugged Torran's attention back to the present. Staring at the empty doorway shimmering in an ominous pale gray in the night vision filter, Torran gathered his thoughts, and then switched the comm again. "Base, I have lost all communication with my squad and they're being reported as KIA. We are under attack from the abnormal Inferi Scourge. We need immediate backup to this location."

The popping and static echoing through his helmet sent a surge of adrenaline through his system. For several seconds, he feared there wasn't going to be a response, but then a voice said, "Master Seeker, you're to hold position until we can send a tiltrotor with reinforcements. All units are all presently engaged."

"We can't hold this position," Torran answered curtly. If the rest of the squad was dead, then he had to save Goodwin and Jonas as well as himself. He'd been a sole survivor of a squad before and the burden of that label still weighed on his soul.

"You have your orders to secure and hold that area," came the reply.

"We're dealing with a pocket of the Abscrags—"

"You have your—"

There were footsteps in the hallway.

"—and we are about to be overrun!"

Jonas and Goodwin lifted their weapons simultaneously.

"Come out. Join us," a deep voice called from somewhere in the corridor.

The woman at the SWD command center was still droning on about orders. Torran killed the comm link. He needed to concentrate on the situation at hand. First, he had to find a way out of the building and that wasn't going to be easy with the Abscrags in the hallway.

Somewhere nearby, a Scrag howled.

Signaling for the two squad members to cover him, Torran crept toward the door. The night vision's inverted perspective illuminated the hallway with an eerie gray glow.

A shadow flickered across the threshold.

Darting forward, he kicked the door shut and hit the lock. Instantly, gunfire started on the other side. The Abscrags now had SWD weaponry. It wouldn't hold very long against the barrage.

Whipping about, Torran pushed past the frightened soldiers and fired at the windows. The bullets punched into the treated glass, forming fist-sized indentations, but the window didn't shatter. "Concentrate your fire!"

Jonas and Goodwin immediately obeyed.

The hot metal chipped away at the glass as the guns roared. Behind the three soldiers, the door buckled. It would give way soon.

"We're going to get out of the building and head toward the subway entrance one kilometer north. Keep moving and do not slow down," Torran said over the noise.

"The rest of the squad?" Goodwin's gun clicked empty and she swiftly reloaded.

"Gone. You see the readout."

"But it can't be true!" Jonas exclaimed. "Abscrags aren't supposed to be that smart!"

"Maybe we're not dealing with Abscrags but something else," Goodwin suggested.

Torran hated that her comment sounded wholly plausible.

Finally, a large enough hole formed in the glass to allow them to crawl out. Rushing forward, Torran bashed at a few loose chunks with the butt of his weapon. Their armor would protect them from the sharp edges. Behind them, the door was starting to give way in the frame. Soon, the Abscrags would be on them, yet Torran was more worried about what was waiting outside the building. The scan of the area still wasn't showing movement, but Torran no longer felt he could rely on the readings. They'd have to trust their instincts and training to survive.

"I'll go first. Goodwin, you follow. Jonas, you bring up the rear." If something terrible waited outside, he'd deal with it and clear the way for the remaining squad members.

It was a bit difficult squeezing through the hole with his helmet on, but Torran didn't dare take it off. Torran held his weapon before him with one hand while using the other to push through the narrow, ragged tunnel. Keeping an eye on his surroundings, Torran wormed his way through the opening. The windows faced a concrete pad that was cracked and sprouting weeds. The drop to the ground wasn't too high, so when he finally pulled his torso through the glass far enough to allow gravity to take control, he fell, tucked, rolled, and shot back onto his feet.

The area appeared clear, but the sight further along the road gave him pause. Revealed through the night vision, Torran saw many bodies sprawled before the heavy doors to the mine. Toggling through his filters, he swallowed hard. The bodies were warm, which meant they were his squad and they were most likely dead. Raising his head, he saw Goodwin squeezing through the hole in the thick glass.

"Hurry," he said, but knew he didn't need to urge the other two soldiers.

Scanning the area, he gripped his weapon ever tighter. The comfort he sought from it didn't manifest as he watched the corpses of his squad in the distance start to jerk and thrash about.

Goodwin crashed to the ground beside him, but rapidly recovered and stood up. Jonas started through the hole, his ragged breathing sifting through the helmet speakers. Thrusting one hand through the opening, he said, "They're almost through! Help me!"

"Cover us," Torran told Goodwin.

Eyes wide with fright, she briskly nodded.

Torran swung his weapon onto his back and raised his hands toward Jonas. He could barely reach the other man and his fingertips scrabbled at the hard, black armor as Torran struggled to get a good grip. Jonas managed to get his other arm through the glass, his firearm dangling from the strap attached to his uniform. Torran clutched Jonas's hand and strove to pull the man through the opening.

The screech of the Inferi Scourge seeped through the feed.

Behind the facemask of the helmet, Jonas' expression was one of stark fear, and Torran's throat constricted with alarm.

"They're in the room," Jonas gasped.

"Goodwin!"

Promptly, she was at Torran's side, her fingers wrapped around Jonas's wrist. Together, they attempted to drag his long body through a ragged gap in the glass. Jonas wiggled about as he tried to find enough traction to push free. Desperation and fear clawed at Torran's mind, but he gritted his teeth and pulled harder. He wasn't about to lose another member of his squad. Especially not one as young and full of potential like Jonas.

"C'mon, Jonas!"

"They got me! They got me!" Jonas thrashed about.

It was difficult to see into the room due to the angle, but Torran thought he saw hands digging at Jonas's waist, or maybe it was a trick of the light and his own nerves.

Planting one boot on the wall, Torran strained to pull Jonas free

Footfalls against asphalt drew Goodwin away from the struggle, leaving Torran to rescue Jonas alone. She whipped her weapon about and fired, the flash from the muzzle illuminating Jonas's terrified face. Torran saw several dark shapes hurtling toward them out of the corner of his eye. Goodwin cut them down, but more appeared out of the tangle of trees encircling the area.

"They're pulling off my boot! They're pulling off my boot!" Jonas screamed.

"What the fuck?" Goodwin shouted

"To infect him," Torran rasped. "Shit! They mean to infect him!"

"No! No! No!" Jonas screamed, the shrill sound squealing through the connection.

Looking up into Jonas's dark eyes, Torran knew the truth instantly. Several pulses of his heart were all it took for the virus to take hold. Torran saw the life in Jonas's eyes extinguish as he went limp. The virus was a quick killer.

With a furious, strangled cry, Torran released Jonas hands and watched his body be dragged back into the building.

"We need to go now!" Torran swung about, lifting his weapon and breaking into a run.

The area was clear for the moment, Goodwin's marksmanship reducing the Scrags rushing them to pulp. Glancing toward the mines, Torran noted the bodies of his former squad continued to twitch as the virus took hold. In a matter of minutes, they'd be reanimated. So would Jonas.

"I don't want to be one of them!" Goodwin rushed alongside the building, the black metal of her heavy firearm gleaming in the moonlight.

"You're not going to be," Torran answered, merging the comm lines so he could call base, but also keep track of Goodwin. "Base, the mining facility is under the control of the Abscrags. We need reinforcements now!"

"We are unable to comply or extract you at this time—"

"Then we'll be dead and you'll have more Abscrags to deal with!"

Torran pivoted about, sweeping the area with gunfire. Two Scrags tumbled to the ground. Meanwhile, dark figures skirted around the corner of the building and one of them raised their arm.

"Goodwin, take cover!" Torran ordered.

There was nowhere to go except into the woods. Torran and Goodwin crashed through the scrub brush and into the copse of fir trees. Torran frantically searched for a place to hide. A second later, a flash of light instantly rendered him blind, and his flesh crawled as a pulse of electricity swept through his armor. The speakers in his helmet squealed with a deafening noise. The display on his visor sputtered and died.

"Shit! Shit! Shit!" Torran hit the tabs on his helmet and swept it off. The cool fresh night air sifted through his sweaty hair as he furiously blinked his eyes. "Helmet off, Goodwin!"

Still unable to see clearly, he tried to get his bearings. Goodwin bumped into him as she flung her helmet aside.

"Sir!"

"I'm here!"

Back to back, the two remaining squad members held their weapons aloft. Torran strained to see through the massive spots obscuring his eyesight. The tapping of boot heels against asphalt sent shivers along his spine. Their enemies were coming closer.

"Alkan!" a voice barked out of the darkness.

"Looking for them, Reese!" a female replied. "They darted into the woods somewhere around here."

"We need them," Reese said in a fierce tone. "Without Martinez, we need more Anomalies to get into the city."

"I know! Back off!"

These Abscrags did not fit the profile he'd been given. They were supposed to be of minor intelligence, able to use tools, and speak a smattering of words. These Abscrags were obviously intelligent and conniving. Therefore, they were much more dangerous.

The footfalls were steadily getting closer, and Torran urged Goodwin deeper into the thicket. His vision was clearing, but it was still difficult to move without too much noise. He doubted that the sound of gunfire from the battles in the distance was loud enough to mask their movements.

"At least the others will be rising soon. They can help us with this hunt," Reese said ominously from the road.

"I'm going into the woods after them," the woman named Alkan said in a fierce voice. "I'll find them."

It was still challenging to see, but Torran knew they couldn't risk staying so close to the road. Tapping Goodwin on the shoulder, he attempted to signal to her, but realized that was foolish. Instead, he gripped her arm and dragged her behind him. Elbow out, gripping his weapon, he held his arm in front of his face and pushed forward through the tree branches. The prickly leaves scratched his face and caught in his hair, but he pressed forward, hoping to get some distance from the creature stalking them. It was tough to find sure footing, but he determinedly kept moving.

Goodwin stumbled along behind him. He got the impression she was recovering a bit slower than he was from being blinded. When the flash grenade had gone off, he'd been in the midst of looking away, so that had helped him not take the full brunt of the burst. It was becoming easier to maneuver through the thicket of pine trees as the spots in his sight cleared.

Nearby, a chorus of Inferi Scourge screeches marred the night. Torran had a suspicion it was his dead squad rising as Abscrags. The thought filled him with remorse and horror. He didn't want to think of Rosario, Jonas, and the others transformed into murderous, smart Abscrags.

As his eyesight cleared, Torran moved faster, towing Goodwin behind him. He was certain they were being followed, for they were definitely generating enough noise, but he didn't see or hear their pursuer. Of course, Alkan hadn't been blinded, so she was able to be stealthier.

"I'm okay," Goodwin whispered, tugging free of his grip. She heaved her weapon upward, ready to fire.

Taking a moment to study the way they'd come, Torran tried to discern if the tree boughs were being stirred by the wind or something much more dangerous.

"Keep close," he said in a hushed voice.

Goodwin didn't answer, but when he started moving, she was right on his heels. Cupping his hand over his wristlet screen, Torran accessed the map of the valley. The charge that had knocked out his armor's electronics hadn't disabled the wristlet. Since each citizen of The Bastion wore the wristlets from birth, they were made to be resistant to all forms of tampering, sabotage, or accidents. Even though he could use the wristlet comm device, he didn't dare try to reach base again with the Abscrag hunting them. According to the readout on the tiny screen, they were headed in the right direction, but what would happen once they reached the exterior door of the subway? It was locked.

If only one Abscrag was following them, then they could eliminate her and make a run for the subway station down the road. Once they broke out of the wooded area, it would be easier to see who was pursuing them, and with this in mind, Torran quickened his pace.

Breathing heavily behind him, Goodwin maintained a close proximity.

By his estimates they were almost to the edge of the thicket when a sizzling noise sent both him and Goodwin scrambling for the nearest cover. Crouching low beside a tall tree, Torran searched for Goodwin in the gloom. It took him several seconds to spot her face down in the pine needles heaped on the forest floor.

The hissing sound continued and it took another few beats of his heart to realize that Goodwin had been shot with an electroshock gun. The weapons were used to subdue food riots in The Bastion. The rifles shot small black discs with barbs that attached to flesh and clothing and sent an incapacitating pulse of energy through their victim. Goodwin's hands and feet beat against the ground as the surge paralyzed her.

Torran gritted his teeth and scanned the trees for the Abscrag pursuing them. One shot from an electroshock gun would render him unconscious. That's how the Abscrags had subdued his people so quickly. But how did they get their hands on such a weapon? Blinking sweat and grit from his eyes, he tried to remember the range on the electroshock rifles. The Abscrag had to be close and definitely had the advantage. If he moved to recover Goodwin, the Abscrag would have him in her line of sight.

Swearing, Torran again dared to poke his head out and surveyed the area for the Abscrag. There was another hiss, and he ducked. The disc hit a tree nearby, bolts of energy crackling against the trunk. A rapid check of his ammunition readout on his weapon did not offer any comfort. He was running low and would have to reload. That would give his enemy an opportunity to rush him.

The night was full of violence. He could hear explosions, gunfire, and the screech of the Scrags in the distance, but the woods around him were strangely muted. The nocturnal creatures inhabiting the forest were quiet, most likely sensing a predator nearby. The Abscrag had no interest in animals though. She wanted Torran. She wanted Goodwin.

The crack of a branch snapping was followed by the audible movement of the Abscrag closing on his location. Taking a chance, he leaned out and fired in the direction of the sounds. There was a grunt, then two more sparking discs flew past him and into the night.

Torran checked his ammo counter again. Alkan knew where he was, but he wasn't sure of her position. He pondered waiting until she made a move to retrieve Goodwin before attacking. His mind spun out possibilities.

Seconds later, they were all rendered moot.

The screech of Scrags filled the woods.

Menacing laughter followed.

CHAPTER 4

Recalling the maintenance cart Castellan Dwayne Reichardt had used to reach the subway station at the end of the line took much longer than Lindsey expected. Vaja had reopened all the security blast doors at the various intersections to keep it running at top speed to where Lindsey and the others were waiting, but it was still a long distance. Her boyfriend was watching the security feed and keeping her updated, but it was challenging not to feel disquieted by the fact that a dead Scrag was in the tunnels. A part of her brain kept wondering if maybe Denman could somehow return to life to attack her and the others.

Hobbes, Giacomi and Franklin stood at the base of the stairs leading down to the subway platform while Lindsey sat on the top step. The advertising vid screens were eerie in the darkness and a few old vending machines sat lifeless and empty on the landing below her. Though she'd seen footage of the old subways when they'd been operational before the valley fell to the Inferi Scourge, that time period seemed unreal to her. She couldn't imagine a world without shortages, a crumbling infrastructure, and antiquated machinery.

"So are they going to fix your bum leg now that we're taking back the valley?" Hobbes asked, plopping down next to her.

Lindsey gave him a long, speculative look out of the corner of her eye. "Why do you ask?"

"It'd be cool to have you back among us now that our duty won't only be patrolling the wall," came the sincere reply.

"Well, I don't know how long it'll take to get our resources to the point where they'll consider fixing it," Lindsey answered honestly. She was afraid to even hope they'd put her on the list for reconstructive surgery.

"It'd suck that they didn't fix it. What the hell happened? Equipment malfunction or something? I heard they shut down the cloning wards for that reason," Franklin said.

"The denial letter said the refusal was due to shortages." Lindsey really didn't want to discuss it. She'd been devastated when she received the official word. She'd wanted to rejoin Maria on the wall, but instead was trapped in the communication hub. If not for her illegal hacking, she'd have died of boredom.

"Sounds like equipment malfunctions. They won't admit to how run down everything is," Giacomi decided.

"SWD has some primo new uniforms though. Did you see them on the vids?" Hobbes shook his head. "Why do they always get the good stuff?"

"I heard they had their own reserves squirreled away before the gate fell. Constabulary is dependent on the city reserves, but SWD has their own thing going," Giacomi replied.

"Is that true?" Franklin asked Lindsey.

"Hell if I know," Lindsey shrugged, but suspected it was the truth. "I'm just a grunt."

"Vanguard Grunt!" Hobbes saluted.

Lindsey refrained from hitting him, reminding herself that she was now their commanding officer. "Vanguard Rooney," she corrected.

The mood sobered immediately.

Resisting a sigh, she realized that they were trying to adapt to the new pip on her uniform as much as she was. An incoming message from command was a welcome distraction. She toggled over to Petra.

"What's going on?"

"There is only one survivor from the squad dispatched to the mining facility. He's on foot and on the run. He's running from what he's calling Abscrags. He says they have electroshock weapons. SWD does not have a tiltrotor in route yet."

"Electroshock weapon? How'd they get that?"

"A tiltrotor was overrun when it set down about an hour ago to dispatch a squad. Electroshock weapons were cached onboard," Petra answered in a grim tone.

Lindsey knew the SWD liked to use the electroshock rifles during riots, but the Constabulary had been opposed to them since the weapons were known to short out the ancient battle armor the Constabulary soldiers wore. There'd been cases of SWD security forces accidentally hitting Constabulary soldiers while trying to break up food riots. The soldier on the run was in dire danger if the electroshock weapon had the same effect on SWD armor.

"What does this have to do with us?" Lindsey asked, wishing she didn't sound so callous.

"He's heading to the subway station. He's requesting that the doors be opened."

"Shit!"

"Lindsey, we'll have to withdraw our hack from the system if the SWD agree to allow him entry."

The maintenance cart rumbled up to the station. It was a squat gray vehicle that rode on the tracks. It had enough room for four people and a large tool box. The trio immediately scrambled down the stairs toward it, only Hobbes hesitating to look after her.

Lindsey waved him on.

"Keep me informed. The second Vaja detects the SWD logging into the subway system, tell him to get out. It'll trap us temporarily, but we'll deal."

"You'll have to proceed on foot if we have to shut down the maintenance cart," Petra reminded her.

"It'll be fine." Lindsey climbed to her feet and shuffled down the stairs. "Just keep me in the loop."

"Understood."

Switching back to her squad's comm line, Lindsey reached the cart and slid onto one of the front seats, adjusting her weapons and cane around her.

"Let's go," she said.

Franklin activated the cart, and it barreled down the track toward the outer doors.

Torran's body tensed as he pressed one shoulder into the tree trunk. His mind searched for a viable plan to rescue Goodwin and get them both to safety. With a sick twist of his gut, Torran suspected there wasn't a way to get to Goodwin without dire risk to himself.

The Scrags – or were they Abscrags? – noisily plunged through the pine trees, screeching as they sought him out.

Goodwin was out of reach and unconscious.

For certain, Alkan was nearby, waiting for him to risk rescuing Goodwin. She had the advantage. Alkan knew where he was hiding, but he still had no idea where she was located.

"It only hurts for a little bit," Alkan called out.

The screeches of the Scrags were drawing closer.

"Just a bite. Pain. Darkness... then... life." The woman's voice sounded frighteningly near.

Daring to take a peek at Goodwin, Torran lifted his weapon, flipped on the scope, and scanned the area. Of course, the Scrags didn't show up due to their low body temperature. The disc that had incapacitated Goodwin was silent now, it's energy expended. Torran should be able to pick her up without being electrocuted, too.

Another disc slammed into the trunk a few inches from his head, spurring him to duck. The disc sizzled, arcs of energy crackling around the clawed edges. Alkan was somewhere in front of him, but where?

The noise of the newly made Scrags crashing through the woods was increasing in volume. He didn't have much time left. Swearing silently, Torran mentally prepared himself for a charge to Goodwin's unconscious form. He'd probably only have a few seconds to swing her over his shoulders and make a run for it.

The next few seconds were a blur.

Torran was just about to plunge into the open when a disc bounced off his weapon and barely missed his face.

The Abscrag had flanked him.

Alkan charged toward him, firing the electroshock rifle. It was sheer luck when he tripped and fell out of her range. The discs hurtled overhead and vanished into the trees.

A howl of fury echoed through the surrounding area.

Scrambling to his feet, he fired at the Abscrag. Alkan was eerily fast and he only caught a glimpse of her white face, dark hair, and battered uniform. Feet pounding against the uneven forest floor, he headed to where Goodwin had fallen while continuing to fire after Alkan to keep her scrambling for cover.

Torran was almost to Goodwin when he stuttered to a stop, breathing heavily.

A dark shape was bent over her.

The screen from Goodwin's bracelet came to life, illuminating the face of a man with very dark skin and bright red eyes. He'd peeled off Goodwin's glove and the motion had activated the wristlet. With a feral grin, he bit into the heel of Goodwin's hand.

"No!"

It was sheer instinct that prompted Torran to action when he heard the hiss of the electroshock rifle firing. Throwing himself to one side and into the shelter of trees, he heard the discs soar past him. Again he fired at where Alkan had taken cover. The bullets sent the branches of the pines in motion, making it more challenging to discern if Alkan was on the move or not.

Goodwin...

He couldn't allow her to become a Scrag. The ugly knot in his throat made it hard to breathe. Once again, he was the sole survivor of his squad.

Carefully skirting through the trees, mindful not to make a sound or brush against the branches, he moved to where he could take aim at Reese, the male Abscrag, and Goodwin. To his disgust, Reese was chewing the chunk of flesh he'd torn from Goodwin's hand while watching the female soldier's body writhe as the virus took hold.

Rage and grief filled Torran's gut, making it hard to breathe, but he had to do the right thing.

Torran was about to fire when something moved just out of his periphery. He spun about to see Rosario rushing toward him at top speed. Her helmet was gone and her cheek was gashed open beneath red eyes. Aware of her body armor, he aimed for her face and fired. Rosario's head snapped back and she tumbled onto the forest floor.

As the transformed SWD soldiers hurtled out of the darkness, a few were downed by the barrage of discs fired by Alkan as she attempted to take advantage of Torran being distracted. Torran sprinted through the woods and past his former squad writhing in the grip of the charge from the discs. The few that Alkan hadn't hit gave pursuit, screeching.

"Fuck!" the female Abscrag shouted.

"Hit him!" Reese ordered.

"I can't! My electroshock rifle is out!" Alkan replied.

"Take mine!"

Torran switched on the light on his weapon, illuminating his way. The Abscrags had him in view and there wasn't a chance in hell he'd be able to find a place to hide before they'd be on him. It was easier to move with the light revealing the obstacles on the forest floor

The Abscrags were relentless in their pursuit. A few managed to get ahead and double backed in an attempt to charge him. Not faltering in his run, he fired directly at their heads, not wasting ammunition on their armored bodies. The faces of friends vanished into clots of bone, flesh, and brains.

The terrified soldier broke free of the trees and dashed across a field flanking the woods. Illuminated by the moonlight, the wild grass undulated in waves around him. In the distance were the spotlights on the high walls of The Bastion. Home had never looked so far away.

Reloading his weapon as he ran, Torran tried to block out the sound of the heavy footfalls that were gradually gaining on him. A few times he stumbled as his foot caught on gnarled roots, jagged rocks, and uneven patches hidden by the grass. Each blunder lost him valuable ground and time.

Activating his wristlet, Torran opened his comm to the SWD command. "Base, the squad has wiped. There are Abscrags at my location. They are armed with electroshock weapons. I need immediate evacuation."

"Master Seeker MacDonald, find shelter and hold your position until we can dispatch a tiltrotor to retrieve you," came the answer he did not want to hear.

Torran leaped onto the road that cut through the open fields toward the underground subway station. The asphalt was uneven, but at least he could see where he was going. A few seconds later, the sound of additional heavy boots slapping against the blacktop reverberated through the night.

"I'm in route to the entrance to the subway station. Please relay request for the doors to be opened."

"Are Inferi Scourge in pursuit?"

Torran didn't have to look over his shoulder to know that they were. He could hear their screeches and the pounding of their feet as they advanced on him. Yet he still needed to report in his status. He shot a quick look behind him. The Abscrags were definitely closing the gap. Their weapons hung at their sides, but his former squad seemed to have no interest using them. Instead they were snapping their teeth and growling out one word: "Hungry."

"I have at least twenty in pursuit," he answered truthfully, and knew he was sealing his fate.

"Find a secure location and contact us for evac," the woman on the other end answered without an iota of emotion in her voice.

"There's no way I can shake these—"

Torran realized base had killed his comm connection when the wristlet went dark.

"Shit!"

Lungs and muscles burning, Torran surveyed the area ahead. The scorched remains of Inferi Scourge were in piles along the road along with bins filled with items salvaged from the bodies. The special ops unit had obviously cleared this area before the final push. If the Abscrags weren't so close, he might have been able to hide among the bodies.

Footsteps of an Abscrag were directly behind him. Torran hoped it was only one closing the gap. Lifting his weapon, he came to a hard stop, letting the butt of the heavy duty firearm punch over his shoulder. There was a loud grunt as the Abscrag collided with his body. Torran's weapon slammed into the face of his pursuer, knocking the Abscrag back. Pivoting about, Torran used his weapon as a shield to knock the his attacker completely away before firing at the head of a man he'd once had drinks with in an illegal pub. The creature fell at his feet.

Three more Abscrags closed in and Torran took a deep breath, aimed, and fired rapidly at the exposed faces of all three. More were coming and there was no time to strip the weapons or ammunition off the bodies if he were to keep ahead of them.

With nowhere else to go, he ran toward the subway station.

CHAPTER 5

The maintenance cart zoomed along the track and through the endless blackness. Lindsey fought against the suffocating fear the absolute dark inspired within her. It was far too easy to imagine the Inferi Scourge hiding in the murk, ready to seize her as she passed and drag her into the rough ground to infect her, but the sensors on her helmet only revealed the track unspooling through a long tunnel.

The dread twisting her insides made it difficult to not be overly imaginative. She didn't seem to be the only one disquieted by the surroundings. The others with her had lapsed into nervous silence too.

Opening the comm to Petra, Lindsey queried, "What's his status?"

Though Lindsey didn't want to ponder the survival chances of the lone survivor outside the wall, she couldn't help but do exactly that. To open the doors was a huge risk, not only to her small squad, but possibly the city.

"They're leaving him to die," Petra answered. She sounded like she was gritting her teeth. "All the SWD forces are concentrated on the areas visible to the news feeds. They're putting on their big show. Vaja says there is a lot of concern about the squad wiping because of something they're calling the Aberrations. SWD command is working on an idea to deal with the threat, but they're calling the squad a loss."

"So he ran into some of those Anomalies that Dr. Curran was talking about."

"The soldier's calling them Abscrags."

Lindsey exhaled. Obviously the squad had known about the Inferi Boon that had gone bad and nicknamed them Abscrags. The word fit. "What are the commandant's orders?"

"Vanguard, this is your call," Commandant Pierce answered over the comm, surprising Lindsey. "You have a better read on the situation than I do."

"Let me see his location."

Vaja had already hacked The Bastion security grid to mask Lindsey and her squads' whereabouts. It would be easy for him to locate the soldier on the run.

A new map fed onto her faceplate and showed the location of the soldier's wristlet signal. His name glowed in green lettering over a glowing yellow dot: Master Seeker Torran MacDonald. The Abscrags also showed up on the screen as small red dots. The sight sent a chill down Lindsey's spine. Red indicated a dead citizen. It was how The Bastion made sure to remove civilian corpses immediately after death for fear of the Inferi Scourge Virus becoming airborne and creating a new outbreak. Yet on her visual the red dots were in clear pursuit of the living person. The risen dead seeking to infect the living.

She shuddered.

Glancing toward the small screen on the console of the maintenance car, Lindsey saw that it was swiftly approaching the subway station. Calculating the distance to the station and the progress of MacDonald, she extrapolated that they could possibly make it out of the station and close the blast doors behind them before he reached the outer steps.

"We'll help him," Lindsey decided.

"You can't bring him inside The Bastion, Vanguard. We can't risk a possible infiltration by the Scrags," Commandant Pierce replied.

"But we can kill the Scrags after him and give him a chance to find shelter."

There was a pause. Then Pierce said, "Agreed."

"What if he tells the SWD about the rescue?" Petra asked, her tone anxious.

"Master Seeker MacDonald used to be Constabulary," Commandant Pierce said. "He'll know to keep the rescue to himself. Good luck, Vanguard."

"Petra, let the Master Seeker know we're on our way," Lindsey ordered.

"Yes, sir," Petra said, then closed the comm link.

Switching over to talk to her people, Lindsey said, "We're heading outside the blast doors on a rescue mission.

"Do we get to shoot something?" Franklin asked, excitedly leaning forward from the back seat. Then after a beat added, "Sir."

"A whole lot of somethings. Hobbes, as soon as we hit the station, I'll need a ride up to the doors. We need to be fast and outside before our party guests arrive. No flamethrowers. Setting them on fire is only going to jeopardize us. They used to be our people, so expect them to be in full armor. Aim for the spots where you don't want to get hit." Lindsey unclipped her flamethrower and handed it to Giacomi, who promptly stored it in the empty tool locker.

"Neck, underarms, and inner thighs," Franklin muttered. "But it's SWD armor. They probably have better protection."

"Then get creative. We can do this," Lindsey snapped. The sick feeling in her gut was only growing in intensity. Though she didn't want to put any of her squad or herself at risk, there was no way in hell she was going to abandon one of their own like the damn SWD was clearly willing to do.

Hobbes grinned at her through the facemask of his helmet. For a second, he reminded her of Ryan, her long dead friend. Lindsey instantly regretted the comparison. She didn't want to lose Hobbes just like she'd lost Ryan. It was hard enough that she was losing, Maria, her closest friend, and Dwayne, who'd been an ally over the last few hard months.

The maintenance cart slowed to a halt before the old platform. Hobbes leaped out as Lindsey edged off the cart. Giacomi and Franklin bounded onto the track, then ran toward the blast doors. Much to Lindsey's embarrassment, she allowed Hobbes to toss her across his broad shoulders and sprint after the other two soldiers.

A second later, the blast doors started to slide open, the emergency lights embedded in the track flickering on. Just inside the growing opening was a dead Constabulary soldier.

Medic Michael Denman.

Giacomi and Franklin advanced on him warily until they saw the large wounds at the back of his head.

"Don't move him," Lindsey ordered. "We need to avoid any possibility of contamination."

The two soldiers stepped around the dead body and eased onto the stairwell, weapons at the ready. Hobbes set Lindsey down and she rapidly lifted her weapon. It hurt like hell, but she left her cane behind. She'd limp and the pain would be terrible, but she'd be able to hold her own as long as they weren't forced to run.

If that happened, she was as good as dead.

She wondered if the commandant now regretted sending her.

Torran's muscles protested every step. Running across uneven terrain was far different from running on the treadmills in the SWD workout center. One misstep had driven a shock of pain through his joints and now his back ached. The humid air clogged his throat and made each breath feel like a gasp for air. To make matters worse, his armor had taken damage at some point and the coolers weren't working, so he was beginning to overheat.

Of course the Abscrags following him were undeterred by such things. He could hear them closing in again.

Already, he'd stopped twice to thin the herd chasing him. The numbers of those hunting him weren't diminishing, but swelling. It wasn't only the undead members of his squad he had to worry about now, but regular Scrags, too. The long undead creatures rushed out of the dark to join their comrades in their mission to capture and infect him.

At least, Torran assumed they wanted to infect him. After seeing Reese eating Goodwin's flesh and the awful remains of Cormier's body, he wasn't too sure anymore. The Inferi Scourge weren't supposed to be cannibals, but carriers. Something had gone wrong and created the Abscrags.

There wasn't a sign of Alkan and Reese yet, but he had no doubt they were in pursuit. He'd been fortunate enough to get a head start on the smartest and deadliest of the Abscrags, but he wasn't sure how much longer he could keep ahead.

Again Torran halted long enough to take down the nearest creatures. This time, his shots killed regular Scrags and just one of his former squad members. It was easier to slay the ones whose faces he didn't recognize.

rinting, he saw the entrance to the subway looming ahead, a
ete structure with broken vid screens on the side facing the road.
It was a gray block against the desolate landscape. Low barrier walls
framed the exiting stairs.

Torran's mind spewed out ideas: maybe he could climb on top and
fire down at the Scrags; maybe he could take cover behind the low wall
and kill all of them before the most dangerous Abscrags caught up: or
maybe he should just save a bullet for himself.

His wristlet chimed and he swiftly swiped the screen.

"Master Seeker MacDonald, this is Commandant Pierce. Proceed to
the subway station entrance. A Constabulary squad dispatched to the
area will assist in eliminating the Inferi Scourge."

"Yes, sir!"

Relief flooded him, though it was a shock to hear the voice of the
highest-ranking officer in the Constabulary. The last time he'd seen the
formidable commandant was when she'd pinned a medal on his chest
before he retired.

"Once the situation is under control, you will wait for evac by the
SWD."

There was a hint of a warning in her voice that made it clear that
something was irregular about the situation. Torran knew from his
debriefing that none of the Constabulary forces were included in
clearing of the valley, so the fact that grunts were in the area was
probably unknown by the SWD command. If that was the case, it
meant the commandant wanted him to keep his mouth shut.
Considering that it was the Constabulary coming to his rescue and not
the SWD, he had no problem complying with her wishes.

"Understood," he answered, huffing along.

"Very well."

The connection ended.

Dragging in deep breaths of humid, bitter air, Torran fired at a
Scrag charging at him from behind one of the bins flanking the road.
The bullets struck the gruesome creatures shoulder, but it didn't falter.
Snagging another clip from his bag, he ejected the spent one from his
weapon with his other hand. The Scrag, a male with short dark hair
and a thick gray beard, charged him again. Torran was just slamming
the new clip home when a bullet sheared off the top of the Scrag's head
and sent the being spinning about before another bullet found its mark
and killed it.

Whipping about, Torran saw four Constabulary soldiers positioned
in the entrance of the subway station. The blast doors creaked closed
behind them. One soldier stood close to the overgrown pathway,
shooting any Scrag daring to emerge from the murky landscape.

On a second rush of adrenaline, Torran sprinted the last few meters
to join the group. The tall one firing at the Scrags with impressive
accuracy was a woman with very dark skin and dark eyes. She didn't

even glance at him as he leaped over the low wall and landed on the steps.

"Master Seeker, good to see you," a woman with vanguard pips on her armor said with the flash of a smile behind her faceplate. Her voice sounded a little odd coming through the exterior speaker of her helmet and he detected one of the accents from the Isles.

"You have no idea how good it is to see you, sir," he answered breathlessly.

"Approaching horde of indeterminate number arriving in two minutes," a man said, then added to Torran, "You got a procession following you."

"I could've done without the escort." Torran slid his pack off and opened it so he could easily remove his last clips. Grabbing a pouch of water, he tore off the top and gulped it down. Torran spotted the nameplate on the commanding officer's armor: Rooney. It explained the lilt in her voice.

"Give the situation status." The woman in charge stared at him. The faint light from her helmet readouts illuminated her features, revealing a grim line to her full lips and incredible hazel eyes.

"The Abscrags...which are thinking Scrags—"

"I know what they are," Vanguard Rooney interjected.

Torran regarded her in surprise. "Oh, well, they have electroshock rifles."

"From a downed tiltrotor," Rooney said with a nod.

"So *that's* how they got them. When my squad split up to cover the area, the Abscrags used the rifles to immobilize them. Then they infected them."

"One bite is all it takes," Rooney muttered. "So even though they're... Abscrags... they still want to infect?"

"Yeah, but for their own reasons. A soldier running with me took a hit from one of the rifles. I didn't realize she was down until I took cover, and then I couldn't get to her. One of the Abscrags took off her glove and bit into her hand."

"Shit," Rooney swore.

"They're making more Abscrags because they want more numbers to their cause. They want into the city."

"They won't make it," Vanguard Rooney replied, her eyes hard.

Torran appreciated her determination. "The two most dangerous ones are in Constabulary uniforms. A white woman and a black man. I heard their names: Alkan and Reese. They're a lot smarter and faster than the rest. The only really stupid thing they did was take off the helmets of most of the squad to infect them. Which means it's a lot easier to kill those particular infected. Though, three bullets to the faceplate of a helmet will shatter it."

Rooney nodded. "Understood. Hobbes, get to the top of this structure. Giacomi, watch our backs. Franklin, join Hobbes. You're our best sniper. MacDonald, you're with me."

"Yes, sir!" was the chorused reply.

The man named Hobbes sprang onto the top of the wall, then leaped and caught the edge of the roof. Boosting his body up and over the lip, he disappeared out of view.

Behind the clear facemask of her helmet, Vanguard Rooney was obviously assessing the information scrolling across it. She was young, blond, and had a fierce look in her hazel eyes that Torran instantly respected.

Franklin's weapon continued to bark out single shots while swiftly following in Hobbes wake. Giacomi and the vanguard took over weeding out the strays while Franklin ran along the back wall and jumped to grab Hobbe's hand. He easily swung her up onto the roof.

The newly made Abscrags sprinted into range, screeching at the top of their lungs. In the mix were a few of the older Scrags, but Torran saw far too many of the faces of people who'd been comrades and friends. There were many more in the herd than he'd anticipated and, unexpectedly, the chance of any of them surviving was questionable. Yet now that he was in cover, the illusion of protection made it harder to pull the trigger. Gritting his teeth, he fought his hesitation, fired, and watched the bullets shred through human flesh and skulls.

On the ground, the three soldiers had their weapons at full auto. On top of the structure, Hobbes and Franklin took up sniper positions.

"Aim for the heads," the vanguard growled, her frustration clear as a few Scrags managed to evade the bullets peppering the ground.

Six Abscrags raced through the killing zone and straight for the three soldiers taking cover below the low wall. They were all former SWD soldiers and their weapons slapped against their backs.

"Hungry," their voices growled through din, animalistic and terrifying.

"If they're so smart, why aren't they using their weapons?" Giacomi pounded up a few steps and fired directly at the helmets of several of the approaching Abscrags.

It was a legitimate question. Torran had already seen two of the Abscrags, the more intelligent ones, using weapons. His mind whirled at the possibilities.

A second later, Giacomi gasped and toppled over.

CHAPTER 6

Lindsey heard Giacomi's voice rasp through her helmet speakers, then caught sight of her crumpling at the top of the steps. Straightaway, she climbed upward to grab Giacomi and drag her back into cover. "Hobbes, Franklin, cover me!"

The bark of the weaponry was reassuring as she reached for Giacomi. A Scrag toppled to the steps not far from her, thrashing violently until another bullet killed it.

"Don't touch her!" MacDonald exclaimed, grabbing Lindsey's arm to prevent her from doing so. "An electroshock disc hit her!"

Following the invisible line from the tip of his pointing finger to Giacomi, Lindsey saw the small black disc clinging to the old Constabulary armor, sparking with energy. It took only a second for Lindsey to realize what was happening and skirt back down the stairs.

"Shit. They're herding the dumber ones to distract us while they move into position! Hobbes, Franklin, get down here!"

The two soldiers scrambled to comply.

Franklin let out a startled cry.

Lindsey's heart skipped a beat.

"It just dinged my helmet," Franklin said breathlessly, dropping down.

It was impossible to hear the electroshock rifles discharging over the roar of the heavy weaponry firing around her. Lindsey aimed for an older Scrag rushing toward them just as Hobbes landed with a hard thump behind her.

"They got Hobbes," Franklin exclaimed, scrambling to get into a better position to fire, yet stay out of sight. She used the railing as a foothold and lifted herself into a better spot.

Lindsey gave Hobbes' vibrating body a brief look, but knew she couldn't touch him until the disc ran out of juice.

"They'll try and flank us," MacDonald said to Lindsey. "That's what they did earlier."

"Then cover our asses," Lindsey answered briskly.

MacDonald immediately scrambled to comply.

Lindsey continued to fire, aiming purposefully at the helmets of the former SWD squad and the exposed heads of Scrags. Their numbers were diminishing, but the swarm continued to rush their position. A few fell just a scant foot from their cover. So far, only one had made it over the wall, but for how much longer?

Behind her, MacDonald was firing at the creatures attempting to attack from the other side. One Abscrag in black SWD armor raced past the others and threw itself at the wall. Lindsey ducked as he flew over her head, landing on the stairs. Writhing about, it instantly scrabbled at MacDonald's legs, trying to gain purchase. The man was without a helmet, his left cheek missing.

"Fucking hell," MacDonald grunted and shot his former comrade in the face, turning his head to avoid the splatter.

"Did you get any on you?" Lindsey grabbed his shoulder and jerked him about.

"No, I'm good," MacDonald answered, his thin face fierce.

He was furious, that much was clear. Lindsey didn't blame him. Life was being horribly unfair to him. Heaving his weapon into position, he fired at the Scrags rushing him.

Discs pelted the stairs from the side and Franklin dropped from her perch as she attempted to avoid the incoming danger. "Shit!"

Lindsey fell back across the steps, the impact jarring the breath from her lungs, but she kept her weapon aimed at the darkness looming at the top of the stairs. Someone was out there, skirting the main battle to fire at them from the side. The blackness of the night was hazy, and Lindsey checked her map on the corner of her helmet. There was no wristlet signal emanating from where the discs had to have originated.

"The two dangerous ones, Master Seeker. Did they have wristlets?"

MacDonald was flush against the wall lining the steps, his gun aiming overhead in case a Scrag bounded onto the stairwell. "I don't recall seeing any."

Lindsey studied the red dots still on her helmet. Only two were still moving, but they weren't the intelligent Abscrags they needed to worry about. "Franklin, we got two left. Attempting to sneak up on our blind spot. They're not on our sensors."

"I'll find them. They're mine," came the brisk answer. Franklin was also lying across the steps, wary of any more shots fired from the electroshock weapons, but she started to rise.

"No, hold position." Lindsey hated that they were pinned down, but it was a risk she'd taken when she decided to rescue MacDonald. Quickly analyzing all possibilities, Lindsey realized they couldn't leave their position without risking the lives of Hobbes and Giacomi and themselves. If they opened the blast doors, they risked the Abscrags charging to get inside. Then she realized what she had to do.

"Can you move Giacomi?" she asked MacDonald.

Keeping his body flush against the steps, he dared to poke his head up to look at Giacomi. "Disc is dead. I'll get her."

While he crawled upward to retrieve the fallen soldier, Lindsey checked on Hobbes. The disc clinging to his armor was still sputtering, but was terminating. "As soon as it's dead, we need to move him above us."

"As a barricade?" Franklin asked incredulously.

"They want to disable and infect us. Giacomi and Hobbes are already knocked out."

Lindsey was not comfortable with her decision, but if the three of them were hit, too, it was over. Lindsey continued to watch her screen and the two red dots of the remaining members of MacDonald's squad.

They were rushing about the area in a zigzag. She suspected they were trying to find more Inferi Scourge to direct to the subway entrance. It's what she would do if she were the clever Abscrags. Gather a bunch of the mindless undead, drive them at the enemy, and then take advantage of the commotion.

MacDonald wiggled back down the stairs, dragging Giacomi with him. A few seconds later, the disc died. Hobbes was huge, so it took both women to scoot him up the stairs just as MacDonald reached them with Giacomi. A few discs ricocheted off the walls and steps, but fell short of their position. Realizing what they were doing, MacDonald angled Giacomi on her side above Hobbes. The three remaining soldiers squatted on the lower landing in front of the closed entrance.

"They're going to cause a stampede with the regular Scrags." Lindsey kept an eye on the two red dots on her screen as they separated and headed in opposite directions.

"I see it," Franklin agreed. "They'll hit us from both sides and the Abscrags will come down the center."

"Right. But we're not going to give them that chance," Lindsey replied.

It was evident by how far away the two dots were from the subway that the two turned SWD soldiers were having difficulty rounding up Scrags. That was definitely a good sign. She opened the comm to Petra and merged it so Franklin could hear. She felt bad to exclude MacDonald. "Petra, I need you to open the blast doors."

"Vanguard, I can't—"

"Not all the way. Just open it to about a meter, then shut it. We're pinned down and I need to draw out the intelligent Abscrags in charge of the others. They're the ones left over from the failed Inferi Boon missions."

"Do it," Commandant Pierce's voice ordered over the line. "Kill them and destroy their bodies."

"Understood." Lindsey leaned toward MacDonald. "Did you hear any of that?"

"Opening the doors as bait," he whispered back.

She barely heard his voice, but could read his lips.

"Not all the way," she answered him.

"Understood," MacDonald said, nodding.

"Franklin, cover the right. MacDonald, the left. I've got center." Lindsey glanced up at the top of the structure. "No way up to the roof other than scaling the low walls, right?"

"Correct. They'll have to hit us by coming over the walls or down the stairs," Franklin answered.

"Then we keep our backs to the doors." The two red dots on Lindsey's screen were still a safe distance away. "Petra, open it up."

The blast doors behind them shuddered as the gears within twirled and opened the locking mechanism. A second later, the doors started to part.

"Let's see how desperate they are." Lindsey adjusted her crouch and pressed against the steps, her gun resting on Hobbes' shoulder. Her leg and hip were on fire with pain, but Lindsey ignored the discomfort.

Franklin and MacDonald also tried to minimize how visible they were from the top of the stairs and lifted their weapons.

The doors continued to yawn open.

Lindsey could only hope that the Abscrags took the bait. It wasn't just her life on the line, but those of her squad, MacDonald, and the city. The intelligent Inferi Scourge would cause serious trouble for the forces clearing out the valley. If the Anomaly Scrags continued to ambush squads and transform them, a new outbreak would cause delays The Bastion couldn't afford. The very survival of The Bastion's populace depended on the valley being retaken and the lost resources being reclaimed. Humanity was hovering on the brink of extinction.

The Abscrags had to die.

"Where are they?" Franklin's voice whispered through the feed.

"Watching," Lindsey answered.

If she were her enemy, she'd be weighing her options. They were under duress to make a choice and soon, which meant they might act on impulse.

"I have to shut the doors, Vanguard," Petra said.

"Understood." Lindsey knew this would be the pivotal moment. Once the doors started to close, the Abscrags would have to make a decision.

"They're going to rush us now," MacDonald said with certainty.

A loud Scrag screech sliced through the night. The two red dots on Lindsey's readout started to turn back. Body tensing, Lindsey aimed at the top of the stairwell.

The attack came from both flanks. The two Inferi Scourge bounded over the low wall at the same time from opposite sides. The Abscrags hadn't dared to fire on the three soldiers below in fear of losing precious seconds they needed to get into the subway station. The woman, Alkan, landed on top of the insensible forms of Hobbes and Giacomi, lost her balance, and slammed backwards onto the stairs.

The male, Reese, landed in close proximity to Franklin, almost striking her, but she managed to roll to one side. Landing awkwardly on one leg, there was an audible snap as his femur took the brunt of his weight. Howling, Reese lost track of his weapon as he toppled over.

It was all happening so fast.

Lindsey attempted to aim at the female, but Alkan swung her electroshock weapon toward Lindsey and MacDonald and fired in short bursts. Ducking, Lindsey hunched behind her two unconscious friends. Hobbes' body seized as a disc struck him. Flinching, Lindsey mentally apologized to him.

Behind Lindsey, Reese grappled with Franklin. Lindsey gritted her teeth and lashed out with one leg, her boot slamming into the side of his head. With a terrifying screech, he turned on her, red eyes illuminated by the light from Lindsey's weapon. Her finger started to pull on the trigger just as Reese was struck by one of the discs. Collapsing, Reese's body fell toward the closing doors. Franklin grunted as she kicked him with both feet, knocking him away from the entrance.

"I'm good, I'm good," Franklin said breathlessly. She had apparently only received a minor shock. With a grunt, she fired a single bullet into Reese's head.

Meanwhile, next to Lindsey, MacDonald attempted to get a good shot at Alkan. The female Abscrag was relentless and had MacDonald pinned. He couldn't even risk lifting his head for fear of being hit. The second she had to reload, Alkan had to know she was as good as dead. Lindsey and MacDonald both waited for that inevitable moment, fingers ready on the trigger.

Instead, Alkan gave the unconscious bodies at her feet a mighty shove while continuing to fire. Hobbes rolled onto Lindsey, pinning her to the steps with his weight. Meanwhile, the blast doors continued to close and the female Abscrag was single-minded in reaching it. Leaping over the tangle of bodies, Alkan fired at Franklin at nearly point blank range, paralyzing her instantly.

MacDonald flung off Hobbes' legs just as Lindsey rolled out from beneath him. Alkan hurtled her body toward the doors.

Lindsey realized in that moment her plan had failed.

Torran ascertained that the female Abscrag was going to make it through the doors if he didn't act. He and Lindsey were jumbled up at the bottom of the stairs with her unconscious squad members. Shoving off the heavy legs of the man, Torran watched as Alkan leaped over them and toward the opening only to be momentarily thwarted by Reese and Franklin. The insidious little black discs embedded in both the living and the dead soldiers were sparking, meaning she couldn't touch either one.

Attempting to drag his weapon out from under Hobbes, Torran shouted, "Alkan!"

The woman whipped her head toward him in surprise.

"You're not going in," Torran shouted.

Alkan shot at him just as he expected.

And the vanguard shot Alkan just like he hoped.

As the Abscrag crumpled to the ground, Torran flinched as the evil black disc unleashed its current into his armor, causing his limbs to spasm. A second later, it was knocked into the wall with the butt of Rooney's weapon.

"How are you?" Rooney asked, leaning over him her hazel eyes wide. "You still with me?"

"Yeah, yeah." His head felt heavy and he was fairly convinced his legs and arms had fallen off. A second later, his limbs reconnected to his brain and he rubbed them in an effort to get rid of the disquieting fizzing in his muscles. "Just got a nip of it."

The doors shut with a boom.

"We've got the two remaining Abscrags from your squad heading back here. I don't know if they're bringing company. I need you. The others are..." Rooney glanced toward her downed squad. "It's you and me."

Climbing unsteadily to his feet, Torran nodded and his brain sloshed around in his skull. It was definitely not the best feeling. He didn't even realize he was slanting to one side until Rooney put her hand on his arm and pushed him upright.

"MacDonald, I need you," she said sternly. "Focus."

"I'm good. I'm good." Torran cleared his throat and narrowed his eyes. The disc must not have fully discharged, since he was still on his feet, but it had him off center. Lifting his weapon, he concentrated on his surroundings.

Rooney grabbed the rail with one hand and pulled herself up the steps. It took Torran a second to realize she was injured. He swiftly tucked an arm about her waist to help her.

"Don't. Keep alert. I'll handle myself." She gently pushed him away, and then pointed up. "They're coming around. They regrouped. Without them--" her eyes shifted toward the dead pair at the base of the stairs "—I don't think they'll know what to do."

The screech of Scrags sounded nearby. It was only a few voices though, and there wasn't a responding cry from others in the area. The special ops team had done their job, and well. The Scrag population was nearly wiped out.

"Not too many left, Vanguard."

Rooney smiled slightly. "No. Not too many. The special ops did their job..."

"I was just thinking that, too." Torran found himself matching her labored stride up the stairs. It was hard not to try to help her, but he could see she wouldn't accept it.

In the distance came the sound of explosions.

"They're wrapping it up with a big fiery bow," Rooney decided.

"A big booming bow," Torran agreed, "on the big nice present of no more Scrags."

"Let's finish our part," Rooney said. "You and me. No more Abscrags."

They were almost to the top of the stairs. Looking up, Torran forced his leaden feet to move. Maybe it was just the electroshock disc, exhaustion, or the hangover from his earlier adrenaline rush, but he just wanted to sit on the stairs and doze for a few minutes.

"And here they are," Rooney whispered.

Bullets tore through the night, punching into the cement over their heads. Immediately, Rooney and Torran crouched, weapons raised.

"They weren't doing that before." The vanguard almost sounded offended.

"They don't have someone to give them orders anymore. They may be falling back to old bad habits I taught them. Like shoot at the enemy."

"Hungry," a voice he recognized shrieked.

"Fuck," Torran cursed.

It was Goodwin.

"Why are they saying that?" Rooney demanded.

"They're cannibals," Torran replied.

"Scrags bite to *infect*."

"These do more than that."

"Fuck! Could it get any more complicated?"

"Probably, but don't tempt fate, Vanguard."

"You know them, MacDonald. Talk to them," Rooney insisted.

Not sure what she expected to happen, Torran obeyed. "Goodwin, it's me. Master Seeker MacDonald."

"Hungry!"

Two voices.

Jonas was with Goodwin.

"Jonas, Goodwin, glad to see you're okay." Wincing at his words, he lifted his weapon higher. The spot at the top of the stairs was ominous. They could appear at any second and either he'd kill his former companions or be killed.

"Hungry. So hungry." Goodwin's voice again.

"Yeah? Me, too. I'd love a nice plate of potato salad."

Rooney edged up the stairs, grimacing in pain.

"Hungry!" It wasn't quite a word. More of a screech.

Torran carefully climbed. Sweeping his gaze over the opening above his head, he feared them coming over the wall. Rooney touched his knee, and then pointed left. Her large, heavily fringed hazel eyes seemed particularly vivid in the gleam from her helmet readout. If she was scared, she wasn't showing it. The wall that flanked the stairs was a mere three feet tall at the end of the opening. If he stood, his six-foot-two height would allow him to easily spot and fire at the remaining Abscrags. Of course, it would also put him in their sights.

Wincing, Rooney moved past him toward the opening. She'd fire from low and around the base of the wall.

"You know that place where we'd go get that great veggie sausage and potato salad? I hear they're having a special tomorrow on fried okra." Did his former squad members even understand what he was saying? They'd been able to take orders from the smarter Abscrags, but was it because they were the same breed?

Rooney reached her position and signaled for him to stop. He nodded and prepared to take the lives of yet more of his squad.

A single gunshot startled both of them. Rooney's eyes widened slightly.

"Hungry," Goodwin screamed. "Hungry!"

Rooney lifted her fingers and counted down.

As soon as she reached zero, Torran shot upward and aimed at where the voice of his former comrade had come from. His finger stilled on the trigger. The light from his weapon illuminated Goodwin. Her helmet was gone and her short red hair clung to her round cheeks. The young woman leaned over Jonas, tearing at his neck with her fingers. Ripping flesh from his body, she stuffed it into her mouth, rocking back and forth in anguish.

"What the fuck?" Lindsey was clearly disturbed, but she hadn't seen Cormier's body.

Torran darted around Lindsey and onto the old sidewalk. Goodwin continued to weep and feast on her bloody meal. Her weapon dangled at her side.

"You want me to do this, don't you?" Torran called, aiming at her.

Goodwin didn't answer, but stuffed more strips of meat into her crimson mouth. She hadn't wanted to be a Scrag. She'd vowed to never let them get her. Yet, here she was: not only dead and transformed, but worse than an ordinary Scrag. Bright red eyes turned toward him, the blood smeared across her face bright in the light cast by his weapon.

Torran heard Rooney limping to his side. He kept his weapon trained on Goodwin, but struggled to pull the trigger.

"It's the kind thing to do," Rooney said.

Pressing his lips together, Torran aimed for the center of Rooney's still child-like face. She was so young. Only eighteen.

"There's no cure, MacDonald, and this is worse... far worse than just being a Scrag."

Again, he and Rooney were of the same mind. It gave him some comfort that she understood how hard it was for him to pull the trigger.

"Sorry, Goodwin," he said sorrowfully.

He pulled the trigger.

Goodwin's body fell with a thump.

Rooney lightly touched his shoulder, then shambled past him. She was obviously in great discomfort, but she moved with purpose, her weapon at the ready.

Torran followed.

Reaching the bodies, Rooney went very still. "Very different from regular Scrags. Their eyes..."

"Yeah."

Rooney slightly bobbed her helmet. He could see her lips moving and knew she was talking to the Constabulary. She finished, then turned her attention back to him. "You'll have to destroy the bodies."

"Okay, but how?"

"We have flamethrowers. We're fixing the inventory so one of them will become a lost weapon of the final push. If you're asked, say you got the weapon off of one of the Abscrags. Understand?"

Torran stared into her eyes and saw only steely determination. He appreciated that in the face of such terrible circumstances. It kept him from sinking into the mire of his own thoughts. "Yes, I do."

"Your squad should be destroyed, too, but..." Rooney sighed. "You probably should keep close to the subway station and not try to track down all the bodies."

"Destroy them, too? Why? Oh, you're concerned about..." He lifted an eyebrow. "Ah. Samples."

Rooney's eyes narrowed. "Why would you say that?"

"Burning specific bodies. Wanting my squad destroyed, too. Seems like you don't want the SWD getting a hold of tissue samples. Of the variations of the virus."

Giving him a scrutinizing sidelong look, before looking toward the high walls of The Bastion, Rooney exhaled.

The mountain range encircling the vast valley made even The Bastion seem small, yet it was home. The only home they had.

"I won't say more." Torran bent down and removed the weapons from both bodies.

"Do you think she understood you were going to kill her?" Rooney was staring at the body of Goodwin.

"Yeah," Torran replied. "I think she did."

"But she wasn't herself anymore."

"That's the hell of it. I think a piece of her was still in there."

A dark shape emerged from the subway entrance. It was Hobbes.

"Linds, we good?"

"That's Vanguard Rooney to you, and yes, we're good. Keep watch. We got bodies to deal with."

"Linds..." Torran glanced down at Rooney. "Lindsey?"

"That's Vanguard Rooney to you, too." She hesitated, then gave him an unexpected smile. "But, yeah, it's Lindsey, Master Seeker MacDonald."

"Torran MacDonald."

"Good to meet you, Torran." She held out her hand to him.

Torran shook it, then lifted his eyes. "It's nearly over."

"The battle?"

"The night."

Together, they gazed toward the thin line of pale blue sky spreading beyond the high mountain tops.

"Then let's finish and go home, Torran."

CHAPTER 7

Lindsey didn't like leaving Torran behind. The man had suffered incredible losses and had spent a good portion of his night attempting to survive. Watching him speak with SWD command on his wristlet, she leaned against the walls lining the stairwell. The pain radiating up and down her leg was almost unbearable. Torran stood at the top of the stairs, Hobbes and Giacomi keeping watch for stray Scrags. Franklin sat on the wall watching the tiny specs in the air circling in the far distance. The tiltrotors were starting to pick up the ground troops. It was almost time for Lindsey and her squad to go home.

Torran finished his conversation, killed the comm line, and rushed down the stairs to where she stood trying to look like she wasn't in excruciating pain.

"They were surprised to hear from me, but they've got a tiltrotor on its way."

"Fantastic." Lindsey gave him a wry smile. "We're all going home."

Glancing significantly at the smoke rising from the nearby pyre, Torran said, "Well, some of us."

"I'm sorry about your squad," Lindsey said truthfully. "I've lost people, too. It's never easy."

"No, it's not. I thought I'd never go through this again, but..." Torran ran a hand over his sweaty, dirty brown hair.

"Again?"

"The final push. The failed one. A year and a half ago."

"You were there?"

"My squad was wiped out. I was the sole survivor."

"Same with me. Well, not sole survivor. Only me and my best friend Maria made it out. The rest of our squad died. We lost a lot of good people that day."

Torran nodded somberly. "Yeah, we did."

"Time for us to go. Got your story straight?" Lindsey observed the man's internal struggle. He didn't like lying, but she could see him coming to terms with the fact that he had to do just that.

"Yeah. I do. I still don't understand why the Constabulary wasn't part of this whole operation to begin with."

"You will," Lindsey promised him. The worm would be going out in a matter of minutes. Soon the entire city would know all about Admiral Kirkpatrick and the SWD's attempt to take over the government.

"The body in the subway...I wasn't going to ask about it, but..." Torran stared at her pensively. "He was one of them, wasn't he? An Abscrag?"

"Something like that."

"And he got into the city and someone shot him?"

Lindsey pressed her lips together, her mind racing. He would know soon about the Inferi Boon, but she didn't want to incriminate herself any more than she had already. "There was a breach. It was dealt with. We're the cleanup crew."

"And you ended up saving me," Torran said.

"We don't leave people behind." Lindsey signaled to Giacomi and Hobbes and switched the comm in her helmet. "Petra, open the doors."

"There is so much more going on than I know about, isn't there?"

Lindsey laughed. "Well, yeah. Isn't there always? It wouldn't be The Bastion if not for the intrigue."

As the doors slid open, much easier now that they'd had a bit of use, Lindsey finally pushed off from the wall. It was difficult standing on her leg and she wobbled. Torran started to reach out to steady her, but Hobbes caught her about the waist and lifted her off the ground.

"Got you, Vanguard," he said. "I'll get you to your cane."

"Cane?" Torran looked at Lindsey sharply.

"The final push," she answered, shrugging.

"I suggest you get on the roof," Franklin said to Torran as she walked past him. "Just in case."

"Thank you. All of you." Torran's lean face was sorrowful, but also sincere.

"See you around, Master Seeker MacDonald."

"I look forward to it, Vanguard Rooney."

Hobbes carried her over the threshold and Lindsey glanced back as the door started to close. Torran was already scaling the wall, heading for the roof. She hated that she couldn't bring him back into The Bastion, but she was also certain he'd be safe until the tiltrotor arrived.

"He was kinda cute," Giacomi decided as they trudged toward the maintenance cart.

"For a skinny guy," Franklin agreed.

"He wasn't that skinny," Giacomi protested.

"I could bench press him." Franklin shook her head. "Besides, aren't you still seeing that one girl?"

"We're not exclusive. She's got a guy on the side."

"I volunteer for being a guy on the side," Hobbes said with a grin, helping Lindsey down the steps.

"Uh huh," Franklin gave him a dark look. "Don't you have enough women?"

Lindsey listened to the friendly banter, remembering all the times she and Maria gave Ryan hell. She missed both of them so much it was a physical ache in her chest. Knowing Maria and Dwayne were out there somewhere together was a small consolation. At least they had a chance at a life beyond the walls of The Bastion.

Settled into the cart and clutching the cane Hobbes had retrieved, Lindsey turned her attention to her wristlet. It was only a matter of minutes now. Maybe seconds.

After the four Constabulary soldiers settled into the cart, it zoomed down the track toward the bowels of the city.

A minute later all four wristlets chimed.

It was time to change the world.

Torran crouched on the roof of the entrance of the subway station. Weapon at the ready, he surveyed the vast land around him spotted with the bodies of the dead and bins of salvage. The Bastion was behind him, majestic and dour in the early morning light.

In his hand, he held the dog tags of Special Sergeant Amber Alkan and Special Constable Gareth Reese, along with those of Goodwin and Jonas. He had plucked the tags from the smoldering remains and intended to turn them over to his superiors during his debriefing. The mysterious and highly intelligent Abscrags had destroyed his squad and nearly killed him. If not for Vanguard Rooney and her squad, he'd be an Abscrag.

It was a very sobering truth.

Cocking his head, he watched the tiltrotors approaching from the south. There were still fires on the far side of the valley from where the last Scrag herds had been blasted with fire bombs. There was aircraft moving over the fires, long curtains of water flowing out behind them. It'd been years since he'd seen emergency fire control vehicles of any type.

The job wasn't done yet though. There were large portions of the valley where firebombs were not allowed due to coal deposits and the underground fuel refinery. Would he be sent out again, too? Given a new squad of fresh eager recruits? Or would he be found guilty of not making wise choices for his squad and be relieved of duty?

There weren't signs of Scrags near him, but along the foothills to the north the wooded areas could easily be hiding some. It wasn't the Scrags he was worried about anymore, but the Abscrags. What if Alkan and Reese had made more?

His wristlet chimed, surprising him. Glancing down, he saw multiple files rapidly downloading and unpacking.

A second later, a computerized voice said, "Details on the Coup d'état organized by Admiral Kirkpatrick have now been downloaded to your device."

"What the hell?"

Torran touched the screen and immediately a simple, but detailed menu popped up. All sorts of files had been sent not only to him, but appeared to be copied to every citizen of The Bastion. It only took him a few minutes after reading two files for him to finally understand why the Constabulary had not been involved in the clearing of the valley. Admiral Kirkpatrick, the leader of the SWD, had made a grandiose play for power and someone had uncovered it.

A message dinged into his wristlet. It was from Vanguard Rooney. He quickly opened it and her face appeared.

"You knew," Torran said.

"Your tiltrotor is being redirected to the Constabulary." Lindsey hesitated. "I'm sorry, Torran, but all SWD officers are under suspicion and are going to be debriefed by the Constabulary. If you like, I'll be the one to escort you."

"No. Don't do that. Keep your distance," Torran answered. "I'm not a part of this treason. I'll be fine."

"Very well," she said in a gentle tone. "Good luck."

The sound of the approaching tiltrotor nearly drowned out her voice.

"I'll see you around," Torran said, hoping that it was true.

Vanguard Rooney was gone.

Standing slowly, Torran waved to the approaching tiltrotor pilots.

In one night, so much had changed. The valley had been reclaimed and there was hope for the future once again.

Viewing the dog tags still clutched in one hand, Torran wondered if he'd ever really know the full truth.

"Vanguard Rooney, excellent job," Commandant Pierce said when Lindsey entered the Constabulary Command Center.

Barely able to walk even with the help of her cane, Lindsey saluted. "Thank you, sir."

Commandant Pierce returned her gaze to the display of monitors in front of her. "President Cabot is safely in his office. Constabulary forces escorted him there with the media in tow. Admiral Kirkpatrick is sequestered within the SWD Facility and is denying the details transmitted by the worm. He's also refusing to give himself up to the Judiciary Authority."

Scanning the Command Center for Vaja, Lindsey couldn't help but beam a bit. It was her sleuthing and her worm that had protected the rightfully elected government, even if President Cabot was a jerk. Not spotting her boyfriend among the uniforms, she focused instead on the surveillance feed coming in from around the capitol building.

"Commandant, we're in control, aren't we?"

"To some degree. SWD forces are still returning from their mission and there are squads occupying The Bastion City Command Center. It's touchy, but we're gaining the upper hand through the media coverage. The Inferi Boon are receiving a lot more sympathy and coverage than we anticipated."

That allowed Lindsey to relax with some measure of relief. She wanted people to look at the list of Inferi Boon names and feel sorrow. She'd never see Maria again in this life and it cut her to the core. The Inferi Boon had given their lives to save The Bastion and she wanted the population to feel the weight of that loss.

"I'm sure that makes you happy," Commandant Pierce said, glancing at Lindsey again.

"Do you think they would've felt the same way if Admiral Kirkpatrick had told the citizens that the Inferi Boon willingly gave up their lives to save us all?"

"They would've felt pride in the Inferi Boon, Vanguard."

"But what if Kirkpatrick said that they had to be killed to stop a possible infection? Do you think the population would have agreed with him about killing our own people?" Lindsey hated that she believed that the citizens of The Bastion wouldn't have felt grief.

"I guess we'll never know, will we?" Commandant Pierce gestured toward the myriad of screens. "The social networks are filled with irate citizens protesting the abuse of power by the SWD. That's exactly what we wanted. You're a hero, Vanguard Rooney."

"No one will ever know that." Lindsey rested one hand on her waist and leaned on her cane. "And that's how it should be. The real heroes are Maria and her squad. All those names up there. Omondi, Denman, Martinez, Mikado..."

"Agreed." The tall woman with intense ebony eyes motioned to an empty chair near a console. "Sit down, Rooney, before you fall over."

Begrudgingly, Lindsey obeyed.

Commandant Pierce sat in her own chair and bent toward Lindsey. "For the next few days, there will be a continuous explosion of indignation and denials. President Cabot knows that the Constabulary just saved his ass. He's going to do everything he can to keep this in the forefront of the media and the city. But already the media wants to know where the leak came from. There will be a witch hunt."

"Is that why Vaja isn't here?"

Commandant Pierce lifted an eyebrow. "He left once the worm went out. He doesn't have the stomach for this, does he?"

Lindsey wasn't sure she did either, but there was no way in hell she wasn't going to fight for her city.

"There's no way they can track it back to us, Commandant Pierce. I made sure of it. I even routed it through the SWD system." Lindsey was particularly proud of that part of her plan.

"At some point fingers will be pointed."

Lindsey leaned her elbow against the armrest of her chair and stared at the commandant. "Who's taking the fall?"

"I don't like doing this, Vanguard Rooney."

"Who?"

Commandant Pierce sighed. "Castellan Reichardt is missing from the city."

"Oh, fuck me," Lindsey muttered.

"We both know he's not coming back. President Cabot is already demanding a full accounting and demanding to speak to the castellan, since it's his job to protect the city. Once it's discovered that Dwayne is not inside the wall, it's only a matter of time before they'll investigate him. And they'll uncover his affair with Maria."

"And it will look like he created the worm out of spite."

"He was a part of all of this. When I shift the blame onto him, I won't be lying."

"But you're saving your ass!" Lindsey flinched. "Sorry, sir."

Commandant Pierce's eyes blazed with anger, but her voice was calm when she answered. "I saved all our asses. In the end, I have to protect not only my own ass, but yours, Vaja's, Petra, and every other person in this command center. And beyond that, the city."

Lindsey didn't dare say anything. She had to remember that even though circumstances had made her and the commandant allies, in the end, Pierce was her commanding officer.

With an exhalation, the other woman slumped in her chair. "The city will survive because of us, the SWD be damned."

"There are good people in the SWD," Lindsey said, thinking of Torran. "The man we rescued is one."

"MacDonald started off as one of us, but yes, I'm sure there are good people in the SWD. Just separating them from the traitors will be difficult."

"What will happen?" Lindsey asked.

"Trials. Most likely by tribunal. And if they're found guilty, they'll end up serving their lives in a small cell tucked into the wall." Commandant Pierce shook her head. "We're all that's left of humanity and yet there are people who will fight to have power over the masses no matter how small those masses might be. We serve the people, Vanguard." Pierce pointed at the screens. "We serve the people out there. If we ever forget that, we're doomed."

"Will they see the castellan as a hero?" She wanted people to see Dwayne for what he was: a noble, good, decent man who sacrificed so much for not only the woman he loved, but The Bastion.

"I hope so," Commandant Pierce answered.

Lindsey believed her.

"Now, go home. Rest. I'll need you back on duty in ten hours. We have a lot of work ahead of us and I'll need you in the mix. Also, I sent this to President Cabot's secretary today." Commandant Pierce tapped the pad at her side, then handed it to Lindsey.

Lindsey stared at the screen in surprise. "I don't understand. I thought they couldn't fix my leg because of resources."

"President Cabot wanted there to be wounded veterans of the final push as a symbol of the Constabulary's effort to protect the people of The Bastion. He ordered that any soldiers that had visible disabling injuries be denied medtech assistance."

Anger, raw and fierce, flamed inside Lindsey and clawed up her throat. She had to swallow hard to keep from swearing aloud.

"You were propaganda," Commandant Pierce said, lowering her eyes. It was clear that this order was not one she'd agreed with.

Unable to speak, Lindsey stared at the request for her leg to be repaired.

"President Cabot will do this for me. He now owes me," Commandant Pierce said confidently.

"Why waste that leverage on me?"

"It's not a waste when I need you ready to assist me in saving this city."

Lindsey smiled just a tad and tucked a loose strand of hair behind one ear. "I do appreciate this, sir. Immensely."

"Well, you've proven that even with your injury you're a brave and capable soldier. Master Seeker MacDonald would vouch for that, I'm sure."

"Is he going to be all right?"

Commandant Pierce gave Lindsey a questioning look.

"His whole squad was wiped out by Curran's Anomalies. It wasn't his fault. Those things were... clever."

"There will be an investigation and the review board will make a decision."

"Which review board? SWD? Or Constabulary?"

"There will probably be an independent board assigned by President Cabot in the interim. There will be a lot internal reviews and reordering of the duties of both the SWD and Constabulary."

Lindsey sighed. "It was awful seeing those soldiers transformed like that."

"The question is: did you get all of them? Another reason I need you up to full strength. The Constabulary will have to be a part of making sure each and every Scrag is destroyed. We can't risk an outbreak again."

The thought of a new plague was enough to send a shiver through Lindsey.

"Now, go home, Vanguard. I'll see you later."

Lindsey stood, picked up her cane, and reluctantly departed.

The streets were still packed with people. Whereas earlier, when word of the final clearing of the valley had sent the citizens into the streets to celebrate, news of the attempted coup had people clustered around portable vid screens while discussing the latest development.

Since the trains weren't running, Lindsey had to walk home. Usually Vaja gave her a ride on the back of his precious bike, but he was nowhere to be seen when she left the Constabulary headquarters. She had waited for a bit in the spot where he usually picked her up, but after he didn't show up, she started the trek home.

No one seemed to notice her for a few long blocks, then a young woman with a bright green kerchief wrapped around her head spotted her.

"Hey, you!" the woman said, hurrying to Lindsey's side. "You need a ride?"

Lindsey tilted her head and stared curiously at the stranger. "I would love one, but I don't see how—"

"Wait right here!"

The redhead vanished, then returned a minute later with a tall, bald man with large shoulders and enormous arms. The woman now carried colorful oversized pillows that had been patched numerous times. "Boris will take you home, officer."

"How?" Lindsey asked, eyes widening. "He's not going to carry me?"

"No, no," the man guffawed. Popping open a storage unit tucked into the side of a building, he pulled out a wheelbarrow.

The redhead set the pillows in the bottom and Boris motioned for Lindsey to get in.

Not sure if she should feel awkward or relieved, Lindsey just giggled.

"Let me take you back to your home. You've done so much for us," Boris pleaded. "Tina agrees. Tight, Tina?"

The redhead named Tina nodded. "Please?"

"Okay! Why not?" Lindsey awkwardly settled onto the pillows and grimaced as her leg protested. With some discomfort, she managed to get situated in a position that didn't cause her a lot of pain.

Boris lifted the handles and easily rolled her down the street with Tina rushing along at his side.

"Now, where do you live?" Boris asked.

Lindsey told him, grateful at the kindness. It wasn't the most comfortable way to travel, but it would have been very difficult for her to make it home alone. Several drones rolled past, flashing vids of the epic battle for the valley while also broadcasting a short, looped speech from President Cabot. Lindsey felt the eyes of many people on her as Boris wheeled her up and down the narrow, congested streets. Many reached out to pat her and a few shouted words of thanks.

"See! You're a hero!" Boris said with a giant grin on his face.

"I'm just doing my job."

"We're going to have a farm," Tina said to Lindsey excitedly. "We already applied this morning as soon as they put the applications on the net."

"No more road repair for me," Boris said happily. "I'm going to grow wheat so I can have good bread again. The kind my mother used to make."

"Everything is different now. Can't you feel it?" Tina grinned, the flush of her cheeks blending into her many freckles.

Lindsey tilted her head to watch a tiltrotor fly overhead. "Yeah," she said. "I feel it."

When they arrived at her flat, Vaja didn't meet her at the door. There wasn't a sign that he'd been home yet. Tina and Boris only left after making sure she was safely inside.

Exhausted, Lindsey took a hot shower before climbing up the stairs to her bed tucked onto the platform over her computers and desk. Her flat was very small and it was stuffy. She turned on a fan and checked the time. There would be at least three hours of circulated air before the rolling blackouts hit her area of the city. Adjusting the pillow under her head, she wondered where Vaja had gone. It felt strange to be alone in her small space after so much had happened. Tina and Boris were right. The world had changed, but she had no one to share the experience with.

Her wristlet chimed and she instantly swiped the screen.

It wasn't Vaja.

It was a message from Torran.

It said one word: *Thanks.*

PART 2

COLD WARS AND ALLIANCES

Lindsey stared at her leg for a long moment, then slowly extended it, pointing her toes. She'd painted her nails bright blue and they were a definite contrast to the gray concrete floor of her flat. Flexing her ankle, she was amazed by the lack of pain. Bending her knee, she did a few sharp kicks. Everything worked perfectly. After almost two years of being disabled, it was wonderful to actually be able to move without the endless gnawing pain. She'd been unconscious for nearly twenty-four hours while they had replaced nearly every part of her leg and stitched her back together. She had only experienced dreams toward the end of her sedation. In those dreams, she'd been running away from Scrags on legs that actually worked properly. It had been a relief to awaken in the safety of the Med Center, free of pain and without a Scrag in sight.

A week of rehabilitation was all it took to get her back in fighting form. The cocktail of drugs they'd pumped into her system had definitely accelerated the healing. The first time she'd run on the treadmill, she had started to cry tears of joy. Now, staring at her leg, she felt tears again.

The door chimed.

With a frown, she scrambled off her bed and walked over to the door. A quick glance at the screen next to the door showed Vaja on the doorstep. She palmed the primary lock and unlocked all the extra locks she'd installed to allow the door to slide open.

"You've got five minutes," she said gruffly, turned on her heel, and strode to her computers. She plopped onto the old chair and turned on the newsfeed. The media was camped outside of the SWD main building, still waiting for Admiral Kirkpatrick to surrender himself to the authorities.

"Lindsey," Vaja said in a soft, desperate voice. "Please, we can make this work."

"No we can't, Vaja. And why do you want it to? You've got how many other girlfriends?"

"This is about me leaving you that morning, isn't it? You're not forgiving me."

"You mean when you left me to walk home on a bad leg after I had risked my life to rescue someone and was in a shitload of pain?" Lindsey gave him a wide sarcastic smile. "Why would I possibly be mad about that?"

"Lindsey, please."

"No, Vaja. No 'Lindsey, please.' You left me in more ways than one that morning. I needed you, Vaja, just not to get home, but because of what I'd been through. What the entire fuckin' city was going through. Instead you disappeared for two fuckin' days and then I find out you're safe with one of your other girlfriends."

"Okay, so maybe I should have told you about the others." Vaja stood in the center of her small flat in his ragged, yet somehow stylish clothes with his amazingly sexy, floppy dark hair and smoldering blue eyes giving her a look that used to make her melt into his arms.

"Yeah, you think?" Lindsey shook her head and hooked one heel onto the edge of the seat of the chair. Resting her elbow on her knee, she watched the news and pointedly ignored Vaja.

"You look beautiful, Lindsey. Seeing you there with your leg looking so perfect. *You're* so perfect."

"I'm sure your other girlfriends are, too." Lindsey ignored him and pondered making herself some coffee. But knowing Vaja, he'd serve himself and she wasn't about to share her precious stores with him anymore.

"I always like it when you wear just your panties and tank top. It's very sexy—"

"Stop!" Lindsey held out one hand in his direction, palm facing him. "No more. I'm done. You're not staying here. You're not sleeping in my bed, eating my food, or sharing my space anymore. And you're certainly not fucking me again."

Vaja exhaled with frustration. "Lindsey, how can you doubt my love?"

Exasperated, Lindsey stood up, opened up her clothes locker, jerked out his knapsack from the bottom and started throwing his clothing into it. "If you won't pack, I will."

"You really want this to happen?"

"Yes!"

"It's because of that guy who sends you messages, isn't it?"

Lindsey gave Vaja a sharp look.

His narrow handsome face was unexpectedly flushed with anger. "I saw you checking your wristlet. I know it's a man."

"It's a fellow soldier who's going through a rough time. He gives me small updates so I know he's okay. Why am I telling you this? It's none of your business!" Fuming, Lindsey shoved Vaja's second pair of boots into the knapsack then tossed it at him. "Get out."

"I need my books."

Lindsey stalked over to a small shelf and plucked several worn journals off and handed them over. She'd been tempted to burn the things, but couldn't bring herself to destroy Vaja's writings. Even if she did find his poetry far too insipid now that she knew he was a lying cheater, she wasn't that petty.

"Lindsey, I wrote many of these for you."

"Right."

"I did."

"Are you sure you're not confusing me with your *other* girlfriends?" Lindsey stormed over to the door, glad to be able to stomp on both feet. She palmed the lock and it slid open. A gush of cold air made her shiver, but she wasn't moving until he was out of her flat and life. "Why don't you go read it to *them?*"

"Lindsey, I have so much love to share—"

"I don't care, Vaja!" She really didn't. He had abandoned her when she'd needed him most. He hadn't even gone to the Med Center when she had reconstructive surgery. Jittery over his involvement in the coup d'état revelation, he was constantly scurrying away from Constabulary and SWD security forces. If she'd known how terrified he'd be, she never would have brought him in. What was worse was that Commandant Pierce had trusted her when she'd vouched for Vaja. A part of her sometimes worried that throwing him out would make him turn on her, but he was far too terrified of the authorities to report Lindsey's hacking. At one point, Lindsey thought she might love him, but now she wondered what she'd been thinking. Maybe her mistake had been looking for love instead of friendship. She missed Maria a whole lot more than she'd miss Vaja.

"You won't see me again," Vaja said, as though that mattered anymore.

"Good." Lindsey smiled at her neighbor walking past her entrance. She waved, and the old man tried not to look at her near nudity. He failed miserably.

Vaja heaved his bag over his shoulder and glowered at her. "We could have had the greatest of loves."

"We had fun for a while. You were reasonably good in bed. You helped me out of a tough situation. But let's call it what it was. A relationship built on lies. I can't love someone who lies to me. So get out."

Hesitating in the doorway, Vaja gazed into her eyes. "I do love you."

Lindsey stepped back and put her hand over the lock. "I *don't* love you."

With one last sorrowful look, Vaja trudged down the stairwell.

Lindsey shut the door and exhaled. "Asshole."

After making some coffee and heating up some oatmeal, Lindsey returned to her computers and watched the latest updates pouring in from the news media and her other resources. She was also compiling snippets of information to send to Maria's wristlet. Though her friend was far away, Lindsey didn't want her to feel completely disconnected from The Bastion.

Now that Vaja was gone, she accessed the secret program buried in the wristlet's operating system. There weren't any new messages, but she had expected as much. The only one that was there was the one she'd received soon after Maria had disappeared. She hadn't found it for days, too unnerved by the chaos enveloping the city to dare to open the program that might provide connection to her friend. It was a program she'd created for Dwayne to use to speak to Maria while she had been part of the Inferi Boon special ops mission.

Tapping the simple message, Lindsey read it over quickly.

Linds, I love you. Please take care of yourself and remember to look for the good things in life. Make sure The Roses have plenty of business. Tell my mother I love her and I'm sorry. When you finally live outside those damn walls, think of me. Remember me. Know I love you. Forever your friend and sister, Maria.

Blinking back tears, Lindsey closed the message, wishing there had been another, but understood that they had to be very careful. The time stamp on the message indicated it had been sent twenty-four hours after Dwayne had departed the city. Lindsey hoped that meant the couple had safety made it out of the valley. She wanted to believe they were both alive and well somewhere out there in the world.

Lindsey had the day off, so she didn't need to check the duty roster, but went ahead and did so anyway to check on her friend's assignments. There was a lot of activity outside of the wall now that the valley was close to being declared uncontaminated. Sometimes, she watched the footage of the massive vehicles destroying old settlements and piling the debris onto the back of trucks for recycling. The act of destruction held a certain amount of fascination for her. Hobbes, Giacomi and Franklin were all on patrol outside the wall near the old hydroelectric plant. Torran was not on the roster for the SWD. He hadn't been since the day he'd returned from his failed mission.

It was amusing how jealous Vaja had seemed over simple messages from Torran updating her on his debriefs. Vaja had other women, but he'd been jealous of her fellow soldier. The man was ridiculous.

A quick cleanup of her dishes was followed by a shower. Lindsey tugged on some frayed blue jeans, a big brown sweater, an old pair of leather lace-up boots and a heavy black jacket. A cold front had blown in during the night, and it was rather chilly outside. Tucking her long blond hair into two messy fishtail braids that hung over her shoulders, she tugged a floppy dark green wool hat onto her head. Picking up a velvet box, which was the reason for her journey across the city, she tucked it into one of her coat pockets. It felt odd not reaching for her cane when she neared the door, but it was also a relief. A black nylon bag with half her uniforms stashed inside waited for her beside the door. Grabbing it, she let herself out of her flat and secured the locks.

The brisk air and muted sunlight gave the gray city an even more somber mood despite all the people rushing about to their various tasks. The roads tucked between the tall, narrow, nearly featureless buildings were clogged with people of all ages. The only bright spots were the makeshift gardens made out of old plastic containers hung from balcony railings and the laundry hanging on wash lines.

A drone ambled by with yet another message from President Cabot. She hadn't heard this one yet and partially paid attention while watching two little girls in matching red coats jumping rope in an alleyway. One little girl was dark-skinned with pigtails and the other was blond with braids. For a moment, Lindsey thought of her and Maria, though they'd not known each other until they'd enlisted. The sight of the two little girls looking so happy together brought a smile to Lindsey's face.

A few blocks down the way, she ventured up a rickety staircase to the building where Maria had once lived. All buildings had entrances on the second floor and were only accessible by retractable stairs. If there was an outbreak, the stairs were pulled up to keep the Scrags from entering. The steps wobbled under her as she ascended. Maria had often complained about them, but apparently nothing had been done to fix them yet. That was the way things worked in The Bastion. But all that was soon to change. At least she hoped so.

Entering the narrow hallways, she followed the heavy scent of chemicals until she reached an open doorway. Inside were two older women Maria had affectionately called The Roses. The married women were both named Rose. One was Rose Bergman, the other Rose Garcia. Lindsey called them Rose B and Rose G. This morning, the two women were busy ironing uniforms at mismatched iron boards. Both wore their hair long and tucked under colorful scarves. Rose B's was pure silver, while Rose G's curly hair was dark grey with strands of white. Maria had introduced Lindsey to the two women who did laundry in exchange for credits, food, and appliance repairs. Lindsey always tried to leave a little extra so Rose B could get her herbal remedies and medicines from the Med Center. The Roses usually tried to dissuade her from giving them too much, so she always had to figure out ways to sneak an extra credit or two into their hands.

"Oh, look! It's Lindsey!" Rose B hurried over with excitement while her wife watched grumpily. "And you're not limping!"

"Yeah, they fixed it last week," Lindsey answered, grinning. Rose B always wore her emotions on her sleeve, and Lindsey found it to be endearing. One always knew where they stood with her. The older woman's genuine delight was infectious.

"I'm so glad they finally did right by you! I always told Rose—"

"All the damn time," her wife grunted.

"—that you're a hero! You should get the best medical care in the city. It's only fair."

"Well, thank you. It's very, very nice to finally be able to move around without pain."

"I can only imagine." Rose B clapped her hands together happily. "I'm so happy for you."

"It's very appreciated."

"So what do you have for us today, Lindsey?"

"Uniforms. Just the regular. It's my day off, so I'll try to come back and get them this evening if that is fine."

Rose B gave her wife a wide smile. "Oh, that's perfectly okay, isn't it Rose? We don't have a lot of work today."

Rose G scowled. "Well, we never turn down a customer... even if they demand a rush job."

"Don't mind, Rose. She's just grumpy." Rose took the bag from Lindsey and rushed it over to the big stainless steel pot where they washed the clothing.

"Well, I'm grumpy because of the news. We should all be grumpy. We lost Maria because of those assholes." Rose G attacked a stubborn wrinkle with the heavy iron. Lindsey wasn't sure if the woman was scowling about 'the assholes' or the crease.

"I miss Maria," Rose B whimpered. "She was always so nice to us. Did you know she gave us all her remaining provisions when she left? We were so worried when Dwayne dropped the box off. I knew it was bad. I told Rose. Didn't I, Rose?"

"No, *I* told *you* something was wrong. I felt it in my gut." Rose G continued to fight the crinkle in the shirt she was ironing.

Rose B sighed sadly. "You must miss her so much, too, Lindsey."

Tears flooded her eyes and Lindsey nodded.

"She died bravely." Rose hugged Lindsey tenderly.

Lindsey accepted the embrace, then withdrew from the older woman's grip while struggling not to cry. It was difficult being so close to Maria's old flat and not being able to drop in for a chat.

"Rose, she shouldn't have died at all! There was a cure for her and the other Inferi Boon!' Rose G set her iron aside and rubbed her fingers. "Those fuckers killed them."

"That's why Dwayne did what he did." Rose B sighed. "He loved her so much. We'd see him sneaking in and out of her apartment all the time. It was obviously not just a hook up. The look in his eyes..." Rose B smiled lovingly at her own wife. "We could see it, couldn't we?"

"Yeah. Yeah." Rose G carefully hung the shirt on a hanger and placed it on a nearby rack.

"I like to think of them together in heaven."

"You think Dwayne is dead?" Lindsey was curious what regular people like The Roses thought about the whole situation. There was a lot of speculation on the news about the castellan's whereabouts. Some suspected he was in hiding in the city.

"Oh, yes. He wouldn't have gone on without her. I know exactly how he must have felt. If something happened to my Rose..." Rose B turned a loving gaze toward Rose G. "I don't know what I'd do without her."

Rose G's usually grumpy expression melted just a bit and she actually smiled. "I feel the same way."

"I'm going to see Maria's mother today." Lindsey leaned her shoulder against the doorframe to the flat. The air was stuffy and pungent with the smell of the cleaning solution. "I was asked to deliver her medals to her mother since she refuses to come to get them."

"Is that why she wasn't at the big ceremony?" Rose B asked, biting her bottom lip.

"Maria's mother declined the invitation and forbade anyone else in the family from attending. Commandant Pierce asked me to deliver them, since I was Maria's friend. She'd offered to take them herself, but Lourdes Martinez cut the call." Lindsey sighed sadly. "I can't blame her mother for being angry."

"Even though what the SWD did was wrong, she should at least take Maria's medals. She was so sweet and brave. I miss her." Rose B sniffled and wiped her eyes on her apron.

"She was the best. In every way," Lindsey agreed.

"She always paid on time," Rose G said, turning away, and Lindsey suspected the woman was discreetly dabbing at tears, too.

"Well, I better get going. I have a long walk to the Espana Sector." Lindsey withdrew her wallet and pulled out some credits. "I'll pre-pay. If for whatever reason I can't make it back tonight, just have Thad deliver, okay?" The Roses used a teenage boy for deliveries. He was at the stage where he couldn't stop staring at a woman's breasts. Lindsey always ducked her head downward so he was forced to meet her eyes. She slipped in enough credits to cover the delivery and still leave a little extra.

"We can do that." Rose G answered. "Can you tell Mrs. Martinez that we send our condolences?"

"Oh, yes! Please do! We loved her daughter!" Rose B clasped her hands to her heart. "We really did."

"I'll let her know." Lindsey pushed off from the doorframe and backed into the hallway. "I'll see you later."

As she strode back to the apartment entrance, Lindsey blinked the tears from her eyes and wiped them away with the cuff of her jacket. Even though she and Maria hadn't seen each other as often as they'd liked, at least Lindsey knew she could always depend on her for a shoulder to cry on and a bit of advice. Without Vaja lurking in her apartment, Lindsey felt lonelier than ever.

Stepping out onto the trembling staircase, Lindsey stared at the crowded city streets and wondered how she could feel so apart from so many people.

Torran dodged about a massive cart weighed down with produce from a private garden. A screen on the side of the cart flashed prices and a few people hurried to make purchases. The vendor wasn't quite to the big open market just ahead, but he stopped to sell some of his wares. His long dark coat fluttering around him, Torran clasped the long strap of the leather bag slung across his chest, and skipped ahead of the growing congestion. He was anxious to get past the market and onto the main road to the Espana Sector of the city.

It was a relief to finally be out of the SWD Facility. After weeks of debriefings, reports, and dealing with oversight committees, it was glorious to be out even if it was overcrowded and reeked. His long brown scarf caught the wind and he snagged the end and tucked it back into his collar. Treading along in battered boots, jeans, and a navy sweater, he felt more human than when he was in the starched perfection of his black SWD uniform. Also, regular attire allowed him to blend into his surroundings without drawing attention. Anyone in uniform was instantly surrounded by civilians wanting to discuss recent events. It made it increasingly difficult for the patrols on the street, and new rules had been instigated about approaching those clearly on duty around the various security stations.

"...these are difficult times, and though many believe they know the way to our salvation, we must come to the table and work together..." President Cabot's voice drifted past as a drone slid by.

"Admiral Kirkpatrick is still sequestered in the SWD headquarters and is refusing to comply with the..." the newsfeed from a vid screen in a small café declared over the din.

It was impossible to escape the fallout of the revelation of the attempted coup. The Judicial Authority was deep into their investigation, but was remaining tight-lipped as the seven judges poured over the evidence against Admiral Kirkpatrick and the SWD. The president was making a great show of respecting the findings of the Judicial Authority and not interfering, but Torran was wise enough to know that what the public saw and what was really happening were most likely two different things. He heard rumors of the battle at the top levels of the government, but he was uncertain of what was truly occurring. It was easy to be skeptical of the official story when he had lied about his own experiences outside the wall.

Torran had just turned a corner and started up the long, wide road leading to the next section of the city when he spotted a familiar face. Surprised, he wove his way through the mass of people trudging along the cracked asphalt. Uncertain if he'd really seen Lindsey, he searched the crowd for blond hair. Finally, he spotted her near the beginning of the bridge that spanned the reservoir. It took only a few jogging steps to catch up with her.

"Fancy meeting you here," he said.

Looking up, Lindsey gave him a startled look, then grinned. "MacDonald!"

"Rooney!"

To his surprise, she hugged him. "Wow! So good to see you!"

Torran returned the hug, the layers of clothing between them creating a comforting shield. "Good to see you, too. Did you get my message yesterday?"

Looking bashful, Lindsey nodded. "Sorry I didn't answer. I was in a bit of a drama with my boyfriend... I mean ex-boyfriend. We broke up last night. Officially. He came by and got his things this morning."

"Ouch. Sorry to hear it," he said. The words were slightly dishonest. He'd vividly remembered Lindsey's eyes staring at him from behind her helmet, but he hadn't realized how much he'd wanted to see them again until this moment.

"Well, he's an asshole." Lindsey shrugged. "Sometimes you just have to let the bad stuff go."

"I hear you loud and clear on that." Shoving his hands into his coat pockets, he looked toward the far end of the bridge. "You heading to the Espana Sector?"

"Yeah, I am. I've got an errand that way."

"It's a long walk. Mind if I tag along with you?"

"Of course not!"

With a grin, Lindsey started forward. They walked close together, heads angled so they could speak with some privacy among the throng. The stomp of footsteps and loud conversations created a buffer of white noise around them.

"MacDonald, I have to admit: I felt awful leaving you out there."

"You saved me. I wouldn't have made it if not for you and the others. We both know that." Torran couldn't help but shiver in his coat. That night lived in his nightmares. He often lay awake wondering what he could've done differently.

"Yeah, but still... I hated reentering the subway system without you coming with us."

"You had your orders. Besides, it would have been tough to explain why you were there, right? I didn't want to discuss it on here," Torran said, tapping his wristlet, "but you knew about the Inferi Boon before the worm transmitted. That's why you were there. You were going to destroy Denman's body because he was Inferi Boon."

Lindsey sighed. "The Constabulary discovered the truth, but was unable to save the Inferi Boon. I was dispatched to destroy Denman's body for exactly the reason you guessed. We didn't want SWD getting samples of the virus."

"Because it had mutated?"

"Something like that."

"It's so fucked," Torran shook his head. "I look at that list of names and I know how easily it would've been for mine to be on it."

"If they had asked you to volunteer, you would have done it just like the rest of us."

"Well, it sounded good, didn't it? Immunity to the virus, ability to kill the fuckin' Scrags with impunity, and first dibs at a nice chunk of land and a house?" Torran exhaled. "Hell, who wouldn't have taken that?"

"My best friend, Maria, took it."

"The vanguard?" Torran hadn't even thought about Lindsey having close ties to any Inferi Boon, which meant they had even more in common than he'd realized.

"Yeah. She wanted a new life for herself and Dwayne."

"The castellan and the vanguard. Their love story is kinda epic, isn't it?"

"Or scandalous. It depends on which news feed or commentator you're reading or listening to."

Torran had managed to catch bits of the newscast once he'd been 'absolved of any misdeeds,' as the official document had stated. The whereabouts of the former castellan and his ladylove was a huge mystery. Many believed he'd killed his beloved, buried her, then returned to the city and was now in hiding. Others believed he'd killed Maria, buried her, then killed himself and his body would be found eventually. There was also speculation that Dwayne had allowed himself to be infected and that eventually the cleanup squads would find both of them as Scrags and be forced to kill them. There were the dreamers that hoped that if they were Scrags, they'd be captured and Dr. Curran's cure would still somehow work.

"What do you think happened to them, Rooney?"

Pursing her lips slightly, Lindsey shrugged. "I don't know. I know he loved her. Desperately. She never told me about their affair, but I know she must have loved him, too. I saw them talking on the vids during one part of the mission and you could..." She trailed off, averting her eyes.

"See it." Torran gently guided Lindsey around a snarl of people gathered around a downed bicyclist. A few were bending over to help the girl up while others tried to reattach the wheel to the frame.

"Yeah. So in my head they have a happy ending. Somehow." Lindsey laughed lightly. "I suppose that sounds foolish considering all of this." She glanced significantly over the rail at the churning brown water rushing through the reservoir below. It was runoff from a massive thunderstorm the night before and on its way to being recycled.

"In a year, it will all be different, you know. People will be living outside the city. There will be farms. Ranches. Fresh food. Running trains." Torran grinned at the thought. "A whole new world to experience."

Lindsey tilted her head to gaze up at him. "Yet, we'll still be in the valley."

"Well, it's a small world." Torran wasn't sure if it was the gray weather or the long weeks of constant questions, but he felt very restless. It was a good day for a very long walk with a new friend. "So, Vanguard Rooney, what's your pleasure today?"

"A long walk, a visit with Maria's mother, maybe a stop at a pub at some point, and apparently, company and conversation. And you can call me Lindsey."

"And you can call me Torran."

"I like MacDonald better," Lindsey said with complete seriousness.

"Really?"

Laughing, she poked his side. "It'll be hard adjusting to calling you by your first name. You're MacDonald in my head. And on my wristlet." She swiped her screen and pulled up her contacts menu. "See."

"Well, you could type in Torran. It's very simple you just..." He took her arm in hand and started typing on her wristlet screen. When he finished changing his name, he put a mark next to it so his messages would get top priority.

"You're rather bold, don't you think?" Lindsey stared up at him through her thick, dark lashes with amusement.

"We're going to be the best of friends. You saved my life. I saved yours." Torran winked at her.

"I *am* glad you're okay. I'm also relieved they were wise enough to comprehend that it wasn't your fault." Her face sobered. "You couldn't have known how the mission would turn out. You didn't have all the facts."

The heavy weight of guilt wasn't about to diminish any time soon. Just the mere memory of Goodwin eating Jonas after she shot him in the head was enough to make him want to retch. Torran embraced the pain instead, hoping it would make him wiser and more cautious should he ever face such horrors again.

"Well, it was pretty obvious they hadn't warned me about the Abscrags that were the result of the failed Inferi Boon missions or about the downed tiltrotor. So when all that was factored in the line of questioning became much less confrontational."

"Bu they gave you hell at first, didn't they?" Lindsey frowned.

"Well, it's the second time I was the sole survivor of a squad."

"So they were suspicious."

"Yeah, but the story you asked me to tell them helped me more than you probably realize."

"I don't know if it was fair of me to even do that. Asking you to lie." Guilt weighed down the corners of her lips.

"Well, having a mysterious figure come out of the subway and help me fight off the Abscrags before disappearing into the night would have seemed a bit farfetched if not for Castellan Reichardt's departure from the city."

"You put a lot of trust in me when I asked you to do that."

Torran ducked his head so he could see her expression. "Hey, you saved my life. It creates instant trust, right? Besides, if Commandant Pierce wanted me to relay that information, she had to have a plan."

"Actually," Lindsey said with a wince, "I told you to say that without getting it cleared with her."

Surprised, Torran stopped in his tracks. "Oh my."

"Well, I knew that they would assume it was the castellan, so that's why I had you say that. It felt like a much more likely story than you fighting off the Abscrags singlehanded."

Uncertain if he was miffed or not, Torran stood in silence for a few long beats. Glancing toward the immense city spreading out all around him and the high mountains on the horizon, he considered all the possible ramifications of what she'd asked him to say. At last, he realized, she'd been very clever.

"Are you mad?" Lindsey stared up at him worriedly.

"Nah. You actually gave me the best story other than the actual truth. Plus, it made the castellan that much more heroic, right?" Torran rested his hand on her shoulder, urging her to walk on.

"I guess that's why I've been so worried about you going through the debriefings and reviews."

"I thought it was because I'm roguishly handsome and charming."

Lindsey rolled her eyes.

"Nah, I get it, Lindsey. I was worried about you and the others, too. With all the tension between our two forces, the coup, and the basic hell of living in The Bastion, it feels like everything is a potential landmine." Torran hated the unease that never left his system. Even walking among the citizens of the city made him a bit nervous. He'd seen the old historical vids and knew how fast the Inferi Plague Virus could spread in a populated area. Nowhere ever really felt safe anymore. It was an exercise in mental fortitude to not see everything in the city as a potential threat.

"I'm glad you kept me updated, Torran. I was worried. So many lies have been said to keep people safe that it makes me anxious."

They finally reached the end of the bridge and turned up a street that cut through a warehouse district where heavily armed guards watched over what few provisions were left. The high fences, cameras, and soldiers in riot gear inspired the crowd to speak in hushed voices. Even Torran felt wary of the guards with their black SWD uniforms and opaque helmets.

Lindsey's hand brushed against his and he automatically took it. She didn't flinch, but wrapped her fingers around his. Understanding her misgivings, he squeezed her hand gently.

If the valley wasn't secure soon, this area of the city would be filled with violence as food riots broke out among the starving masses. The people around them had no idea that the city was on the brink of starvation in a matter of months if there wasn't a significant change. That change was the valley.

"It's worth it," Torran said, leaning over to whisper into Lindsey's ear. "All the death, the pain, and the lies...if we can save these people. It's worth it."

Lindsey turned her head upward and smiled. "Absolutely."

CHAPTER 9

The small café was packed with people and it was hard to find a place to sit. Lindsey dispatched Torran to find a battered table while she joined the ordering line. He'd handed over his protein ration for the day and she had fished her own out of her coat pocket. The line moved along rather quickly as a young woman took orders and passed them off to the two cooks behind her. It was hot inside the small area with the ovens in use, but Lindsey didn't dare shrug off her coat. Thievery was a major crime in the city, especially during bad weather, and coats were one of the most commonly stolen items.

"Order, hon?" the woman behind the counter asked.

"Barbecue with potato salad and greens on the side. Do you have bread right now?"

"We have several loaves left, but that's extra."

"Okay, we'll have four slices with that order. And two herbal teas." Lindsey handed over the protein and the credits. She never ate at a café that didn't have the cooks in plain view. It was well-known that some cafés skimmed off bits of protein to sell on the black market.

"It'll be out in ten minutes." The server studied the credits Lindsey had handed over for a second, then returned a few. "Military discount."

"How'd you—"

"Only military people have such clean money," was the answer.

Spotting a tip jar, Lindsey shoved the returned credits into it. "Thanks."

A blue plastic tarp was stretched under the ceiling and a bucket in the corner was slowly filling with water running off one corner. Another sign of the decay of the city and the civilian resourcefulness.

Lindsey spotted Torran at a wobbly metal table in one corner. She hurried over and fell into the chair across from him. It was uncomfortable, but after their long morning walk, she was fine with resting for a bit. Shrugging off her coat, she tied one sleeve to the chair leg.

"I know it doesn't look like much, but they actually make really good food here. The entire roof is an herb garden. The only reason they have bread here is because for two years all they did was grow wheat and store the grain in one of the rooms upstairs. At least, that's the rumor I heard." Torran gestured toward a heavily-chained doorway tucked to one side of the kitchen area. "Hence the tight security to the upstairs area."

"I heard that long ago, bread was the staple food of famine."

"Now it's tasteless protein slabs." Torran grimaced.

Lindsey leaned her elbows on the table and glanced toward the vid screen in a dry corner of the café that was showing the latest news.

"How bad is it inside the SWD right now?"

"Among the security forces, it's rough. Demoralizing. They busted their asses only to be maligned by what the admiral and his minions did. The glory they anticipated after their great victory has been dimmed a bit. Now they're sharing duties with the Constabulary, so that natural rivalry is even more pointed."

Lindsey wasn't fond of the SWD after what they did to Maria, but she understood how hard it must be for those who had enlisted in the SWD in hopes of building a better life for everyone. "I suppose you don't know what the deal with the higher ups is?"

"I know absolutely nothing other than what the news says about the admiral being holed up in his residence with his advisors and supporters, and that if he leaves he'll be arrested instantly by the Constabulary. And I also know, for the moment, Dr. Curran seems to be the face of the SWD."

"She's not a very nice woman."

"No, she's not." Torran hesitated, then asked, "Did she really have a cure for them?"

Lindsey hated lying, so instead she shrugged and changed the subject. "Is it rough for you now? Being SWD and not Constabulary?"

Torran regarded her solemnly. Did he notice her dodge? "Not at all. I believe that science will alleviate our suffering and that much good can come out of the SWD. I volunteered to help them create the search and destroy security forces once it became clear that they were going to be putting lives at risk. Better to prepare the search and destroy troops than watch them die because of lack of sufficient training."

"So you don't miss the Constabulary?"

"No." Torran shook his head. "I didn't agree with a lot that I saw and it was clear I couldn't be a part of any effective change. I did like the idea of being part of some sort of change in the SWD. Taking a different approach from the Constabulary."

Lindsey had to admit her devotion to the Constabulary seemed a bit foolish at times in light of all that had occurred. Commandant Pierce was a good person at heart, but she'd compromised herself quite a bit for the better good of The Bastion.

"Lindsey, it's not that the Constabulary and the SWD are bad organizations, it's that there is a disease in the upper echelons of power that rob their effectiveness and put lives at risk."

She lifted her eyes to see he was worried he'd insulted her. "I get that. I just wish there were absolutes, you know?"

"There are absolutes. The Scrags need to die. Humanity needs to work together to survive."

With a sad sigh, Lindsey said, "Yeah, but we're not really working together, are we?"

"Well, you and I are."

It seemed strange to be spending so much time with someone she'd met on the battlefield and had messaged impersonally just a few times over the last few weeks. Yet, she felt like she'd known Torran for a long time.

"Torran, did we ever meet when you were in the Constabulary? We were both part of the final push."

"I don't think so. I would have remembered a pretty girl with devastatingly gorgeous eyes."

Lindsey chuckled. "Charmer."

"In all seriousness, there were so many of us that the faces of those outside my squad are a blur. That bothers me sometimes when I look at the list of names on the memorial. There are so many I didn't know that died right alongside my friends and squad members." His expression was haunted and one she understood well.

"One of my best friends is on the memorial. His name was Ryan. I had an awful crush on him."

"I hope he was a wise man and crushed back," Torran said with twinkle in his eye.

"We had our fun times." Lindsey's cheeks flushed slightly at the memories. "It just feels odd that we served together and never met."

"But we've met now. It's all good, right?"

"Absolutely."

Lindsey fell silent as their food was set before them on the table. The spicy smell of the barbecue sauce made her even hungrier than before. The protein almost looked like meat. The female server set down a basket of bread slices and Lindsey noted a few extra pieces had been added. There was also extra ice in their teas.

"Thanks, Rebecca," Torran said to the server.

With a smile, the woman hurried away.

"So is the special treatment here because they know you or because we're military?" Lindsey wondered aloud.

"Probably a bit of both." Torran made a sandwich of the cooked protein and greens.

"Do you always venture so far out?"

"I'm adventurous. Plus, I get bored staying in just one section of the city for too long. Also, you'd be amazed at how much the cityscape changes. It's little things, but I enjoy seeing what people are up to."

"Like what?"

"New vendors. New shops. New pubs. New gardens on buildings." Torran shrugged slightly, but Lindsey could see the enthusiasm in his eyes.

"An adventurer by heart, huh? Which would explain being in both the Constabulary and SWD."

"Maybe." Torran grinned. "Now eat your lunch. We still have a ways to go before we hit Espana Sector."

Lindsey didn't want to think about her grim task. Though she hoped Maria was far away and safe with Dwayne, it hurt to accept she'd never see her friend again. How much worse must it be for her mother?

After they finished eating, Lindsey continued her long trek with Torran at her side. Instead of talking about the news, Torran pointed out all his favorite things along the trek. There was a clothes shop that sold vintage military uniforms, a café that specialized in teas, a rooftop orchard of apple trees, and the occasional mural by talented artists that created a colorful landscape in an otherwise dreary world.

Each sector in the city was sectioned off by walls, bridges, and massive gates. The gates remained open unless there was a riot, but Lindsey found the formidable entrances a little disconcerting. Heavily fortified and guarded, the gateways to each sector were a reminder of the world they lived in. Though the gates were used in case of riots, they'd been built in case of an outbreak of the Inferi Scourge Plague Virus.

A clever graffiti artist had painted flags over the entrance of the former countries represented by the population within the district.

"That's new," Torran said, pointing at the artwork.

"I hope they don't cover it up. It adds flavor."

Walking beneath the entrance, Lindsey felt the slight vibration of her wristlet as it sent a transmission to the monitors at the gate. Another entry into the log of her passage through the city. The only time she didn't feel like she was under constant surveillance was in her flat, but that was because she was clever enough to get around the monitoring systems.

"Well, this is where we split up," Torran said with a sigh.

"Thanks for the company."

"I hope your visit goes well."

Lindsey pushed her hands into her coat pockets. "I'm not sure what 'going well' will mean."

"It's never easy dealing with grief."

Realizing that Torran was the one to notify his squad member's families of their loss, she reached out and set her hand on his wrist. His skin was warm beneath her fingers. "I'm sorry. I've never had to do this before." Though Lourdes Martinez knew her daughter was missing in action and presumed dead, it was not going to make the task any easier. When Lindsey had lost her own family, she remembered the faces of the officers who'd come to notify her at her school. They'd looked so calm until she'd noticed their hands were shaking. At sixteen, she'd lost her entire family to one of the few train accidents in the history of The Bastion. An orphan for over a decade now, it didn't diminish the pain or the loneliness. Maybe that's what she needed to keep in mind. Nothing she said was going to assuage the pain that Maria's mother felt.

"You'll do fine," Torran assured her.

"Thanks." Lindsey drew away and checked her wristlet for the directions to Maria's family home. "I'll message you and let you know how it went."

"We'll talk later." Torran gave her a slight smile, then strode in the opposite direction.

Lindsey walked on alone.

The last leg of her journey was shorter and filled with new sights, scents, and sounds. Spanish, French, and Portuguese mingled in with the common language of English. Music poured out of speakers set up at kiosks and there was a bit more color in the surroundings. Artists had covered many of the bland gray walls with murals and panoramic paintings of the old world.

Maria's childhood home was a four story building surrounded by brightly colored metal tubs sporting flowers, small trees, and herb gardens. Someone had painted the entire building a light blue color. Walking up the stairs, Lindsey stepped aside as children rushed down. At the entrance, she found the security system still in effect and waved her wristlet over the panel and said Maria's mother's name. A second later, the doors opened and she stepped into the small lobby with a stairwell on one side and an operational elevator on the other. Wary of the lift, she took the stairs.

The Martinez residence was on the fourth floor and took up all the units. Maria had said her brothers lived near her mother, but Lindsey didn't realize she meant the same floor in the same building. She recognized a dark skinned man with lots of curly hair repairing a light panel at the far end of the hallway.

"Hey, Mariano."

"Lindsey!" Setting aside his tool, he reached out to shake her hand. "What brings you here?"

"Commandant Pierce asked me to bring Maria's medals."

Mariano grimaced. "Oh. Wow. I'm not too sure how my mother is going to take that."

Digging the case of her pocket, Lindsey stared at the embossed velvet lid. "Maria would want her to have these, you know."

"Yeah, I know. But my mother is still really angry with her. Furious, actually."

"Even though she's..." Lindsey hesitated. "Even though she's missing?"

"You mean dead." Mariano ran his hands over his hair, leaving it in uneven tufts.

With a sigh, Lindsey nodded. "I'm sorry."

How could she lie like this when she knew there was hope? Of course, it was best if people believed Maria and Dwayne were dead. It was safer for them and the city as a whole.

"My mother is a very emotional woman. She loves very deeply and when Maria volunteered for that mission, Mama knew it was going to end with her daughter dead. So she has a lot of resentment not only toward the government, the SWD, and Constabulary, but at Maria herself."

"Commandant Pierce requested I give these to Maria's mother personally with her condolences."

"I get it, Lindsey, but Mama is going to give you hell."

Considering the secret she was keeping, Lindsey admitted to herself that maybe she did deserve some wrath directed at her. "I'll deal with it."

Mariano exhaled, swore in Spanish, then walked over to a door and jabbed the panel. "Mama, it's Mariano. Maria's friend, Lindsey, is here to see you."

Several seconds later, the door opened to reveal a woman who looked startlingly like an older version of Maria. It never failed to amaze Lindsey how much Maria resembled her mother. She'd often teased her friend that Maria already knew exactly how she would look in thirty years, but now Lindsey wondered if Maria would age at all. Was Dr. Curran correct about the virus preserving Maria? Giving her immortality?

"Hello, Lindsey," Lourdes said, her voice slightly clipped. Her long raven hair was streaked with more white than Lindsey remembered and was wrapped into an ornate bun at the back of her head. "How can I help you?"

Behind Lourdes was a small living room with a large painting of the Virgin Mary on one wall and portraits of the Martinez family. One photo was of Maria in her dress uniform. It was draped in black silk. A candle burned on the table beneath it.

"I just want you to know how sorry I am about Maria," Lindsey started, fumbling for words.

"I got your messages. Thank you," Lourdes said, her dark eyes regarding Lindsey suspiciously.

"I wanted to make the memorial service, but I was in surgery that day." Lindsey had been furious over the scheduling, but had been at the mercy of the Med Center.

"I noticed. No cane this time."

For some reason, the woman's words made Lindsey feel guilty. Maria was missing in action and Lindsey had a new leg. It seemed unfair. "Yeah, they fixed my leg finally."

"It took them long enough," Lourdes said sourly. "Those assholes."

"Mama," Mariano muttered.

"Well, they took my husband and my daughter. I don't have anything kind to say about them."

"Maria volunteered. She's a hero," Mariano protested.

Rage filled Lourdes eyes. "I will never forgive her."

"Mrs. Martinez, Maria loved you so much—"

"But she didn't listen to me and now she's dead, Lindsey. Why else are you here?" Lourdes folded her arms across her chest and glowered at Lindsey.

"Commandant Pierce—"

"You can go now." Lourdes moved to shut the door.

"Please, Maria earned these. She'd want you to have them." Lindsey thrust out the velvet box.

Lourdes regarded Lindsey with contempt. "It's not enough. Nothing the Constabulary or President Cabot do in her memory is enough! She's dead. She's gone. They killed her!"

"Mama, she gave her life for us."

"They took her womb. They took her future. Then they took her life!"

Lindsey flinched when Lourdes slapped the box out of her hands. It struck the floor on one corner, popped open, and spewed the four medals onto the floor.

"Tell your Commandant Pierce I don't want them. I want my daughter! I want her whole, alive, and living the life she deserved!" Lourdes shut the door and it audibly locked.

Squatting down, Lindsey collected the medals. Mariano crouched next to her to help.

"Sorry, Lindsey."

"It's okay." Guilt was eating at her again. Lindsey wanted to open the door and tell Lourdes that Maria was alive, immune to the Inferi Scourge, and probably out in the world beyond the mountains with the man she loved. But Lindsey knew that if Lourdes was told the truth, she'd take that information to the authorities, and demand Maria's return. That would put Maria and Dwayne in jeopardy. That knowledge didn't help her feel any better.

Standing, Lindsey offered the box to Mariano. "Please take it. Let Maria's nieces and nephews see what she earned through her service."

With shaking hands, Mariano took the box. "My father and Maria both died to save this city. They were both turned into something terrible. Was it worth it, Lindsey? Did they save the city? Are we saved?"

Unable to answer for a moment, Lindsey swallowed hard, then nodded. "We're close to it now. Because of them. The valley will soon be cleared and the farms will bring in fresh food. We'll be able to flourish again."

"But for how long?" Mariano wondered aloud. The question seemed directed at the universe and not at Lindsey.

"We'll find a way. Humanity always does." Or at least she hoped so.

"Take care, Lindsey. Don't let them fuck you over, too."

"I'll keep that in mind." She lightly touched his shoulder, then headed back toward the stairs.

"The castellan..."

Lindsey turned around. "Yeah?"

"He loved her a lot, right?"

"With all his heart. And she loved him."

"Then she was happy." Mariano held the medals to his chest. "I'm glad to know that."

"Me too." Lindsey gave him a wistful smile, then headed down the stairs.

Torran exited the narrow shopping area tucked between two apartment complexes. The blue tarps that were strung overhead to keep out the sun and rain flapped in the breeze. His purchases safely secured in his bag, he hurried down the road toward the entrance to the Espana Sector.

"...is said to be ready to surrender only to law enforcement officials dispatched from the Judicial Authority. If Admiral Kirkpatrick surrenders this evening, it will bring an end to the standoff between forces loyal to the SWD leader and the Constabulary forces dispatched by President Cabot..."

Glancing at the big vid screen perched above the district square flanked by the local government and security buildings, Torran wasn't sure if he felt relief or not. Trials were inevitable at this point, but he feared they would only segregate the population. Admiral Kirkpatrick was a very charismatic man. During the last few weeks he'd probably been crafting a defense with his legal counsel and supporters that would be aimed at destabilizing the Cabot presidency.

Another pedestrian bumped into Torran, spurring him onward. The pillars of the meeting hall in the center of the square were draped in black banners and a large granite wall was erected in the front. People clustered before it, some openly praying or weeping. An older woman stood a few feet away with bins full of wildflowers for sale for a few credits. Torran hurried over to her and looked over the wilting display.

"For a loved one?" the woman asked with a heavy accent. Dark eyes tucked into heavily wrinkled lids regarded him with curiosity. She was clothed in what appeared to be tribal garb and her thick silver hair was plaited to her waist.

"A friend, actually. She came from here. Rosario Smyth."

"She's on the wall. I've seen her face. So sad." The woman pulled some flowers that were still in fresh condition. They were bright orange and pretty.

Torran handed over a few credits. "She was a good person."

"They were all good people."

Nodding, Torran weaved through the mourners toward the placards on the wall. Each one contained the official photo of each soldier lost in defense of The Bastion along with a commemoration beneath it. A narrow metal vase was welded to the corner of each one. Some people hung rosaries or other mementos from the vases, but many were filled with flowers. When Torran found Rosario's memorial, he was saddened to see her vase was empty. Rosario had been raised in a foster home after the death of her parents during one of the flu epidemics. He'd sent notice to her foster parents, but had never received any sort of reply. His heart heavy for his lost friend, he carefully arranged the flowers in her vase.

"At least Kirkpatrick did something about the Scrags, right?" a guy said to Torran. The dark skinned man with a shiny bald head stared somberly at the image of a soldier who looked quite a bit like him, just younger.

"It was a joint effort," Torran answered.

"Yeah, but Kirkpatrick had the balls to do make the hard call. You really think there was a cure? That was bullshit. He did what he had to do."

Torran peeked at the name on the memorial the man was regarding. The name on the memorial was Jose Gutierrez and he'd been in the SWD. It was a name he recognized. "Your family member was Inferi Boon?"

"My brother. And yes. But he knew what he was doing. He willingly gave his life. No questions asked. He died a hero out there."

"They all did. The question is: did they deserve to die?"

Torran wondered if the man would answer, but he didn't. Instead, he kissed the image, said something in Spanish, and walked away.

As the crowd briefly parted, Torran saw Lindsey standing at the far end of the memorial, tucking flowers into a holder. Pressing his way through the throng, he drew close enough to see she was leaving flowers for Maria Martinez.

Unwilling to bother her, Torran took a few steps back and tried to not disrupt the mourners. It hurt to see families gathered at the memorial. One woman was carefully cleaning rain spots from the image of a male soldier while a gentleman pressed his forehead to another and prayed.

There were monuments of this type all over the city. Death was such an enormous part of the life of The Bastion that elaborate rituals had grown up around it. Memorial walls and yearly observances of various battles or epidemics were just as common as holiday decorations and celebrations.

Lindsey took a few steps to the right and slid one flower into the holder of another portrait. It was of a man with dark skin and hair. Torran realized it was probably the elder Martinez. He'd read all about Maria and her father's sacrifices for The Bastion on the news feed.

When the blond woman finally turned away, she spotted him. Feeling a bit awkward, he gave her a small wave. Hands tucked into her coat pockets, she walked to him. Her hair was escaping the braids resting over her shoulders and her hazel eyes looked more green than brown in the muted lighting.

"Sorry to intrude," he said.

"You're not." Lindsey sighed, looking sad and a bit tired.

"My friend, Rosario, she's on the other end." He pointed, feeling slightly flustered. He didn't want to appear as though he was following Lindsey or expecting her to just come along with him. Though he admitted a certain amount of attraction to her, they were just becoming friends.

"Did she die that night?"

"Yeah. She was turned," Torran said, blinking rapidly so tears wouldn't form.

"I'm sorry."

"Yeah, well, we did our best."

"We did." Lindsey stepped beside him, facing the opposite direction, her back to the memorial. She bumped his arm lightly on purpose. "Ready to head back?"

"Yeah. Yeah. You sure you want to walk back together?"

"Don't be silly," Lindsey chastised him, rolling her eyes. "Like I really want to walk alone in my own dire thoughts of doom and gloom instead of having company and good conversation."

"When you put it that way..." Torran offered her his arm and was pleased when she tucked her hand into the crook. "How'd the visit with your friend's mother go?" Torran asked after they'd departed the square.

"Good. I guess. She's very..." Lindsey shrugged and looked as though she was trying to find the right words. "Well, she's one of those people who feels very strongly that everyone should do what she says and when they don't comply, she's not very pleasant."

"Sounds like most of my commanding officers," Torran said with a wink.

"And mine," Lindsey admitted with a wry grin. "Maria enlisted against her mother's wishes. She'd already lost Maria's father, and didn't want to lose her only daughter, too. And now she's gone."

"And her mother's angry." Torran nodded, understanding.

"Not just at the Constabulary or the President. But at Maria."

"I can see that. It's hard to see someone you love putting themselves at risk."

"I foolishly hoped that giving her Maria's medals would make her feel better, but I think I only made her angrier."

"Well, her daughter was made into Inferi Boon. That can't be easy to deal with." Torran gave Lindsey a significant look. "It can't be easy for you either."

Coming to a stop near a subway station, Torran observed that the doors were open, but had a big sign indicating it was under repair. He wondered how long it would be before the trains were running again and his long walks would no longer be necessary.

"It's not easy. I miss her. She's my best friend. I sometimes think about how she must have felt when she first realized what they'd done. And then I think about how she must have felt when she understood she'd never come back to the city. That they were going to kill the Inferi Boon." Lindsey brushed her bangs away from her eyes, her gaze set on the city wall in the distance.

"They're going to pay for that, you know. The trials will happen soon. The news is reporting that Admiral Kirkpatrick may surrender to the Judicial Authority soon."

"It doesn't make it easier," Lindsey responded.

"I know. It doesn't."

"Can I ask you a question, MacDonald?"

"Torran."

"Torran, can I ask you a question?"

"Go ahead."

"When you transferred to the SWD and you knew they were preparing for an assault against the Scrags, didn't you fear it would go the same way as the final push?"

"What you're really asking is why I put myself in the same spot as before. Face to face with the Scrags."

Lindsey nodded. "Yeah."

"Because someone has to do it," Torran said, shrugging. "And if we don't, who will?"

"So true."

"So what do folks like you and me do? We volunteer. We do it again and again, because it's what we do."

"It's what makes us better."

"Not better. Just different."

Lindsey squeezed his arm. "Nah, we're better."

Torran couldn't help but laugh.

They'd lapsed into silence a few times along their long walk out of the Espana Sector, but the further away they were from the memorial and the ghosts that haunted it, the more relaxed they became and conversation gradually returned.

The crowds moving on foot through the streets of The Bastion were the only bright colors against the endless drabness of the buildings. Lindsey allowed herself to be swept along at Torran's side. He was taller, and despite his slenderness, the people parted in front of him faster than they did for her. She supposed it was his bearing. Torran wasn't in uniform, yet he carried himself with authority. Meanwhile, she deliberately slouched in her long coat and tried to look like an average person.

A throng of kids all under the age of ten rushed along the street, chasing a bright red ball. Laughing and shouting, the children darted around Torran and Lindsey, but nearly toppled an elderly couple wheeling a small metal cart down the road.

"Hey!" Torran shouted after the squealing youngsters. "Be careful!"

"Meant no harm!" a redheaded boy replied.

"Yeah, well, watch out for your elders, all right?" Torran gave the passing couple a brief nod.

The couple returned it thankfully.

"Didn't see them," another boy with a rakish grin and blond hair answered.

"Well, we're not as fast as you and can't duck out of the way like little monkeys the way you can," Torran pointed out.

"Do you play football?" one of the girls in blond pigtails asked. Lindsey wondered if she was the other boy's younger sister.

"Oh, back in the day when I was your age," Torran admitted. "I'm a bit rusty. Toss it my way and we'll see."

The response was one of the little girls kicking the ball right at him. Torran expertly kicked it back, much to the delight of the children.

Lindsey laughed as the ball was knocked back and forth between the kids and Torran, but then one of the drones turned down the narrow pathway and instantly the game was over. While the kids scrambled out of the way and down a side street, Torran and Lindsey circumvented the drone flashing the latest news on the sanitization of the valley on its big screens.

"I thought you were going to thrash them," Lindsey remarked. She was relieved he hadn't. Though the kids had been thoughtless, they were also just children. The city was hard to live within and there was not a lot of space to play. In her younger days she'd played plenty of street football.

"Nah, they're just little people with way too much energy." Torran shrugged, his narrow face somber. Running a hand through his brown hair, he left the longer ends near his forehead sticking out at charming angles. "They just need to be reminded to watch out for others."

"True. If the last few months have proven anything is that we need to stick together."

"I hear ya on that," Torran said in his faint Scottish accent.

Lindsey's boots splashed through a puddle from a water main a group of female techs were trying to repair. The old equipment was obviously giving them issues and the group looked agitated. At least there was hope for new equipment in the near future.

They hit a snarl in the foot traffic caused by the break the water main, and Torran reached back for her hand. She surprised herself by taking it. Maybe it was just her loneliness, but she was enjoying her day despite some of the more dramatic parts.

"So what do they do?" she wondered aloud, indicating the bustle around her. "People who don't have assigned jobs. How do they busy themselves? All day? The streets are always so full."

Pulling her up to his side, then releasing her hand, Torran said, "I'm not sure, honestly. I suppose most are looking for food other than the rations. Maybe clothes. Equipment. Making credits any way they can. Or maybe they're visiting friends. Shagging."

"Shagging?" Lindsey laughed at that comment. "I suppose that makes a lot of sense. Especially with men being so outnumbered by women, I'm sure a lot of you guys keep really busy."

Torran chuckled. "Well, yeah."

Lightly gripping her arm, he tugged her into what may have once been an alley, but was now a walking path. It wasn't as congested as the main road and led to a steel staircase. Tilting her head, Lindsey saw the monorail station looming ahead. The entrance wasn't closed off and people were walking along the narrow tracks.

"Ah, a shortcut," she observed.

"I know a few around here."

"So, you never told me what you're doing on this side of town," Lindsey noted. "Isn't the Scottish borough on the other side of the city inside the Isles Sector?"

Torran patted the leather bag hanging from his shoulder. "I was picking up some supplies, actually. An old girlfriend got me hooked on tortillas." Flipping up the flap, he revealed two packs of the delicacy.

"You walked all this way for tortillas?"

"Oh, yeah. Definitely."

Intrigued, Lindsey said, "So are they good?"

"You've never had tortillas?"

Shaking her head, Lindsey hoped he'd maybe offer her one. She was a little hungry.

"Well, if you like I can make you a taco sometime." Then, as if expecting rejection, he said, "No strings attached, of course."

"Strings are fine actually," Lindsey replied, surprising herself a bit. He was definitely her type with a long, leanly muscular build and dark hair.

"Oh?" Torran gave this thought. "Oh, well. That's good."

"I mean, if you want to attach strings, that is." Lindsey felt her cheeks flush, not quite sure where she was going with the conversation. "Friendship strings."

"Friendship strings are good. But I am single. I was sorta seeing this one girl, but she wanted too much."

"Oh, she was getting too serious?"

"Well, she wanted me to get serious with her and her four sisters."

Clanking up the steps toward the monorail station, Lindsey lifted an eyebrow. "Oh?"

"Well, with the man shortage she felt it was only right for her to share me with her sisters. They even had a schedule worked out. Including...conceiving babies." Torran winced at the last word.

Hesitating on a step, Lindsey stared at Torran with wide eyes. "You could have had five women at your beck and call and you turned it down. *Really?*"

"No, no, you're seeing it wrong. I would have been at their beck and call. Besides, I'm just not wired up that way." Torran slipped by her and continued up toward the monorail station, his long dark coat swinging around his frame. "I'm a one gal bloke."

"Ah. Well, if it makes you feel any better, I just dumped my boyfriend because he felt I should be willing to share, too."

Lindsey joined Torran at the top of the steps and gazed out over The Bastion. The view took her breath away. It was so vast, so gloomy, and yet so filled with life. And that life would hopefully continue. Thanks to the Inferi Boon, there was a chance now. It filled her with optimism, yet left her yearning for more.

"So you weren't into sharing?" Torran asked, pulling her attention back to him.

"Well, I, like a lot of women of my age, like to fool around. I've had my fair share of fun. And I also recognize that men have the upper hand when it comes to actual relationships. But Vaja seemed different. He was really into me and we had a lot of mutual interests. We met on one of the social feeds and it seemed like we could make a strong go of it. So I let Vaja move in with me. I shared my life with him. I expected him to share his with me. I thought that was our arrangement."

"And it wasn't?"

"Not on his end. He has three other girlfriends in different parts of the city. He likes to live with one girlfriend for a bit, then move on to the next. When he moved in with me, he didn't tell me I was girlfriend number four. And when he finally did..." Lindsey thought of Dwayne risking everything to save Maria. She'd seen the love in his eyes when he spoke to Maria over the comm. Was it too much to want the same? "It wasn't enough. Now, if he had just wanted to fuck around on occasion and had told me that from the beginning, it would have been a different story. I might have considered it."

"Gotcha." Torran regarded her thoughtfully. "Maybe he thought you loved him too much to turn down his proposed arrangement."

"I liked him. I didn't love him. I realized that when it was really easy to show him the door."

"You're tough. I knew I liked you for a reason."

"Other than I look amazing in combat gear?" Lindsey teased.

"Oh, that's a big reason, too."

Torran strode onto the track platform and sauntered after a group of young people. The tracks had curved sides and handrails to keep people from falling. Even though the intention of the builders was for The Bastion to flourish, there had been some anticipation of difficulties. Making the tracks safe for walking traffic if the grid was down was one of the smarter things the engineers had done. Only a few tracks were powered, and those were used by the military and government. Lindsey kept pace with him, walking at his side. They strolled along in silence for a bit, listening to the patter of the many feet pounding against the walkway. The sun was low on the horizon and soon the streetlamps would be turning on. Down below was the ceaseless chatter of people and the announcements from the drones.

"So, how is the leg?" Torran asked abruptly.

"Fine, now that it's all new hardware," Lindsey replied. "Seriously, you remember my limp after meeting me just once?"

"I thought it was odd that you were a hero of The Bastion, but yet disabled."

The anger returned, but Lindsey fought to keep it under control. "It was done purposefully. Apparently, some higher ups decided that the civilians would be comforted by seeing veterans of the big push with war wounds."

"That's fuckin' crass," Torran muttered.

"I was told they didn't have the resources allocated. Instead it was all a publicity thing." Pressing her lips together, Lindsey again felt remorse that she'd help save the presidency of the man who had ordered her to be disabled for over a year. Of course, it would have been worse if Admiral Kirkpatrick had taken over. "The procedure was recently sanctioned so I could be a shining example of our situation improving. New leg. New hope. As always, the government uses us for their propaganda. They're as bad as the SWD." She instantly regretted her words and looked at him sharply. For months she'd hated the SWD as an entity, but now she had to remember that individuals made up the organization, and she rather liked one of them.

Torran hesitated in his steps, allowing the people behind him to push past. Lindsey joined him next to the handrail. Tilting his head to look down at her, he said, "I may be a part of the SWD, but I serve The Bastion."

"I didn't mean that you're—"

"Remember, I was part of the failed final push, too. I watched my squad get wiped out when the expansion perimeter collapsed. I barely made it to the wall and ascended the rappel lines to safety."

"I remember you saying that. I'm sorry if I made you feel that I don't appreciate what you've done. I do remember how awful it was. I remember the sacrifices people made." Knowing that Torran had been a part of the final push did make a difference to her. It meant he understood what she'd seen and endured.

"We lost a lot of good people that day, Lindsey."

"We did." Lindsey remembered Ryan sacrificing himself so that she and Maria could survive.

Torran continued: "And we lost a lot of good people *afterward*. I don't want to see that happen again."

Blinking against the sun reflecting off the glass and metal of the towering government buildings, Lindsey asked in a soft voice, "Why are you telling me this?"

"Because I like you. And I know that the SWD is not everyone's favorite organization. Especially right now." Torran gazed directly into her eyes. "I don't approve of using people's injuries as propaganda, I don't approve of altering people without their consent even if it's to save humanity, and I want to be a part of a positive change. I meant what I said over our meal earlier."

"I admit you're not a dick like most of the SWD personnel."

"Blame my Constabulary roots," Torran said with a laugh, then sobered. "The people working for the SWD want to save humanity, too. Maybe not the Admiral Kirkpatricks, but the rest of us."

"You sound like you're trying to sell me something," Lindsey decided, placing one hand on her cocked hip.

"I am," Torran admitted. "A chance to make you a taco."

That elicited a giggle from her. "You're doing okay so far."

Torran grinned. "Excellent."

Continuing on their trek home, Lindsey tucked her hands into the pockets of her coat. It had been a long time since she'd simply hung out with someone that wasn't Vaja. She recognized now how much she had leaned on her ex after Maria had departed on her secret mission. Though she had been fine with throwing Vaja out, the emptiness that had suddenly filled her life after he abandoned her had been more depressing than she'd anticipated. The smattering of conversation with Torran during the rest of their journey to the Central Sector of the city was mostly small talk, but it was comforting.

The shortcut deposited them close to the alley where her small flat was located. Lindsey again cast a thoughtful look at sun the dipping below the mountain range. The streets weren't as busy now that the citizens were sitting down to evening meals or watching shows on the vids.

"I'm over this way," Lindsey said, and pointed to the rectangular box of a building she called home.

"Ah, okay. Well, thank you for the company on our long walk."

"Did you really walk all that way for tortillas?"

"Well, not just tortillas." Torran gave her a sheepish smile, and opened the bag again. Shoving the tortillas aside, he revealed a bottle filled with clear liquid. "Tequila. Very rare. Very expensive. The same ladies who make the tortillas also grow agave."

"That's *real* tequila?" Lindsey marveled at his connections. "Wow."

Torran gave her a wide cocky grin. "I have refined tastes."

Glancing at the door of her flat just a block away, Lindsey twisted her mouth to one side while pondering her next move. Not one to play games or be coy, she made up her mind. "Want to come home with me?"

"Eh?" Torran regarded her as if he wasn't quite sure what she was asking of him.

"Want to come home with me? Get *naked?* Have *sex?*" Lindsey raised her eyebrows, awaiting an answer.

"You're after my tortillas and tequila," Torran said, teasing her, but clearly interested.

"Maybe. But it was nice spending time with someone today and I don't want it to end. Plus, you're handsome and sexy with that gorgeous floppy hair which is completely not regulation, and you have cute freckles."

"I do have cute freckles," Torran agreed with a nod.

"No strings. Just... fun. I don't have four sisters and I don't want babies."

"And I'm not looking to add a fourth girlfriend to my roster."

"So... a shag... tequila... and tacos?"

"Yeah," Torran said, with a toe-curling charming grin. "Yeah."

CHAPTER 11

The flat was colder than Lindsey expected and she shivered upon entering. With the rolling blackouts there was no point in leaving the heat on anyway. The lights flicked on, revealing her small space, and Torran glanced around with interest.

"Do you have a flat outside the SWD Facility?" she asked shrugging off her coat.

"I had one, but lost it after the divorce. But that was also before the big push. I could have applied for a flat, but that's when I decided to go ahead and retire, then enlist with the SWD."

"So... divorced?" Lindsey hung up her coat in her small locker, then took Torran's as he handed it over.

"Yeah. She decided she was the female Vaja." Torran shrugged. "We were young, stupid, and got married far too young and far too fast. And also: the whole idea of a family flat was very appealing."

"It's how they get you to breed," Lindsey commented with a smirk.

"It really is. Have a family. Get a bigger place. Sheer bribery." Torran set his bag on her narrow counter. "So... tacos."

"I don't know if I have anything we can put in them." Lindsey crouched to examine the contents of a small refrigerator.

"I do." Torran pulled out the tortillas, tequila, and then a small padded container. With great flourish, he opened the container and showed her something that made her eyes widen in disbelief. Wrapped in strips of cloth were three brown eggs. "Am I amazing or what?"

"I'm so impressed right now."

Setting the eggs aside, he drew out a small bag of spices. "So, eggs, spices, tortillas. Breakfast tacos. Maybe not like they used to exist, but..."

"Close enough."

"Exactly."

While Lindsey watched, Torran made them a nice little dinner of tacos and fried potatoes that Lindsey donated from her provisions. Sipping cinnamon tea spiked with tequila, they ate mostly in silence while the news feed on Lindsey's computer related the latest updates and speculation.

"Are you going out there soon?" Torran asked.

"Beyond the wall?"

"Yeah."

"I'm going in for another physical, then I should be cleared for duty. I'll get a new squad and probably start doing my duty out there. You?"

"Next week I get a new squad. Not quite sure how happy they'll be to learn about my last two."

"We're soldiers. We know how it is. And if they don't, they'll learn." Lindsey shoved the last of the taco into her mouth and relished the moistness of the eggs. She couldn't remember the last time she'd had real eggs.

Picking up the tequila bottle, Torran poured more liquor into her tea. "At least the future is brighter now than it was."

Lindsey wasn't sure if he was talking about the city or their newfound friendship. Giving him a long look from beneath her eyelashes, she sipped her tea. It was more cinnamon flavored liquor than actual tea.

"That look is devastating."

"What look?"

"That slightly lowered eyes gazing through the eyelashes look. You do it quite well, and it's amazing."

Rolling her eyes, Lindsey flipped him off.

Torran guffawed.

With her stomach full and the liquor warming her up, Lindsey had to admit it was the most relaxed she'd been in ages. The gnawing anxiety that had bothered her for so long was diminished, much to her relief.

"I'm taking a shower," she announced.

"My cue to go," Torran said standing.

"Oh, no. I meant it." She pointed at him. "You're staying the night."

"I don't want to take advantage of you. We're both a bit lonely and down."

Lindsey took off her sweater and tank top at the same time and tossed them aside. Torran's protests died on his lips as he stared at her breasts.

"We're becoming friends. You're a man. I'm a woman. Yes, I'm a bit lonely, but I'm also very much aware of what I want. Right now, I want you. Naked. In the shower with me."

"Okay," Torran stammered.

Lindsey walked to her small sanitary station and popped open the narrow door that opened to the small space. The toilet was retracted into the wall and she swiveled the little sink into its cubby in the wall to get it out of the way. The pale blue walls of the small space were covered in rubber decals she'd found in a bazaar. They were the silhouettes of sea creatures Lindsey would never see in real life. She activated the shower controls so the water in the tank could heat.

It was strange to disrobe in front of someone new, but also exciting. The mistake she'd made with Vaja would not be repeated. She'd concentrate on friendship instead of romance and have fun when it suited her.

Peeling off the last of her clothes, she checked the time. "We have about ten minutes until the next rolling blackout."

Lindsey checked on Torran to see he was very slowly undressing. He'd only taken off his sweater and scars from previous injuries puckered the skin on one arm and the side of his chest. It was very nicely muscled and Lindsey appreciated the lines of his slim waist. The throb of desire was a pleasant distraction from all the troubles of her world. The tips of her unraveling braids brushed over her hardening nipples.

"Well?" She placed a hand on her hip.

"I'm waiting for you to change your mind," Torran confessed.

"Are you serious?" With a laugh, Lindsey walked the few short steps him, grabbed him by the belt and started to undress him while giving him the most flirtatious look she could muster. If he liked it when she looked up at him through her eyelashes, it was time to use it to her benefit.

"You're quite wicked, you know. Taking advantage of me and my resources. First tacos, then tequila, and now my cock."

"Yeah, well, that's just how I roll." Giving him a coy look, she reached into his jeans and was pleased to find he was very hard. "You don't seem to be protesting."

"Not at all." Torran bent over and pressed a kiss to her lips.

Stroking him, she responded to the caress of his lips and tentative forays of his tongue against hers. She sucked on the tip of his tongue and pushed his jeans and boxers downward. Wrapping her arms around his neck, she pulled him down for a deeper kiss. He tasted of cinnamon, tequila and spice.

It was divine.

With one last flick of her tongue against his, she stared into his face. His eyes were hooded with desire, yet a little distant. It was a look that was familiar to her. There were guards up between them. After so much loss, it was hard to be completely open with another person. Those protective boundaries suited Lindsey perfectly. She wanted physical comfort and company. Torran could have her body and her mind, but her heart and soul were hidden away.

"You done being a wanker?" she asked.

Kicking his shoes and clothes away, he lifted her easily in his arms. "Absolutely."

Giggling as he carried her into the sanitary station, Lindsey wrapped her legs around his waist. "It'll be a tight squeeze."

"My favorite kind," he answered, and managed to get them both inside the small cubicle.

The door slid shut. Setting her feet down on the rubbery floor, Lindsey held her hand over the controls. "If we're lucky, warm water. If we're very lucky, hot water. And if we're not lucky, cold."

Torran stared at the showerhead over his head. "I'm feeling lucky. Go for it."

Lindsey hit the on button and the hot water splattered over their bare skin. "You're lucky."

"In more ways than one."

Sliding her fingers over his short hair, she pulled him in for another kiss as his hands traveled over her body. It was always awkward at first with a new lover, but Torran didn't take very long to discover her most sensitive places. When he dragged his fingers lightly up her spine, she nearly squealed with delight. Tangling his fingers in her hair, his lips assailed hers with an unhurried passion that she found intoxicating. He was taller and stronger than Vaja, and the space was cramped. When they bumped the controls and soap poured over them, they both laughed aloud.

"Oops," Lindsey said, then used the soapy suds as an excuse to glide her hands over his torso to his hardness pressing into her thigh.

"We could probably slip and die in here," Torran decided pressing his forehead to hers as he gasped.

"What a way to go though, huh?" She stroked him firmly, loving the feel of how thick and hard he was in want of her.

"The best."

"And would you hurry up and fuck me," she whispered against his lips.

With a little growl, Torran lifted and pinned her to the slippery wall. Kissing her feverishly, he angled himself to enter her. For a split second, Lindsey wondered if this was the wisest thing for her do in light of her break up with Vaja, but then struck down that thought. Life was short and full of pain. Pleasure was a gift to be enjoyed.

Comprehending Torran was waiting for her final invitation, she sucked on his bottom lip and rubbed the slick folds of her core against the head of his cock, before pressing herself onto him. Closing her eyes, she dug the tips of her fingers into his shoulders and clung to him as he started to thrust into her. His wet hair hanging nearly in his eyes, he kissed her cheeks, nose and lips before bending down to capture one of her hard pink nipples between his teeth.

The confines of the shower only made their situation more erotic and somewhere in the back of her mind Lindsey was glad she'd never lured Vaja into the shower with her. This was her and Torran's unique little tryst. When she came hard against him, she clung to him with her arms and legs to enjoy the almost overwhelming sensation of him plunging harder into her as he stroked his way to his own orgasm. Just as he let out a guttural moan of pleasure and came inside her, the rolling black out hit the small flat. They were instantly plunged into darkness.

Torran's lips found hers again and he kissed her passionately as he finished filling her. Legs trembling, she slid them down over his hips to settle on the floor. Still in the dark, she panted from both pleasure and exertion.

"So," Torran said after a second. "Is there a manual release on this shower door, or are we stuck in here?"

"We could go for another round," Lindsey answered in a husky voice.

In the darkness, she swore she saw him grin. "Well, not opposed to that..."

She found the manual release and the door creaked open. "But let's do that in my bed where it will be a lot warmer."

With a grin, Torran hoisted her up in his arms and carried her out.

Exhausted, panting, and sore as hell, Torran lay on the bed next to Lindsey, listening to her breathing. The rolling blackout was over and after three solid hours of the best sex of his life, he almost wished the lights hadn't come back on. But it did give him an obscenely great view of Lindsey's ass as she leaned over the rail of the bed in an attempt to reach the tequila bottle they'd left on her small counter.

The walls of her flat were covered in glossy images she must have cut from old magazines and books, or printed from the photo archives. Caught in the illumination cast by the lamps, the pictures of long dead people and lost places made him curious about why Lindsey collected them.

"Got it!" She sat up, holding the half-empty tequila bottle in one hand. She took a swig, flinched, then handed it to him.

Torran dragged her over to him, poured the liquor over her breasts and lapped it off her nipples. This elicited a delighted giggle from her, which is exactly what he'd wanted to hear. He loved her laugh. It was without restraint, just like Lindsey. He'd met some powerful and smart women in his days on earth, but she was rather fearless in a way that terrified and enthralled him at the same time.

"What the hell was that?"

"I improvised," he replied with a wink.

Her hair was a mess, sticking out of her now completely destroyed braids. Only a few strands were still clinging to her original hairdo. She was beautiful, and he knew that he was in awful danger if he stayed with her the rest of the night. Lindsey had made it very clear that they were at the start of a friendship, not a romance. The sex had been about physical pleasure, and he knew that. It had been fun fucking her, but he'd been very aware that it had been just that. And he also knew that if he wasn't careful, he'd want it to be more. Right now he couldn't afford to invest his heart. Too much in life was uncertain, and he'd rather just enjoy the better moments and not fixate on making anything permanent in his life. The thought of venturing beyond the wall filled him with dread. Someday, it would be his turn not to return.

Taking another long sip, Lindsey straddled his hips and grinned down at him. This time she did the pouring, and he lifted his head to catch the stream running off her elongated nipples.

"I'm really, really drunk now," Lindsey confessed.

"You don't have duty tomorrow, right?"

"No, do you?"

"Not until the afternoon."

"Plenty of time to sober up then."

Lindsey shook out her hair, finally freeing it entirely. It was still a bit damp, but looked insanely sexy. Her wetness against his stomach was making him hard again. He was convinced she was going to be the death of him.

Their wristlets chiming simultaneously startled them, and Lindsey accidently spilled some liquor on her as she quickly activated the screen. Torran sat up and licked her arm to catch the trickles of tequila before checking his own wristlet. The saltiness of her skin tasted good with the liquor.

It was a city-wide announcement.

"So he surrendered," Lindsey said, relief in her voice.

"It's the right thing to do." Torran read the release from the government swiftly. It was carefully worded, but it was clear President Cabot would not be swayed from portraying Admiral Kirkpatrick as a traitor.

"Who's Legatus Martel?" Lindsey glanced at Torran curiously.

Catching up with her reading, he said, "That was the title Admiral Kirkpatrick was supposed to have before they granted him the right to keep his former rank. Martel is a name I'm not acquainted with, but she must be the new leader of the SWD."

"Marilyn Martel." Lindsey frowned. "So is this one of President Cabot's appointees?"

"Most likely."

Lindsey ran her fingers gradually through her hair. "It's a familiar name though."

"No inclusion of her bio. Weird."

Lindsey lifted her eyes and pouted. "Very."

"We'll worry about it tomorrow," Torran said, his fingers tracing down her arm gently.

"More unknowns. I hate not knowing something." She frowned, her fingers tightening on the neck of the bottle.

Carefully selecting his words, Torran said, "Well, sometimes the unknown isn't bad, right?"

Cocking her head to regard him, her somber expression was a little unsettling. Then he realized she was actually quite deep in thought. Her eyes were fixated beyond him. It was a look he'd seen on her face when they'd been outside the wall. It was almost like watching a computer at work: cold, aloof, dealing with the facts. She blinked once and her focus was clearly back on him.

"Well, I like the known better," she said teasingly. "Like when I wondered what was in those jeans of yours and now I know."

Torran melted into her kiss. He didn't even mind when the tequila bottle toppled over and soaked the blankets. Dragging her into his arms, he told himself he was just having fun, but already the cracks around his heart were letting her essence slip in

Lindsey awoke with a start. It took her a second to comprehend it was her wristlet vibrating that had awakened her. Activating the screen, she saw the message was incoming from her secret program. Instantly, her heart started to beat wildly with excitement. Still a little tipsy from the tequila, she edged out from beneath Torran's long leg and arm and scooted to the ladder.

Once on the main floor, she sat at her computer array beneath the elevated bed, and she logged into the program. After several long, excruciating seconds, the message downloaded. It was from Maria. Twisting her mouth, Lindsey quickly scrolled through it. The message was short, but worrying.

Lindsey, Dwayne and I need to talk to you and Commandant Pierce ASAP. Call tomorrow at exactly 1600 hours.

Realizing she needed to be careful with how many times she contacted Maria, Lindsey hesitated, weighing whether or not she should respond or just wait until the designated time. Finally, she typed in a short note signaling she'd received the message and logged out of the program. Gnawing on her thumbnail, she stared at the screens. She wanted to hack into the SWD and government sites and search out information on the new Legatus, but didn't dare do it while Torran was around.

"You look worried."

Lindsey gazed upward to see Torran peering at her over the rail of her bed.

"I'm always worried in the back of my mind." With a sheepish smile, she shrugged slightly. "Well, not worried exactly. I'm always got some fixation lodged in the gray matter."

"Sort of like you got a computer program running in the back of your mind sorting things out?" Torran ventured.

Surprised that he got it so right, Lindsey gazed at him in awe.

"You get a look in your eyes. Like you're processing something." Torran slipped over the side of the bed and dropped down. "Considering your very nice computer display, I'm going to guess that you're good at working with them, too."

"My father was a programmer. He taught me everything I know."

"But you had the natural talent, too, huh?"

"You can say that." Lindsey uneasily shifted her weight on her chair, not willing to let Torran too far into her personal headspace.

"But you're a grunt. Not a programmer."

Lindsey swiveled toward him and shrugged. "I wanted to do something different. I didn't want to follow in someone else's footsteps but make my own path."

With a slight nod, Torran rested his hands on the edge of her bed and stretched. It was very provocative and she was distracted by the muscles shifting beneath his skin. She wanted to be distracted. Fear was a tight knot in her gut.

"And you don't want to talk about it."

"Nope."

"Is this where we draw lines?" Torran asked, tilting his head.

"Yep." Lindsey slid to her feet and ran her hands down his chest. "We're getting to know each other. We're getting to be friends. But not only did I lose the stupid ex, but my best friend. I need a new friend."

"A friend with benefits." Torran stared into her eyes somberly. "I'm there with you."

"Are you?" Lindsey really hoped he was, because she liked him.

"This life is too uncertain," he said at last. "Better to keep things simple. Uncomplicated."

"Let's enjoy the rest of the night before we have to go back to the real world." Lindsey rubbed her lips against his chin softly.

Torran cupped her face and kissed her lightly. "I better go."

"Torran..."

"No, Lindsey. I should. You see, if I stay any longer I won't want to go back to the real world."

Frowning, she feared she'd made a misstep with him.

"The thing is this... you're a great girl. And I think we're going to be great friends. But we need boundaries. Sleeping here tonight... a little too much over the line."

"So don't sleep." Lindsey gave him the beguiling look that seemed to affect him so much.

"Oh, that's playing so dirty." Torran laughed.

"One more time, then you can go home." Lindsey turned up her flirty look, her fingers lightly touching his hip.

"Fine. But... boundaries."

"Right."

His kiss rendered her breathless.

Hours later, Lindsey woke to an empty bed and flat. Her bed was still damp from the tequila she'd spilled, but she didn't mind so much. Torran had helped her past the heartbreak of Vaja and given her something she'd been missing for a long time.

Friendship and understanding.

Now she just needed to find a way to distract herself during the long wait to find out what Maria and Dwayne needed from her and Commandant Pierce.

With a sigh, Lindsey wished Torran had stayed.

CHAPTER 12

Commandant Pierce paced her office with her hands tucked behind her back as Lindsey finished securing the room in preparation for Dwayne and Maria's transmission. The small implants under her fingertips vibrated as she performed her final scan. It was the one thing Vaja had done that she could still appreciate. He had put her in contact with a black market surgeon who had made small modifications to her body. If Lindsey didn't have to deal with regular health checkups, she'd be tempted to make more modifications. There was only so much she could hide from the medical sensors.

Lindsey's search revealed that someone had imbedded more spying devices in the commandant's office. These were clever little bugs that constantly changed frequency channels to evade detection. Lindsey had deactivated all of them and removed one for further study. Every time she extracted one, Commandant Pierce's frown deepened.

Tucking the extracted bug into her small tool kit, Lindsey pulled out one of her modified pads and checked the suppression system she'd installed. It would take someone a few weeks to bypass it, but by then she'd have something new to confound them with. Excitement burned inside her as she worked. She loved outwitting other techs.

Commandant Pierce stopped, turned, and tilted her head, eyebrows rising in a question.

Lindsey held up three fingers and continued working on her pad. She'd been avoiding hacking into The Bastion system out of fear of detection, but now she regretted that decision. There were a lot more security locks in place, and it took her longer than usual to slip through them without leaving a trace. She had to make sure that no one could hack the wristlet signal when the secret program activated.

It was difficult to describe what she actually saw while foiling the security nets. Though her eyes were concentrated on her pad, her mind translated all the incoming information into a surrealistic panoramic view that enabled her to spot exactly what she needed to accomplish any of her set goals. Vaja had once tried to get her to describe what she envisioned in detail, but she hadn't been able to. Vaja had labeled her an artist, not a hacker. She suspected he was right. Tapping at the screen, in her mind she saw a dark mass of information separate into malleable parts that she reconstructed to her needs.

With two last keystrokes, she saw the new configuration start to perform the task she assigned it.

"Done." Lindsey climbed to her feet and hurried over to the commandant's desk.

"Just in time. They transmit in two minutes."

"I've been staying out of the grid," Lindsey replied. "So it was messier than usual." Hooking her pad up to the commandant's vid screen that was used for conference calls, she made sure all the connections were working properly.

"We're all being cautious," Commandant Pierce replied wearily.

The strong lines of her beautiful face were tight with worry. There was obviously much going on that Lindsey didn't know about. It was time to start sleuthing again.

The last thing Lindsey did was redirect the feed from the hidden program in her wristlet into the pad. "Everything is set."

"Good." Commandant Pierce pushed a chair toward Lindsey. "Take a seat."

Lindsey obeyed and Commandant Pierce settled into her leather chair. On the corner of her desk was a photo of the Commandant's teenage daughter. For some reason, Lindsey had a tough time imagining Commandant Pierce as a loving mother. She was so intimidating it was hard to visualize her as anything other than an officer. Lindsey deactivated the pads in her fingers and tucked the stray strands of her hair back into her bun. It was a little strange to realize she wanted Dwayne and Maria to see her as a dignified soldier. After a second, she realized it was because they'd both seen her at her worst, and she wanted them to be consoled with the idea she was fine in their absence.

The secret program activated and immediately redirected itself to the pad. Lindsey leaned forward and answered. Instantly the vid screen filled with the image of Dwayne and Maria seated side by side. Dwayne's arm was draped over Maria's shoulders, and she leaned into him slightly. Behind them was an array of consoles. The couple appeared to be in an aircraft or city control center. Both were clad in plain black t-shirts and Maria grinned the second she saw Lindsey.

"Linds!"

Forgetting all about protocol, Lindsey grinned and waved. "Maria! It's good to see you."

"As you can see, we're alive," Dwayne said with a broad smile.

"Castellan, you've never looked so... young." Commandant Pierce lifted one eyebrow in surprise and glanced at Lindsey. "Am I right?"

Dwayne appeared to be in his early thirties. The gray was gone from his brown hair and the lines in his face were diminished. Instead of a handsome man in his early fifties, he looked just a little older than Maria.

Affectionately, Maria laid her hand on his cheek. "A perk of the virus Dr. Curran gave me."

Dwayne kissed her palm, then leaned toward the camera. They, too, had rigged their vid screen to capture the wristlet's transmission. "Though we're happy to see both of you, we wouldn't be breaking our radio silence if we didn't feel it was of dire importance to the city. We accept that we're on our own out here."

"You appear to be doing well," Commandant Pierce noted.

"The Scrags don't even look at us. We're fine," Maria answered. "We've been receiving your messages, Linds. And we have some concerns about what's going on with Admiral Kirkpatrick."

"He surrendered last night," Lindsey said.

Dwayne frowned. "That's even more worrisome then. It's probably a part of whatever plan he's concocting."

"You think he's planning to somehow continue his coup d'état?" Commandant Pierce folded her arms across her chest.

"There have been pulses emanating from The Bastion activating the surveillance grid in the outside world," Maria answered. "They're looking for us."

Sickened at the thought, Lindsey pulled out a smaller pad from her uniform pocket to take notes. "Are you sure?"

"We're in Beta City until this transmission ends, then we're leaving. The pulses are weak, so they have limited range. We plan to be beyond their reach," Dwayne answered. "There were four pulses yesterday that activated the grid for two hours. We're in a secure spot, so we weren't detected."

Beta City was actually an enormous evacuee camp with all the luxuries of a small city. It had been a holding area for the civilians that were eventually moved to The Bastion. That meant Maria and Dwayne were closer to The Bastion than Lindsey liked.

"We're actively shielding ourselves from all types of scans." Maria lifted both hands to reveal that the wristlet was gone. "We're going to have to keep them off and in a shielded container. One of the pulses delivered a program that attempted to hack through any we'd installed to hide ourselves or allow communication with the city. Lindsey, you're the best, but they almost got through."

Scribbling down notes with her stylus, Lindsey nodded. "Can you send me a copy of the pulse and the program?"

"Already on its way," Dwayne answered. "We got four more minutes on this transmission, then we're leaving."

"And you can't tell us where," Commandant Pierce instructed somberly.

"We've accepted that we can't go back to The Bastion. Especially after the pulses yesterday," Maria said, sadness in her big dark eyes. "They're looking for us, which means they know we're alive, and that we have a different virus in our veins than the others."

"Dr. Curran talked." Commandant Pierce shook her head. "I knew that woman couldn't be trusted."

"If they find us, we'll never see the outside of a SWD lab again," Dwayne said pensively. "We have transportation with stealth tech. In a few hours, we'll be gone. It took us two weeks to get this old girl up and running, but she'll keep us safe until we're out of the reach of the pulses."

Though Lindsey was relieved that her friends were alive and together, she realized they weren't truly safe yet. It would be up to her to make sure they were.

Silence fell over the four people as the enormity of the situation weighed down on them. Maria scooted forward and placed her hand on the vid screen. Lindsey slid out of her chair and placed her hand over Maria's.

"Linds, we know you'll do your best. We will, too. But we want you to know that one way or the other we're going to be okay, and we want you to be, too."

"Maria, I'll stop the fuckers from finding you," Lindsey vowed.

"I fucking love you, my sister," Maria whispered with emotion.

"I've got your back, sister," Lindsey answered.

With a very dour look on his face, Dwayne also bent toward the screen. "Lindsey, Commandant Pierce, if they do find us, we'll transmit our location to you so you can dispatch a Constabulary team to destroy our bodies. We'll take care of our exit ourselves when they get here. Though the virus in our veins has been… miraculous so far, we have no idea how it will continue to evolve or change us. The Bastion must survive as humans, not as Scrags. Boon or not."

"Agreed, Castellan. Honestly, I wouldn't let you back into the city anyway. We can't risk an outbreak."

Dwayne nodded. "You're wise, Sir."

"I'm paranoid, Castellan. But it does sound as if the SWD is not finished with its attempt to take over the Bastion. That being said, let's not ever receive that final transmission," Commandant Pierce replied.

Staring into the eyes of her dearest friend, Lindsey felt her own eyes filling with unshed tears. With their hands pressed against the vid screens, it was almost as if they were touching. It had been foolish to believe the SWD wouldn't turn their attention toward the missing castellan and vanguard. They were listed as MIA, not dead. That made them a valuable resource of The Bastion in the eyes of the SWD.

"The Bastion's reach is going to be limited, but we can't be sure of how far the SWD will try," Dwayne continued. "We'll be far away by nightfall."

Lindsey finally dropped her hand and started to scribble on her pad again. "I'm going to make a quick program for your wristlets. It'll redirect the transmission to a node where I will drop all the city updates. It'll be a floating data cloud, so they shouldn't be able to track it back to you. I'll have to work out the kinks and—"

"Linds, we trust you," Maria said in a soothing tone.

Raising her eyes, Maria could see her friend's concern. "One month intervals. Okay?"

Dwayne directed his attention to Maria, who met his worried look with a slight smile. "Lindsey can pull it off, babe."

With a short nod, Dwayne agreed to the arrangement. "We won't be sending anything back unless it's of vital importance. If things go to shit, we'll send a direct transmission on the open frequency."

"We could always try to persuade the population to side with you and Maria," Commandant Pierce suggested.

"I'm sorry, Commandant," Dwayne said, "but we can't put our faith in a public outcry. These are our lives. And if the virus in us mutates, or even if there is a slight chance it would adversely affect another person, we can't take the chance of returning to the Bastion."

A faint beep sounded on the other end and Maria reached out to touch a control panel out of sight. "We need to go. A pulse just hit the outer junction."

Before Lindsey could even utter goodbye, then screen went dark.

"No more playing by the rules," Commandant Pierce said in a fierce voice. "Hack into the SWD and rummage through their guts. I want to know what's going on. Immediately. It's obvious they haven't given up yet, and neither are we."

"Yes, sir." Lindsey stared at the faint imprint of her hand on the vid screen and wished fervently she could have said goodbye.

Gnawing on a chalky protein bar that was supposed to taste like chocolate, Lindsey stared at the computer in front of her. Tucked into a tiny unused office, she was occupied with peeling away all the layers of secrecy inside the SWD. Her mind plucked the words from the screen and transformed the data into images within her mind that made it much easier to collate and process.

Fingers tapping over screens, Lindsey pieced together a story that chilled her to the bone. A cup of coffee was ice cold at her elbow, and she set the bar aside without finishing it. Leaning forward, her fingers flew across the display.

"Fuckers," she whispered in anger.

Continuing to swipe the pertinent information onto one drive, Lindsey almost wished she wasn't discovering just how deep the rabbit hole went inside the SWD.

The door chimed and Lindsey checked the security feed. Commandant Pierce stood outside with her hands resting on her narrow hips. Lindsey unlocked the door and it swished open. Once the officer was inside, Lindsey shut and locked the door.

"What did you find?" Commandant Pierce asked, staring at the computers Lindsey had dragged into the small space. The air conditioner was on high and the commandant shivered. "How bad is it?"

"Oh, it's bad. Really bad," Lindsey answered. She'd only brought one chair into the office, so she offered it to the commandant. "Take a seat?"

"I'll stand. Show me."

Lindsey quickly saved everything she needed and disconnected from the grid. "Well, the delay in Admiral Kirkpatrick surrendering was on purpose. During that time period, food stores were transferred out of several warehouses to another location."

"The SWD stole food?" Commandant Pierce arched her eyebrows.

"Yes and no. All the transfers were made using the president's authorization and the food was relocated to the shelter in the basement of the president's residence."

"What are you saying?"

"Well, the SWD forged the president's authorization and stole vast stores of food and planted it in the president's own home using the city's delivery system. They set him up." Lindsey organized the screens for the commandant to study. "It wasn't easy to trace, but I found the origin computer where the forgeries were created and traced the route through the system. Someone did try to scrub the info, but there were still data packets lodged in various nodes along the path."

"I have no idea what you're saying."

"Well, they wiped the computer where they did the forgery. But like a train moving through the city, the orders had stops at various stations along the way to its destination. That's how I was able to trace backward. The code used to secure the message left little data stamps at each junction."

"Like a train tripping proximity sensors?"

"Yeah, kinda."

"So they're trying to make the president look like a thief."

"They're trying to set him up to look like he's hoarding food and preparing to cut off the rest of the city and only save himself and others in power. Admiral Kirkpatrick has a speech written that discusses his discovery of the president's 'theft' and his own plan to send SWD squads into the dead world to retrieve food stores." Lindsey's hands shook slightly and it wasn't just from the shock of her discovery. She needed food after forgetting to eat all day. Picking up her bar, she took another bite.

"So Admiral Kirkpatrick will look like a hero of the people and President Cabot the villain."

Lindsey forced herself to swallow the dry lump. "But that's not the real reason for the squads moving out into the dead world. It's an excuse." Pulling up another document, she pointed at several lines. "They're going after Maria and Dwayne."

"The pulses."

"Exactly. They're trying to locate them using the pulse. This document is from Dr. Curran to a Mrs. Petersen."

"Mrs. Petersen?"

"Commandant, there is an entire section in the SWD where every person is called Petersen. It's to protect the core group working together to take control of The Bastion."

"So the Mr. Petersen we were dealing with isn't the only one?"

"No. And I looked into the documentation being prepared by the Judiciary Authority. The Mr. Petersen they're preparing to charge is not the one we encountered." Lindsey touched the screen and the bland face of man with dark skin and hair popped up. "This is the man who has been in talks with the Judiciary Authority and performing as an assistant to Admiral Kirkpatrick."

"That's not him. That's not the same man."

"The Mr. Petersen we dealt with doesn't show up on any security footage from any meetings. He was excised from the vids."

Commandant Pierce frowned as she read the information on the screen. "So you think the one we were dealing with is still in charge?"

"Definitely. Legatus Martel didn't have a history in the SWD databases until a week ago. Then she simply appeared and was included in the files sent to President Cabot when he made the move to appoint a new leader of the SWD. I looked at those files. They were skewed to make him select Martel."

"Where did Martel come from?"

"Well, I had to go outside the SWD to find her. She's a real person and I found her civilian records. She studied with Dr. Curran at the university, and then she just vanished. I suspect she joined the SWD and became a Petersen. The reason I recognized her name is because Dr. Curran sent her a communique during the Inferi Boon project. It was of a personal matter, so I didn't pay attention to it. They were arranging to have dinner at the Luminous Restaurant. The one that actually has real meat! Anyway, Dr Curran said the reservation was under the name Martel."

Commandant Pierce was silent for a very long moment. "SWD has always operated apart from the Constabulary."

"Because of Admiral Kirkpatrick's influence."

"Which has provided them the opportunity to create this elaborate network of lies."

"They have a very specific agenda."

"They want Maria and Dwayne."

"And created a cover story for a fleet of tiltrotors leaving the city."

"And when they retrieve them?"

Lindsey tugged nervously at her hair. "They're to be secreted into the labs."

"Of course."

"Also, Dr. Curran got samples off the Abscrags. She's experimenting again."

Shaking her head, Commandant Pierce looked older than when she'd entered the room. "Of course."

"This is enough to take to the president, right?"

"Absolutely. I'll deal with it immediately."

Lindsey quickly compiled all the information onto a data drive and handed it to the commandant.

"You look about how I feel," the other woman said with a wry smile.

Glancing toward the screen where the SWD deployment roster glowed, Lindsey sighed. "It's not a day for good news."

"You've been in here for hours. You've got enough to counter the SWD. Take a rest, Rooney. Go get a drink."

"I'll probably do that as soon as I finish doing something."

"Make sure you do. Now let me out of this damn claustrophobic room."

Lindsey rapidly unlocked the door and watched the commanding officer depart. Once the door was shut and locked, she returned her gaze to the SWD roster. The names of those selected to track down Dwayne and Maria glowed ominously.

Master Seeker MacDonald sat at the top of the list.

Reconnecting to the grid, Lindsey hacked into The Bastion security files and searched for Torran's wristlet identifier.

CHAPTER 13

The illegal pub was swarming with off duty SWD personnel and civilians. It was near the SWD Facility and Torran liked to grab a drink after a rough day. Still clad in his uniform, he felt the eyes of the junior officers and enlisted people on him, but he didn't really mind. It had been a rough afternoon. He'd spent most of it getting acquainted with the faces, names, and profiles of his newly acquired squad. Though he didn't want to admit it, he wasn't looking forward to meeting them.

Staring at the pale gold liquid in his glass, he wished it was tequila, but he had no regrets with how his bottle had met its demise. It had been a great night.

The long bar was made of old shipping containers and the lights strung along the pipes gave the basement pub a very post-apocalyptic vibe. Considering they were living in a post-apocalyptic world, he supposed it was perfect. He did miss the old pub in the Scottish Borough that actually resembled a pub from Scotland. Rumor was it had been moved brick by brick from Aberdeen.

The old stool beside him creaked and he glanced over to see Lindsey settling onto it. Her bun had slipped off the top of her head and was a jumble at the nap of her neck. Her bangs and wisps of hair framed her tense face. Still clad in her Constabulary uniform, she was drawing some downright hostile looks from the SWD security forces.

"Are you stalking me?" Torran asked.

"Yep." Lindsey took the glass from his hand, drank the remains of the liquid, flinched, then signaled the bartender for two more. "I hacked into the city security grid and found your wristlet identifier. Then I made a program in my wristlet to track you. And as soon as I was off duty, I followed it here. So, yes, I'm stalking you."

Staring at her, Torran wasn't sure whether he was flattered or a little afraid. Maybe he was both. "Why stalking?"

The big hazel eyes he adored so much filled with tears. "I need a friend."

"I'm your friend," Torran assured her while setting an elbow on the counter and claiming his drink.

Lindsey pushed some credits to the bartender, and the slim woman, with a shaved head and wearing a wisp of a black dress, claimed them without a word. Even the SWD prejudice affected their favorite bartender.

"For that amount, get her two drinks," Torran said to the bartender.

The woman scowled but poured another.

Torran set it next to Lindsey's other drink. "Bad day at the office?"

Lindsey made a noise that was halfway between a snort and a laugh. "Putting it lightly."

"Can you talk about it?"

Shaking her head, Lindsey picked up the drink and took a quick sip. She flinched at the taste, but took another. "It's just... complicated."

"Like life," Torran offered.

"Yeah. What about your day?"

"New squad assignment. Spent the whole day looking at very young faces. I meet them tomorrow. Fresh out of training. New recruits dying to get out there and kill Scrags."

Lindsey was silent for a long moment, then finally said, "Hopefully there aren't any more out in the valley."

Torran nodded and gulped down his drink. He still had a slight hangover, but didn't mind flirting with another. "I hope for the same. Did you see those crazy walls they're erecting around the cleared areas?"

"I missed that. Was that on today's news feed?"

"Yeah. Kinda like those damn walls they tried to put up during the doomed final push. The mesh ones. By the time they get done, the valley will look like a maze with all those sections."

"Just like the Bastion."

"Except the walls will be around farms, ranches, the mines..."

"But more walls."

"I'm kinda sick of walls," Torran decided.

"Though I suppose it's better than the outside world, huh?" Lindsey almost sounded wistful, yet also afraid.

The vid screen in the corners of the bar continued to display the latest developments and Torran was sick of watching the same looping information. To his relief, the music filtering through the old speakers strung up in the corners of the narrow bar overwhelmed the voices of the news anchors.

"Are you sure you don't want to talk about your day?" Torran asked. It was clear that something was weighing heavily on her. He could almost see the computer in the back of her mind whirring away despite the emotional turmoil in her eyes.

"Torran, even if I could talk about it..." She licked her lips and steadied herself against the bar. "... I couldn't tell you. I don't even know if I could put into words what I feel."

"You look so sad. So hurt."

"And helpless." Lindsey took another long sip from her drink.

"You're not helpless. You're capable. You saved my life."

Lindsey's finger danced over his hair, fringing his high forehead. "This is so not regulation." She obviously wanted to change the topic.

"SWD is much more lax than Constabulary about the whole hair thing. Though looking at your hair, I got to wonder if they're slacking off."

Touching her fallen bun, Lindsey rolled her eyes. "I tend to tug at my hair when working. Vaja says I should chop it off."

"Vaja... is back?"

"No, no. I should say he used to say that. But my dad always liked my hair long. He used to brush it before I went to sleep when I was very little. Of all the things from my childhood, that is the one thing I remember. My dad brushing my hair..."

"It's a lovely memory." Torran tugged at a hairpin holding her bun together and her long locks unraveled around his hand. "It looks nice down."

"You're drunk." Lindsey decided.

"Yep."

An SWD officer brushed past them and his foot hit Lindsey's stool, nearly toppling her off it.

"Hey!" Torran shouted after the man, but the only response he got was a dark look before the customer went to join his friends at a table.

"I should go," Lindsey said swiftly. "I am in 'enemy' territory."

"I'll come with you," Torran said, downing his drink and sliding to his feet.

"You don't have to."

"Yeah, I do. I'm feeling surly."

Lindsey gave him a grateful look. When he took her hand, she didn't protest, but followed him out of the packed bar. They both ignored the disdainful looks cast in their direction. Torran hadn't fully realized how much anger was brewing in the SWD against the Constabulary, but he had been out of the loop for the last few weeks.

Without any real direction, they walked for a few blocks through the impressive buildings that ringed the SWD Facility. This area of the city was cleaner and less crowded than the rest of The Bastion. Most of the buildings housed offices for government officials.

Night had cast a thick blanket of darkness over the city and fog filled the streets. Only street lamps illuminated their way. Torran didn't like that Lindsey had walked all this way alone. Rape and assaults were rare, but did happen.

"Torran," Lindsey said softly.

Turning toward her, he saw tears on her face.

"You're going beyond the wall soon." It wasn't a question.

"Yeah."

"Come back, okay?"

"Lindsey..."

When she kissed him, he knew it wasn't out of love, but out of need. The pain, loneliness and fear poured out of her and matched his internal turmoil. After a few seconds, he pulled away and instead held her tightly in his arms.

"I'll come back," he whispered.

Lindsey initially felt foolish seeking Torran out at the bar, but as he walked her back to her small flat, she let go of those feelings. He obviously did care about her and his presence was a comfort. Whereas Vaja would've been hounding her to disclose what was going on in her head, Torran allowed her to be alone in her thoughts and only divulge what she was comfortable telling him.

Of course, there was no way she could tell him about Maria and Dwayne being on the run from the SWD. Nor she could she tell him that she'd discovered what the SWD was planning and how Torran fit into their designs. When she'd seen his name on the roster of those selected to venture into the outside world in pursuit of Maria, it was as if the air had been knocked out of her lungs. Commandant Pierce had all the information Lindsey had collected, but she wondered if the Constabulary would be able to counter what the SWD had planned. She was still processing all she'd learned for it was very overwhelming.

Clutching Torran's hand, she wondered if she should disclose what she'd discovered. Of course, that would be revealing her illicit activities. That was something she did not want the SWD to know, and she was still determining if she trusted Torran with that information or not. Of course, she couldn't warn him that she'd do everything possible to prevent his mission from being a success.

So instead of talking, they walked in silence.

When they reached the narrow alleyway that lead to the stairs to her flat, she pulled him to a stop. "Torran, you don't have to walk me all the way home if you don't want to. I'm sorry I showed up being an emotional mess—"

"That's not a problem. I'm glad you came to me. But do you want me to go and leave you be?" Torran asked in such a way she knew he'd respect whatever she said.

After a beat, she admitted the truth. "No."

Wrapping his arm around her shoulders, he guided her toward her small flat. "Lindsey, I don't know what happened today, but I'm here for you. That's what friends do. Right?'

"You know, Maria would have adored you," Lindsey said, and felt the pang of loss like sharp dagger in her gut once again.

"I *am* a likable bloke," Torran said teasingly.

Nearing the stairs, Lindsey realized that someone was sitting halfway up the steps clad in a dark coat with a hood over their head. Torran immediately stepped in front of her, which partially annoyed her.

"Hey, you there. You can't sleep there. Go to the nearest shelter," Torran called out.

The figure lifted his head and Lindsey recognized Vaja's slim face in the dim light cast by the street lamps.

"I live here, asshole," Vaja answered sharply.

"No you don't," Lindsey snapped, darting around Torran to confront her ex as he came down the steps to meet her.

"Lindsey," Vaja said in such a way that it made her want to slap him. He sounded like an adult tired of a child's temper tantrum. "Can we just go inside? We need to talk."

"No, we don't."

"Look, you need to leave," Torran said to Vaja in a stern tone.

"I'm her boyfriend. Who the hell are you?"

Torran and Vaja glared at each other over her head.

"Vaja, you're not my boyfriend and he's just a friend," Lindsey interjected.

"Are you fucking him?" Vaja asked pointedly.

"If I am, it's none of your business!" Lindsey gave Torran a sharp warning look, but he just appeared grim.

Pointing at Torran accusingly, Vaja said, "He's that guy. The one always messaging you."

"He's my friend who does message me on occasion, and it's none of your damn business anyway!"

"Lindsey, we need to talk!"

"No we don't, Vaja. You need to leave!"

"Lindsey, I left the other women for *you.*" Vaja reached for her, but she stepped out of his grasp.

That elicited a scornful chuckle from Torran.

Lindsey tossed Torran another warning glare.

Vaja pointed to his bag tucked under the steps. "I've come home to you and only you. I want to be with you. I love you."

The words were exactly what she had wanted to hear from Vaja two days before. Even though the delivery was heartfelt and Lindsey was surprised to see love burning in Vaja's eyes, she realized she no longer wanted him to make declarations of fidelity. At one point, she'd believed she loved him, but she knew she'd been deceiving herself. Maybe a few days ago she would have let him stick around for companionship, hoping one day she might love him, but she didn't have the luxury of time anymore.

"Lindsey, say something," Vaja pleaded, giving Torran a dark look.

"Go to a shelter, Vaja. Get a flat assignment. Leave me alone," she replied in a weary voice.

"It's him. He came between us."

Lindsey and Torran exchanged looks. He lifted his eyebrows slightly, but said nothing.

"No, he didn't. Your lies did. Torran is my friend."

"You're fucking him," Vaja said with scorn.

"If I am, you can't say a word about it." Lindsey grabbed Vaja's bag from under the stairs and shoved it into his arms.

"Yes, I can. Because our love is real, Lindsey. I realized it after you made me leave. I couldn't bear the thought of not being with you." Vaja brushed his fingers lightly over her cheek.

Lindsey shivered from the touch, the memories of all they had experienced swirling around in her mind and tangling with the darker thoughts of his deception. She detected Torran circling around behind her. It was natural for him to move into a position to provide backup. They were both soldiers after all.

Setting her hands on her hips, Lindsey stared into Vaja's beautiful ice blue eyes and ignored his touch. At one point she'd melted at the very sight of him, but now she was just sad.

"I'm not in love with you, Vaja. I'm not in love with anyone."

That elicited a mirthless chuckle from her ex. Looking at Torran, he said, "Sucks to be you, huh? How long will you last?"

"We're friends," Torran replied.

"Sure you are." Vaja jumped off the stairs, swung his bag over his shoulder, and stared at Lindsey. "I'll come by tomorrow so we can talk without him."

"Don't bother," Lindsey called after him, but had the sinking feeling that Vaja wouldn't listen.

"Asshole." Vaja flipped off Torran, then trudged down the narrow passage to the street.

Unlocking the door, Lindsey slipped into the flat. Torran followed and palmed the door locks. He didn't say anything. Instead, he leaned against the door, arms folded over his chest, and waited.

Lindsey unbuttoned her jacket and struggled to find words and speak coherently. At last, the only one that slipped free was, "Fuck!"

"Exes. They're complicated."

Torran said the words so deadpan it made her snicker. The sound of her laughter provoked a smile to break out on Torran's lips. The sight made her stomach clench again. She hated that she knew what he did not.

"Should I go?" Torran asked, misreading her expression.

"No. Stay." Lindsey set her coat on the back of her computer chair. In her mind's eyes she saw his name again on the SWD roster.

"What's happening?" Torran ventured to ask.

Lindsey slid her fingers through her long hair and stared at him in silence.

"You know something. Like how you knew about the Inferi Boon and the castellan leaving the city. The night you saved me, you knew so much more than I did. It's happening again. I see it in your eyes."

"You see things others don't. It's a little disturbing," she said half-jokingly.

"Lindsey, are you in danger?"

"No. Not directly."

"Am I?"

Lindsey pressed her lips together and weighed her options. "In about an hour the whole city will know what I'm about to tell you. That's when the press conference will occur outside of the SWD Facility. The SWD will tell the Bastion we're on the verge of starvation because of President Cabot's inept handling of our reserves. Then it will be announced that using the resources gathered from the valley, the SWD is sending troops out to gather food from the dead world."

"How do you know this?" Torran stared at her with alarm.

114

Tears filling her eyes, she said, "I know things because I can't stand not to know what's happening."

"You hacked into the SWD. You saw their plans. You saw that I'm on the roster," Torran muttered, then said, "Shit."

"Torran..." Lindsey couldn't find words anymore. She cared about him. He understood her and already felt like a dear friend. In her imagination, she could see him hanging out with her, Ryan, and Maria. He would have fit in so flawlessly. Why had it taken so long for them to find each other? Now he was leaving on a mission Lindsey wanted to fail.

"Can you show me?"

"I shouldn't show you any of it," Lindsey retorted. "I shouldn't have even seen it."

"But you did. Because that's what you do. You see what others don't. It's what you've done with me, you know. You see things others don't." His voice was clipped, his expression pained, but he wasn't being cruel. "I suspected you were some sort of spy or hacker. That computer always running behind your eyes."

Pressing her lips together, she finally nodded. Sitting at her computer, she disconnected it from the grid. Pulling out her small pad, she accessed the hidden files and relayed the information to the bigger screen. She only showed him the stolen speech and the roster. She didn't show him the secret intel on Maria and Dwayne.

Leaning over her, Torran studied both of the open documents on the screen. After several long minutes, he finally said, "Okay."

"It's not okay."

Torran pointed at several abbreviations at the bottom of the roster. "Experimental stealth armor. They think they have a way to protect us."

"Torran..."

"So, that increases our chances right there..."

"Torran!"

Lindsey tilted her head so she could see his face. Eyes wide, his dread was clear.

"What do you want me to say? That I won't go? Because I have to go. It's what people like you and me always do, Lindsey. Even if we might die. We go and do what we need to do."

Standing, she wrapped her arms around him and pressed her face into his chest. His arms went around her and he laid his cheek against the top of her head.

"We just met..." he said, and left the words drop away.

Lindsey couldn't speak. She was torn between wanting his mission to fail and having him return. Caught between her love for Maria and her growing attachment to Torran, she was distraught.

"You didn't want to tell me," he said at last.

"No, I did. I just... I want to trust you, Torran. But if the SWD internal security found out—"

"They won't. I won't tell a soul," Torran swore. Releasing her, he took her by the arms and stared down at her. "I promise that."

"When I went to find you, I just... I was going on emotion." Staring at the emblem of the SWD on the collar of his black uniform, she hated that she was stuck once again at the center of the battle between people who cared more for retaining power than helping the citizens of the Bastion. "I wanted to be near you before you found out and it all changed. I know we just met a few weeks ago and haven't spent a lot of time together, but we share so much in common. You actually seem to get my weirdness."

"You're amazing," Torran protested. "You're such a good friend. A good soldier. So clever. So amazingly talented." He waved a hand at the computer screen. "And I'm glad I'm finding out from you. It makes it more... bearable."

Touching his cheek, the sorrow she felt within her startled her with its depth. Maybe she was more attached to him than she allowed herself to believe. Rising up onto her toes, she kissed him tenderly. Torran responded with a soft brush of his lips against hers. Peering into her eyes, he must have seen what she felt: boundaries falling. The kiss that followed was searing with emotion and passion. It was far more intense and consuming than the kisses they had shared the night before. Lips and tongues meeting in torrid passion, they clung to each other as if the world would tear them apart.

With a sob in her throat, Lindsey realized it *was* tearing them apart.

"I had it all wrong," she whispered against his lips, her fingers gripping the collar of his jacket.

"How?" he asked, a tiny frown between his eyebrows.

"It's not that life is so short we shouldn't risk getting attached... it's that life's so short we should take every risk no matter how terrifying."

"They'll call me in tomorrow morning," he said in a quiet voice.

"Then stay here tonight with me," she urged him. It was quite hard to speak, and it hurt to think too far into the future. She just wanted the here and now to be everything that could have been if they just had time.

"If I stay," Torran said cautiously, "I want more than to just fuck you. I want to know what it is to... love you. Okay?"

With a sorrowful giggle in her voice, she answered, "Again, you seem to read my mind."

"Forty minutes until broadcast."

"Let's make it count," she said, her fingers playing with his clearly not regulation hair.

CHAPTER 14

Torran was still tucked inside Lindsey's warmth when their wristlets chimed. He attempted to roll off her, but she kept him pinned to her hips with her legs. Gazing up at him with eyes that made him want to slay an entire world of Scrags just to be with her, Lindsey brushed the sides of his face with her fingers.

"Just one last kiss before the world changes," she whispered.

Bending his head to hers, he gave her a long, deep kiss that caused him to stir inside her.

She moaned with pleasure.

The wristlet chimed again.

A sigh escaping his lips, he swiped the screen of his wristlet to see the flashing emblem of The Bastion and a countdown timer to the announcement. Lindsey moaned when he slipped out of her to lay at her side. Reluctantly, she activated her own wristlet, rolling onto her stomach to watch the feed. Torran set his wristlet next to hers and nestled into her side. Pressing gentle kisses against her temple, he waited to hear the announcement of his fate.

When the emblem dissolved, instead of Admiral Kirkpatrick before the camera it was President Cabot. standing in the rotunda of the Capitol complex.

"Citizens of the Bastion, good evening. I apologize for interrupting your evening rituals or wakening you, but recent events have compelled me to speak directly to you tonight. Though we are unified under the banner of humanity, recent events have revealed that elements within our city do not serve the needs of people, but only their own selfish desires. Troubling information of a duplicitous nature came to light tonight.

"Admiral Kirkpatrick and his associates originally planned to speak to you at this hour in order to spread falsehoods about my administration. Their allegations included the gross mismanagement of Bastion food stores and secret plans for survival of only a select few. It is true that our food stores are limited at this time, but with the reclamation of the valley, which I ordered, there is hope for the future. Also, like our predecessors we have emergency contingences to ensure the survival of humanity. Admiral Kirkpatrick and his supporters hoped to skew the truth to appeal to your fears in an effort, once again, to rob the legally elected government of The Bastion of its power. He'd devised to propose a plan where SWD forces would venture into the dead world to retrieve food stores from long abandoned food depots. Depots that were beyond our capabilities of accessing until our fuel reserves were once more available to us due to our victory in reclaiming the valley.

"I concur that this is a viable alternative now that we have the ability to once again venture outside of The Bastion and the valley. But I believe that our strength as a people lies in working together.

Therefore, I have requested that Commandant Pierce of the Constabulary and Legatus Martel of the Science Warfare Division formulate a plan that will utilize squads from both branches of our military to carry out a mission to secure these depots."

Torran felt Lindsey tense beneath his touch. Casting a nervous look at him, she scrambled off her bed.

"Linds," he called after her.

When she didn't answer, he followed.

Torran found Lindsey reconnecting her computer to the grid and activating screens faster than his eyes could follow. Fingers flying over screens and keys, Lindsey moved so quickly he was in awe. Her eyes tracked across the readouts with an intensity that was almost frightening. Tapping her fingers against one screen, she twisted her lips.

"Lindsey, what are you looking for?" Torran peered at the display, but could only make out a few things.

"The roster changed," she answered, lifting her eyes finally. With the sweep of her hand, all the screens vanished.

Squatting before her, Torran rested his hands on her waist. "Am I still on it?"

Lindsey nodded.

Torran could see the computer behind her eyes whirling away, then saw it finally flick off. It was a relief to see her return fully to him.

"So, nothing has changed," he ventured.

"Oh, no. It's changed." Lindsey shrugged slightly. "Now I'm on the roster, too."

The despair he'd felt when she had told him the news about his name being on the initial roster had been pretty intense, but it didn't compare to the thought of her life being in danger. "They can't."

"They can and did. I'm in charge of the Constabulary squad. You're in charge of the SWD." Lindsey pressed her forehead to his and cupped his face with her palms. "We're going out there together."

Torran struggled to find the right words to say, but his mind failed him. He wanted to console her, but also rage against the powers that were using the enlisted as pawns in their games. Covering her hands with his, he heard the president speaking through the feed filtering through their wristlets.

"At least we'll be together," she said finally.

Lifting his eyes, he saw that she was giving him a sweet smile. "I'd rather you were here. Safe."

"But, Torran, this is what people like us do, right?"

Torran hated that his words had come back to haunt him, but she was right. "Yes, this is what people like us do."

"And this is why we have a connection. We understand each other, what we must do, the sacrifices that must be made."

Nodding, Torran kissed the palms of her hands.

"So we'll do our duty." The sadness in her eyes was unbearable.

Torran stood and dragged her into his arms. Holding each other close, they could hear the last lines of the president's speech and the anthem of The Bastion playing before the feed ended.

Their wristlets chimed, then turned off.

The world had altered around them yet again.

Watching Torran sleep, his head tucked beside hers on the pillow, Lindsey's mind spun out all the possibilities of what could possibly occur on their mission. The SWD's secret mission to retrieve Dwayne and Maria would not be so easily subsumed. The SWD would find a way to split the squads apart.

What would Torran do when he discovered his mission was actually to retrieve Dwayne and Maria?

Lindsey suspected she already knew the answer, and it filled her with dread.

CHAPTER 15

"Of course I was going to add you to the roster once President Cabot agreed that the Constabulary must be involved," Commandant Pierce said, regarding Lindsey calmly from behind the pristine desk. Legs crossed, arms folded, the higher-ranking officer emanated confidence and power.

Standing before the commandant, Lindsey was silent. She'd fully expected to be called in to speak with Commandant Pierce, so the early morning summons on her wristlet hadn't been surprising. Even after hours of lying awake with her overloaded brain processing everything she'd learned, it was difficult for Lindsey to unravel her twisted emotions surrounding the imminent mission and deal with them adequately. She was scared, of course, but also devastated by the fact that she and Torran were now set against each other even if he didn't realize it yet. All night, she'd struggled with the conundrum before her. Would the SWD abandon their plan if the Constabulary was involved? Should she tell Torran about Maria and Dwayne? About what the SWD was planning? There were so many questions, yet she doubted she would be provided with the answers she needed to make wise choices.

As though waiting for her to say something, Commandant Pierce continued to regard Lindsey in silence.

"You're sending me because of my skills," Lindsey said at last, her voice unsure.

"Of course. I'll need you out there thwarting any attempt the SWD may make to find the castellan and vanguard."

Troubled at the thought of this task, she said, "That may be difficult, since it's a joint effort."

"I *know* you'll find a way. My only concern is whether or not you'll pass the physical the SWD is demanding each soldier must pass in order to be involved in the mission."

Lindsey bristled a tad. After more than a year struggling with a disability, she was sensitive about her health. "I've maintained my fitness despite the injury, and since the repair, I've been working on strengthening my leg."

"Then hopefully you'll pass their tests." The commandant hesitated. "Or make it look like you did."

Lindsey puffed up just a bit at the reference to her hacking abilities. It was nice to be praised for her skills even though her physical aptitude was in question. "I assume they expressed concerns that I just came off the disabled roster?"

"Oh yes. But they have concerns about *every* soldier I put on the Constabulary roster."

"By 'they' you mean Legatus Martel."

Commandant Pierce's gaze turned absolutely cold. It wasn't directed at Lindsey, but it was unnerving just the same. "Yes, Legatus Martel. She's an interesting woman. Her dossier makes a lot of claims about her military training within the SWD under Admiral

Kirkpatrick's elite guard, but I'm not certain I see the attributes born of such a career in her demeanor or interactions."

"A bureaucrat in soldiers' clothing..."

"...does not make a soldier." Commandant Pierce smirked, and it was rather terrifying. "What has been agreed upon so far is that each soldier, both SWD and Constabulary, must meet a certain criteria, both physically and mentally. President Cabot wants each participant to be a veteran of an actual conflict. In other words, the survivors of the final push and the recent clearing of the valley are the prime candidates. I suspect this is for multiple purposes. One being that the squad will have some combat experience and, therefore, handle the rigors of the mission better than a green squad. The second is probably for propaganda purposes."

"The heroes of The Bastion going out to save humanity once again."

"Exactly. The one major victory I've won is that one of our own chief defenders will be in charge of the mission. I have submitted a list of ten names to President Cabot and Legatus Martel."

"Will the chief defender know about the SWD secret mission to retrieve the castellan and vanguard?"

Exhaling slowly, Commandant Pierce leaned forward to rest her elbows on the desk. "No."

"Is that President Cabot's order?'

"President Cabot doesn't know about the secret mission."

Lindsey widened her eyes in surprise.

"If President Cabot suspected that immortality was within the veins of Dwayne and Maria, what do you think he'd do?"

"Oh." Lindsey frowned. "He'd be ready to assume a presidency for life. An eternal life."

"Exactly. My job is to keep the city and the valley safe for humanity, not the government. President Cabot's job is to make the people feel he is working for their best interests. Until recently, the Bastion was running smoothly because of how the founders laid out the framework for the powers at the top. Constabulary protects the people. Judiciary Authority enforces the law. The SWD develops new tech to fight the Scrags and keep humanity healthy. And the President and the council speak for the people in all governmental matters. It worked for a long time, but now the power has shifted and created this... mess."

With a scowl, Lindsey said, "Why are we helping him again?"

"Because the people elected him." Commandant Pierce sighed. "Woman to woman, Lindsey, I've played the game of the upper echelon for the last few years. I've compromised myself a few times. I've done things I regret. I was silent when I should have spoken up, and spoken up when I should have been silent. In this case I plan to maintain my silence on the matter of Dwayne and Maria to not only protect myself, you and the others, but humanity."

"And if the SWD says something to the president?"

"I'll act as though it's new information, then argue that they should never be recovered because we don't know what that virus in their veins will do to the general population."

"Do you think he'll listen?"

"No. Which is why I need you out there thwarting the SWD at every turn."

Setting her hands on her hips, Lindsey drew in a deep breath, then slowly exhaled to calm her fraying nerves. "Into the dead world..."

"The SWD has developed new armor they believe can protect the team from attacks."

"Not a real comfort when you toss in the word 'believe' with no real assurances."

"Every step of this mission will be carefully planned out by you and the master seeker. The safety of the combined squad is of the utmost importance. Let's be honest here, Vanguard: the city is on the brink. We're already at Level Three rationing. Most of the city is reliant on food they grow themselves or barter for. With the winter months ahead, we're going to have to implement Level Four rationing and people are going to start becoming very hungry once their personal stores start to run low. The protein supplements only go so far slaking hunger. The new castellan is already preparing for food riots."

"We have a new one?"

"Her appointment will be announced later today."

Lindsey made a mental note to snoop through the Constabulary system more often.

"Castellan Julia Bruner will do an excellent job. Of that I am certain."

"How much will she *know?*"

With a low chuckle, the commandant sat back in her chair. "You, Vanguard, are a very, very bold woman."

"I'm aware I'm probably overstepping my bounds, but as you pointed out—"

"We're strange bedfellows." Commandant Pierce shrugged. "She'll know what I feel she needs to know. At this time, Julia needs to concentrate on maintaining peace in the city. Not the SWD. Not the Scrags."

"And my job is to thwart the SWD at every turn and keep Dwayne and Maria far away from the city."

"I don't even want to imagine the chaos that will rain down on us if they're found. The mere thought of an immortal governing body exalted over the rest of humanity for eternity is too abhorrent to even consider. Of course, those in power would lie to themselves, believing they're above corruption and ruling for the benefit of all people, but we all know the old saying."

"Absolute power corrupts absolutely?"

Standing, Commandant Pierce tucked her hands behind her back and strode over to Lindsey. "What little power I have corrupts me. Bit by bit. Bite by bite. I have to be diligent at all times to not let myself fall into the traps it lays before me. I am an imperfect person. I'm not the wisest, the cleverest, or the strongest. I am anchored by the fact I am a mother. I want the best for my daughter. I want her to live in a world where she can have a full stomach, a career of her choice, the chance to love, and the freedom to vote on her future. Trust me: there are times when I want to play the dirty game that surrounds me. To win. To be stronger. Smarter. More powerful. To outwit those I consider weak. I say this to you as Adeleke, the woman, not the commandant. Every day, I fight for my daughter's future, and it's a battle I find worth fighting for. The Bastion benefits from my devotion to her. So my question to you, Lindsey, as you go out into the dead world: who are you fighting for?"

Pressing her lips together, Lindsey thought of the little girls she saw playing in the streets, the people clustered in the cafes, the mourners at the memorials, and Torran fixing her tacos. "The chance for life."

"The SWD will be under pressure to deliver food and resources to The Bastion, but I doubt they'll give up their quest for the virus. There will be an SWD Sci-Tech team going with you."

Dread filled Lindsey and she regarded the commandant fearfully. "Who's on it?"

"Dr. Beverly Curran and ten assistants."

Lindsey drew in a sharp breath.

"When they make their move, you need to be ready." Commandant Pierce's dark eyes narrowed. "This is when it becomes difficult to have power and not fall into its trap."

"Do you want me to let them die? Kill them?"

"I leave that to *your* discretion."

The burden set on her soul was heavy and suffocating. Lindsey swallowed.

"I trust you, Vanguard Rooney. Not just because of your stellar record, or your uncanny ability to discover the secrets of The Bastion, but because Castellan Reichardt did. And other than my husband, he's the noblest man I've ever known. You'll do what you need to do out there. I trust you."

"Thank you, sir."

"Now make sure you blow them away with excellent results in all your tests."

"Oh, I can assure you. I will."

"One way or the other?" The officer raised a sleek eyebrow, an amused smile on her shapely lips.

"One way or the other," Lindsey answered, already pondering how she could change her test results if she failed any of them.

"You are dismissed," Commandant Pierce said, and returned to her chair behind the enormous desk.

Lindsey saluted and let herself out of the office and into the smaller area that housed the commandant's new assistant. Petra sat at her desk, tapping away on a pad.

The woman glanced up at Lindsey and gave her a knowing look. "Always interesting in The Bastion, isn't it?"

Lindsey wondered how much information Petra's resources had already fed her. Petra was almost as good as Lindsey with finding out what was going on behind the scenes.

"It wouldn't be The Bastion if some conspiracy wasn't brewing in the dark recesses of the halls of power," Lindsey answered.

"So very true... But at least there are good people doing their best for the city. For our children." Petra's voice held a trace of fear.

Lindsey's gaze shifted to a small family photo on the corner of Petra's desk, then she noted half a protein bar sitting near it with small bites along the edges.

"Petra, you don't eat all your rations, do you?"

Swiveling her chair toward Lindsey, Petra crossed her very slender legs. "You're observant."

"You give it to your children. The part you don't eat."

Nodding, Petra said, "Of course. My husband and I always make sure our children aren't hungry."

A tiny bit of guilt seeped into Lindsey's thoughts. As a single person, she only worried about herself. Though she was aware of the population of the city hurrying about in their lives, she never really thought about all the small sacrifices they might be making daily to ensure their children survived.

"You're going on that mission, aren't you, Lindsey? To find more food?"

"Yeah, I am."

Petra toyed with the plain paper wrapper that her bar sat on. "I've never been so scared and yet hopeful in all my life."

"I'll make sure the mission is a success, Petra."

"Myra."

"What?"

"Myra Petra. That's my name. You can call me Myra."

Chuckling with embarrassment, Lindsey responded, "For some reason I thought Petra was your first name." Chances were Lindsey would continue to think of the woman by her surname. Torran still corrected her when she called him MacDonald.

"I know." Petra stood up sharply, peering out into the corridor past the glass doors. "The new castellan is here."

Across the hall a slim, tall woman hesitated as she spoke with her newly appointed assistant. She was a redhead with a streak of pure white hair that originated at her widow's peak before sweeping up into her bun in an attractive swirl. Dressed in a charcoal gray uniform, the woman was striking in appearance.

"What do you think of her?" Lindsey asked.

"I don't know yet. She transferred in from the Southern Garrison. Her record is impressive. She was part of the final push, too. She's the one who ordered the rappel lines to be lowered."

"So she's the reason Torran lived," Lindsey muttered.

"Torran MacDonald? The one you rescued?"

Lindsey responded with a dip of her head.

"You seem to know a lot about him considering you met him once," Petra observed.

"We talked," Lindsey replied, her voice neutral.

"Then your mission should be all the more interesting. He's on the roster."

Deciding to leave before her personal life was cracked wide open, Lindsey dug a protein bar out of her pocket and tossed it onto the desk. "For your kids."

As she strode briskly out of the area, she felt Petra's inquisitive gaze following her.

Entering the conference room, Torran was not surprised to see Legatus Martel sitting at one end of the highly polished white table. A blond woman in a white coat was seated to the right of the Legatus and a dour-looking older man with fortis prime strips -- the highest rank in the security branch of the SWD -- sat on the other side.

Early that morning, soon after Lindsey had received her summons to see the commandant, Torran's wristlet had chimed with orders of his own. They'd hurried to get ready and shared a pot of coffee. When he'd arrived, he'd found the SWD facility bustling with activity and excitement.

"Master Seeker MacDonald, take a seat," Legatus Martel instructed. The inflection of her words implied that she often spoke French.

Torran sat in the chair indicated and set the beret of his uniform on the table. Resting his hands on his lap, he waited in silence.

Legatus Martel looked impeccable in her black jacket with its white collar and cuffs. Skin almost as white as snow and ice-blue eyes granted her an ethereal beauty. Raven locks drawn into an ornate chignon at the back of her head only emphasized her heart shaped face and large eyes. Torran thought she looked rather doll-like, but the sternness in her stare swiftly eradicated any impression of her being delicate.

"Master Seeker MacDonald, your record is impressive. It reveals a man of great fortitude when facing danger. You've been decorated numerous times for your bravery while serving both the Constabulary and the SWD. Your recent survival against incredible odds is admirable."

Torran fought the urge to interpret her words as mocking. Guilt wrapped thorns around his heart and shaded his perception. He hated being a lone survivor.

She continued uninterrupted: "Fortis Prime Trevino hand selected you for this mission based on your exemplary performance. Congratulations."

"Thank you, sir."

"As you know, the SWD under the command of Admiral Kirkpatrick instigated a plan to procure food from depots abandoned during the mass exodus to The Bastion. Though his motives for such an effort are questionable, President Cabot has deemed the plans viable. Therefore, we are now in a joint effort with the Constabulary to implement the plan with some adaptations. The roster before you is the proposed list submitted by Fortis Prime Trevino."

Torran glanced down to see the roster appear on the sleek black glass of the table.

The two other people in the conference room remained quiet as the Legatus continued. "Everyone on this list will need to undergo testing to prove they're ready to face the battlefield beyond the valley... except for you. Based on your recent performance evaluation, we're not concerned about your battle readiness."

Torran almost chuckled at the words 'performance evaluation,' since he'd basically been on trial for being a sole survivor, but he maintained a straight face.

"You and Vanguard Rooney, if she's cleared, will be in charge of your combined squad, but will answer to a chief defender, who has yet to be named. This mission is of paramount importance to the survival of The Bastion. It's also a chance to elevate the SWD above the recent debacle."

"Understood, sir."

"Our predecessors went to great lengths to develop tech that would enable them to store food for extended periods of time. Let's hope they succeeded. A Sci-Tech team will also be included in this mission. Dr. Beverly Curran will be in charge. They will be responsible for ensuring the food you retrieve is not contaminated." Legatus Martel's eyes did not waver from Torran's face. "The Sci-Tech team must be protected at all costs."

Clearing his throat and leaning forward, the Fortis Prime said, "Master Seeker MacDonald, you came face to face with the Anomaly Inferi Scourge, and you're aware of the Inferi Boon."

"Yes, sir."

"And you understand Dr. Curran's role in creating them." Trevino's dark eyes observed Torran thoughtfully.

Torran finally looked toward the stern-faced blond woman. "Yes, sir."

"Then you fully understand who she is and why you must protect her."

"Yes, sir. I am. I've seen her interviews on the news vids."

Dr. Curran's lips quirked into a small smile.

"Honestly, I'm surprised that someone with such importance to The Bastion would be willing to leave the security of the city," Torran dared to continue.

Martel's gaze shifted rapidly from Dr. Curran to the fortis prime, then she clasped her hands together and set them on the table. "Master Seeker, the information we're about to impart to you is top secret. You will not speak of it to anyone other than Dr. Curran while on assignment," Martel said firmly.

"Yes, sir." Torran pushed the palms of his hands against his knees to keep them steady, uncertain he wanted to know what was about to be revealed.

"It's our belief that Vanguard Maria Martinez is still alive and with the castellan. As you know from the news vids, they were secret lovers."

Blinking, Torran shifted in his chair. "So she's alive? Like a human is alive? Or alive like a Scrag?"

"Human," Dr. Curran answered. "She returned to life."

"How is that possible?" Torran frowned slightly.

"Apparently, the virus mutated in her system. We're also certain that the castellan is also infected now with the new strain," Dr. Curran responded. "ISPV restores a semblance of life to its victims. But this modified virus actually returns life fully with the additional bonus of being immune to the Inferi Scourge Plague Virus and being virtually invisible to the Scourge."

"How do you know the virus mutated?" Torran asked.

Dr. Curran's eyes slightly narrowed. "We monitored the Inferi Boon. Her results differed from the others indicating she was returning to life."

Trying to wrap his mind around the concept, Torran flicked his eyes back and forth, surveying the people before him. "You want to retrieve them, don't you?"

"We believe that the cure to ISPV is in their veins," Martel explained.

"A cure for all the Scrags? To like return them to life?"

"No, Master Seeker. Not quite. The Inferi Scourge already have the original virus in their veins. Therefore, they're inoculated against the variant. There is no cure for them," Dr. Curran said. "But we believe that we'll be able to create an immunization shot that will allow humanity to walk among the... uh... Scrags... without fear of attack or infection."

"Like the Boon did." Torran wasn't sure how he felt about this news. Something about the scenario made him uneasy.

"Yes, but they won't be Boon," Dr. Curran corrected. "They'll be humans that are immune."

Trevino leaned forward. "Think of it, Master Seeker. We could reclaim the world. Kill the Scrags without fear. Clean away the vestiges of the destroyed world and create a new civilization outside The Bastion."

Though he'd never seen Scotland outside of vids, Torran instantly thought of his family being able to return home. "It would be amazing to be able to do so."

"Under the umbrella of the primary mission, a secondary secret mission will be underway. You will seek out, find, and return Vanguard Maria Martinez and Castellan Reichardt," Martel ordered.

Torran stared at the roster on the table to gather his thoughts. "What if they don't wish to return?"

"Then you'll place them under arrest and return them for desertion of their posts," Trevino replied.

"Sir, we did try to *kill* the Inferi Boon," Torran pointed out.

"Admiral Kirkpatrick did," Martel said.

"Yes, but if the castellan hadn't left the city and rescued the vanguard, she would be dead. And so would the hope of immunization."

"What is your point?" Trevino asked, an edge in his voice.

"Couldn't we just ask them for a blood sample? Let them be."

"No," Dr. Curran said simply. "We need them for testing."

"Like... lab animals?"

"Are you questioning your orders?" Legatus Martel asked sharply.

"No, sir." Torran sat back in his chair and tried to sort out his conflicting thoughts.

Trevino regarded Torran darkly. "Master Seeker, they'll be treated with the greatest care. They're a valuable asset to this city and to humanity. But they are also deserters, and when returned, will be incarcerated and tried for that crime."

It took all of Torran's willpower to point out that this sounded like a very convenient way to allow Dr. Curran to do her experiments. Yet, everything that was being said was true. Admiral Kirkpatrick had ordered the elimination of the Inferi Boon. The castellan and vanguard had abandoned their duties *if* they truly were still alive. And the possibility of finding a way to immunize humanity against ISPV was beyond exciting. The ramifications of such a discovery were astounding.

"We can depend on you," Trevino said, but it wasn't truly a question.

"Of course, sir. I'm just..."

"It's a lot to absorb," Dr. Curran interjected. "The couple being alive. The possibility of a cure. Retrieving the food stores."

"Yes, ma'am," Torran agreed.

Legatus Martel studied him for several long moments, then slightly nodded. "Tomorrow, we will have confirmation of the makeup of the final roster. Planning meetings will start tomorrow afternoon. The mission will launch next week, so be ready for long days as we prepare."

"Yes, sir."

"You're dismissed."

Torran could feel the eyes of the three on him as he stood, picked up his beret, and turned to the door. Walking out of the conference room, he swallowed down his trepidation and fear. If all that had been revealed was true, then maybe one day he'd be able to live in a free world far away from The Bastion.

CHAPTER 16

Torran was returning to his quarters when his wristlet chimed. Swiping the screen, he was pleased to see Lindsey was calling him. Her face popped onto the screen as soon as he answered.

"Where are you?" Her hair was damp and coiled on top of her head. Already, tendrils were escaping and curling along her jaw.

"On my way home. You?"

"SWD Facility. I had to run on a treadmill for an obscene amount of time. I just got out of the shower."

Lifting his gaze, Torran surveyed the main edifices of the facility. They were made of white granite with imposing black windows. The sharp angles and wide swooping curves made them stand out against the black rectangular buildings that served as housing for the SWD personnel. Lindsey was probably located in the nearest one that was five floors high with a sharp roof that reminded him of a mast on an old ship.

"So you're in Building C, right?"

"Right."

"Okay, I'll meet you at the quad near the obelisk."

Glancing over her shoulder, Lindsey lowered her voice as she said, "Think it's safe to hang out?"

"Well, at this point we both know that we're going on the mission if you don't flunk your physical—"

"I passed with flying colors, thank you very much."

"—so we should be fine."

Lindsey pondered his answer for a second, then nodded. "Then I'll see you soon."

A few minutes later, Torran watched as she strode toward him in her charcoal-colored uniform. More of her damp hair had escaped her hairdo, and he found it rather endearing.

"Master Seeker MacDonald," she said briskly.

"Vanguard Rooney," he answered, then fell into step beside her. Tucking his hands behind his back, he looked down at her. "So you passed."

"What did you expect?"

Torran tried not to sound disappointed. "Well, that you would pass. But I'm not certain that's a *good* thing."

"Oh, so you're the only one who can put their life on the line for The Bastion?" Lindsey gave him a disapproving look.

"It's not that," he said, though it really was.

"Right." Lindsey looked around the very quiet area. The white flagstone courtyard was eerily empty of people. "Is it always like this?"

"Well, during shift changes it gets busy."

"So much space..." Lindsey's voice held a hint of an accusation.

"It's not like they can bring civilians in to camp out in the quad, Lindsey."

"It's just that SWD always gets the best."

"Nah. They don't have you."

Lindsey gave him a sharp look, then laughed. "You're such a charmer."

"C'mon. My place is over here."

"We're flirting with danger," Lindsey chided him.

"Nah, just flirting."

Since she had shared her home with him, he was a little nervous, yet excited to show her his abode. His small flat was at the top of a narrow flight of retractable steps in the far corner of one of the giant black buildings. The windows and stone matched, giving the impression of it being one solid structure.

"It's a bit imposing, isn't it?" Lindsey remarked, gazing up.

"It's home." Torran unlocked the door and it slid open.

Lindsey edged around him and glanced into the flat as the lights flicked on. "Now I know why you didn't want a city flat."

The main room of Torran's home consisted of a small kitchen with a dining area attached and a large living space with an office alcove. Paintings by Torran's mother decorated the walls, and an afghan she'd made was draped over the black leather sofa. Lindsey walked to the center of the room, staring at the place in awe. When she spotted real books lining a small bookshelf, she hurried over for a closer look.

"My father kept those in the evacuation. When his family was airlifted from Scotland, he took only one change of clothes and used the rest of his suitcase for books. He loved to read, but wasn't keen on pads. His mother wanted to throttle him."

"Amazing." Lindsey lightly touched one of the worn spines. "You do realize that you're living in the lap of luxury."

Torran shrugged. "I wasn't about to turn it down."

"So," Lindsey looked around. "Does the sofa become a bed? Where is your sanitation station?"

Walking over to a slightly recessed door, Torran touched it. It slid open to reveal his bedroom. "In here."

"Get out!"

Lindsey hurried through the door as he turned on the lights. Staring at his neatly made bed, she exhaled. "I hate you. Let me guess. No sanitation station, but an actual bathroom."

Torran touched another door and it slid open to reveal the very small, but nice bathroom. "The shower is *very* roomy."

"You're a perv," Lindsey chided him, but peered inside.

Touching her waist lightly, he was both pleased, yet a little nervous about having her in his flat. It was much more sterile than her tiny place. Though his personal treasures were on display, his place somehow seemed devoid of the energy that filled Lindsey's. It was a bit of a shock to his system to realize that it was because he'd never allowed himself to feel at home in the flat. He'd always regarded it as temporary, yet he really hadn't considered where home might be.

"So much space," she said, glancing at him. "Yet when we're out there, the world is going to seem so vast."

"The valley felt like that when I was stuck out there. Enormous. Vast. Scary."

"I hated leaving you," Lindsey said softly.

"You say that often, you know."

"It haunts me. Leaving someone behind."

Torran's thoughts drifted to his secret mission and he averted his eyes. How would Lindsey regard the situation once it was revealed? Would she see it as a betrayal, or would she understand it was for the better good? Maria was her best friend, and guilt nipped at his conscience. Yet, he had to help humanity survive, didn't he?

Lindsey's kiss startled him since he'd started to fall into a spiral of anxiety. The touch of her lips against his drew him back from plunging too far. Deepening the kiss, he pulled her close. After a few intense moments, they separated, a little breathless.

"What was that for?" he wondered.

"You looked sad," Lindsey answered.

"I'll look sad more often then," he teased her, grinning.

She gave him another firm kiss. "I like kissing you when you're happy."

"So I'll do that more often, too!"

"That's the spirit!" Looking about his bedroom, she bit her bottom lip. "So... now what?"

"How about I make some fake tacos for dinner and we can watch vids for a bit?"

"After," Lindsey said, her fingers playing with the buttons on his coat.

Taking her hands into his, he stared down at her sadly. "We can't keep doing this when we go out there. We have to put distance between us."

"When we're on duty and doing our job. Not now." Lindsey's eyes looked dark and mysterious in the lighting of his room.

Kissing her fingertips, he nodded. "Okay. I just don't want to make it harder for us."

"Harder how?" Lindsey raised her eyes, and the look within them seemed to warn him to caution.

How easy it would be to spill his heart out and hope she accepted the offering. Instead, he gave her a cocky smile. "Well, you're going to have to break the habit of giving me those come hither looks and trying to get me naked every chance you get."

"I'll break it later." Lindsey slipped her hands free from his and started to unbutton his coat again. "For now, I insist on you getting naked and fucking me senseless."

Torran didn't argue further.

Feet propped on the low table set in front of the older, yet still very nice leather couch, Lindsey regarded Torran through her lashes while he finished dinner in the kitchen. He was chatting away about special spices and his cooking expertise, but she was admiring him and not really paying attention. She was pleasantly sore from exercise and sex and wanted to pretend all was right with the world for the rest of the evening.

On the vid, the news was discussing the mission to retrieve food. It was the biggest story, even removing Admiral Kirkpatrick's upcoming trial from the main headlines. Dressed in one of Torran's black undershirts and her panties, she stretched her legs out, admiring the new limb.

"...that is how I get the protein to taste almost exactly like meat."

The news changed to cover a small food riot at one of the distribution centers. Lindsey frowned as she watched the footage of the SWD security forces shooting electroshock discs into the crowd of frightened people. According to the reporter, a false rumor of the warehouse nearly being out of food had resulted in terrified parents rushing to the facility.

"...so it gets just the right consistency. Salsa is a very delicate process..."

Recordings of the continuing clearing of the valley took the place of the riots. The mesh walls now stretched across large swaths of land and Sci-Tech teams were dispatched to test the soil and approve areas for planting.

"...it's really very difficult to find an avocado..."

"Torran," Lindsey called out.

Glancing up, Torran lifted his eyebrows. "Yes?"

Lindsey slid off the couch and walked over to him. She loved the way his eyes followed her. It was if every movement she made mattered to him. Staring into his brown eyes, she knew they'd made a terrible mistake, but that there was no going back.

Tilting her head, she gazed at him through her eyelashes. "Can we really do this mission together?"

He returned to warming up tortillas on his small stove. "You said we could, remember? So, yeah, why not?""

"Because we're falling in love with each other." There. She'd said it.

"Yeah," he drawled out in an especially thick Scottish accent. "What of it?"

"So you admit it?" It had taken Vaja until their break up to swear his love to her.

Torran glanced at her. "Yeah. I do."

"That you're falling in love with me?"

"I admit *you're* falling in love with *me.*" He flashed a devilish smile at her.

"Asshole."

"Nah, not an asshole. I just planned to say the words at a little more appropriate time. Earlier, in fact."

"I know. I stopped you."

"With sex."

"Mind-blowingly good sex," she amended.

Torran finished warming up the tortillas and started scooping the brownish protein mush he'd concocted into the center of them. "It really, really was. But, yeah, I was going to tell you earlier because—"

"We're complicating things."

"Exactly."

Lindsey sighed. "We could tell them we're involved."

"They'll pull one of us off the mission."

There was no way Commandant Pierce would allow them to remove Lindsey, so that meant Torran would be removed. The idea was tempting.

"I want to go," Lindsey said, and meant it. She was scared, but she knew she had to keep Maria and Dwayne out of the hands of the SWD.

"I do, too." Torran finished making the tacos and set them on small plates.

Lindsey stared at him and wondered when or if he'd know about the Sci-Tech's mission. Maybe he already knew. She wanted to ask him, but didn't dare. A hard knot of sadness formed inside her as she realized already the mission was dividing them.

Torran swiveled toward her and set his hand gently on her waist. Bare chested and only wearing pajama bottoms, he was insanely sexy in her eyes. "When this started between us, we didn't know about this mission. And even if I had, I wouldn't have stopped. The moment I saw those beautiful eyes of yours, I was already halfway gone. The truth is that we're both highly qualified for this mission, and we can make it a grand success. The only question we must ask ourselves is if we can put our feelings aside and allow ourselves to do our job."

"In other words, not fret over each other's safety." Lindsey traced her fingers over his lightly.

"Can you?"

It was a difficult question to answer, but even more so because Lindsey knew that at some point they might have orders that contradicted each other. Yet, she couldn't allow the SWD to find her friends. And the reality was that it would be easier on her nerves to be near Torran.

"You could stay," Lindsey dared to suggest.

"But I can't," Torran answered simply. "Because this is what we do."

"Exactly."

Sliding her arms around his waist, she stared up at him. "Then we'll have to do our jobs and do them well so we both come back."

A faint smile touched his lips. "Nothing about this life is easy."

"Nope."

"So we go do our job. Come back. Have celebratory sex…"

"Sounds like a good plan."

"Then why do you look so worried?" Torran asked.

Making a mental note to hide her feelings better, Lindsey realized she had to lie. Though she was willing to admit she was falling for Torran, she couldn't discuss what she knew about the SWD mission with him. Or maybe she was afraid to discover he agreed with the secret mission to bring back Dwayne and Maria.

"The food riots today upset me." It was a half-truth to cover her real misgivings.

"Yeah. But we'll fix it." Torran kissed the tip of her nose.

"And be heroes," she said, smiling.

When he kissed her, she clung to him with a need that frightened her.

The tacos were very, very cold by the time they finally ate them an hour later.

PART 3

THE MISSION

"There is no option to fail," Lindsey said gravely. "Our success is imperative to the survival of The Bastion."

The combined squad of SWD and Constabulary soldiers stared at her somberly. Torran was positioned to the side, hands clasped before him, surveying the people gathered in the room. It was shaped like a small amphitheater with a dais in the center where Lindsey and Torran stood. Constabulary gray sat together on one side, SWD black on the other, and a smattering of white Sci-Tech in the middle. Dr. Curran was not in attendance, which didn't surprise Lindsey. Most likely, the doctor would be busy with her own agenda when out on the field and had little interest in the actual mission.

Torran stepped forward to continue: "The Scrags track humans by movement and sound. They're also drawn to vehicles that they acquaint with humanity. This is information gleaned from the daily logs of Chief Defender Omandi and Vanguard Martinez during the Inferi Boon Special Ops Mission. Sound stirs the Scrags out of their stupor, and they become immediately restless and hostile. They attacked the Inferi Boon until the Boon removed their helmets and the Scrags were finally able to visually identify them as one of their own. Unfortunately, this did not always stop Scrag attacks. The Inferi Boon soldiers witnessed the Scrags even attacking each other when overstimulated by the perceived presence of humans. The more riled up the Scrags become, the more dangerous they are."

There was some restless movement among the squad members. A few faces on the Constabulary side worried Lindsey. Some of the original selections on the roster had not made the cut, and replacements had been called. Franklin and Hobbes sat among the Constabulary. Whereas before she'd been glad to be among familiar people, it bothered her now that she was so emotionally invested. She cared about the safety of all the squad members, but her heart was a bit more on the line when it came to friends.

"Therefore," Lindsey said, stepping to one side to allow the soldiers a better view of the screen behind her, "we will be only be deployed at food depots that have the highest security and are on the outskirts of major cities or towns. The approach of aircraft will stir the Scrags out of their torpor. They will then follow in the wake of the tiltrotors. This phenomenon was witnessed during the recent clearing of the valley on numerous occasions. One tiltrotor was lost when it set down and was instantly swarmed."

"We'll have limited time, people. The operations under this mission will be under the gun and we'll have to be in and out in a short amount of time." Torran's grim tone and expression matched perfectly.

Again, the squad shifted uncomfortably.

"The SWD created stealth armor in anticipation of a mission of this type," Lindsey explained. "The suits were originally created to clear the valley, but were not viable for close encounters with the Inferi Scourge due to a time limit of their effectiveness. Because aging tech had to be used in their construction, the suits only offer invisibility for ten minute intervals."

Torran activated the vid screen. "The stealth function of your suits will render you invisible to Scrags from a distance. Up close, they may be able to see through it if you move. The technology is not perfect."

Lindsey glanced over her shoulder as the screen revealed a dummy wearing the stealth suit. The armor gave the dummy the appearance of water contained in the shape of a human when it switched on, then blended into the surroundings. Inferi Scourge were dispatched into the testing room a few seconds later. The Scrags were slightly riled from being transported, but soon stilled while letting out mild, questioning screeching noises. The dummy's legs and arms started to move slowly, gradually picking up speed to imitate the gait of a person. Abruptly, a Scrag let loose a shriek and attacked the dummy. The others instantly followed.

The squad members stared intently past Lindsey and Torran at the screen. Lindsey let them absorb what they'd seen, then said, "If the Scrags somehow manage to remove a part of your armor, you're dead and a Scrag."

Torran stepped in front of the screen as it went blank. "The suits were made for the sole purpose of resisting bites and keeping you hidden from the Scrags should you end up in close proximity to them, so you're not bullet and shrapnel proof. Remember that."

"It's not like the Scrags will be shooting us," someone muttered.

Lindsey and Torran exchanged looks. As far as anyone knew, the Abscrags were now all dead. The valley was close to being completely cleared for resettlement and there had been no sign of the clever variation of Scrags.

"No, not likely, but we should remain vigilant," Torran finally said. "We will need to clear each food facility before transport of the supplies can begin. If the facility is breached, then you will activate your stealth suits."

"Your weapons will have the same cloaking ability. A small electrical charge begins the cycle of invisibility. You will be trained on how to use this tech." Lindsey set her hands at her waist and regarded the group, studying each face. She was satisfied to see they were attentive. "Our goal is to not make the natives too restless. Once the squad dispatches from the tiltrotor, we will immediately secure the depot. Once the storage area is cleared, we will extract as many food containers as possible before the situation becomes too perilous."

"And it *will* become *perilous* very quickly." Torran pointed to the screen as it flashed to life and showed old footage of a food depot that had been an evacuation point. Despite the concrete and fortified fences, the perimeter collapsed and the depot was swarmed, thousands of evacuees being lost in a matter of minutes. "This is what we can expect. We are talking about hordes of Scrags that number in the hundreds of thousands. Gates and walls will not hold against them for long. Most of the food depots were built to keep out marauding humans, not creatures that don't give a care as to whether or not they're crushed to death in a stampede."

For the first time, Lindsey saw the squad reacting with frightened looks. Maybe it was memories of their own skirmishes with the Scrags that made them uncomfortable, or maybe it was sympathy for the long lost victims, but they looked disturbed and maybe a little afraid. "Do not waver from your assignment. We must work like the intricate pieces of a machine. Dependent on one another to make all the forays into the dead world a success."

Stepping closer to Lindsey, Torran said, "Forget the SWD and Constabulary rivalry. This is about more than petty squabbles. This is about saving humanity. The Inferi Boon Special Ops were both Constabulary and SWD and they're the reason we're about to finally start to resettle the valley. Soon, farmers will be harvesting crops because of the sacrifices of the Inferi Boon. We honor their memory by making this mission a success. By ensuring humanity survives."

There was a solemn silence among the squad members. No sarcastic comments or mocking looks were exchanged. It was a nice shift from the usual hostile atmosphere that existed when Constabulary and SWD were in close quarters.

"Training begins tomorrow at 0800 hours. We'll see you in Training Room Five. Dismissed." Torran's Scottish accent was heavy, and the usual twinkle in his eyes was missing.

Lindsey stepped aside to observe the departing squad. The faces of the soldiers of all genders and various races were sober and thoughtful as they filed out. When the doors shut behind the group, Torran pivoted toward Lindsey.

"Fuck, they look young," he groused.

"Or maybe we're prematurely old," Lindsey suggested with a wry smile.

Torran pulled his pad out of his pocket and irritably stabbed at it with one finger. "At least they were all attentive. I didn't see any wandering eyes."

"I'm concerned about the Sci-Techs though. Did you see them shifting uncomfortably during the discussion of the armor?"

"Yeah, but that could be based on the fact they've never had to *wear* armor before. Or because they've never been in any sort of battle. Tomorrow will give us a better idea about how they'll cope." Torran shook his head. "We've got six days to make it work."

Tugging her own pad out of her pocket, Lindsey called up the preliminary reports gathered for the mission planning. "I hate that we're going to Beta City first. There's going to be a high concentration of Scrags around the depot due to it being near the final evac site."

"There will be two fence lines between us and the Scrags. It'll slow them down."

Lindsey's fingers glided over the slick surface as she ran various time estimates. "The fences will come down for certain."

Torran studied the information she beamed at his pad. "I see where your concern is."

"We have three aircraft entering the area. The two cargo transports and a tiltrotor. They will draw a lot of attention. I see a definite weak spot on the north side facing the evac site. In the last images taken by the evac aircraft you can see where one fence was already listing. It may have come down already." Lindsey skewed her lips to one side, concentrating on images and how they translated into the plan.

"The good thing is that the Beta City depot won't have as much to transport as depots in major cities. We can make it work."

"We need to be in and out in twenty to thirty minutes, MacDonald."

"We can attempt to push another location as our first mission," Torran suggested.

Lindsey regarded him through her eyelashes. "You really think they'll let us go for a bigger target?"

Exhaling through his teeth, Torran pondered her question. Finally, he said, "No. They won't. The further out we travel, the more likely we are to run into unexpected complications. They will not want delays."

"My thoughts exactly."

"We do think a lot alike, Rooney. Kinda scary."

"Great minds, huh?"

Torran shrugged. "I wouldn't say great... Scheming maybe."

Lindsey gave him a sharp look while wondering if he knew about the secret mission that would be launched at some point during their excursions into the dead world. If so, what were his thoughts?

"What's that look for, Rooney?"

"What look?"

Torran pointed at her face. "That look. Very intense. Very pointed."

The corner of Lindsey's mouth twitched upward. "Just estimating odds of success."

"And how are we doing?"

"Are you a betting man, MacDonald?"

Running his hand over his hair, Torran lifted a shoulder. "Sometimes."

"The odds aren't exactly in our favor, but we'll make it work."

"Because that's what people like us do."

"Exactly."

The doors opened to reveal a short woman with dusky skin and wavy black hair streaked with silver chopped short at her chin. In Constabulary gray, she had chief defender markings on her collar and arm.

"I'm Chief Defender Solomon. I've been assigned to lead the mission."

"It's good to see you again, sir," Torran said.

A smile tugged on the woman's thin lips. "And good to see you. Though I'm saddened that you're not in a Constabulary uniform, MacDonald, I'm glad we're working together again."

Shifting his attention back to Lindsey, Torran said, "The chief defender and I enlisted at the same time. We were even in the same squad until just before the final push. She was promoted and transferred to her own squad."

"It's good to meet you, sir," Lindsey said.

"Vanguard Rooney, I've heard a lot about you. All of it glowing and impressive. I look forward to getting to know you and working with you. I'm a little behind on the mission specs due to the length of time it took to select me for the job, so please bring me up to speed."

"Should we adjourn to the mission prep room?" Torran gestured toward the door on the opposite side of the briefing room.

"Lead the way," Solomon replied.

Inside the room was a bank of consoles, vid screens, and a table with a holographic image floating above it. Lindsey and Torran had spent much of their day studying all the intel and creating the mission dossier. Solomon glanced at some of their work, then settled her gaze on the image hovering over the sleek black table.

"Our first objective," she observed.

Lindsey docked her pad into the side of the table as Torran gestured for her to take over. For the next hour, she gave a briefing on the mission parameters set by the higher ups, and the plan that she and Torran had been piecing together.

"We're evaluating every bit of intel gleaned from satellite feeds before they expired a few years ago to identify any potential danger points," Lindsey explained while indicating several spots on the satellite images projected on the table.

"It's all danger points," Solomon said with the shake of her head. "Let's be honest with each other. This is a political mission. The food we return will only delay the inevitable elevation to Ration Level Four. I realize our orders are to bring back the maximum amount of food, but we won't sacrifice lives for it. MacDonald, how good are the stealth suits?"

"Honestly, I'm not sold on them. I do think they might help if we've got a little distance from the Scrags, but up close, we're fucked."

"More flash for the civvies," Solomon groused.

Lindsey was in absolute agreement with the chief defender and liked her quite a bit already. "Yes, sir. I do believe so, sir."

"Okay, so we take what the higher ups are tossing us and make it work," Solomon said.

"Agreed." Torran gave Lindsey a quick, questioning look.

She got the impression he wanted to see if she approved of Solomon or not. "My major concern for Beta City is how close the food depot is to the evac site."

"That fence line is a worry. We could request an aerial drone to scan the area now that they're flying again." Solomon folded her arms over her chest and tilted her head as she observed the hologram of the depot. "Rooney, what are the chances of the Scrags following an aerial drone?"

"Honestly, I have to look up that data."

"Do it. Now that we have access to fuel again, let's take advantage of it."

Torran lifted his pad and did a quick search. "There are several aerial drones patrolling the valley. The rest are mothballed. We might be able to requisition one for the mission. But it won't be able to make it over the mountains by itself. We'll need a tiltrotor to ferry them over."

"I might be able to swing it. We'll want more than one," Chief Defender Solomon decided. "I also want a new test run on those suits. This data stamp is two years old. This isn't acceptable."

"Yes, sir." Lindsey slid onto a chair at a console and activated a screen.

"Until we have a dependable report on just how good those suits are, all training room scenarios will be without them. The last thing we want is for our squad to be dependent on faulty tech."

While the chief defender continued to issue orders and toss out questions, Lindsey stole a look at Torran. He was obviously pleased and so was she.

Finally, the mission didn't feel like it was doomed to failure.

CHAPTER 18

The bar was bustling with activity, and no one glanced at Torran and Lindsey when they entered in their civilian clothing, ordered drinks, and sat at a table in a corner. Exhausted from the long day, Torran had considered going home to bed, but hadn't wanted to turn in just yet. He needed time to decompress from all the preparation they'd done during the day. Much to his relief, Lindsey had agreed to meet up with him after dropping by her place for a shower and a change of clothing.

Working with Lindsey was interesting and rather intriguing. Her brain sometimes seemed to process faster than the computers they worked on. Also, she had an uncanny ability to read his expressions, or maybe they were just that similar. She always seemed to know what he was thinking or about to suggest. He'd rather enjoyed the lengthy planning session, but he wanted to spend time with her without the veneer of rank.

Though Lindsey was visually striking in her uniform, he preferred how she looked in her olive cargo pants, black sweater, and battered boots. Her blond hair was twisted into two small messy buns on either side of her head and her bangs fell into her face as she slumped in her chair with a tired but happy look on her face.

"You know, the unkempt look suits you," Torran remarked.

Lindsey laughed. "Why, thank you. And you look like you're in uniform even when you're not."

"Ouch."

"It's true."

Torran pointed at his shoes, a pair of lace up canvas sneakers. They were dingy, ratty, and would probably soon expire, but they were incredibly comfortable. "Not regulation."

"And neither is that hair."

"You like my hair. You like me. I charm you." Tilting his head, he gave her his best cheesy smile.

"Maybe I'm just using you for sex."

"Nah. You like me."

Lindsey poked her fingers in her drink, then flicked droplets at him. "You're far too confident, cheeky boy."

"So, work today..."

"Ugh. My brain still hurts." Lindsey pressed her damp fingertips to one temple.

"So what did you think of Solomon?"

"She's going to kick our asses, and that's a good thing. She's clever. I like clever. Clever is very, very good."

"Which is why you're seeing me, right?"

"Still digging for a compliment, I see," Lindsey teased, then sipped her liquor.

Torran winked and downed his own drink before signaling for another. "Shit, I'm so damn tired, but I have no desire to go home yet."

"It's no walk in the park for me either. Being in the SWD facility all day is... tiring. Everyone is so prim and proper."

"It's because you're Constabulary. They're trying to impress you."

Lindsey rolled her eyes at his comment. "I'm no one to impress."

"Well, it's clear that the Constabulary has the upper hand in all this. Hell, I used to be Constabulary. So that means all three leaders of the mission were trained by the Constabulary. And there are lots of rumors floating around about the SWD possibly being absorbed into the Constabulary."

"Really? I hadn't heard that gossip." Lindsey played with the lip of her glass with one finger. "I don't' really see that happening, though."

Slouching in his chair, Torran bobbed his head. "True. The government will want to keep the tension between the SWD and Constabulary to inspire productivity."

"Exactly."

Nearby voices were rising in distressed tones. Lindsey's eyes flicked toward the possible conflict, then lifted to regard the screens overhead on the wall. "Torran, this isn't good."

Torran followed her gaze. "Shit."

"Level Four already? That can't be true!"

"Can someone turn that up?" Torran shouted over the increasing racket.

Already other customers were clustering beneath the vid screens. The music came to an abrupt stop and the feed from the vid screens shifted to the speakers.

"...a warehouse in the Isles Sector apparently had a malfunction in the refrigeration units and the protein stored within was spoiled. An investigation has been launched..."

"Someone leaked the news," he said to Lindsey.

"What?"

"Someone leaked the bloody news!" Torran gestured toward the screen in disbelief.

The voice of the newscaster was instantly drowned out by angry voices. A second later, everyone's wristlets started to chime.

Torran quickly checked his to see a city-wide announcement on the ration change.

Lindsey looked up from her wristlet, her expression troubled. "But why leak it to the news?"

"Hell if I know."

Again, Torran's wristlet chimed. This time was it was an order from the SWD to return to the facility immediately.

Lindsey's chimed a second later. "I've been ordered to the SWD facility," she said, confused.

Torran slid out of his chair and held out his hand to her. She reached for him, and just as their fingers touched, chaos erupted near the front doors. Several men and women engaged in a loud confrontation just inside the entrance.

"We're closed!" the bartender yelled from where she stood on top of the bar. "Everyone out!"

A scuffle broke out. Not near the front door, but toward the rear of the bar. Torran caught sight of several people grabbing bottles of liquor from the shelves as the bartenders attempted to stop them. Blows were exchanged and, instantly, there was a massive surge toward the exits.

"We need to get out," Lindsey exclaimed.

Tables and chairs clattered to the floor as the rush to either loot the bar or escape into the street commenced. Torran dragged Lindsey into an alcove as several large men shoved their way past them toward the bar. A female patron hurled a chair at one of the bartenders. Another man struck out with a full bottle in his hand, blood bursting from his victim's ruined face.

Using his height and slim build, Torran skirted along the edges of the throng, pulling Lindsey behind him. The squeeze through the doorway was a bit laborious, the elbows and knees of strangers pushing into his body. He managed to break through the tangle and out of the bar with Lindsey's hand still clasped in his. Caught in the entrance between the doorjamb and a large man, Lindsey cried out in pain. Her fingers slipped from Torran's. The man was trying to carry several bottles out under one arm and cuffed Lindsey in an attempt to push past her.

"Don't touch her!" Torran shouted, shoving the man.

The brawny guy with a shaved head and tattoos stumbled back into the people behind him. Lindsey darted out into the street, and Torran followed. Behind them, the thief engaged in yet another brawl with someone trying to grab the liquor from him.

Clutching Torran's arm, Lindsey pressed her body into his side to avoid the heavy flow of people around them. "This is really bad, Torran."

The streets were crammed with distraught citizens. Tempers flared and fear filled the eyes of those standing near Torran and Lindsey. Some were crying openly, while others heatedly argued. The situation was clearly becoming dire.

A drone rumbled around the corner and trundled down the center of the street flashing warnings on it screens. "Citizens of The Bastion, please return to your homes. Do not loiter in the streets. This is for your own good. Citizens of The Bastion..." the drone instructed.

On the balconies, the street residents were hastily pulling their hanging gardens up over railings. The cries of children in the flats above drifted into the night. Torran caught sight of people standing guard over their rooftop vegetable and fruit plots with makeshift weapons in their hands.

"Shit, this is awful," Lindsey muttered at his side.

"We need to keep moving," Torran replied recognizing the growing chance of mob violence.

Pushing their way through the mass of people, the two found themselves at a disadvantage. They were moving against the flow. At some point, the mass of people had decided on a purpose.

"They're heading toward the food warehouse south of here," Lindsey called out above the noise of the commotion.

Torran's wristlet kept chiming with incoming messages. He dragged Lindsey up a stairwell into a narrow doorway. Accessing the wristlet, he saw a city-wide announcement of martial law.

A few seconds later, SWD troops marching in formation appeared further down the street. They were garbed in riot gear and held electroshock weapons.

"Torran," Lindsey gasped.

"I see them."

To make matters even more worrisome, aerial drones whirred over the tops of the buildings, their long metal wings and spidery legs glinting in the gleam of the streetlights. They could compress themselves into very small spaces, but also lift a grown man off the ground. The drones sported four tiltrotor wings that always reminded Torran of dragonflies. With their long limbs extended, they were over six feet tall, but often flew with their legs and wings retracted making them appear much smaller. The aerial drones were in full battle mode, so the end of each long spindly leg carried electroshock weaponry.

"Get out your armband," Torran ordered.

Each Constabulary and SWD soldier carried an armband with them at all times for situations such as this one. Torran pulled his out of his battered wallet, unfolded it, and slipped it over his coat sleeve. It adjusted to his bicep, and when he tapped the emblem, it glowed. Lindsey followed suit, and they both activated their distress beacons on their wristlets.

"Citizens of the Bastion," the overhead drones called out in unison, "you must immediately evacuate the streets."

Dread gnawing at his calm, Torran rapidly read through his communiques. Some were city-wide announcements, one was from his worried mother, but the rest were from the SWD ordering all off duty personnel back to the facility.

"We need to go," Lindsey said, leaping down into the street and pushing her way toward the city center.

Torran followed in her wake. The approaching SWD allowed them to pass due to their armbands, but people in the flats above were angrily screaming at the troops. The sound of the electroshock rifles firing sent chills down Torran's spine. Looking back, Torran saw the aerial drones firing on the rowdier crowds further up the road.

Another message chimed into their wristlets.

"They're closing the sectors," Lindsey called out to him

She was just ahead of him, skirting around a family rushing down the street. Torran hoped they were heading home. A second later, there was a loud whoosh and a flash of heat.

Spinning around, Torran saw fire licking up the side of the building and several SWD soldiers engulfed in fire. Their armor took the brunt of the assault, and they dropped to the ground to smother the flames. It took only a second for him to realize that some of the customers in the bar had turned the stolen liquor bottles into makeshift bombs. Torran started back toward the fray to help extinguish the flames writhing on the liquor-soaked ground and crawling up the buildings when Lindsey grabbed him and jerked him away.

"They'll deal with it. We need to make it back before Central Sector closes!"

Torran understood the wisdom of her words, but it was difficult to abandon soldiers in need. Several people threw more bottles of liquor at the already spreading fire. In the distance, the sirens of emergency crews cried out.

"Torran! We have to go!"

At last, Torran turned away and raced after Lindsey as she sprinted up the road. As people retreated into their homes and drones flew overhead, it became easier to run along the narrow roads toward the inner wall that encircled the Central Sector that housed the government buildings, Constabulary Central Command and SWD Facility. Darting up alleys and rushing along emptying streets, the two soldiers aimed for the nearest entrance.

The soft fluttering sound of an aerial drone drew Torran's gaze upward. It darted toward them.

"Citizens, you are in violation of martial law," it called out, the electroshock barrels lowering and aiming at them.

Torran held up his arm, the armband in view. Lindsey did the same, breathing heavily with fright at his side. Either the armbands worked, or the signal from their wristlets registered for the aerial drone retracted its weapons and flew off.

"Shit," Torran grunted.

"We really need to get off the streets." Lindsey pointed at a flock of aerial drones flying over the nearby buildings.

Together, they dashed up the sloping road to the massive entry point to the Central Sector. Others were hurrying inside, and Lindsey caught sight of Hobbes and Franklin among some of the Constabulary squad members. The group rushed through just as the large door started rolling down.

"Just in time," an SWD soldier shouted at Torran and Lindsey from the guard post, waving them through.

Lindsey and Torran sprinted the last few feet through the entrance before the barricades rose out of the ground to prevent anyone else from attempting to enter.

"You know what this means," Torran panted.

Lindsey flinched. "They're going to send us out sooner."

The massive door slid shut with a loud thud that reverberated through the night.

"Why can't anything be easy?" Torran asked the world in general. Lindsey lightly touched his arm. "Because this world is fucked." With a sigh, he nodded. "Let's find out how bad it all is." Together, they walked toward the SWD Facility.

Lindsey slung the bag filled with newly issued uniforms, underwear, and toiletries over one shoulder, left the small dorm room she'd been assigned to, and trudged across the quad to Torran's flat. Until the crisis was over, she was not going to be able to return to her home. Though the dorm room was nice enough, she wasn't going to spend the night alone. She'd messaged Torran, so she wasn't too surprised when the door immediately opened for her.

Slipping inside, she saw the news playing on the vid screen. "How bad?"

"Riots in most of the sectors," Torran answered as he locked the door behind her before returning to where he'd been sitting watching the news.

Lindsey tossed the bag of her new possessions onto a chair and collapsed onto his couch. Checking her wristlet, she saw more incoming data from both the Constabulary and SWD command centers. By morning, she was certain the specifics of their mission would be changed.

Slouched next to her, Torran glared at the screen. "It was a deliberate leak. Someone told the media before the government could initiate crowd controls. Someone wanted this to happen. The wanted the bloody chaos in the streets."

"Kirkpatrick's people?"

Torran shrugged. "Who the hell knows anymore? But then again, who else would it be?"

Lindsey didn't dare name her second suspect. Maybe Legatus Martel decided to speed up the primary mission to launch the secret one in a faster time frame. Or maybe Lindsey was just being paranoid.

"How's your folks?" Lindsey knew Torran's family was near one of the warehouses under siege by rioters.

"Fine for now. Ma is terrified. Da is pragmatic. He moved their garden tubs into the kitchen as soon as they got the news. My brother and an uncle are helping them guard."

"Your sister?"

"Their building pulled up the stairs and are working together to protect their resources. The kids are scared, and no one is certain how they're even going to get their rations with things as chaotic as they are."

"Shit. This is awful."

"The question is: will the higher ups give us twenty-four hours of prep, or thirty-six? And the altered schedule isn't about allowing us enough time to get ready. I'm sure if they had their way, we'd already be leaving right now. It's about giving the president time to roll out a big production around our departure."

Slumping into his side, Lindsey exhaled with fatigue born of both mental and physical exertion. "You mean we'll have to smile for the cameras."

"Look somber and resolute for the cameras, you mean." Torran slung his arm about her shoulders, snuggling her against his body.

"First my leg then this... I fucking hate propaganda." Lindsey shut her eyes, blocking out the images of the civilians panicked in the streets. Some mothers and fathers had risked the curfew to take their children to the Central Sector gates to hold up their crying children for the media cameras to record. Closing off the sectors had only made the crisis worse. Now rumors were spreading through the feeds that only certain sectors would be receiving food rations.

The Bastion was engulfed in turmoil.

"Someone is playing a very dirty game," Torran said at last.

"And we're at the center of it."

"Yeah." Torran kissed her forehead, then said against her skin, "but we can't give up hope. We're so close to so much good happening."

"You mean the first crops being planted? Our mission?"

"I'm sure other good things will come, too."

Lindsey stiffened slightly. Did he mean capturing Dwayne and Maria? "Like what?"

Tilting his head back to rest it on the rear of the sofa, Torran pressed his fingertips to his bloodshot eyes. "Hell if I know. I just hope something positive comes out of all of this."

Teeth tugging on her bottom lip, Lindsey stared worriedly at the live coverage. They were safe behind their walls, far away from the pandemonium. It seemed wrong until she realized that very soon they'd be facing the Scrags for the sake of the people rioting in the streets.

"Linds, we should sleep. I'm sure they're going to call us in early."

"You don't want to wait up for the president's speech, Torran?"

"Nah. It'll be the same old, same old. Smoke and mirrors. I'd rather fall asleep with you in my arms than listen to him yammer on."

Lindsey kissed his chin tenderly. "You're such a romantic."

"Another reason why you like me." Torran lightly brushed his lips over hers. "Admit it."

"I admit to nothing but wanting to sleep!"

The playfulness between them was fun, but she found herself studying him as they switched off the news and set about readying for bed. Would she be able to tell when he was informed of the secret mission? And how would the SWD and Constabulary teams end up being split apart out in the field?

When Lindsey snuggled into Torran's side a short time later, she wondered if the night's events were just part of some greater conspiracy that she wasn't yet aware of. Her mind churning, she was half-tempted to climb out of bed and hack into the grid. Instead, sleep snatched her from the waking world, and she fell into a deep slumber.

CHAPTER 19

Torran watched the squad moving rapidly through the training room. The holographic projection of the loading site at the Beta City depot looked disturbingly real. The exterior of the building was flawlessly rendered. Lindsey had created the simulation using the crystal clear images downloaded from the drones. Sunlight poured through the open bay doors and the shriek of the Scrags filled the air. The interior schematic was to specifications found in the databases, but shouldn't have changed over time due to being sealed off.

From Torran's position on the observation deck, he saw a few of the SWD soldiers drifting off their assigned path.

"Carter and Ramirez, you've overshot your objective," he said into the comm.

The two soldiers' immediate course corrected.

"Could you have made the Scrags a little less noisy?" Torran asked Lindsey.

The simulated screeches from the Scrags clearly had some of the soldiers rattled.

"I matched the sound frequency of the hordes outside the walls," Lindsey answered with a shrug.

"Of course you did."

Both officers were dressed in the stealth armor. There wouldn't be any updated trials on the suits and the first real test would be on the field. A good chunk of their day had been spent maneuvering with the squad through the simulation multiple times. There were still issues with the team, so Lindsey and Torran had retreated to the observation deck to observe and come up with solutions.

Chief Defender Solomon had been called away, which Torran was certain was not a good sign. The bureaucracy wanted its fingers in the mission, and the chief defender had spent long hours in conferences while the squad practiced.

Several of the Sci-Techs ignored two large containers, continuing toward the next one.

"Thompson and Grier, why are you ignoring those two containers?" Lindsey asked into the comm.

"They were contaminated the last three missions," came the reply.

"We can't afford to skip any containers in the real mission, Grier. Check them." Lindsey glanced at Torran. "How many hours?"

"Fourteen straight. They're tired and it's affecting them." Torran picked up a packet of water and tore off the top. "We have to let them get some sleep before deployment."

"I wonder what the word is on that?"

Torran gulped down the water and tossed the packet into the recycle bin. "Damned if I know. Can't you do your..." He mimicked her typing, insinuating she should be doing her hacks.

"I wish, but I have a job to do."

Isolated in the training rooms, they weren't privy to the news reports on the unrest enveloping the city. When Torran had awakened, the SWD had already restricted the feeds to his and Lindsey's wristlets. It was common practice for when soldiers were on the battlefield so they wouldn't be distracted by incoming messages from family and friends, or vids from the news or entertainment sites. It had annoyed Torran even further when he realized they'd done the same with his vid screen. The SWD Facility was on lockdown, and the communication blackout was unsettling.

"Initiate a Scrag breach," Torran said to Lindsey.

"They're tired," she remarked.

"They'll be tired out there, too."

"True."

Fingers sliding over the console in front of her, Lindsey modified the program. A minute later, the simulation altered as Scrags poured into the food depot. Instantly, the pilot of the tiltrotor (who was strapped into her own simulation) reported the breach. The soldiers reacted by activating their stealth suits. Small cameras within the lining of the armor filmed the surroundings then projected the images onto the fabric -- which was basically a malleable screen -- creating the illusion of invisibility. This time, the squad responded much speedier than before.

Torran pointed to the Sci-Tech team located near one of the containers. Their suits were working, but one of them was attempting to move behind the container. The pattern on the suit shifted and instantly drew the attention of one of the A.I. Scrags. It let out a screech, then attacked.

With a sigh, Torran killed the simulation. The hologram instantly vanished, leaving the soldiers standing in a large room with blank walls. Their armored suits flickered, then returned to their normal appearance.

"Shit!" someone grunted.

The Sci-Tech that had been attempting to hide covered his facemask with one hand as those around him let their annoyance be known.

"Okay, I will explain one more time. The suits are only useful when the Scrags are in close proximity if you stand still." Torran set his hand on the top of the console and leaned forward to stare into the room. "Once they are up close and personal, your suits will not be able to properly stealth your movement because the internal cameras will also be recording the images of the Scrags. Since the program dictates that the suit is not to record life forms, it will struggle to delete the Scrags from the projection, which causes it to flicker. Which means..."

"You're now a Scrag, Tech Harrigan." Lindsey gave him a thumb up.

"Or a nice bit of paste in your suit," Torran added.

Shoulders slumping, weapons dangling at their sides, the squad grumbled as they wandered about. The pilots stepped out of their smaller sim rooms on the second level and leaned over the railing.

"We going again, sir?" one called out.

"Negative, Scoggins," Torran responded. "Let's take a break. Protein shakes and water are in the mess hall."

Torran glanced over at Lindsey to see her watching the playbacks of all the mission sims side by side on the screen stretching across the console panel. Below, the squad unhooked their weapons and pushed them into the armaments locker, where a robotic arm swiftly grabbed the firearms and tucked them into the racks.

Sliding his fingers through his hair, Torran exhaled as the last soldier exited the room, leaving him alone with Lindsey. "Bloody hell."

"It's not that bad. They're doing better than they should be, considering all the distractions," Lindsey said, not looking up. "We're just having issues with actual coordination between the three divisions."

"But they're one squad." Torran grunted.

"Not yet, but they're getting there." She gave him a quick sidelong look. "You should go get a protein shake, too. And bring me back one."

"I shouldn't leave you with all the work," he answered.

That brought a smirk to her lips. "I like work. It makes my brain feel... happy."

Torran scoffed playfully. "We can't all be extraordinary geniuses with minds like computers. Yet, I do okay with my regular old brain."

"Yes, you do. It's lovely." Lindsey paused the playbacks and pointed. "There is a direct view from the storage area to the outside once the loading door is open. In each simulation, the program extrapolates that this zone as a problem spot." She specified a corner of the outer fence. "We're in line of sight."

"Which stirs the Scrags up."

"In the original images, there was a series of sheds here. Over time, they collapsed. Now they're bunched up against the fence. We've been worried about the evac site, but this is where our breach will be."

"But if we close the doors, we add time to our removal of the containers because we'll have to reopen the entrance again. Which will definitely ensure we get rushed by the Scrags."

Lindsey set her hands on her hips and her fingers tapped against her armor. "We have to cut our mission time down and expect the breach."

"Fuck," Torran muttered.

The doors behind them opened and Chief Defender Solomon entered. Her short hair was pushed back from her face by a black headband, giving her an even sterner appearance.

"Where is the squad?" she asked.

"On break," Torran responded.

"Dismiss them. We leave in seven hours. We need to be at the depot at daybreak."

"We have a problem in the mission specs," Lindsey said, gesturing to the playbacks.

"Then resolve it before morning." Solomon's voice was tight. Torran wasn't sure if it was with fury or some other emotion. "President Cabot himself will be attending our departure. He has made it implicitly clear to me that success is of vital importance, and nothing short of success is acceptable."

"He'll have it," Lindsey replied.

Torran wasn't too sure he shared Lindsey's confidence, but he nodded. "Consider it done."

"Excellent. I'll see you in the briefing room in the morning." Solomon turned to leave, but then turned back. "Rooney, I want the revised mission specs to me within the hour. Then get some sleep."

"Yes, sir."

When the doors shut behind the chief defender, Torran swiveled toward Lindsey, his arms crossed. She was staring at the playback footage with a thoughtful expression on her face.

"I'll dismiss the squad and get us shakes and water. Then we'll do this *together*," he informed her.

Lindsey nodded, her eyes never wavering. She had the look that frightened yet intrigued him. Daring to risk the cameras watching, he kissed her cheek.

Startled, she looked up at him, then slowly smiled. "Thanks."

Torran gave her arm a light squeeze before striding out.

The squad didn't complain when he dismissed them upon entering the mess hall, but they did look disgruntled at the news of their early morning departure. Grabbing two shakes from the dispenser and several bags of water, Torran hurried back to the training room.

Entering, he saw that the simulation was running again. Lindsey stood near the doors with her pad in one hand, craning her neck to gaze up.

"The cargo ships are going to cause a big commotion when they land, right? Which is why weren't not letting them set down until the last minute and we're disembarking on the roof."

"Right..." Torran handed her a shake, already opened.

Looking faintly annoyed by the interruption of her train of thought, she took it.

Though he hadn't said anything, she was looking slimmer than when they'd first met. A lot of it had to do with stress. He'd noted that she tended not to eat when fixated on a problem.

"Drink. One swallow."

Lindsey scowled, but obeyed. Once she gulped some of the liquid, she instantly continued her litany. "So we're coming down along the exterior catwalk and stairway, right? Part of it is over these loading doors we have to open to enter the storage area."

"Right." He tapped the bottom of the protein drink she was holding.

With a sigh, Lindsey guzzled down the whole thing and handed him the empty container. "I checked the SWD inventory, and I've got good news."

"You've lost me."

"This stuff..." She pulled on the material that was attached to the exterior of his suit. "They have more of it. Bolts of it. So we just need a screen big enough to cover the doorway. We can hang it from the rail above. I already have the dimensions we need. We just need a roll of the stuff and an aerial drone to take a snapshot of the closed doors to display on the screen."

"It's clever and might work."

Lindsey sighed. "We don't have enough time to make the screen to the exact specs we'd need to ensure success. The internal workings of this suit are impressive, but it's all old parts. But if the screen can hold up for the ten minutes allotted to check the containers, it could work to buy us time before the Scrags come over that fence."

"You're a genius. You know it. Send that to the chief defender. She can crack the whip to get it made. And let's call it a night."

Glancing into the fake daylight, Lindsey sighed. "I still think this should be a night mission."

"We've got no choice. The higher ups are worried about the aircraft. They've been mothballed for a long time and the pilots are used to sim craft, not real ones."

Lindsey exhaled, then lifted a shoulder. "Our people haven't been out on the field all that often either. Cloak of night would greatly reduce the visibility of our squad."

"Preaching to the choir," Torran said, then took a sip of his own protein shake. It was rather tasteless and far too thick.

Lindsey was silent as she sent her updates to the chief defender. When she was done, she showed him the message. She'd included his name. He appreciated her devotion to their partnership in leading the squad.

"You need to drag me out of here before I find something else to fret over," she said to him.

"Sleeping over?" he asked escorting her to the door.

"I want a hot shower, sex, and several hours of blissful sleep snuggled into your side," she answered.

"Yeah. So demanding." He playfully ruffled her hair.

"You're the one who said hello on the bridge that day. This is all *your* fault."

"You didn't have to say yes to my invitation to a walk."

"You didn't have to say yes to my invitation to hot sex."

"Yes I did. Otherwise I'd be certifiably mad."

Lindsey laughed as the door opened. "Well, don't you know? We're all mad here."

"Ah, a Louis Carroll quote. Another reason to tolerate you."

Together, they left the training room.

CHAPTER 20

"Scrag concentration around the food depot is higher than reported," the pilot's voice said through the comm unit.

"Scoggins, direct the feed to my screens," Lindsey responded.

The tiltrotor shuddered as the aircraft sluiced through the wind gusts billowing before an oncoming storm front. The aerial drones had already been recalled to the tiltrotor due to the harsh weather. The small aircraft were unable to fly in the bad conditions and were now attached to the tiltrotor's outer hull like insects. The screens on Lindsey's console altered with the new data streamed from the long-range sensors. They weren't as clear as they fresh feeds from the aerial drones, but they would have to do.

Again, the tiltrotor rocked. A few of the soldiers strapped into the seats in rows behind her let out agonized grunts. The flight over the mountains had been difficult and treacherous. A few times, Lindsey had been convinced the tiltrotor was about to be smashed into the summits. The pilot had done an amazing job -- considering the bad weather conditions and the fact she'd only flown an actual aircraft a handful of times -- and ferried them safely over the mountain range. Now the tiltrotor rushed over a thick, green forest toward the towers of Beta City in the distance.

The chief defender sat at her own console across the aisle, while Torran sat directly behind Solomon communicating with the cargo aircraft that was trailing twenty minutes behind the tiltrotor and just about to crest the mountains. The workstations received intel from not only the tiltrotor, but Beta City sensors being activated by the pulses being sent out by the Bastion. Torran and Lindsey quickly evaluated the information, then transmitted the vital details to the chief defender for her review.

Again, the tiltrotor hit a pocket of rough air and pitched to one side. Lindsey glanced at Dr. Curran at the Med Console. The blond woman was intently watching the vitals of the soldiers under her care. Curious, Lindsey examined the incoming information from the Med-Con transmitted to her screen. Dr. Curran had the suits administering anti-nausea medication to most of the squad. Each suit was outfitted with med packs with small dosages of various types of medication -- such as antihistamines, anti-nausea and pain relief -- that were administered when needed. Lindsey noted that neither she nor Torran required a dose, but the chief defender did. For some reason she found that amusing.

"The Scrags have definitely shifted," Lindsey said into the comm. "Evaluating the situation now."

The mob of undead had moved closer to the front of the complex, and Lindsey wondered why. Had the aerial drones caught their attention? The relocation of the mob actually worked to their benefit. A lower concentration of Scrags near the likely breach point in the rear of the complex would possibly buy them a little more time. She sent the updated information to the chief defender with her suggestion to alter their approach in order to avoid pulling the mob toward the rear of the complex. Several seconds later, Solomon gave the order to tweak the flight plan.

The cameras from the exterior of the tiltrotor continued to feed data to her screens, while Lindsey struggled to not be distracted at the vastness of the land spread out below them. The forest was broken by small bodies of water, pastures, and crumbling towns. The world appeared to stretch out forever in every direction. It was awe-inspiring. For so long, her world had been a single city in an isolated valley. She wished the tiltrotor had windows so she could peer out and see the panorama with her own eyes. Instead, she watched through the electronic eyes of the cameras.

There had been some discussion about having a reporter embedded with the squad, but the idea had been scrubbed. Also, a media remote camera had been eliminated as an option. Lindsey was glad. If the citizens of The Bastion saw what she was witnessing, their unrest would only grow. How could she ever return to the gray world of The Bastion after seeing such beauty?

Her gaze shifted to the footage of the Scrags, and her reverie was over.

It was a beautiful and incredibly deadly world.

"We're on final approach," Scoggins announced.

"Get ready to deploy," Torran ordered.

Lindsey swiped the feed onto her wristlet and unfastened the straps on her chair. As the tiltrotor descended, the rear door opened as the ramp extended.

"Make this fast and smooth," Chief Defender Solomon commanded, making her way past the squad rising to disembark.

Dr. Curran also stood and gripped the handhold overhead. Her gaze met Lindsey's briefly, and her expression was difficult to discern. Lindsey wondered if Dr. Curran resented having to go on missions not associated with her quest to reclaim Maria as a lab rat. The thought brought a smile to Lindsey's face. Dr. Curran gave her a questioning look, then turned away.

A blast of air struck the soldiers as the exit widened and the tiltrotor hovered over the roof of the food depot. The squad dropped a few feet onto a catwalk that stretched along the length of the building and past two towers that were the tops of granaries. The steel and black exterior was covered in a thick layer of grime. Years of weathering had eroded some of the protective paint, allowing spots of rust to form.

Lindsey tugged the mask of her stealth suit over her head, claimed her weapon, and followed the others out. The stealth suits looked very different in the direct morning light. The sunshine added an odd shimmer to the dark gray fabric. The feed in Lindsey's helmet revealed that everything was going as planned so far. Behind Lindsey, two squad members pulled a long tube out of the undercarriage of the tiltrotor while two aerial drones dispatched and skimmed along the roof to peer over the edges to scan the perimeter.

"You know what to do. Let's make this fast and painless. I don't want any deviations from the plan. No sightseeing. This has to be fast, people. We have two cargo transports in route, and we need to be ready for them," Chief Defender Solomon instructed before leading the squad along the catwalk in the direction of the stairwell that would deposit them near the loading doors.

A rumble in the sky jerked Lindsey's attention upward. The storm was moving in much faster than anticipated. Hopefully they'd be done and out of the area before it hit in full force. Moving swiftly past two rooftop entrances into the food depot, Lindsey was relieved that the doors were secured. There'd been some discussion about descending through the roof and sweeping through the upper floors of the depot, but the plan was deemed too much of a risk. Final reports from the depot had indicated there was an outbreak inside the building. At last, it was agreed that the main storage area would be easier to enter via the loading dock doors. Also, it would give the squad only one area to clear instead of the entire building.

The food depot was three stories high, taller than most of the structures around it. The evacuation center to the east was a modified airport. The main building appeared to be in decent condition, but the landing pads and surrounding field were filled with Scrags. The approach of the tiltrotor had been masked by the wind blowing away from the Scrags, but some creatures along the edges of the crowd had witnessed the arrival of the team and were rousing out of their stupor. Meanwhile, to the west, the Scrags that had clogged the streets awakened as the tiltrotor flew over. The undead streamed toward the food depot.

The wind buffeted the squad as they sprinted across the rooftop. The stealth suit helmets were more like hoods with a flexible faceplate, and when another strong gale hit the squad, Lindsey grunted as her visor smacked into her nose. The suits had worked fine in the training room, but now Lindsey wondered if they were suitable for the missions. She was beginning to long for her Constabulary armor even if it was old and clunky. The suits didn't have an oxygen system like the regular armor and the air filters tucked into the sides of the hood only fed them fresh air. The smell of rot and ozone drifted through the filters. That wasn't particularly comforting. She'd rather smell the stale air of recycled oxygen in her old suit.

Running with the squad, Lindsey kept an eye on those carrying the stealth curtain. It was a bit bulky, but she was glad it had been made in time for their departure. It would hopefully deceive the Scrags and postpone them breaching the fences.

The Scrags filled the area between the old warehouses and equipment storage depots. Air gusts carried away their terrifying screeches, but the noise was loud enough to tease along the edges of Lindsey's hearing.

"There's so many," Hobbes said in awe.

"The world is filled with them," Torran answered sadly.

An aerial drone skipped alongside the squad, bobbing on the choppy air currents. When the soldiers reached the platform above the loading dock, the drone flew ahead, its long legs extending to catch the rail of the catwalk and perch where it could capture the static image that would display on the curtain.

So far, everything was going as planned, which both elated and terrified Lindsey. If things were going this well, did that mean they would succeed, or was it just a setup for a catastrophic failure? It was hard to believe in good things when so much had gone wrong.

Franklin swept past Lindsey, peering at the Scrags through her weapon scope. "They're getting rowdier."

"That crowd isn't the one we need to worry about. It's that one." Lindsey pointed toward the Scrags located in the rear of the complex that had yet to fully register their arrival.

Sweeping her weapon toward the Scrags clustered in the back, Franklin scowled. "They're quiet for now."

"Let's hope it stays that way," Lindsey replied.

Reaching the catwalk, the squad separated to allow the soldiers hauling the screen through to the railing. It only took a few seconds to secure the enormous piece of fabric and unfurl it. Lindsey and Torran stepped to the rail, peered down, and exchanged looks. The projection of the closed doors flicked on, matching the area behind it.

"It looks good," Torran said approvingly.

"Let's go," Chief Defender Solomon ordered.

The metal lattice fastened to the frame of the stairway hid the soldiers from the eyes of the undead creatures, but the pounding of footfalls against the metal steps of the stairwell rattled Lindsey's nerves. Thankfully, they were far enough from the Scrags that the wind carried away the sound.

Arriving at the concrete pad before the loading doors, Lindsey checked the status of the departing tiltrotor. Yates, one of the squad members, hurried to use a key-hacker on the doors. Another soldier, Carter, carrying a small remote generator on his back, joined her. The generator would produce a wave of energy that would power the doors and lights temporarily.

"How's your eagle eye view?" Lindsey asked Scoggins after switching over her comm.

"Main activity continues to be on the west side, but more have arrived from the north. They have yet to reach the fence, but are closing in," the pilot answered.

"Keep me informed."

"Yes, sir."

Lindsey updated the chief defender and Torran over their dedicated channel.

Solomon looked pensive at the news. "How soon before the Scrags hit the fences?"

"Within five minutes, but that's within our anticipated parameters," Lindsey replied.

"We're on schedule," Torran added.

Examining the heavy curtain obscuring the squad from the view of the Scrags, the chief defender said, "This screen seems to be working."

Lindsey studied her readouts. "Agreed. Aerial drones are showing no significant movement among the Scrag crowd near the possible break point."

"We do have unexpected trouble along the northeast side. They're against the retaining wall," Torran said, his tone turning grim.

"Show me," the chief defender ordered.

Torran passed along the drone information to both women.

Lindsey tabbed through the images being transmitted by the drones by clicking on her wristlet that was linked into her hood's screen. There was a massive amount of Scrags up against the wall that separated the complex from another warehouse, and it was already showing signs of stress. Blood sprayed into the air as those Scrags unlucky enough to be up against the concrete barrier were squished like ticks.

"How does the data affect our mission time?" the chief defender asked.

Lindsey ran a quick calculation in her head, not bothering with the suit's tech. Again her mind sifted through the miniscule details, revealing the important bits in a simplistic tapestry. "Four minutes less than estimated."

"Relay that to the aircraft, MacDonald. We need them to take a more direct path and not bother circling the area."

"Yes, sir."

The large metal door in front of them shuddered to life.

"Let's hope they actually did store the food to last a hundred years," the chief defender muttered, "and that it wasn't just hype."

As soon as the doors slid open far enough to allow entry, the squad hurried through with weapons raised and ready for whatever lay on the other side.

"We have bodies," Franklin's voice said tersely. "Long dead. Not Scrags."

Lindsey slipped into the building and saw several deceased lying on the ground. They'd been dead for so long, the corpses were mummified. It was clear that all had died to a gunshot to the head.

"Were they Scrags?" Hobbes wondered aloud.

"Possibly," Torran answered. "Keep alert. You know what to do."

Lindsey studied the vast room warily. The simulation had been eerily close to the actual storage area except for the corpses and four loaders that were pushed up against the interior doors. The barricades were confirmation as far as Lindsey was concerned that they'd been smart not to enter through the roof entrances. It would have taken far too long to clear out the building.

Towering storage units painted in bright blue rose to the high ceiling. Each unit was designed to maintain the perfect environment for food storage and were not connected to a central power grid. There were plenty of places to hide, but Scrags didn't like to hide. The minute they detected humans, they stirred to life. Of course, they were a little sluggish at first, so it was better to error on the side of caution. How long would it take for a Scrag who'd been locked up for nearly half century to wake up and attack?

Lindsey hurried with the rest of her team to clear the right side of the room. Row upon row of the storage units filled the enormous room. The remote generator spurred the lights overhead to glow, but there were still disturbingly dark spaces. Quick, precise sweeps cleared the areas as they advanced toward their objective. The small group skirted between a row of containers and the wall. The doors on both ends of the room were closed and had loaders jammed against them. There were several empty spots on the floor where storage units had stood, indicating that during the evacuation some of the food had been moved. So had the crew in the loading area held off the Scrags while the cargo ships carried off what they could? The evidence seemed to support that idea.

Along the way, they discovered more bodies at the base of one of the storage units.

"Shots to the head like the others," Hobbes said grimly.

Lindsey glanced at the mummified bodies. They were wearing uniforms from the armies of the old days. Flags from long gone countries decorated their shoulders.

"There was no hope." Franklin pushed one of the bodies over with her foot, then squatted to gaze at the desiccated face. "It was either a bullet or starvation."

"Shouldn't they have gone with the others to The Bastion during the evacuation?" Carter, another SWD soldier, asked. He was a wide-set man with heavy features, pale blue eyes, tan skin, and short dark hair.

"There wasn't enough room," Lindsey answered. "Some volunteered to stay behind once it was determined that there weren't enough aircraft in the area to evacuate everyone. There was mass panic when Beta City fell. It happened so suddenly. They never saw the attack coming."

"So all of these people are the heroes." Hobbes' voice filled with admiration.

"The very best of us," Lindsey said, glancing at Torran across the room.

"Clear on this side, Vanguard Rooney," Chief Defender Solomon's voice said through the comm.

"Progressing toward objective," Lindsey responded, and signaled her group to continue forward.

As the squad advanced, Lindsey focused on the far end to the darkened recessed area where the control room was. There was a lot of concern about this particular spot. It was the only part of the room that the portable wireless generator was too weak to reach with its wave.

"What if they're in there?" Hobbes asked. "Waiting?"

"Well, there's one way to find out," Lindsey said, then struck the storage unit beside her. The clank resonated through the room. "Let's give them a wakeup call."

"Vanguard?" the chief defender's voice queried.

"They're attracted to sound and movement," Lindsey answered, then hit the unit again.

The dark space before them remained quiet.

"Light," Lindsey ordered.

Hobbes pulled a small flashlight from his belt and shone it at the spot she pointed to. One of the other things she disliked about the modified weapons was since they were covered with the same material as the stealth suits, the lights had been removed along with the long-range scopes. The beam barely penetrated the murk, but it appeared that the control area was empty.

Advancing, Lindsey could hear the rest of the squad calling out that their section of the vast storage room was clear.

"Corpse on the floor," she said, indicating the pair of boots hidden behind a workstation.

Hobbes and Franklin scooted past her, moving into position to charge into the enclosed area. The door was open, which Lindsey hoped was a good sign. With well-practiced ease, Hobbes and Franklin slipped into the control room with Lindsey right behind them. The space was narrow, cramped and devoid of life. Two bodies were on the floor and were long dead.

"Nothing to shoot," Franklin grunted.

"We're clear," Lindsey said, relief in her voice. Relaxing her shoulders, she returned to the main floor.

"We've got a schedule to keep. Get to work," the chief defender ordered.

The Sci-Tech team immediately started their scans of each storage unit as Dr. Curran observed their progress. Lindsey caught the doctor briefly glancing her way with one of her inscrutable expressions. Deciding to ignore the woman altogether, Lindsey directed her gaze at the barricaded doors. The heavy-duty loaders were squat vehicles with long metallic limbs that ended in claws. The arms enabled the driver to pack the vehicle with heavy cargo and cart the products to loading areas. The loaders in front the interior entrances to the storage area had the arms extended and the claws set against the doors.

Torran stepped to her side and gestured toward the loaders. "Why barricade the doors?"

Lindsey studied the barricade before answering. "Interior doors don't have the high security locks reserved for the outside doors. If the reports of a Scrag outbreak inside the building are true, they had to do what they could to keep them closed."

"We need those to load the cargo transports," he said. "Which means moving them away from the doors."

"And Scrags are still in the building..." Lindsey took a deep breath. "Shit."

Torran gestured to an entrance across the room. "I checked the doors on the other side. The locks didn't activate. The only thing keeping the doors closed are the loaders. Can the remote generator get the door locks to work?"

Scrutinizing the four doors that were blocked off and the distance between them, Lindsey shook her head. "It's too low powered. The wave is keeping the lights on, but it doesn't have that much juice. The auto-locks should have flipped on before the power went out."

"But what if they were sabotaged?" Torran raised his eyes.

Lindsey followed his gaze to the area above the storage containers. Scorch marks decorated the ceiling where power junctions had been blown out. "This is bad."

"Dr. Curran, what's the status on the storage units?" Torran asked, opening up the comm to the doctor and including Lindsey.

"Only a third are viable," Dr. Curran answered.

"Why only a third?" Torran asked, his brown eyes meeting Lindsey's.

"Sabotage took out quite a few of the units."

Lindsey sighed. She should have known things were going a little too well.

CHAPTER 21

"Keep us updated," Torran said, then cut the scientist out of their conversation. Looking at Lindsey, he could see the computer behind her eyes already whirring to life. He trusted that look implicitly.

"The power junctions were sabotaged, meaning they couldn't lock the doors," Lindsey said. "They barricaded the doors to keep the Scrags in the building trapped while they got a few of the containers onto the transports before shutting the loading doors."

That sounded about right, so Torran gave her a quick nod. "So the question is: did they then kill themselves?"

Lindsey glanced at the bodies around her, then opened a direct link to Hobbes and Franklin. "Check all the bodies in the room. See how many have holstered weapons."

The two soldiers hurried off as Lindsey squatted in front of one of the piles of dead soldiers. A Sci-Tech and his escort were just finishing at the nearby storage unit. The tech marked the unit with a large red X, then moved on. Another sabotaged unit.

Crouching beside her, Torran asked, "What are you thinking?"

"I suspect there was a battle. Some of the people in here were defending the food depot. The others weren't." Lindsey pointed at the weapons still holstered in the belts of the bodies in front of her. "Indications are that they were ambushed. They're nearest the control center. Exit wounds look like they're in the front of the head, not back."

"Shot from behind most likely."

"Killed unexpectedly. Then I think there was a skirmish."

What she was suggesting seemed to make sense in the light of the sabotage and bodies around them. Torran didn't like where the investigation was pointing at all.

"Vanguard Rooney," Hobbes said, running up, Franklin on his heels. "Most of the bodies around the control room had weapons on them, but they were not drawn. Toward the loading docks, those bodies were armed and appeared to have additional wounds other than the head shot."

"Neither side truly won, but the saboteurs failed. That meant someone managed to kill them before they were able to finish their job," Torran decided.

"Why destroy the food? Why murder these people?" Lindsey directed her focus to the people at her feet again. "Who would do something like that?"

With a frown, Torran said, "The Gaia Cult."

"The people who wanted humanity to die?" Hobbes asked.

"People who believed humans had outwitted their extinction event and overstayed their time on Earth," Franklin amended. "They wanted to save the planet from us."

"So they destroyed the resources we might need to survive," Lindsey straightened and glanced toward the loaders. "Maybe they're the ones who started the Scrag infection in the building."

The cult had been responsible for opening the gate and letting the Scrags into the valley that surrounded The Bastion. Their ardent belief that humanity's time was at an end spurred them to horrific acts of terrorism. This seemed to be yet another one.

"It had to have been the Gaia Cult," Torran decided. "This looks like their work. They just didn't get to finish. What is beyond those doors?"

"Those are basic interior doors," Lindsey said. "They swing outward. Enough force will push them open."

Torran tapped on his wristlet screen and summoned one of the drones. "Then we should be able to peer under it." He gestured to the tracks in the floor used to move food from the processing part of the facility to the storage. "I got a drone on its way."

"I have an update on the containers," Dr. Curran said through the channel to the three in charge.

"Report," the chief defender's voice ordered over the comm.

"A little less than half of the containers are still operational and have viable food products within," Dr. Curran answered.

"That's a much smaller haul than anticipated," Solomon groused.

"The containers were sabotaged. There's not much we can do about that," Dr. Curran replied, her voice clipped.

"It'll have to do then. MacDonald, Rooney, what is our status?"

The aerial drone sped past Torran and headed toward one of the doors. Its long spidery legs extended from under its body as it settled on the cement floor. "Running a scan on the hallways. We can't move the loaders yet."

"Transports arrive in two minutes," the chief defender said briskly.

"Understood," Lindsey said, glancing at Torran. Her expression was very tense.

A small beep in Torran's helmet indicated he was about to get a new feed. A second later, the data from the small scanner the aerial drone had scooted under one of the doors appeared in the corner of her faceplate. It took several tries with the filters for them to finally get an adequate scan. Torran's heart thumped harder in his chest.

The image was of countless feet standing perfectly still.

The Scrags were outside the doors. Fear filled his veins with ice. Swallowing the hard lump that formed all at once in his suddenly tight throat, he toggled over to the chief defender directly.

"What is it?" Solomon asked. From across the room, she directed her gaze toward him.

"There are Scrags in the lower left hallway. We're checking the others w now. We'll need to move the loaders, which will make sufficient noise to waken them." Torran kept his voice surprisingly steady despite the dread clawing at his insides.

"I need details within one minute," Solomon answered briskly.

The aerial drone lifted off and flew to the next door after Lindsey sent it fresh commands. Torran watched the feed as the drone slid a sensor into the narrow space under the door. He exhaled as he saw that the hallway was empty. Lindsey issued more commands and the small drone darted overhead, resembling an oversized insect, to the other side of the room.

"We'll use the loader in front of the empty hallway to push a sabotaged storage container against the doors," Lindsey said.

Torran surveyed the barricades, then nodded. "Yeah. That should work."

"It'll affect our egress time schedule." Lindsey slid her pad out of her uniform and started tapping away on the screen.

The drone sent an updated feed.

The next hallway was packed with Scrags.

"Well, that makes it simpler," Torran said, sarcasm hiding his nerves.

"Fuck," Lindsey grunted.

The aerial drone skittered just above the floor to the next door. The squad members were busy unlocking the food containers from their storage units, but a few gave the small drone worried looks.

This hallway was filled with corpses. It appeared that someone had set off some sort of explosive device. Bits of bodies littered the hallway and the ceiling and walls had partially collapsed.

"There is a God," Torran said with relief.

"And She is good." Lindsey flashed him a smile.

Together, Lindsey and Torran hurried to the chief defender's side. The woman was watching the final prep for the removal of the food.

"Situation is not as dire as it could be. Southeast door and northeast doors are breach points. One hallway is blocked, the other is empty," Torran explained.

"The empty hallway leads straight to the granary and only has one other entrance to it. Maybe someone managed to lock it," Lindsey added. "If we use the loader from the blocked hallway, we can move damaged food containers in front of the doors that have Scrags on the other side. They'll wake up, but they'll have trouble getting through."

"We've got six loaders. Two will be needed to block doors. That will affect our load time," Torran finished.

At that very moment the three aircraft sent their approach status. They were about to arrive.

"Do it. Make it fast. We still have that potential breach in the rear of the facility and the Scrags about to take down the wall on the northwest side. MacDonald, get the doors blocked and the loaders prepped. Rooney, I want you to run a fresh scan on all approaches to the facility. I want to know exactly how much time we have before Scrags are on us," Solomon ordered.

"Yes, sir."

Torran gave Lindsey the briefest of glances. He didn't expect her to be looking his way since she was always so intent on her tasks, but her gaze met his for a second. It was enough to make him feel a bit more grounded. They cared for one another and wouldn't let each other down.

"Carter, Ramirez, Evins, Yates, you're with me."

Immediately the four SWD soldiers hurried to his side.

The aerial drone zipped past Torran and swooped after Lindsey.

Reaching the doors to the blocked hallway, Torran swiftly explained exactly what their assignments were, then signaled for more of the squad to come join him. As he talked, he saw Lindsey leading Hobbes and Franklin toward the front doors. The aerial drone darted around the curtain to the outside. He'd just finished with his instructions when Dr. Curran approached him.

"What's this I hear about Inferi Scourge behind the doors?" she demanded.

"There was an outbreak in the building. They're still in here with us, but the doors are blocked off."

"But the loaders—"

"We got a plan."

Dr. Curran gave the chief defender across the room a hard look. "I was told this mission was going to be safe."

"You do realize where you are, right? You're in a dead world. A world that humanity had to abandon to save itself. Nothing out here is *safe.*" Torran pinned her with his fiercest look. "Don't ever think you're safe, or you will make a terrible mistake that may cost not only your life. but the lives of others."

"Are you done lecturing me?" Dr. Curran asked, lifting her chin haughtily.

"I hope so. Get back to your position. We're leaving in about one minute."

Torran made sure the self-important doctor was obeying him before he opened a link to Lindsey. "Rooney, what's the status?"

"They're inbound and landing within thirty seconds. Scrags near the possible breach are now waking up. And the storm is about to hit."

"The curtain..."

"Its usefulness is done. It did the trick, though I wonder if we even needed to project the image. The Scrags are a bit dumb," Lindsey ruminated.

"Well, better safe than sorry. They've been staring at the damn door for how long? Any major alterations may have jarred them awake."

"You're a clever man." There was a beat of silence, then Lindsey said, "Here we go."

A second later the sound of the massive cargo transports approaching filled the room. The air around the soldiers vibrated as the aircraft neared. The Scrags would definitely now awaken.

It was time.

Immediately Carter started the loader blocking the door on the ruined hallway. It groaned to life, then its long arms retracted from the doors and curled into their stationary position. With a satisfied grin,

Carter drove toward the next door where Ramirez waited in the driver's seat, her fingers nervously tapping on the controls while other soldiers provided cover. Carter edged up behind one of the ruined storage units and a Sci-tech ejected the container. The damaged container slid out of the tall blue cylinder and Carter expertly extended the mechanical arms of the loader to fully extract it.

"How long before they awaken?" Torran asked over the comm.

"According to Vanguard Martinez, it will be within a minute," Lindsey answered.

The woman he loved and feared for was on the other side of the room, watching Evins maneuvering one of the faulty containers into position. Meanwhile, Yates waited with her loader in front of the door hiding the mass of Scrags. The tension in the air was palatable. Everyone was staring at the doors, waiting for a sign that the Scrags had awakened.

The loader Carter was driving swiveled about toward the door where Ramirez waited to move her loader. The engine revved louder as Carter put some speed into it, expertly weaving around the other storage units. Even over the rumbling engine, Torran heard the exact moment the Scrags awakened.

The terrifying screech of the Inferi Scourge emanated from behind the closed doors seconds before they shook violently under the onslaught of the undead.

"They're awake," Lindsey said, her voice catching in her throat.

The doors keeping out the Scrags shuddered under the intensity of their attack. Every muscle in her body tightened in anticipation of battle as she directed Evins toward the quaking doors. Yates started up her loader, but didn't retract the arms yet. Checking on the progress across the room, Lindsey witnessed Carter scooting the large container into place as Ramirez slowly edged the loader away, while keeping the arms in place against the doors. Though the two people had never practiced such a maneuver, they were doing a great job with the very difficult dance.

Meanwhile, the Sci-Techs clustered in the center of the room away from the potential hot spots. They weren't soldiers, and though they'd been taught to fire their weapons, it was best to keep them from the potential fray. The curtain over the doorway began to flutter wildly as the transports and tiltrotor descended. The roar of the aircraft landing blocked out nearly all other sound. When the curtain was abruptly torn from its fastenings and snapped away by the wind, Lindsey saw the underside of one of the transports come into view.

"I need those doors blocked now!" the chief defender ordered.

Ramirez retracted the arms on her loader as Carter finished setting the large storage container in place. The doors continued to quake, but did not give way to the attack on the other side.

Torran whipped around and gave Lindsey the all-clear signal.

Turning her gaze to Evins and Yates, Lindsey's breath caught in her throat. The hinges on the left door were popping out of the wall under the ferocious assault of the Scrags.

Outside, the transport set down. Carter and Ramirez were already extracting food units while other soldiers kept watch over the shuddering doors. Dr. Curran and the Sci-Techs rushed outside to the waiting tiltrotor, their jobs completed.

"They're getting through," Yates exclaimed. "The door is coming off the wall!"

"Abandon the loader," the chief defender ordered. "We'll make do with what we have."

"I suggest we put the container Evins is carting against the loader," Lindsey said, her voice a bit breathless.

Yates jumped off the loader and dragged her weapon upward just as the door on the left side popped its top hinge entirely. Only the bottom hinge was still holding onto the wall and the top of the door slanted outward. The desperate clawing hands of the Scrags shoved through the opening.

The first freight pallet arrived inside the storage room, driven by one of the crew members of the transport. Each food unit was to be placed on the pallet and then moved into the cargo transport.

"Evins, drop the container where you are and start loading now!" the chief defender ordered. "Rooney, take care of that doorway. MacDonald, get those pallets loaded!"

Signaling her group, Lindsey ran toward the doorway. Hobbes and Franklin fell into step behind her along with a few others. Yates stood at the ready, feet planted apart, her weapon aiming at the slowly expanding gap at the top of the door. In a perfectly choreographed ballet, the other loaders rushed to pack the freight pallet.

The door bent under the assault of the Inferi Scourge. Lindsey knew that the bottom hinge would give away at any moment. How many Scrags had been in the hallway?

"Pallet is ready," Torran said briskly.

The information on her helmet updated as the pallet retracted onto the loading platform and another took its place. Twelve food units down. Forty to go. They didn't have enough time to retrieve all of them.

"I'm moving the arm," Lindsey said before she realized she had formulated a plan. "Cover me!"

Running to the loader, Lindsey ignored the buckling doorway. In another few seconds the Scrags would be able to scramble over the top of the toppling door. Jumping into the seat of the loader, Lindsey scanned the controls. They were basic, but the arms were a little more complicated than she anticipated. Starting up the loader, she seized the arm adjusters. The clawed ends of the arms were pressed to the middle section of the doors, allowing the upper half to bend outward. Lindsey hesitated, realizing that if she miscalculated, the Scrags would topple the doors and she'd be caught in their onrush into the storage area.

"What are you doing?" Torran demanded over a secure channel only to her.

"Something incredibly stupid," she answered.

Maintaining pressure on the door, she slowly slid the giant claw upward. The top of the door slanted even further outward, the metal groaning. A Scrag appeared, clawing his way through the opening. Lindsey caught sight of his screaming mouth and murky eyes as he dragged himself part of the way through the doorway. A second later, one of her people shot him through the head and his body slumped.

"Got him," Franklin said.

Lindsey continued to glide the end of the loader arm up the door at an agonizingly slow pace. She didn't want to put too much force into the arm and have it shove the door into the hallway. The body of the Scrag vanished, but two more replaced him. They Scrags were crawling over each other in an attempt to get out of the hallway and into the room where the living were located. Franklin's sure shots took out one, but the other managed to topple over the edge and onto the loader.

With a shriek, the Scrag launched itself at Lindsey. She brought her arm up in front of her face, just before he slammed into her. Through the visor of her hood, the dead eyes of the man were wide and glazed as he bit down on her forearm. Realizing he was not rending flesh and infecting her, he shook his head violently. The pressure from the bite elicited a cry of pain from Lindsey, but she didn't dare let go of the control for the loader arm.

Checking her suit stats, she was relieved to see the armor was holding up against the attack, but for how much longer? She was aware of Torran shouting orders, but she directed her gaze past the Scrag at the screen on the loader. She had a job to do.

It was Hobbes that grabbed the Scrag off her and wrenched him onto the ground. With a furious grunt, Hobbes kicked the creature in the head, then shot it point blank.

Still in pain, Lindsey gripped the controls with both hands and nudged the arm up as more Scrags poured over the top. Though Lindsey was terrified, she had to trust her squad to protect her as she finished her task. One bounced off her and hit the ground. It scrambled to its feet and whirled toward her. A second later, it was dead on the ground from a bullet. Gunshots resounded in the room.

Lindsey grinned fiendishly when the metal door straightened under the press of the loader arm and caught one Scrag as it tried to come over the top Pressing higher with the arm, inch by inch, the buckled door flattened. With a sickening crunch and meaty ripping noise, the Scrag was severed in half. The torso flopped onto the loader, then slid to the ground in a wet, bloody heap.

Hobbes shot it in the head.

Locking the loader arms in place, Lindsey slid out of the vehicle and avoided the blood and guts pooling on the ground. To her shock, she realized more Scrags had come over the top than she'd realized. Her forearm throbbed with pain. A second later, there was pressure against her thigh as the suit injected her with a painkiller. It took only a brief moment for it to take effect, and she was grateful.

A second pallet exited the storage area and a surge of relief flooded Lindsey. One transport was full. Now to finish loading the second. Harsh air currents swirled into the building as the transport lifted off. There was a moment of brevity as everyone cheered, but one hard look from the chief defender had them scrambling to finish the work.

Lindsey stabilized her breathing and redirected her focus to the feed. The aerial drones were still monitoring the perimeter and it was looking grim not only in the rear where they expected a breach, but along the walls and fence lines. Listening to the incoming reports, it was quite clear that they were virtually out of time.

"We have to go now," the chief defender said. "Commence egress."

Watching the feed of the wall on the north side of the complex crumble, Lindsey's heart stuttered in fear. The pallet from the second transport was almost loaded, but they would have to leave without several of the viable food containers.

Carter rushed to put his final container on the loader.

The aerial drones documented the Scrags racing through the wall breach and along the sides of the complex. There were other fences blocking their way, but when Lindsey saw the first one go down in a matter of seconds it became clear that the mission was over.

Torran and Lindsey overlapped each other as they barked out orders, hustling the squad toward the exit. It was clear the soldiers didn't want to leave so much food behind. The freight pallet driver withdrew from the area before Carter could get this container onto it.

"Carter, we're done! Go!" Lindsey motioned for him to follow. "Franklin, cover us. We got Scrags on their way."

"The south fence is down," Scoggins said tersely.

"Cover us," Chief Defender Solomon directed. "We need to get the last pallet on board."

Aerial drones spun through the air, recording the Scrags sprint toward the back of the complex. A rapid calculation in Lindsey's head revealed that they only had two minutes before the area was overrun. She rushed to the doorway of the facility and nearly froze. A wave of Scrags was speeding from the downed fence line in the rear. The loud clatter of the tiltrotor firing at the horde fought with the whine of the pallet being hoisted into the belly of the big gray transport. The tiltrotor was hovering two feet above the ground covering the squad and the other aircraft.

Sprinting under the wings of the cargo transport, the squad rushed for the tiltrotor. The sound of the approaching Scrags pieced even through the roar of the engines.

"Pallet is loaded! Transport lifting off," Torran exclaimed.

The tiltrotor was eighteen meters away, holding position as the transport ascended. The horde of Scrags was approaching fast, but still weren't in firing distance. Several aerial drones flew past Lindsey and her feed updated to reveal the Scrags rounding the building's corner and running at full speed after the squad. There were so many undead the shock of the sight stole her breath for a second. Another drone, circling overhead, revealed a terrifying sight. Scrags were rushing toward the tiltrotor and the squad from every direction.

"Set her down!" the chief defender ordered.

The violent downdraft from the transport's departure nearly knocked Lindsey off her feet. Someone caught her arm and pulled her upright. It was Torran. The expression in his eyes almost took her breath away with its ferocity. In that moment, she knew he'd do anything to keep her safe.

The tiltrotor's extended legs touched the ground. The rear guns were silent, unable to fire yet since the squad was occupying the space between the Scrags and the tiltrotor.

The screech of the Scrags intensified as the transport flew over the complex and the sound of its engines diminished. In Lindsey's head, she counted down the meters to the tiltrotor. The reek of the Scrags made her want to gag. All around her were the undead of every race, gender and age. All were screaming, all wanted to bite, all wanted to infect, and all were drawing closer.

The squad opened fire. In a phalanx, they faced outward, still moving, shooting at the Scrags. The undead were closing the gap far too fast.

"Go! Go! Go!" the chief defender ordered just as they reached the underbelly of the tiltrotor.

The guns on the tiltrotor discharged in a thunderous roar. The higher caliber weapons reduced the edge of the Scrag horde to bits of mush. Lindsey kept shooting, her firearm jolting her wounded arm. It didn't hurt, but her aim was off. The screeching, twisted, rabid faces of the Scrags filled her vision. Many were half-naked from years of exposure to the elements, but the virus had retained their nearly lifelike appearance. The dirty, murderous creatures had no fear and ran into the barrage of bullets fired by the tiltrotor.

The squad scrambled up the ramp into the aircraft. Lindsey was one of the last to clamber up into the tiltrotor just as it ascended. The Scrags leaped for the retracting ramp and the doors started to close. Lindsey fired at one trying to lunge for her. She saw its face disintegrate just as the doors thumped shut. Sagging against the closed exit, she watched the feed from the aerial drones as they caught up to the tiltrotor and attached to it. The Scrags filled the area, howling at the retreating aircraft. There would be no coming back to this location. It was completely overrun. The remaining food stores were a loss.

Lindsey closed her eyes and listened to her heavy breathing inside her suit.

"...returning to The Bastion. No fatalities. No infections..." the chief Defender's voice was saying.

Swiveling about, Lindsey walked on shaking legs to her console. Torran was already at his, but his concentration was on his readouts. Collapsing into her seat, she looked down at her arm. Where the Scrag had bitten her armor were deep indentations.

CHAPTER 22

The hours after their arrival at The Bastion were chaotic and a bit of a blur. The squad had to go through decontamination and endure a thorough scan before being allowed out of the hanger. She was ISPV free, but bruised. Dr. Curran personally administered a few shots to speed up the healing. Though her arm was already feeling much better, her nerves were frayed. Had the Scrag been able to bite through the armor, she'd be dead.

Lindsey's stealth suit was claimed by the SWD Sci-Techs for examination, and she was glad to be rid of it.

The debriefing was long and tiring. The chief defender, Torran, and Lindsey were immediately separated. The officers in charge of the questioning were thorough, but she disliked their tone when they discussed the food containers left behind. Throughout the process, she'd wanted to tell them to go out and get the containers themselves if they were so convinced they'd been retrievable, but she held her tongue.

Six hours after her return, she was finally given a protein bar and a bag of water and sent back to her quarters. She still hadn't seen anyone else from the mission. It aggravated her that they'd performed a great deed for The Bastion but were made to feel almost like failures due to a truncated raid.

It was difficult to believe it was merely mid-afternoon when she trudged across the quad to her dorm room. She'd been tempted to go to Torran's flat, but she doubted he was there. The comm on their wristlets had been switched off upon their return to prevent them from discussing the mission and contaminating their points of view. Though she could hack hers, Torran's was still off.

When she entered her tiny dorm room, she yanked off her boots and sprawled across the bed. Shaking, Lindsey endured the aftermath of the adrenaline rush that had kept her moving throughout the day. What was worse, her mind turned out alternate outcomes to the excursion. It was almost as if she couldn't quite accept they'd all survived. Images of Scrag faces assaulted her mind's eye, and the sound of their screeches haunted her hearing. Her stomach was a quivering mess and tears obscured her vision. No one had died, and no one had been seriously injured, but they'd come so close to failure.

Eventually, she drifted off into a light sleep filled with nightmare creatures that truly did exist.

Lindsey was roused by the door chiming about thirty minutes later. Groggy, she slid off the rumpled bed. The muscles in her back were aching, since she carried her stress along her spine. Unlocking the door, she watched it slide open through bleary eyes. Torran stood on the other side with a pensive expression on his face. She waved him in and slumped against the wall as he brushed past her.

The door slid shut, leaving them in silence. The look on Torran's face was difficult to decipher. His jaw was clenched and his gaze was directed away from hers. What was going through his mind? Was he angry? Upset?

"That could have gone worse," she said at last, trying to start a conversation.

Torran took her by surprise when he gripped her arms, tugged her against him, and rendered her breathless in a scorching kiss. Her lips parted beneath the hungry caress of his mouth and his tongue swiped against hers, causing her to moan with delight. Clutching his arms with her hands, she hungrily responded with equal passion. The depth of her desire for him surprised and frightened her. She'd never experienced such longing in her life. It was more than physical desire, and almost beyond description.

Shaking, Torran raised his hand to her face and broke the kiss. "I thought I might lose you when that Scrag bit you. I wanted to save you, but I couldn't," he muttered against her lips.

"I'm fine, Torran. I'm still here," she managed to say, still gasping for breath.

"I can't lose you," Torran whispered, his brown eyes downcast. His fingers were trembling against her cheek.

"You won't. Ever," she promised, though she knew it was empty. Life could be so cruel.

The next kiss was sweeter, but just as intense. She laid her hands against the sides of his neck and his rapid pulse beneath her palms said so much. The terror of that awful moment still beat in his heart. Now she understood the complexity of emotions in his expression when he'd entered the dorm room. The look upon his face mirrored her emotions. The fear and stress they'd experienced on the mission had been exacerbated by their affection for each other. Now that they'd returned and were safely alone, all those jumbled feelings were pouring out of them.

When his fingers swiftly unfastened her uniform, she didn't resist despite her mental and physical fatigue. He needed the reassurance that she was still with him, still alive, and still in his arms. Meanwhile, she wanted to feel his love, his desire for her, and his need to protect her. It wasn't until he'd pinned her to the wall and slid his cock into her already wet core that Lindsey finally managed to escape the horrors of their mission. Pleasure filled her senses and wiped away the terrors she'd experienced. The sound of their labored breathing as Torran shoved into her and she thrust against him replaced the terrifying screeches. The fragrance of his skin replaced the reek of death. The exquisite sensation of him plunging in and out of her and his mouth consuming hers replaced the pain of the Scrag's bite. Torran wiped away all the horrors and replaced it with him.

When he finally came inside her, Lindsey was lightheaded with bliss. Sagging in his arms, she buried her face in his neck. "Don't leave me," she whispered.

"I won't," he replied in a ragged voice. "We don't report until morning,"

It wasn't what she'd meant, but she was a little afraid of how easily the words had slipped out. It was a confession of how much she needed him and how much of her heart she'd invested in their relationship. He kissed her again, but this time the touch of his lips was gentle and sweet. They spent several more precious moments just kissing tenderly as they disengaged their bodies and slowly finished undressing.

After climbing naked into bed together, they fell asleep almost immediately. The nightmares returned, but Lindsey only had to drift close enough to wakefulness to realize Torran was at her side and be reassured by his presence. He awakened her a few times by muttering in his sleep while twitching. Holding him tight, she tried to give him comfort as he maneuvered through his own terrible dreams. They were both plagued by what they'd endured, and in some ways, that was a comfort. That understanding made their connection stronger.

It was nearly midnight when Lindsey woke up to Torran's tender kisses on her neck. With a small moan, she tilted her head away from him so he could nibble his way along the curve of her throat.

"Done with nightmares for a bit," he said against her skin.

"Me, too." Tangling her fingers in his hair, she enjoyed the sensation of him kissing and licking his way down her body. "A girl could get used to this."

"And you will," Torran said, his Scottish brogue making him all the more sexy in the moment.

He spent a delicious amount of time adoring her hard pink nipples with his tongue. In the muted light cast be the bedside lamp, she felt no fear knowing he was near. The day and all its terrors faded away and all that existed was her small dorm room. Soon his ministrations had her arching her back while she rubbed her pussy against his thigh in desperation.

"Hurry up and do something. You're driving me mad," she pouted.

"Nah. I'm taking my time."

With a teasing smile, he leisurely covered her stomach and hips with little bites and kisses. Intoxicated by his touch, her nipples and clit were already painfully erect. Just one flick of his tongue against her wetness sent her spiraling into an intense orgasm.

"Okay, I really, really want to get used to this," she panted.

"Not done with you yet."

Grinning at his masterfulness, Torran wrapped his arms around her thighs and devoured her until she was almost screaming. Torran was just climbing back up her body with the most satisfied look on his face and a rock hard erection when their wristlets chimed. Instantly, they were both quite sober. Sitting side by side, they reviewed the incoming message.

"They can't do this," Lindsey said, her heart sinking.

"Yeah, they can."

Lindsey's brain already hurt at the thought of all they had to do to prepare for the next raid. Already, packets of information were downloading to her wristlet, along with a new schedule. "This is ridiculous!"

Torran's scowl deepened, the lines between his brows revealing his own tension. "Two fuckin' day's prep for a major excursion."

"And they're doubling the squad." The vein in Lindsey's temple throbbed with stress. "Fuck me."

"That's a good idea. We'll deal with this shit later," Torran said with a nod.

"I didn't mean literally," Lindsey responded, but couldn't help but give him a flirtatious smile.

"Well, if you don't want me to cajole those sweet little noises out of ya, I'll just—" He pretended to move to get off the bed.

Lindsey seized his arm, pulled him back toward her, and kissed Torran while straddling his body. She was so ready for him, and despite the bad news, he was still mightily aroused. His hardness slipped into her with ease. Breaking their kiss, she stared into his eyes, rotating her hips against his. "I'll make sweet noises if you do that growly sound."

"You've got a deal."

With a smile on her lips, she kissed the man she loved with all her heart.

With a loud grunt, Torran fought his way out of a nightmare, not escaping entirely until he swung his legs off the bed and activated the small lamp next to it. Breathing heavily, his pulse pounding, Torran pressed his sweaty palms to his equally sweaty face. It took every ounce of self-control not to bolt to the door to make sure it was secure. His hands felt empty without a weapon and he clenched them into fists. The dream had been vivid, brutally so, and had shaken him to his core. Sweeping his gaze over the room, he anchored himself to reality. He wasn't on the field of battle and was in a safe place. The dreadful images from his dream were starting to recede, but he could remember one very clearly.

It was Lindsey as a Scrag.

Glancing over his shoulder, he saw that she was still asleep. Her fingers were slightly twitching, but she otherwise appeared peaceful. Lindsey tended to kick off all her covers when she slept, and the vision her pale form against the dark blue sheet was comforting. Her golden hair half covered her face and he gently swept it away with one hand. The full pink lips he loved to kiss were slightly parted in her slumber, but her breathing was easy. At least she was having good dreams. She wasn't a Scrag, but alive and well. The strength of her body was evident in her muscled limbs and taut tummy. But he also loved the femininity of the roundness of her hips and slope of her breasts tipped with pink nipples. The scars from her reconstructive surgery had nearly faded into her skin and he touched the largest on her inner thigh. She'd experienced so much pain, yet was so strong. Torran was certain she was the most wonderful woman in the world.

Yet, her beauty was marred by the thing that haunted his dreams: that horrible bruise left by the maw of the Scrag. The mark on her forearm was nearly gone. At least the designers of the suits had been clever enough to add additional protection to the sleeves. Torran knew from old reports that most Scrag bites were inflicted on hands, wrists, and forearms. The natural inclination of any human was to raise their arm in defense when a creature was lunging at them.

The image of her arm caught in the jaws of the Scrag would never leave him. It had taken all his willpower to trust Franklin and Hobbes to save her and not abandon his post to rescue her. Though he'd done the right thing, guilt still lingered. He should be the one to protect her. Lindsey had saved his life. He owed her so much. It should be his duty to make sure she was guarded against all threats.

Of course, it wasn't just the fact she'd saved his life that elicited the need to protect her against all harm. Torran recognized he had fallen for her. It was almost painful how much he'd come to love her. Everything about her was enthralling. From her saucy humor, intelligence, kindness and strength of will, to her beautiful golden hair, sensuous lips and enticing body.

Checking his wristlet, he saw that he only had a few more hours to sleep before they'd return to duty. Though he enjoyed working with her, the reality was that Torran was tired of hiding how he felt about her. If the city wasn't on lockdown, he'd already have taken her to meet his folks. Torran wanted a life with her. Not a shared duty. An actual life.

Lying next to her, he lightly brushed his palm over her bare hip and rested his head against her shoulder. She stirred enough to mold her body against his while angling her head toward him to rest her cheek against his hair. "Everything okay?" she murmured, not really fully awake.

"Yeah. It's good."

"You sure?"

Pressing his lips to her shoulder, he said, "I'm sure. Sleep, Linds."

She didn't answer, and he took that as a sign she'd dropped off again.

Listening to the sound of her deep breathing, Torran agonized over the situation he was trapped in. Though he loved her completely, at oomo point, he was going to betray her trust in him. If the vaccination to ISPV was in Maria Martinez, Torran would move heaven and earth to find her so he'd never have to fear for Lindsey's life again. There were things much worse than worrying for your own life, and that was living in terror of losing the person you loved. Lindsey would never be a Scrag. He'd find Maria to ensure Lindsey's safety. Would Lindsey forgive him? He wasn't sure, but at least she'd be safe.

And if he saved the world along the way, that was something he could live with.

PART 4

THE END GAMES

CHAPTER 23

"This is ridiculous," Lindsey declared.

Commandant Pierce arched an eyebrow, but remained silent as she watched Lindsey stalk back and forth in front of her desk. Lindsey knew she should rein in her temper and show more respect, but it was difficult. She was exhausted, bruised, and mentally worn out.

"Four missions in one week! Four! The sheer amount of intel that we have to collect and then disseminate into a viable plan is staggering. I'm a fuckin' genius, but I'm starting to make mistakes because I'm so fuckin' tired."

"Yet all the missions have been a success with zero loss of life. The commendations you're garnering are impressive, Vanguard Rooney."

"I don't care about them, you know. This is about helping the people. It's not for the higher ups or to decorate my uniform with pretty medals. Frankly, I can barely stand that stupid smile President Cabot gives me whenever I have to attend one of his bogus press conferences."

"Because of your missions, the city is now back at Level Three rationing," Commandant Pierce pointed out. "That's excellent work."

Lindsey stopped pacing, rested her hands on the desk, and leaned toward the commandant. It was so neat compared to her own workstations in the prep room back at the SWD Facility. She used to have neat workspaces, but those days were over for now. "I'm glad the riots are over. I'm glad the city isn't on lockdown anymore, but..."

"But?"

"Do you really think they've given up on finding Maria and Dwayne?"

The commandant shook her head. "No. Of course not."

"Then why aren't they making their move?"

"But aren't they?" Commandant Pierce swiped her desk so that a screen appeared. "According to your report, the remote generators are used on each mission to send out pulses to activate the security grid of each city."

"So that we can use the city scanners to detect the movements of the Scrag swarms..." Lindsey realized she'd missed something vital. The shock of that revelation hit her in a tidal wave that sent her head spinning. With a dazed look on her face, she collapsed onto a chair. "Oh, shit. Of course! How could I miss it? They're looking for them in each city we raid."

"Most likely." Commandant Pierce settled back in her chair.

"I guess I didn't think about what else might be going on for the pulses because it was *my* idea to activate the local security." Feeling ridiculously tired, a bit stupid, and very embarrassed, Lindsey sat in silence. Just because she and Torran were planning the expeditions didn't mean that the SWD wasn't twisting the excursion specs to their advantage. And she hated to think that maybe Torran had a hand in assisting the SWD.

The nearly round-the-clock duty schedule had her on the edge. She wasn't even sure how Torran could stand her sometimes, but usually he just let her rant while agreeing with nods of his head. Then he made her some weird, but delicious meal out of their bars of protein and made her laugh until she forgot why she was so annoyed. The pang in her heart at the thought of him made her situation even more challenging. Were they already on opposing sides?

"They're going to keep us going at this pace until they find them, aren't they?" The thought made Lindsey frustrated to the point of anger. She was tired of the secret games people were playing in which she and Torran were pawns.

"That's probably the plan."

Lindsey clasped her hands in her lap and leaned forward. "Why can't they send out another squad?"

"Resources. We still don't have the fuel depot working at full strength. The mix has to be just right to get the stagnant stores returned to full potency. That's the official word. Unofficial word is that Legatus Martel has convinced the President to keep your squad as the only active one."

"How? I don't get it."

"Legatus Martel has the ear of the president. He likes her quite a lot in spite of my warnings. She's more... accommodating than I am. She tends not to argue as much. Also, she's been very adamant that the one team is sufficient and points to the calmer city population. Each time you return with more food supplies, you validate her viewpoint. The effectiveness of your team actually works against you."

"And he buys into it? You'd think he'd want a bunch of teams out there making him look good."

Commandant Pierce sighed. "It's propaganda, Lindsey. The names and faces of each squad member are known by every civilian in the city. You're heroes. I know you're not allowed to watch the news vids, but you're a celebrity now."

"I really don't like the sound of that," Lindsey grumbled. She had already hacked into the news feed to see how their missions were being depicted. The coverage was what she'd expected. The news vids from the tiltrotors were used to show the heavy infestation in the cities, but never the beauty of the outside world. The president was making sure that all the hopes and dreams of the people were squarely on the survival of The Bastion. She supposed it made sense, but it also made her sad. Hope was important to the human spirit. That was a lesson she was learning as her aspirations for a future with Torran began to solidify. She'd also seen the way the squad was being immortalized, and it made her uneasy to be held up as some iconic figure when she was just a weary soldier doing her job. "Why do they need us to be celebrities?"

"President Cabot is doing his best to ensure his legacy as the savior of The Bastion. That means the propaganda machine is working overtime to create a narrative that favors him. Right now the theme is 'leading against all odds.' So having one specialized team busting their ass to save The Bastion fits that narrative. Limited personnel plus limited resources equals heroes against all odds. Also, Vanguard Rooney, the more people we send out, the more chances there are for failure and death. He's trying to minimize that possibility."

"But we need more food, right? We could haul in so much more with multiple squads running missions."

"Yes, but President Cabot's people assure him that as long as the Level Three rationing stays stable, there won't be any more riots. The supplies you're bringing back will keep the city at Level Three. Plus, the first crops will be harvested in a few months. That may drop us to Level Two." Commandant Pierce cocked her head. "Also, you need to consider that the less people they have going out there, the easier it will be for the SWD to capture Vanguard Martinez and Castellan Reichardt and control that narrative as well."

"Does everything have to be so damn political?" Lindsey huffed, irritably tugging at her braid.

"Sadly, yes."

"I'm a soldier. I'm not cut out for all this intrigue."

"You're doing a fine job, Vanguard Rooney."

"I missed what they might possibly be doing with the pulses," she groused.

"Well, the suspected SWD purpose for the pulses is disguised as a legitimate facet of a well-planned excursion. Honestly, I'm just guessing that's what they're doing. Only you can discern if they're actually looking for them using the pulses."

"Which I will," Lindsey said darkly. She was already planning to study the pulses and take another look at their excursions for any hidden patterns.

"I can see that exhaustion is coming into play. I'll request very strongly that the squad have two days off. I'll make the suggestion to the president in a way that will appeal to him. Like he's showing fatherly compassion or something of the sort."

"We could use two days after today's mission. This one is a big challenge. The Notre Dame Food Depot is massive. We're taking six transports. Luckily, it's well fortified. In fact, all the excursions since the first one have been to food depots that have much better security. Which brings me to this... why all the food depots? If our founders knew they were moving to The Bastion, why not move the food here?"

"The Bastion was supposed to be self-sufficient, remember? Also..." Commandant Pierce hesitated. "Well, Lindsey, there was always the hope we would be going back to claim the world. And part of the plan was to provide resources for the new pioneers."

A cold finger of dread slid down her spine. "So us raiding those resources is us giving up on that hope, isn't it?"

Commandant Pierce looked down at her desktop and the screen glowing there. "Yes, to some degree. We need to concentrate on saving ourselves right now. Returning to the outside world is something that just doesn't seem viable."

Lindsey wondered if it would *ever* be viable.

"I think we're done here," the commandant said finally.

Standing, Lindsey saluted and started for the door.

"Vanguard Rooney, be a little more diligent in the future missions. A little more... inquisitive. And don't trust anyone," Commandant Pierce's voice said, the granite in the words a little frightening. "Even bedfellows."

Lindsey almost turned around, but thought better of it. It seemed Petra was keeping an eye on Lindsey and Torran for the commandant. "Yes, sir."

She left the office and the doors shut behind her.

Petra swiveled about in her chair, her pad in one hand. It was if she were waiting for Lindsey to say something. Anger pricking at her determination to be civil, Lindsey pulled a protein bar from her pocket and set it on the desk.

"For your kids."

"Thank you, Lindsey."

Setting one hand on Petra's desk, Lindsey bent toward her. "Stay out of my private life."

Petra met Lindsey's stare with a calm expression. "Even though your worm has been very good at eradicating all traces of you and Torran in the city security feeds, people have eyes. They see things. Such as you entering his flat and him joining you in your dorm room. And people talk, Lindsey. I know you're completely enmeshed in your tech, but the tech is not always going to protect you."

"How far has the word gone?" Though she hated that Petra knew about her private affairs, she was even angrier at herself for letting down her guard. Now she'd have to sleep alone and only see Torran while they were working.

"I've been keeping a watch on correspondence and nothing official has popped up. So far, it is only idle gossip among a small group. So I would suggest discretion." Petra did appear to actually sympathize with Lindsey's predicament. Her long fingers gently lay over Lindsey's. "You're needed out there. Don't give them a reason to pull you."

With a curt nod, Lindsey straightened, drawing her hand away. "Right."

"And thank you for the protein bar. It's appreciated. I know things will be better soon thanks to what you're doing."

Lindsey just nodded again and made her escape. The twisting knots in her stomach and rapidly building headache were not going to make her day any easier. She was due at the SWD Facility within the hour.

The bustle of people around her in Constabulary charcoal gray was a welcome departure from the black and white uniforms of the SWD. The Constabulary halls were filled with chatter, a rather different atmosphere than the quiet sterility of the SWD hallways. She missed her old stomping ground and wondered when she'd return to it.

"Good job out there," someone said in passing.

"Thanks," Lindsey answered, then ducked into a lift.

Thankfully, she was alone.

Pressing her hands to her queasy stomach, she stared up at the numbers flashing on the screen over the door. The walk back to the SWD Facility would do her some good. The time would let her get her head together and calm her nerves. Her insides were a gnarl of knots.

When she reached the front gates, she was startled to see a pod car sitting near the curb. Ground vehicles were rarely seen on the streets of The Bastion and were mostly used by high government officials. The highly polished white exterior and the curved black windows reminded her of a bug. The door popped open and slid up to reveal Dr. Curran.

"Vanguard Rooney, would you care for a ride?" the blond woman asked.

"I was planning on walking," Lindsey answered, unnerved by the woman's presence

The Constabulary gates shut behind her with a clang.

"You are returning to the SWD Facility, aren't you?" Dr. Curran's fingers tapped on the steering wheel.

"Yes."

A surprising needle of fear pierced through Lindsey. Dr. Curran was the mad genius who had helped save The Bastion with her modification of the ISPV, but she'd also helped doom Maria to exile. Lindsey's heart ached for her best friend, but her reluctance to get into the vehicle wasn't founded in her anger at the doctor, but dread of what the woman might do in the future.

"I insist that you get in. After all, you're a hero of The Bastion." Dr. Curran smiled, yet her eyes remained aloof. "You shouldn't be walking through the streets."

The scientist did have a point. The SWD did have a fleet of small tiltrotors used to ferry officials about, but she'd declined the ride, wanting to enjoy the walk. Lindsey had almost been late to her meeting with the commandant due to being stopped by several citizens during her trek at sunrise. They'd just wanted to thank her personally. It was now later in the morning, and the streets were packed.

"Were you sent?" Lindsey asked.

"I just happened to be in the area."

Already, people were pointing at her and talking excitedly amongst themselves. With a sigh, Lindsey relented, scooted around the rear of the vehicle, ducked under the door the doctor opened for her, and settled into the passenger seat. The security harness lowered over her body and tightened just as both doors thumped shut. With a barely audible whine, the small vehicle lurched forward. Pedestrians scurried out of the way, which was a good thing, for it was obvious Dr. Curran expected people to yield to the vehicle. Lindsey fought the urge to grip the dashboard as the pod car careened through the streets and instead balled her hands in her lap.

"You look as tired as I feel," Dr. Curran stated briskly in an attempt to start a conversation.

"It's been a tough couple of weeks."

Lindsey glanced out the window at the people rushing to avoid being struck by the pod car. To her amusement, she noted their eyes peering at the tinted windows in an attempt to see which high level official was inside. It was so odd to be in a ground vehicle. She'd never been in one before.

"Well, after that first mission, things got a bit easier, didn't they? The squad expanded in number, more aircraft were assigned, more drones... everything improved. Even those damn stealth suits."

"Yeah, much better than those initial suits." The SWD Sci-Tech team had abandoned the stealth suits they'd designed and instead upgraded the SWD armor. It was sleek, easy to move in, and had actual helmets. They'd covered the armor with the stealth material and had refined the covering on the weapons.

There was a long, rather drawn out silence between them. Lindsey thought about starting some small talk but opted against it and focused on the city streets. The people did seem happier. There were smiles and laughter. It was a good feeling to know she was a part of the change.

"Did you ever wonder why we went to Beta City first?" Dr. Curran asked abruptly.

"The higher ups ordered it, so I guess they had their reason," Lindsey replied.

Dr. Curran turned onto the road leading to the SWD Facility. "Did you ask Chief Defender Solomon?"

"No. Not really. She did say something about not having a choice."

"Really?"

The pod car swerved through the entrance of the SWD Facility. The sensors immediately scanned the car and the gates opened once Dr. Curran and Lindsey were identified as having clearance.

"What are you getting at?" Lindsey asked pointedly. The doctor was definitely giving off a very disquieting vibe.

Dr. Curran remained silent for an unnerving couple of seconds, then said, "The chief defender chose the first objective." Pulling into a parking area, Dr. Curran let the words sink in.

"I don't understand," Lindsey stuttered. "Why would she lie?"

Lindsey and Torran had both regarded Beta City as a bad choice for a mission. Solomon had appeared to agree with them. If she'd chosen Beta City, why hadn't she told them? Furthermore, why would she even want to go to Beta City?

Parking the pod car, Dr. Curran's usual stoic expression melted into a more pensive one. "That's what you should ask yourself and then find an answer. You're a very clever young woman. I've noticed that. You should have been SWD, you know. Not Constabulary. Your gifts are wasted. To have your mind on my team..."

"I am on your team, aren't I?" Lindsey's words were clipped. After the warning from both Commandant Pierce and Petra, she was feeling very on edge and defensive.

Dr. Curran settled back in her chair and stared at the black granite wall that encircled the SWD Facility. Finally, she broke her silence. "Those who follow blindly will be blind when danger comes." With that comment, she opened the doors and slid out.

Lindsey immediately scrambled out of the car and rushed around to confront the scientist. "What do you mean? What's going on? What do you *know?*"

Dr. Curran smirked. "That's the thing, Lindsey. I *don't* know what is going on. I'm much in the dark as you are about certain aspects of our mission. At one point, I was foolish enough to believe that at last my eyes were open to all the dark secrets of The Bastion, but now I suspect I am as blind as those poor souls rushing about in the city."

Lindsey gave the woman a dubious look. Wasn't Dr. Curran part of the grand conspiracy? "So what you're saying is that you don't trust the chief defender."

"Ah, Vanguard Rooney. I don't trust anyone."

"But you're talking to me."

"Only because I believe you're clever enough to sort out what is going on and perhaps enlighten *me.*"

That remark definitely made Lindsey uncomfortable. How many people knew about her secret abilities? Perhaps they weren't as secret as she had presumed. It seemed best to not address the hidden meaning laced within the scientist's words. "I have no reason to even like you. Especially after what you did to my best friend."

"I liked Maria," Dr. Curran snapped. "I liked her quite a lot. I did what I felt was best. I erred in some ways, but I had the best of intentions."

The women glared at each other, and Lindsey had the desire to unleash all her frustrations on the scientist, but refrained. It wouldn't benefit her to make Dr. Curran her enemy, especially if things were not quite as they seemed with the chief defender.

"I know Maria volunteered, but you had no right to lie to her. You told her there was a cure."

"The mission was rushed. I wasn't given the time to find a cure."

"But you lied to her, and that wasn't right."

"I understand that, but we had no choice. *I* had no choice. I wasn't pleased with the mission being hurried. I wanted to cure those soldiers. I didn't want them to die. I gave Maria a different virus because I hoped it would return her to life and provide a cure. I actually liked her quite a lot. Her strength of will, character, and athleticism exemplify the best of humanity."

Lindsey bristled a bit. The scientist described her friend like she was a specimen. Yet, she wasn't about to argue that point. Because of the scientist, Maria wasn't safely inside The Bastion but somewhere out in the dead world and the focus of a manhunt.

"The one thing you need to recognize, Vanguard Rooney, is that nothing and no one is what they seem in this city."

With that parting comment, the scientist briskly walked away.

Lindsey considered following, but thought better of it. The ride back to the SWD Facility had bought her a little time before the excursion to the Notre Dame Depot. Her nerves a tangled mess, she hurried along the walkway toward the building that housed the squad's headquarters. The crisp wind tore at her hair, and she fussed with it. At times, she wanted to cut it, but then she remembered her father gently brushing her hair and dismissed the impulse. In a strange way, her long locks were a memorial to him.

Hobbes unexpectedly joined her trek just as she neared the building. "Vanguard Rooney," he said, and the words sounded teasing.

"Hobbes," she said, eyeing him warily.

"So after today's big haul, would you be up for drinks?" Hobbes cocked his head to look down at her, his eyes twinkling with mischief.

"Are you asking me on a date?"

"Well, if the answer is yes, I am. If not, it's totally a group thing. All the squad getting together to celebrate. Master Seeker MacDonald already agreed to go."

"Did he?" Again, Lindsey wondered how much people knew about her affair with Torran.

"So..."

"I will join the squad for a drink," she answered, ignoring the proposed date and the possible poke at her romantic relationship.

"Excellent!"

Hobbes didn't seem disappointed in the decline of a date, but he also never lacked for bedmates. At one time, Lindsey may have considered a little tryst with him, but his dashing good looks and muscled physique didn't appeal to her like they once had. Her heart definitely lay with Torran, and that thought both thrilled and terrified her.

When they entered the building, Lindsey saw that several squad members were already milling about as the hour of their departure drew near. She excused herself and headed for the prep room. Maybe she could find a quiet place to get her thoughts in order and do a bit of snooping. When the doors opened, she found Torran leaning over the console, already at work with a frown on his face. Glancing up, he killed the screen he'd been studying and swiveled about to face her. Again, he had an inscrutable look.

Instantly, Lindsey's heart beat a little faster. What had he been looking at? She was about to open her mouth and ask what he'd been up to when the doors opened behind her.

"We need to leave now," Chief Defender Solomon announced. She was already in her gear. "An unexpected snow storm is in route."

With that proclamation, Solomon retreated into the hallway.

Lindsey took a deep breath, and started to follow.

Torran fell in behind her.

Just as she slipped through the doorway, he lightly brushed his fingers over hers.

Looking up at him, she saw the deep concern in his eyes.

But concern about what?

CHAPTER 24

Torran was not in the best of moods.

He'd been peeved when Lindsey had been summoned to see Commandant Pierce just a few minutes after they'd awakened. He wanted to spend a few more hours alone with her before they had to report for duty. Every time they successfully returned from an excursion, he wanted nothing more than to never revisit to the dead world. Though the squad success rate was one hundred percent and there had been zero loss of life, Torran knew that every time they ventured out the chances of something dire befalling the squad amplified.

As Lindsey had dressed for her meeting, he sat on the bed watching her with a heavy feeling inside. She appeared oblivious to his growing anxiety over her safety, or maybe he was just very good at hiding it. When she finally pressed a kiss to his lips, he held onto her, drinking in the sensation of her in his arms. Chances were they wouldn't be able to share a quiet moment before deployment, so he relished their embrace. With a contented sigh, she snuggled against him and ran her fingers through his hair.

Their last kiss was long, deep, and smoldering.

It took all his willpower to let her out of his arms.

Then she was gone, and he was alone.

His bed, flat, and heart always felt much emptier when she wasn't around.

Sitting in the gloomy room, it was easy to start to dwell on all the possible terrible scenarios that could develop during their excursion to the Notre Dame Depot, so he forced himself out of bed. A shower and breakfast helped him feel a little more stable, but he couldn't shake the anxious haze encompassing him.

After dressing for the day, he decided to check over the excursion specs one more time. Leaving his flat, he trekked across the quad. The heaviness inside his chest was not alleviating, but growing. Something was wrong, and he feared he had missed something important in all the intel he'd been assimilating for the excursion.

Torran was almost to his destination when his wristlet had chimed. Fortis Prime Trevino was calling a meeting, so he redirected his path toward the main building. The buzzing sensation in his nerve endings increased with each step. He wanted to believe it was just his anxiousness over the coming excursion, but the analytical part of his brain whispered that all was not well.

When Torran entered the designated conference room, he was surprised to find himself alone with Fortis Prime Trevino. The man wasn't seated, but watching the staging area several floors below, where the aircraft were being prepped for departure.

"Master Seeker MacDonald, thank you for joining me," Trevino said in greeting, though he didn't remove his gaze from the scene on the ground.

"How can I be of service, sir?" Torran clutched his hat in his hands and waited for the officer to either motion him to sit or join him.

"As you know, we've been searching for the missing vanguard and castellan. The pulses during the squad's excursions have failed to detect living humans."

Since Torran had never been notified by anyone that the pulses had been used for such a search, he remained quiet. Apparently, someone was keeping him in the dark. He'd wondered a few times when the SWD would be called upon to recover Maria Martinez and Dwayne Reichardt, but had maintained his silence according to his directives. Though a part of him had been anxiously awaiting the order to retrieve the couple, he'd also dreaded the moment. He hoped Lindsey would understand that he had to obey his orders. It would be more difficult to explain that he supported their apprehension for the sake of keeping her safe.

Trevino finally looked Torran's way. "The deserters couldn't have gone too far."

"Unless they repaired a vehicle of some type," Torran suggested.

"Yes, but then they'd have to find a way to restore the fuel they'd need to fly or drive such a vehicle. That would take time."

Trevino walked to the table and tapped the surface. A hologram appeared. It was a map of the area around The Bastion. It extended outward and covered the areas where the squad had retrieved food. Torran could now easily see the search pattern. The pulses probably should have turned up the couple by now if they were in the area. Fear strangled him for a few seconds, and he swallowed hard.

"I see your concern, sir." Torran cleared his throat. "If they're alive, they should have shown up on the scans. Do you think they're dead? Or possibly turned into Abscrags?"

"Perhaps. Or there could be sabotage." Trevino transferred his gaze from the holographic map to Torran. "Do you think that is a possibility?"

It bothered Torran that he instantly thought of Lindsey. She was incredibly intelligent and very capable of thwarting the SWD. Again, the thought of being on opposite ends with Lindsey made him very uncomfortable.

"It is a possibility," he replied at last. "But then the Constabulary would have to have uncovered our plans."

"Which is conceivable. They spy on us as much as we spy on them. I have a specialist sorting through the mission records trying to determine if there is sabotage occurring and who's behind it. Do you have any thoughts on who it might be? It might accelerate the process." Pivoting toward Torran, arms crossed over his broad chest, Trevino stared at the Scotsman with an unreadable look.

Torran pressed his lips together and quickly sifted through his thoughts. Finally, he said, "There are a few possibilities. Chief Defender Solomon comes immediately to mind."

"She's on my list, too."

Setting his fingertips on the edge of the table, Torran hated the next words out of his mouth. "Of course, Vanguard Rooney."

"She's at the *very* top of my list. We're already launching an investigation. It's not easy to find any details about her outside of her service record. Which makes me very suspicious."

Torran wondered if maybe there were undercurrents to the conversation. Had perhaps someone seen him and Lindsey together? Maybe they'd become too lax in their interactions with one another. He had to wonder if he was under suspicion and the entire conversation was actually about his loyalty.

Trying very hard to remain calm, he said, "You might as well put the entire Constabulary squad on your list at this point. They'll try to protect their own. Hell, I guess I should be on the list as well, since I once served as a vanguard."

Trevino inclined his head, but Torran couldn't decipher what the gesture meant. "The Notre Dame Depot excursion is one of the most important yet. We strongly suspect the fugitives might be in the city. Calculations indicate this would probably be the furthest they'd be able to travel with their limited resources."

"I will keep my eyes open for any irregularities."

"Excellent. We're depending on you, Master Seeker MacDonald."

Once he was excused, Torran dashed across the quad to the squad's headquarters. Lindsey would be returning soon, and he hoped to speak to her in private. If she was being investigated, it was only a matter of time before their affair would be uncovered. Most likely, Lindsey would be removed from the squad, and though Torran would be happy to have her out of danger, she'd resent the transfer. He hated the idea of any friction happening between them. Yet, he couldn't tell her about the search for her best friend, even though there was a distinct possibility she already knew. And it wasn't beyond reason to suspect she was working against the SWD discovering Maria.

Though he wasn't a violent man by nature, Torran felt like punching something very, very hard.

Instead, he hurried into the prep room and pulled up the mission records on one of the consoles. Though he was not the mad genius Lindsey was when it came to computers, he was more than competent. Swiftly writing a program to search for specific clues, he frowned as he worked. Lindsey was very good at covering her tracks, which would make his search very hard if she was the one behind the sabotage. Yet, things could be missed. He opted not to pay attention to the feed from the aerial drones or remote generators, but the squad's suits.

Torran was deep into his review when the door opened, and it took him a second to register the arrival of another person. Swiftly closing his program, he looked up to see Lindsey standing in the doorway. It seemed to be the day for indecipherable looks on people's faces. He couldn't tell if she was angry, sad, agitated or afraid. Or maybe she was all of those things at once. She started to speak, but the doors opened again.

"We need to leave now." Chief Defender Solomon was already in her armor and held a tablet in one hand. "An unexpected snow storm is in route."

Not even giving them a chance to respond, the commanding officer swiveled about and hurried down the hallway.

Without a word, Lindsey followed and Torran hurried to catch up. His fingers grazed hers and she looked up at him. It staggered him to realize that an unexpected distance had popped up between them just since their parting kiss in the morning. The woman he loved looked wounded, unsettled, and unsure. He suspected he may have somehow lost her faith in him, and the thought left him adrift in a cold void. Words failed him and he stared at her in silence.

"We need to go," she said finally.

"Lindsey," he said in a voice so soft those down the hallway couldn't have heard him.

"We'll talk later," she replied, and then walked swiftly after the chief defender.

Deeply bothered, Torran trailed after her, his stomach a heavy knot in his belly and his nerves buzzing with dread.

CHAPTER 25

The massive transports lifted off from the Notre Dame Food Depot, and the down draft buffeted Lindsey, nearly blowing her over. To keep her balance, she stood with her feet planted apart while watching the feed from the various monitoring sources. The stadium size depot had a retractable ceiling that permitted the transports to land and lift off from directly inside the main building. It made loading the freight pallets much easier and faster. The landing pad and docking area were large enough that they'd been able to fill all the transports at once. All the containers from the storage units had been viable and were now loaded on the cargo transports.

It was a huge victory.

"Time to go, people!" Lindsey shouted over the roar of the engines of the aircraft.

The squad in their sleek armor rushed past her and up the ramps into the two waiting tiltrotors. Torran stood near the one he was assigned to while also supervising the withdrawal. Though she was doggedly concentrating on her duties, she couldn't help but steal an occasional look his way. There was so much they had to discuss, but she wondered when they'd be able to have a personal conversation. The world was ominous enough. Why did she have to lose the one thing that brought her any measure of peace?

But then again, maybe peace wasn't a normal part of the human experience.

During the extraction, Lindsey had spotted a few signs of attempted sabotage. This time, the Gaia Cult had left its calling card with a spray painted message, but it had faded over time and was unreadable. After careful examination, she ascertained the depot security had thwarted the ecowarriors. There were some signs of a battle fought at close proximity and long-dead bodies littered one area of the vast depot. There were Scrags in the building, but their number hadn't been sufficient to cause any great threat to the squad. The few present had been easily dispatched. Since none of the doors or walls had been breached upon their arrival, she suspected the Gaia Cult had been behind the contamination.

Overhead, the massive cargo transports roared away.

Another successful mission with no loss of life.

The aerial drones continued to circle the food depot, scanning the wall that encircled the facility. The perimeter was already being overrun in one area by a massive crush of Scrags. A horde was rushing toward the depot, but they weren't a true threat, since they wouldn't be able to access the interior. The squad would be long gone by the time the Scrags managed to find a way inside, though she doubted they would. The depot would have made a secure safe haven for a small group of people, since it was so well fortified. But considering the attempts of the Gaia Cult to destroy humanity, it was probably a good thing that when the city had fallen, all the survivors had been airlifted to The Bastion.

"Another breach has occurred at the south wall," Torran's voice said crisply.

Lindsey watched the feed and shivered. It was terrifying how unrelenting the Scrags were once they had prey in sight. The transports and tiltrotors had likely stirred up the entire undead populace of the city.

"We're done here. Leave it to the Scrags," the chief defender instructed.

Lindsey swore there was a smile in the commanding officer's voice.

Following her squad into her designated tiltrotor, Lindsey glanced toward the other one. Torran was just ascending the ramp and she saw his helmet swivel toward her. After a brief wave, he disappeared inside as the tiltrotor started its ascent.

Lindsey sighed and ducked into her own tiltrotor as the ramp retracted. The squad was already in their seats, the harnesses descending to snap into place. Hastening up the aisle, she saw Franklin and Hobbes give her the thumps up. When the squad had been split between the two tiltrotors, she'd been relieved that Dr. Curran and the Sci-techs were with the chief defender. Sadly, so was Torran, and she wished he was with her instead of in the other aircraft. At least then she'd have the comfort of his presence even though things were oddly strained between them.

Throughout their mission, Torran had been a tad brusque in his interaction with her. In retrospect, she had left them in an awkward pause. She'd been flustered by how quickly he had turned off the console in the prep room. Even though she told herself she wouldn't snoop when they returned, she knew she would. She had to know what he was hiding. The added stress of knowing she couldn't spend time with him anymore outside of their duty only made the situation more worrisome.

"Prepare for departure," Scoggins said through the comm.

The harness to Lindsey's chair descended and tightened around her. Leaving her console dark, she concentrated instead on the helmet feed. The return journey to The Bastion was always uneventful, but she liked watching the images from the aerial drones and tiltrotor cameras. Most of the terrain was absolutely breathtakingly beautiful even as winter started to set in and the greenery faded beneath of cloak of white. The flight plans attempted to avoid old towns and cities, but once in a while, she'd spot the remains of the old world. Everything about the older human enclaves was so different from The Bastion. Even the city they were in now was very different from their home.

To protect the lower, ancient city, the upper city had been built on enormous platforms supported by pylons sunk deep into the earth. Crisscrossing roadways, walkways, and monorail tracks created an almost beautiful web between the elevated cityscape. Their flight path took them beneath the lattice of metal and concrete. The engineers of the city had created passages for aircraft underneath the upper city.

As the tiltrotor rose out of the food depot, Scoggins followed the flight path of the other departing aircraft. Watching the feed from the cameras under the cockpit, Lindsey was relieved when Torran's tiltrotor cleared the passage and turned over the river that wound through the city. Her tiltrotor was just a few seconds behind, and the harness caught her body firmly as the craft banked to the right.

A deafening explosion was followed by the tiltrotor bucking wildly. Flung to one side, the straps keeping her secure bit hard into Lindsey's armor and the pressure shoved the air out of her lungs. The interior lights flickered on and off, then went dark. The emergency klaxon sang through the gloom.

"Report," she gasped. "Scoggins! Report!"

"...right rotor... engine..." The pilot's voice was garbled.

Another boom sent the tiltrotor into a terrifying spin. The centrifugal force drove Lindsey against the seat as the feed on her helmet flashed wildly. One image, sent from an aerial drone following the tiltrotor, revealed that the cockpit was severely damaged and fire spreading along the right side of the aircraft. Straining to hit her wristlet, Lindsey saw the terrified faces of the squad around her illuminated by the lights in their helmets. Across from her, Hobbes and Franklin clasped hands.

The autopilot flipped on and attempted to pull the tiltrotor out of the sickening downward spiral. Lindsey was tossed forward as an auxiliary engine sputtered to life. Relief flooded her as the tiltrotor stopped its wild rotation and attempted to straighten as the autopilot regained control. Shaking fingers pulling at the release on her harness, Lindsey's mind was already a whirlwind of plans on how she could take over the pilot controls and get them to safety.

The harness release didn't budge.

Again, she pulled at it, desperate to get to the cockpit.

A second later, she realized it was too late when the feeds from the tiltrotor's exterior cameras refreshed on her helmet screen.

The aircraft slammed into the river.

The chief defender's tiltrotor circled the struggling aircraft at a safe distance. Torran watched his feed and listened to the pilot attempting to reach Scoggins. The chief defender's voice didn't even register in his mind as he watched the tiltrotor ferrying Lindsey spinning wildly out of control.

"...emergency protocols should activate..." someone was shouting, then Torran realized it was Dr. Curran.

To his relief, the auxiliary engine extended out of the side of the ailing craft and flared to life. His heart in his throat, he watched the other tiltrotor manage to break its spin, but then a hush fell over the comm as it dropped like a stone into the river below. The aerial drones whipped around the crash as the tiltrotor listed to one side, obviously taking on water, then swiftly started to vanish beneath the dark waves.

"We have to rescue them," Torran shouted. He'd hit the release on his harness and was on his feet before he even realized it.

"We can't rescue them," the chief defender replied, her face and voice tense.

"There are twenty people down there. Our people!"

"The Scrags are already rushing to the crash site. I will not risk this squad..."

The rest of her words became white noise. Torran stared at his commanding officer shouting at him and made his choice. Tearing off his helmet, he ran to the back of the tiltrotor.

"MacDonald!"

Popping the emergency hatch, he saw the dark water of the river below, but knew he had scant seconds before the aircraft would be over the dead city again. Clutching his helmet in one hand while securing his weapon to his armor, he dropped out of the tiltrotor. The wind tore at him as he plunged. He straightened his body, aiming to land feet first, and let go of his helmet. Pulling his arms in tight to his body, he exhaled as the dark river rushed up.

When he struck the water, the impact was jarring, but not painful. Thankfully, the river was deep enough that he didn't hit the bottom. The coldness of the water stunned him for a brief second, then he kicked toward the surface, his helmet bobbing on the ripples left from his dive was his target. When he broke through to the air, he grabbed it firmly with one hand while dragging moist air into his lungs.

Flipping onto his back, Torran floated while reattaching his helmet. The feed immediately started to reboot once it was connected to his armor. The sound of the departing tiltrotor faded into the distance and the impact of his decision sent tremors of fear through him. One look toward the wing of the crashed tiltrotor sticking out of the murky water was enough to spur him into action and ignore the fright blooming in his mind. His weapon bumped against his chest as he swam. The armor's internal regulators switched on and started to warm him. Teeth still chattering, he swam as fast as he could manage.

"...we're almost out of range..." the chief defender's voice said, bursting through the speakers in his helmet as the comm rebooted. "...you're on your own until..."

Torran was fairly certain a rescue team wouldn't be in route until after the convoy had returned to The Bastion. He didn't even attempt to answer. All of his energy was exerted in using his arms and legs to cut through the water. Lindsey needed him and he would not let her down.

When he reached the aircraft it was nearly completely submerged. He was forced to dive and pull himself along the hull toward the ruined cockpit. The severe damage made it easy for him to slip through the ruined canopy and swim inside. One look toward Scoggins revealed she was dead. Swimming past her, he pulled himself through the dark interior. Only the lights from his helmet illuminated his way. Loud metallic groans sent vibrations through the water and the entire craft shuddered. There was a sickening sound of rending metal and Torran grabbed onto a handhold just as the back of the tiltrotor separated from the front.

"Internal suit oxygen is about to expire," his armor announced in a cold, emotionless voice.

"Yeah, yeah," he muttered.

Once the tiltrotor settled again, he swam through the large gap between the broken pieces of the wreckage and pulled himself into the rear of the craft.

"Warning. You have only thirty seconds of oxygen remaining."

Torran had to shove some broken equipment and debris out of his way, but he managed to enter the passenger area. Immediately, he saw it was listing hard to one side, and there was a dwindling air pocket above him. Kicking upward, he broke the surface and tried to orient himself.

The closest squad member to him was clearly dead. Debris had impaled him. The second was also dead. A good portion of a console had imbedded itself in her head. Pulling himself toward the section still elevated above the water, Torran observed that most of the squad was beneath the surface. The harnesses had not released and they were still strapped down. A few were thrashing, attempting to get free. Torran reached up and grabbed one of the manual releases and tugged on it. The handle would not budge. Pulling harder, he grunted with the strain. It didn't relent. Tugging his weapon above the water, he flipped on the light. It illuminated the release and Torran swore.

It appeared to be welded in the locked position.

Again the tiltrotor moaned as it sank deeper into the river. The water rose several inches and Torran pressed his lips tightly together. The struggling soldiers beneath the waves were weakening.

"Shit!" he swore.

"Torran?"

"Linds!"

Immediately, he started pulling himself toward the sound of her voice. Other soldiers reached for him, realizing he was there to rescue them. Only a few heads were above the water line. Lindsey was in her seat, but it had been dislodged from the floor and listed against the wall.

"You need to help her," another voice said.

It was Franklin. She was sawing away at her harness with a knife that was definitely not regulation. She was nearly free. Next to her Hobbes was unconscious and sinking into the water.

"Save who you can when you're free, Franklin," Torran ordered, then swam past her to Lindsey.

Tangled in wiring and pinned by her seat, Lindsey's fingers were tugging at the harness release. "Torran, what are you doing here?" Her voice sounded strained and tiny through the exterior speaker of her helmet.

"Came for you," he answered. Replacing her hands with his own, he attempted to unlock the straps holding her captive.

"Save the others," she said. "They're dying. Drowning. I can hear them through the comm."

"Linds, I can't save them. The emergency release on the harnesses was tampered with. Franklin will cut them loose as soon as she's free."

In the pale illumination of Lindsey's helmet, Torran saw tears glistening on her cheeks and flecking her eyelashes. The sight broke his already battered heart. It also compelled him to hurry. He needed to save her, then as many of the others as he could. Time was running out for all of them.

A loud splash and a gasp sounded behind him. Glancing over his shoulder, he saw Franklin struggling with Hobbes. Only four others now barely had their heads above water. In the darkness he couldn't make out their faces, which he was somewhat grateful for.

"Why won't it unlock?" Lindsey's voice was ragged with fear.

Torran had to push her hands away so he could see the mechanism. It was difficult with the water already climbing over her shoulders. "Hell if I know. I'll get you lose. Don't worry."

"Save the others," she said again.

Torran stared straight into her eyes and said, "No." Maybe she didn't understand, but if she died, he wasn't too sure how he'd muster the will to fight his way to safety. She was everything good in his life, and though he'd never considered himself to be overly romantic, the thought of her not existing in his world was soul-crushing.

The tiltrotor let out a terrifying sound as it started to slowly topple over. Torran covered Lindsey's body with his own to protect her from the panels crashing down around them. The air pocket shifted away from the squad as the back end of the tiltrotor settled onto the bottom of the river. Finding himself under water, Torran feverishly attempted to pull the straps free of the chair. Dim lights drifted close to him and he realized it was from Franklin's helmet. Extending her hand, he saw the outline of her knife and he snatched it from her grip.

"Warning. Oxygen levels—"

"Yeah, yeah," he grunted at the suit.

Through the murky, oily water, he could see Lindsey's big eyes watching him slice at the straps. How long she had before her oxygen ran low he wasn't certain. Her expression was eerily calm and she rested her hand against his shoulder as he worked.

"I got about thirty seconds of oxygen left," Franklin's voice said through the exterior speaker of her suit.

"I almost got her free. Grab any weapon you can and head toward the flight deck. The ship is in half. You can get out that way," Torran ordered.

Franklin's body disappeared into the darkness.

"Torran," Lindsey whispered.

"Don't talk. Save your oxygen." He was almost out of air.

"Did you really come back for me? Alone?"

"Yes." His words were clipped. He was almost through another strap. Just one more across her waist and she'd be free. The muscles in his arm were burning, but he didn't care.

"You're amazing, you know," she said, gasping for breath.

"Stop talking," he commanded.

"Warning. You are now out of oxygen," his suit informed him.

The last strap was digging into her armor, so Torran adjusted his stance and sawed at the section connecting to the chair. Holding his breath, he fought against the oncoming dizziness and ignored the black flecks in his eyesight.

"Give me the knife. I'll finish. Get out," she rasped. "I've got thirty seconds."

Shaking his head, he kept up his assault. There was no way he'd leave her. Even as his vision started to tunnel, he hacked at the strap until it came loose. Lindsey tumbled into his arms, sending them both careening into the silent, swaying bodies still harnessed to their seats. Lungs burning and unconsciousness looming, Torran fought to extricate himself from the tangle of limbs, weapons, and debris.

Lindsey tugged on his arm and jerked him free. Grabbing onto anything that was sturdy, including their dead squad members, she dragged them both through the water to the small air pocket looming above them. The second Torran's helmet broke the surface, the air filters gobbled up the oxygen.

"Franklin, this is Rooney," Lindsey said over the open comm. "I'm free. We're about to come out. What's the status?"

There was a small pause, then Franklin's voice said, "You need to get out here fast. They haven't spotted me yet, but there are several herds of Scrags rushing up and down the banks. They saw us go down."

"On our way," Lindsey answered.

It took every ounce of willpower for Torran not to pull off their helmets so he could kiss her. Despite the blue tinge around her eyes and lips, she was beautiful. He'd never regret coming back for her. Never.

"Ready?" she asked.

"No, but let's go." Torran took her hand and together they sank beneath the waves.

CHAPTER 26

The banks of the river were lined with wide, overgrown boulevards filled with crashed ground vehicles covered in vines and rubble. Crumbling shops and multi-storied houses loomed over the hulking wrecks. The architectural style indicated that the buildings were hundreds of years old, maybe even a thousand. At one point, the structures had probably been quite lovely, but the elements and time had taken their toll. Broken windows and crumbling facades stole the last of their elegant beauty.

Lindsey glanced down into the dark waters, unnerved that she couldn't see what lay beneath. Most likely, the riverbed was home to debris, long dead bodies, and submerged vehicles. Hopefully, nothing moved through the water except fish. She didn't even want to think about Scrags lurking beneath her feet.

Floating behind the tip of the tiltrotor wing that was poking out of the water, Lindsey had a firm grip on the edge to maintain her position. The screeching of the Scrags hunting nearby continually sent shivers of fear through her body and sliced through her brain like a razor. She was muddled by the crash, her earlier headache flaring into something akin to a low-grade migraine. Already, she'd had her suit administer painkillers to dull the worst of the discomfort.

Torran pressed against her back, his arm about her waist to keep himself close. His presence helped steady her nerves. She could feel his protectiveness in the grip he had about her waist. Even if their superiors had set them against each other, they were now unified in their quest to survive. That he had risked his life to save her was so immeasurably touching, it rocked her to the core of her soul. There was no doubt that he loved her, and she knew she loved him. Yet, neither one of them had said the actual words yet. Maybe the words didn't need to be said when they were willing to lay down their lives for one another. If not for his bravery, there was a solid possibility she wouldn't have survived the crash. And if she had made it out of the wreckage, it would've been just her and Franklin against a city filled with Scrags. Though she trusted Franklin's abilities, Torran being at her side was reassuring. They'd already faced death together before and lived. Therefore, Torran's presence made her feel like the odds of their survival had increased drastically.

Nearby, Franklin was sprawled along the top of a piece of the cockpit floating on the waves. With her stealth suit activated, she was invisible to the Scrags rampaging along the banks while she examined the area with the binoculars she'd managed to rescue from the crashed aircraft. The bulky pack on Franklin's back was filled with weapons she'd confiscated from the wreck, and it too was invisible. Despite the stealth, Lindsey could make out the somewhat unsteady outline of the soldier if she stared hard enough.

Franklin opened the comm line. "Vanguard, we can't get out of the water here. We're surrounded by several large herds of Scrags. Further up the river is a stairwell tube to the upper city. I'm not seeing any activity up there."

"Then that's where we'll head." Lifting her chin, Lindsey stared up at the platform rising high over their heads. Tall, glittering buildings resided upon it. Other platforms were scattered over the old city, each one connected to the others by bridges. The impressive structures were engineering marvels.

"Franklin, good job. Now get off there before that suit shits out," Torran added. "Your time is almost up."

Franklin slid into the water, careful not to make noise or cause a big splash.

It absolutely gutted Lindsey that she and Franklin were the only survivors of the crashed tiltrotor. After Lindsey's own escape from the aircraft, she'd wanted to swim down and search for survivors, but Torran and Franklin had stopped her. The tiltrotor was sinking into the mire, and there was the possibility that she could be trapped as the wreckage settled. She didn't want to think about the bodies of the squad in the darkness below her. Hobbes was among them, and it hurt to think of losing yet another friend. They'd never have that drink now, and she'd never see his smile again. Just like Ryan and Maria, yet another friend was lost to the Scrags. It was Scrags that had destroyed the world and forced humanity to hide in The Bastion. If not for them, none of her friends would've died or have been infected, and she wouldn't be trapped in a city filled with the dead.

Lindsey glanced toward the right bank and the dark figures racing through the refuse of the long abandoned world. The undead appeared terrifyingly close. As Franklin swam to the commanding officers, her suit returned to normal.

"Anyone know if Scrags like water?" Franklin asked.

"We're just lucky the other tiltrotor grabbed their attention and drew them away," Torran replied.

"So that means they'll go into the water," Franklin said with a flinch. "Great."

"We'll just need to be cautious," Lindsey replied. She'd seen vids of Scrags rushing into bodies of water to pursue prey. The undead beings didn't appear to know how to swim, but that didn't mean they weren't a threat. She was uneasy being in the murky river waters. It was not difficult to imagine Scrags beneath her feet reaching up to grab her.

"I say we swim straight up the middle of the river and go as fast as we can with the stealth off," Torran said, his voice clipped. "Once we hit the stairwell to the street, we need to activate our stealth suits because then we'll be in plain view."

"What's our destination?" Lindsey tilted her head, trying to catch a glimpse of him through her helmet visor.

"The upper city and any place up there that's safe," Torran answered somberly.

"They're as likely to be up there as they are down here," Lindsey pointed out.

"Not to sound like I'm overriding you, sir," Franklin said, "but higher ground is always best, right?"

"Yes, yes it is," Lindsey agreed.

It wasn't as if she wanted to stay on the ground level of the city, but the climb would be treacherous, since the old technology was no longer operational. Of course, the entire scenario was dangerous.

"Let's move. We need to find shelter by nightfall." Torran pushed off, gliding through the water so only the top of his helmet was visible.

Lindsey released her grip on the tiltrotor wing and sank into the water. She was glad that the SWD suit was not as heavy as her old Constabulary one. Though she had to pump her arms a little harder to keep her eyes above the water, she managed to keep up with Torran's pace as she glided along the surface. The helmet registered her oxygen levels, and she only had to push just a little out of the water to allow the helmet to suck in more air and release the carbon dioxide. Franklin followed behind her, weighted down by the weapons she'd attached to her armor, but she was stronger than Lindsey and easily kept pace.

The screeching of the Scrags continued to echo as she swam, the sound piercing through her already tortured head. The headache was now behind her eyes and nearly unbearable. It had been ages since she'd had a migraine, but this one was determined to manifest. The changing weather was only contributing to her agony. The sky was overcast and the clouds were low and gray. The chief defender had mentioned a snowstorm and Lindsey wondered how much time they had before it reached the city. Hopefully they'd find shelter with access to an emergency generator so she could attempt access to the city grid. Without the constant feed that usually flowed across the sides of her helmet, she was a bit lost.

A footbridge spanned the river ahead. Scrags darted across it, agitated by the aircraft and the crash. The soldiers would have to swim under it to reach the stairwell.

Torran sank beneath the waves. Lindsey warily dove after him and didn't surface until she was shrouded in the darkness beneath the arch. It was frightening to be engulfed in the gloom while hearing the cries of Scrags rushing over the bridge. Maybe it was the shock of the collision, her impending migraine, or the weight of her armor and weapon, but Lindsey realized she was starting to fall behind. She fumbled with her wristlet and hailed Torran, but he didn't answer. Kicking harder, she managed to close the gap between them again. Again, she messaged Torran, hoping he'd answer. Silence was the only response.

When she swam out from beneath the bridge, relief flooded her to be in sunlight, but only for a split second.

There was a loud splash and Lindsey spun about in the water in alarm. Immediately, her comm hissed to life.

"They're jumping into the water from the bridge behind us," Franklin exclaimed.

Lindsey spotted the ripples emanating from the spot where the Scrag had fallen into the water. There was no sign of it now, but the splash had drawn the attention of several other undead creatures. Confused, they stood on the bridge, searching for the source of the noise. Lindsey urgently swam after Torran.

"We're almost there." Torran pointed to the tube housing the stairwell to the platform above. "We need to hurry."

Lindsey despaired at the thought of the climb, but she dragged her body through the water with tiring arms and legs.

The splash of more bodies striking the water sent tremors of terror through her.

The main comm switched off, then Torran hailed her on a private channel. She swiped her wristlet under the water. "I'm coming."

"Lindsey, listen. You're in danger And not just from the Scrags. The tiltrotor was sabotaged. It was meant to crash."

"What? By who?"

"Not sure yet, but this was all done for one purpose. To isolate you and force you to reach out to Maria."

"How do you know?"

"Because I was told," Torran replied.

"Told by who?" Shock and betrayal nearly choked the words in her throat.

Before Torran could answer, Lindsey brushed against something in the water. A second later, a Scrag surged out, screeching as it reached for her.

TEN MINUTES EARLIER—

The screeches of the scrags on the banks of the river ripped through Torran's psyche like rapiers. It just wasn't possible to ignore the horrific noises. Even Torran's helmet being partially submerged didn't help drown out their cries as he pushed off the tiltrotor and started down the river. He paused only briefly to make sure Lindsey was right behind him, then aimed for the stairwell rising to the upper city. Though she hadn't said anything, he could tell Lindsey was hurting. Though it didn't appear that she had any serious injuries, he suspected she was badly bruised and probably had a concussion. Franklin appeared to be in better condition. Hopefully, they could all find somewhere safe to hide until a rescue team came for them.

There was a beep inside his helmet. Franklin was directly paging him. A little surprised, he opened the comm. "How are you doing back there, Franklin?"

"Doing well, sir, since everything is going according to plan."

Torran nearly stopped swimming he was so startled by her words.

Franklin continued: "I have to admit, sir, that I didn't expect the other member of my cell to be SWD, or on the other tiltrotor. I thought it would be another Constabulary soldier on mine."

Franklin's words didn't make sense, but Torran instantly knew something terrible and important was happening. "I used to be Constabulary."

"True. I should have considered that. I know we weren't supposed to know who our other cell member was, but I couldn't help speculating."

"Well, it was best to keep things secret," Torran replied, hoping he wouldn't trip up and expose himself as a fraud.

"Whoever rigged the tiltrotor to crash was a little overzealous. I was worried I wouldn't be able to get Rooney out on my own. I was relieved when you arrived."

"It was a bit messier than expected." Torran's blood felt thick in his veins and his head throbbed with anxiety and anger. Someone had deliberately sabotaged the tiltrotor. The welded locks on the harnesses made sense now.

"The aerial drone we commandeered is scanning the area right now. I have the feed, but it's indicating that you're not receiving data? That I'm the only one online?"

Swimming through the oily, debris-ridden water, Torran concentrated on all the details of the unsettling conversation with Franklin, a person he realized neither he nor Lindsey could trust. "I had some damage from the jump into the river. I had to reboot. I lost the program."

Franklin swore. "Damn. I'll have to send the data packet once we're topside. I guess I'm our only eyes right now."

"What's our status?" It was hard not to sound clueless about what she was talking about, but at least there was one slight reassurance. Franklin apparently had access to an aerial drone and that would be a massive asset in keeping them all alive.

"The drone is reporting low population on the upper platform. Our target location appears to be secure and we should be able to access it with no difficulties."

"Excellent."

Nearing a bridge, Torran dove into the murky depths to avoid the eyes of the Scrags populating the walkway. Sifting through all his conversations with the SWD, Torran struggled to ascertain who could be behind the sabotage. He was convinced it wasn't the SWD. Was it a rogue faction? Or was this some sort of top-secret mission approved by the president? But would the president authorize the murder of the squad? The veins in his temples pulsed with tension.

"Do you really think she'll tell us where Vanguard Martinez is located?" There was a note of uncertainty in Franklin's voice.

"Not immediately," Torran answered. The message Solomon had sent after he dove into the river niggled at him. Boldly, he added, "But she'll get desperate when rescue doesn't come." It was a gamble to say that much, but he decided to risk it.

"Which is exactly what Solomon is hoping for."

"Solomon knows what's she's doing. She's clever."

Pushing to the surface of the water beneath the bridge, Torran tried to regulate his breathing as the air filters drew fresh air. Panic filled him and made his chest tight. He was trapped not only in a city filled with the undead, but in a web of lies spun by someone he should have been able to trust. Why did Chief Defender Solomon want Maria?

Lindsey surfaced behind him, but he avoided looking directly at her. How could he? Half the squad had died to lure her into a trap. That knowledge would crush her.

Torran swam into the sunlight, glad to be away from the darkness. Another beep indicated an incoming request from Lindsey, but Torran ignored it. Half the squad had been murdered and the raw anger burning through his veins was difficult for him to contain. Yet, he would have to in order to find out exactly what was going on. He had to keep calm and draw any information he could out of Franklin.

There was a splash behind him.

The general comm connection popped to life with a burst of static.

"They're jumping from the bridge behind us," Franklin cried out through the link.

Torran swiveled about, lungs and arms treading water to keep afloat. Lindsey gave the crowded bridge one frightened look and paddled furiously toward Torran.

"We're almost there," he called out encouragingly, waving toward the stairwell. "We need to hurry."

As Lindsey propelled toward him, more Scrags leaped into the water. Franklin took up a defensive position behind Lindsey, holding her weapon out of the water. In theory, the firearm should work, and Torran hoped it would if they needed it. Torran popped the tab holding his weapon to his chest and swung it about through the murky water. At the same time, he called Lindsey on a secure comm.

She immediately answered in a breathless voice, "I'm coming."

While Franklin was distracted by the Scrags, Torran knew he had to let Lindsey know what was happening. There might not be another chance. "Lindsey, listen. You're in danger. And not just from the Scrags. The tiltrotor was sabotaged. It was meant to crash."

"What? By who?" Disbelief filled her words.

"Not sure yet, but this was all done for one purpose. To isolate you and force you to reach out to Maria."

"How do you know?"

"Because I was told," Torran replied, realizing he was reluctant to expose the truth about Franklin. After losing Hobbes, he knew the news would crush Lindsey. Yet he had to tell her.

"Told by who?"

Her tone was ragged and possibly accusing.

Torran was about to answer when a Scrag erupted from the water, shrieking as it lunged toward Lindsey. As the creature reached for her, Lindsey kicked out, managing to drive her boot into the Scrag's chest. The impact drove the Scrag away as Lindsey surged backward. The waters closed over the Scrag's head as it disappeared from view. Bubbles and foam flecked the spot where it vanished as the ripples expanded outward.

Torran switched the main comm link. "Don't fire unless you have to!"

More Scrags were hurling into the river from the bridge. They flailed about once they hit the surface, churning up the water as they sank. A few barely stayed aloft with their wild thrashing, but didn't appear know how to advance on the living.

Meanwhile, Lindsey swam in a wide arc toward Torran in an attempt to avoid the submerged Scrag while Franklin trailed behind her.

"Where's the Scrag?" Lindsey gasped. "Where'd it go?"

"It sank." At least Torran hoped it had. He couldn't see it beneath the oily, trash covered surface.

"I think it pushed up from the bottom. The water isn't as deep here," Franklin observed.

Torran jerked his foot upward as something hit against it. "They're under us!"

"Keep swimming," Lindsey ordered.

Arms smacking hard against the water, she aimed for the bank near the base of the stairwell. The enclosed tube glinted in the fading sunlight and now that they were closer, Torran saw that the entrance was definitely secure. The transparent casing of the passageway was covered in years of dirt and grime, but appeared intact. Following behind, Torran struggled to keep his body as close to the surface now that he was aware of the creatures lurking below.

Several Scrags burst out of the water. Clawed hands reached for him and Lindsey. Torran swung the butt of his weapon into the face of one and brutally kicked at the other. He heard Lindsey struggling, but was trapped by the two he was fighting. Slamming the weapon into the heads of both of them, Torran tried to knock the undead away, but the Scrags doggedly grabbed at his arms and torso. The water kept closing over his head, but by forcefully scissoring his legs he managed to bob up to the surface again. The hands of the water-logged Scrags ripped at him, but their sodden flesh tore from the bone. Each time he struck their screeching faces, more skin and muscle tore away.

Lindsey appeared beside him. Her helmet was covered in blood, but it was on the outside and dripping into the river. Grabbing his arm, she swung her body about and planted her feet on the chests of the Scrags. With a violent shove, she broke them free of Torran. Franklin descended on the Scrags from behind and her knife flashed as she furiously stabbed the creatures through the head.

Torran was wondering where the other Scrags Lindsey had been fighting were when they seized him and Lindsey. Together, they went under into the darkness. Terror ripped at Torran, but he fought against its paralyzing power, trusting the armor would buy them a few precious minutes. Using his weapon, he shoved away the grasping hands and snarling faces that were barely illuminated by the helmet lights. Blood filled the space around him and his feet touched the bottom of the river. Driving his boots into the mud, he tried to get enough leverage to knock his assailants completely away. Hands slashed through the bloody, dirty water.

"Got them," Franklin grunted.

More blood filled the water until all he saw was red. Then he was free of the grasping digits.

"Stealth on," he choked out. "And let's get the hell out of here."

CHAPTER 27

Pulling her body slowly out of the water, Lindsey sagged as gravity dragged her to the flagstones on the bank. The weight of her body, armor and weapons made it hard to move at first, but then her muscles remembered their purpose and she yanked her legs out of the water. On hands and knees, she inched along the edge of the river. It was unsettling to see her hands and arms melding into her surroundings, only given away by quivering around the edges. Reaching a stairway that lead to the street, she hunkered beside it.

Without the constant influx of information onto her helmet screen, Lindsey was disoriented. The only feed she was receiving was from the armor of her companions. The dots on her locator indicated they were drawing closer to her location. With her own eyes, she barely made out their wavering forms against the backdrop of the river.

Meanwhile, the Scrags screeched and thrashed in the water as they continued to search for prey in the churning waves.

"They think we're still in the water." Torran lowered his voice even though his external helmet speakers were off and he was on the general comm.

His earlier confession still didn't seem real, but Lindsey trusted he was telling the truth. The squad had been murdered in order to strand her and force her to reach out to Maria. Yet how did Torran know? Certainly not before the crash. He would have never allowed Hobbes and the others to die, or allowed her to be in a doomed aircraft. Which meant...

Closing her eyes, Lindsey shuddered as she realized Franklin had betrayed her. It had to be the other survivor, yet why would Franklin say anything to Torran? Was it because he was SWD? That didn't make sense, since Franklin was Constabulary. Lindsey's head hurt, and she wanted nothing more than to press her fingertips to her temples. If only she could have a second or two to gather her thoughts, she'd figure out what was going on and be able to plan.

Pounding footsteps on the stairs next to her pulled her attention up. Scrags were flowing down the stairwell from the street. Clearly, the creatures were drawn by the commotion of the Scrags splashing in the water. Breath catching in her throat, Lindsey clutched her weapon tighter as the undead streamed toward the river. Fearfully, she searched for Torran and Franklin. She barely saw the disruption of their suits as they darted out of the way of the oncoming rush. The suits started to fluctuate as the helmet cameras attempted to adjust the image the suits were projecting to maintain their stealth.

"Don't move!" Lindsey cried out. "I can almost see you."

The dots on her screen froze in place.

"If they bump us, they'll know we're here," Franklin rasped.

"Hold your position," Torran ordered. "Let the suits adjust."

Squatting against the side of the stairwell, Lindsey set her back against the wall and aimed her weapon at the filthy undead beings. The virus preserved their almost life-like appearance, yet their clothes were mere scraps, their hair a tangled mess, and their bodies were covered in years of muck. Their screaming mouths and wild eyes were nightmarish in their inhumanity. Lindsey gulped, fighting the tremors in her hands. The soldiers were so vulnerable in their position, only hidden by suits that would soon have to recharge.

A Scrag struck one of the soldiers, spinning them both about. On her screen, it indicated that the soldier was Torran. Lindsey sucked air through her teeth, trying not to cry out and make the situation worse by distracting him. The Scrag twisted about, clearly looking for what it had hit. Letting out terrifying shrieks, the male Scrag with a ratty gray beard and bald head stretched out its hands, seeking possible prey. The suits of both soldiers briefly flashed as the projected images again attempted to adjust. Torran was on the ground, and Franklin was barely a few inches from the Scrag. The other undead continued into the water, drawn by the wildly howling and splashing Scrags, but it would take just one creature identifying new prey to draw their attention to the shore again.

"Don't move," Torran whispered. "Franklin, stay still."

"He's almost touching me," she answered sounding close to panic.

"If you move, he'll see you," Torran responded.

"I have you covered," Lindsey promised. "If he touches you, duck."

"You fire, Rooney, and they'll be on us in seconds," Torran reminded her.

The stream of Scrags coming down the stairs was now a trickle, and most of the herd was in the river. They were so agitated, they were fighting with each other.

"We'll make a run for it," Lindsey answered. "They'll have to get out of the water."

The male Scrag swiped at the air again, eyes wide and searching. Franklin held her position, but her breath was ragged. Torran remained on the ground behind her, unmoving as the final few Scrags dashed into the river churning with the flailing bodies of the undead.

The Scrag took a slight step toward Franklin and wildly lashed out. From the slight wavering in the air, it looked like Franklin dodged under his arms.

"He almost had me!"

"I have an idea," Torran said. "Franklin, when I tell you, shove him backward. We'll toss him into the river."

"I might become visible for a few seconds," Franklin protested.

"You're going to anyway when he touches you, and then we'll have to take defensive actions," Torran snapped. "Do it."

"I can't push him that far!"

"Do it!" Torran ordered.

"Obey him, Franklin!" Lindsey rose to her feet and took aim. "I have you covered."

With a cry of fear and frustration, Franklin lunged forward and hit the Scrag with her weapon. The suit shimmered at the impact as the Scrag stumbled back. It stopped a few feet from the edge of the water and screeched. Torran was instantly on his feet and ran at the creature. Lindsey could see his suit rippling as it attempted to adjust to his surroundings. Torran leaped upward, lashed out at the Scrag with one leg, struck the creature in the chest, and knocked him back the last few feet into the water.

"Now run!" Torran urged.

Most of the Scrags appeared to be drawn, yet disoriented by the events on the shore, but a few started to claw at the stone bank to pull themselves up. Lindsey darted around the bottom of the stairwell and hurried up the steps. On her screen, she saw Franklin and Torran rushing after her. The stairwell was L-shaped, and she hit the first landing and looked back. Scrags were crawling onto the shore. With the stealth suits flickering, the three soldiers were in dire danger. Whipping about, she swiftly ascended the final flight to the street level.

The road was filled with the debris of buildings and vehicles. A few Scrags were darting about in confusion, unsure of where to go as the howls of their comrades ricocheted off the structures around them. The tube to the upper city was a block away. The entrance was shut, which was a relief, but also an obstacle. They'd have to force the doors open before the stealth function in their suits had to reboot.

"Rooney, status," Torran said.

"I got a dozen Scrags scattered over the street. Entrance is shut."

"We've got some Scrags on the shore looking for us but not pursuing," Torran informed her.

"That entrance is going to be a bugger opening." Lindsey raised her weapon as she scooted past a decaying pod car and aimed at the Scrag still strapped inside.

"I have a remote generator in my bag," Franklin announced. "I grabbed it on my way out of the crash."

"Excellent work, Franklin," Torran said.

Lindsey glanced toward Franklin and Torran as they reached the street. She could barely make out their forms, which was a good thing. The suits were rapidly adjusting to their new environment, but they were still in terrible danger out in the open.

Fury washed over Lindsey once again. Franklin was the reason so many were dead at the bottom of the infested river, and why Lindsey and Torran were trapped in the Scrag-ridden city.

An undead child stumbled around the remains of an aircraft. It was a little girl around three years old. The bite on its forearm sent a shiver through Lindsey as she recalled the attack at the Beta City Depot. The child was naked and her chubby arms and legs were covered in what appeared to be dried blood. The impulse to protect and comfort filled Lindsey, yet she knew this dirty cherubic creature with masses of dark hair and gray-tinged skin was death incarnate. The tiny lips parted and the horrific Scrag screech emanated from the girl's throat. It was a questioning sound. It was a noise she'd heard before. It was as if the Scrags called out to each other.

Moving very slowly, Lindsey attempted to give the child wide berth. Downed limbs of the horse-chestnut trees littered the cracked and buckled sidewalk, making it difficult to maneuver without a sound. Torran and Franklin caught up to Lindsey's position, and their dots on her helmet slowed to a stop.

"She'll call the others," Lindsey said in warning. "So we need to be careful."

The little girl Scrag crawled over a gnarled branch and gave out another questioning screech.

Further down the road, from where the three soldiers had come from, came the answering shrieks from the Scrags on the bank and river.

A lump formed in her throat as Lindsey watched the long dead child toddle past her. The ugly wound on her plump arm told the terrible story of her demise. Who had bitten her? A parent? Sibling? Stranger? The small fat feet were chaffed and bloody from walking over sharp pebbles and shards of glass. A part of Lindsey wanted to shoot the child and put her out of her eternal misery, yet she also wished she could pick up the little girl and somehow save her.

Franklin moved so fast, Lindsey didn't realize what she was doing until the little girl was on the ground and Franklin was jerking her dagger out of her skull. Breathing heavily, Franklin said, "It's not right to let her live like that."

"You took an unnecessary risk," Torran snapped. "She was almost past us."

"She would have called the others," Franklin retorted, but it was clear that hadn't been her motive.

Had the little girl reminded Franklin of a sibling? Cousin? Maybe herself? Lindsey had to wonder.

Raising her gaze from the dead child, Lindsey saw Scrags stepping off the stairwell onto the sidewalk behind them. Uncertain, the creatures called out, then waited for the child Scrag to answer.

"Keep moving," she directed, then turned toward the entrance.

It was nerve-wracking moving so slowly through the shattered remains of another era. A few times, they had to venture close to the undead pinned beneath collapsed buildings or still trapped in vehicles. A few of the Inferi Scourge that had been wandering about in the street were drawn to the throng still clustered at the top of the stairs to the riverbank. From their hesitant, questioning noises, it was clear the Scrags were uncertain where to go. It was terrifying to realize that they actually hunted for victims. No wonder humanity had been doomed.

Lindsey edged around a rusted drone and was relieved to see she was almost to the entrance. The doors were stained and as she drew closer, she saw that some of the stains looked like smeared handprints.

Nervously, she raised her eyes to examine the long cylinder that housed the stairwell to the upper city.

"What if they're inside?" she asked.

"Hold up and give me a second," Franklin said, sounding less and less like a soldier under their command.

Since she was part of a conspiracy to trap Maria, Lindsey supposed Franklin really wasn't a part of their team anymore.

Franklin withdrew the binoculars from her pack and flipped on the stealth. The three soldiers stood perfectly still while Franklin studied the long transparent passage. From Lindsey's perspective, the smudged tube appeared to be devoid of life. There wasn't any movement near the bottom level at least.

"I don't see any signs of Scrags," Franklin said after a long pause. "There are some areas that look like they're damaged, but we should be able to get past them."

"I don't think we have a choice," Torran replied. "More are coming out of the water, and we'll be visible shortly."

"Let's do this," Lindsey said, and charged forward with the others on her heels.

Reaching the entrance, she gave the exterior a cursory glance. Signs in various languages were plastered over the door. Most were warnings about Infer Scourge infestations and safety procedures. One of the warnings was not to enter the tube if the plague broke out in the city.

Lindsey shook her head. No one would've paid attention to these signs when the Scrag infestation had started. With a sigh, she turned to see the remote generator emerging from what appeared to be slightly shimmering air. It didn't have any sort of stealth protection. Lindsey winced when its sudden appearance drew the attention of a nearby female Scrag shuffling around a pod car.

"We have a problem," she said.

The long, violent shriek of the Scrag rent the air. Instantly, the others answered.

"No time," Torran exclaimed and grabbed the remote generator. Shoving it against the entrance under the panel, he activated it.

The lights above the entrance flipped on, as did several close streetlights.

"Shit!" Franklin shouted, and shot the female Scrag through the head.

Sound no longer mattered.

The lighted entrance was a beacon to the Scrags.

The howls and the thunderous sound of running feet reverberated around the living.

Lindsey scanned the panel as it lit up. "It's locked! City security protocols has it shut down. I'll override. Buy me time!"

"We don't have any!" Torran snapped, but opened fire on the Scrags heading their way a second later.

"I'll take out the closest," Franklin said, wielding her weapon with her usual deadly accuracy.

Lindsey tore her eyes away from the Scrags rushing from the riverbank and concentrated on her tablet. There weren't Scrags coming from any other directions yet, but she had to move fast before they were cornered. Though her head was throbbing painfully, her brain absorbed the information after a few seconds into her examination of the city security protocols and revealed it as an image she could easily disseminate. It took only a few seconds to recognize what she needed to do to unlock the doors, and her fingers sprung into a quick dance.

The sharp barks of the weapons firing escalated. Lindsey glanced over her shoulder just as the stealth suits returned to visibility. Torran was using two weapons to slow down the oncoming rush. He wasn't attempting killing headshots, but aiming to cripple the Scrags and slow them down.

The herd was closing fast, maybe fifteen meters away. The ones in the front fell beneath the barrage of fire, legs shredded and buckling beneath them. The following Scrags tumbled over the fallen, and the tangle of bodies swiftly became an obstacle.

"Lindsey, how are you doing?" Torran asked, his voice sharp.

The entrance shuddered, and the doors opened with a wail.

"Done!" Lindsey darted inside, her weapon aimed toward the frozen escalator. Nothing moved above her. "We're clear at the bottom."

Franklin dashed through the doorway and Torran followed, grabbing the remote generator as he scooted inside. Lindsey hit the door controls. They stuttered to a halt, then reversed their movement.

Aiming at their heads, Lindsey fired at two Scrags about to shove their way through the doorway. The back of their skulls erupted in a volcano of blood and brains. The sight sickened her, but was strangely satisfying. The oncoming Scrags weren't going to make it to the doors on time and she exhaled with relief as they thumped closed. She locked it just as the Scrags hit the doors.

The area the surviving soldiers were in was a rectangular room that enclosed the bottom of four wide escalators: two ascending, two descending. The remote generator didn't have enough juice to activate the underground mechanism, and Lindsey turned it off. The lights overhead dimmed, then blinked out as the generator ceased to function.

Torran stood on the steps above her while Franklin peered out at the Scrags beating their hands against the glass of the long windows on either side of the entrance. It was thick and would take great force to break through, so Lindsey assumed they were relatively safe for the moment. Exhaustion weighed on her, and she took a deep breath to steady both her nerves and wildly beating heart. Meeting Torran's intense gaze, she licked her parched lips and gave him a slight nod.

"We need to keep going," Franklin said briskly. "More are coming."

"How long before the windows or doors give way?" Torran wondered aloud.

"Give me a moment to calculate," Lindsey said, pulling out her pad again.

"I suggest we start climbing," Franklin said shortly. To Lindsey's surprise, the other woman grabbed her arm and jerked her toward the stairs.

"Hey!" Lindsey cried.

"We don't have time to rest!" Franklin pointed at the Scrags clawing at the windows. Their mouths were spread wide as they shrieked. Lindsey was relieved that the soundproofing of the structure blocked out the sound. "They're going to get in."

"There's still a chain of command here," Torran said briskly, pulling Lindsey away from Franklin.

Lindsey didn't like all the jostling and shrugged him off as well. "I suggest we remember we're all soldiers and survivors and must work together. With two commanding officers, this will get confusing fast."

"Then I capitulate to your will, since I'm the only SWD officer here," Torran said. "You're in charge, Vanguard Rooney."

Franklin looked ready to protest, then nodded. "I think that works best, too."

Lindsey was agitated that Franklin even commented. "Fine. Franklin, take the rear. MacDonald, take point."

Lindsey picked up the remote generator. It was lightweight, but she was tired and stumbled slightly. Torran took it from her and signaled Franklin to turn over the heavy pack she was wearing. The tall woman almost protested, but again relented. It was obvious that Franklin was struggling with maintaining the illusion of being cooperative.

Once Torran had the pack on, he started up the still escalator, his boot heels causing the metal steps to ring out. Lindsey trailed after him, her weapon at the ready. Franklin's steps were a reassuring sound behind her. At least Lindsey knew she could count on Franklin's will to survive.

Together, they started the long climb.

The ascent was strenuous, but Torran managed to keep a steady pace despite his protesting body. At each landing, they'd rest for a minute or two before continuing. The stairwell zigzagged within the long cylinder and he could only see one section at a time. The muscles in his legs trembled from the exertion, and he was beginning to tire. After everything he'd endured since waking up that morning next to Lindsey, he just wanted to return to his bed and hold her in his arms.

Instead, he climbed.

The arched ceiling of the stairwell was transparent, but it was still difficult to see through. The thick layer of crud obscured the sunlight and shrouded their ascent in gloom.

"The area below us is still clear," Franklin said as they reached another landing.

This one had a three hundred and sixty degree view of the city. The light was a little stronger in this area, and Torran pressed a gloved hand to the glass and peered out. The snowstorm was definitely moving into the area. Flurries were already dusting the city across the river with white. Tilting his chin down, he saw a sight that chilled him. If not for the soundproofing of the stairwell, he was sure the screeching of the massive crowd of Scrags gathered at the entrance would be unbearable.

Stepping next to him, Lindsey followed his gaze. "Shit."

"They're going to break in at some point," Torran said with a sigh.

"We're pretty high right now," she reminded him. "It'll take some time for them to catch up."

"But we're already tired and they *won't*," he answered.

"Bloody hell," Lindsey mumbled.

"We need to keep moving." Franklin's face was grim in the light of her helmet. Her dark skin was flecked with sweat and her black eyes glinted with determination. "We need to keep ahead of them and reach the higher platform."

"How did the tiltrotor go down?" Lindsey asked abruptly. "How did this happen?"

Torran wished she hadn't asked such a volatile question.

"Probably a Scrag jumping onto it from the upper city," Franklin answered smoothly. "I'm sure you've seen the vids."

Torran and Lindsey had both read the reports of the evacuation when putting together the excursion specs. According to eyewitness accounts, the Scrags had flung themselves from the upper city onto departing craft, sometimes with devastating results when they impacted with the hulls. If the damage was severe enough, the aircraft crashed. Franklin had told a clever lie, probably one devised for her mission. It fit perfectly.

"Yeah, I saw the vids," Lindsey said with a sigh. "I guess that makes sense."

"We're close now." Torran pointed to the underside of the upper city with its crisscrossing maintenance walkways.

"Let's keep moving." Lindsey pushed away from the windows and headed toward the stairs. Torran followed, resisting the urge to touch her. The last thing he wanted was for Franklin to discern was his personal interest in Lindsey. He needed Franklin to trust him and not question his loyalty.

The next part of the climb was a little harder. Though they'd observed shoes, coats, purses, bags, and other items discarded on the steps, there were now piles of personal items littering the frozen escalators. They had to kick the rubbish out of their way to keep ascending. For Torran, it was a little difficult to ignore the abandoned toys. It had been awful enough to see the Scrag child, but now he wondered about the fates of the children who had been evacuated to the upper city so long ago. That speculation was hell on his nerves. Though Torran had balked at the idea of fathering children by multiple women when the offer had been proposed to him, he'd started to consider the possibility of fatherhood when he and Lindsey had become increasingly closer in their relationship. The concept of having a child with her had started to appeal to him greatly, but now he wondered if he'd been foolish to even hope.

Again, he was paged by Franklin on a secure comm line. He answered: "How are we looking?"

"The aerial drone reached the top of the stairwell. The doors are open. Pried open from inside, it seems."

"So we could have Scrags ahead," Torran said.

"The drone is also reporting a blockage near the top. It definitely took damage at one point."

"Can we get past it?"

Franklin hesitated, then said, "It'll be precarious, but yes."

"It's not like we can go back down," Torran groused.

"Once we reach the upper city, the aerial drone has mapped out the best path to our destination. There are Scrags in the area, but we should be able to deal with them." Franklin didn't sound as confident as before.

"This was not the best idea," Torran said angrily.

Franklin was silent.

Torran began to worry that he had overstepped and created suspicion in the woman.

"I didn't like the idea of the crash either, but us being stranded here had to be convincing. There was no way to let the Scrags into the food depot and create a crisis scenario. And we have to make a move now. The further out into the world Maria gets, the harder it will be to track her. Our search area doubles each time she relocates."

"Agreed. Keep me updated. Switching back to the primary comm before Lindsey gets suspicious."

Torran's fury was overwhelming. It took all his willpower to not whip about and demand more answers. He had a gut feeling she'd clam up the minute she realized he wasn't on her side.

Reaching another landing, Torran directed his gaze up at the next long expanse leading upward. It was darker than the other areas, since it was in the shadow of the upper city. Plastic bins, luggage and bags were in a heap at the top of the escalator. Kicking some of the bags out of his way, he glanced at Lindsey. Her big hazel eyes, more gray than any other color now, gazed back at him worriedly.

"It doesn't feel right," she said.

Franklin joined them. "It looks clear."

"Yeah, but it still doesn't feel right," Torran said, agreeing with Lindsey.

"Do you think it was a barricade?" Lindsey pointed at the pile at the next landing.

"An inefficient one, if it was," Torran said, but could see how she'd come to that conclusion.

"They were civilians," Franklin observed. "They didn't know how to protect themselves."

"They were dependent on people like us," Lindsey said somberly. "Keep alert. If it was a barricade and the Scrags aren't below us, it means they're above."

Torran wished he could tell Lindsey what Franklin had reported, but he had to be cautious if he wanted to maintain Franklin's trust in him. Once he had enough information about the group Franklin was a part of and their plans, what would he do then? He supposed he'd weigh his options when the moment arrived.

Climbing, the steps creaking beneath him, Torran's suit adjusted to the increasing cold outside. Every few steps, he had to push bags, luggage and plastic containers to the side to squeeze through. Mindful to stay as quiet as possible, he was careful not to knock the cases down the escalators. As he neared the next landing, he saw it was filled with toppled luggage. Stepping over the objects was nearly impossible since there was so many.

"Definitely a barricade," Lindsey decided.

"And overrun." Torran switched on his weapon light and brushed the illumination over the area. Dark stains were everywhere. Most likely, it was blood.

"MacDonald, clear a path while we cover you," Lindsey directed.

Attaching his weapon to his armor, Torran started swiftly stacking the stuff to clear a path. Glancing at the next portion of their climb, he hesitated. The glass canopy was gone and snowflakes fell through the gap onto the steps. The escalator was bunched into an ugly snarl of metal. To bypass the area, they'd have to climb over the ruins.

"Vanguard Rooney, this isn't going to be easy."

Lindsey stepped next to him and scrutinized the situation. "Shit."

The metal steps were twisted and misshapen, exposing the damaged chains underneath. The rubber that covered the handrails lay in big loops over the devastation. Charred luggage, large pieces of metal and glass from the canopy, and scorched bodies made the situation even more harrowing.

"Grenade," Franklin decided. "Someone set off a grenade."

"Our best chance is to climb the center rail," Lindsey decided. She clambered onto the wide rails set side by side, and she stood, staring at the debris. It reached as high as the broken ceiling in several places. "Yeah, this is our only way up and over."

Torran scrambled up behind her, allowing her to lead the way. Lindsey's analytical mind would probably help them through the ruined area much faster anyway. Lindsey treaded carefully along the handrail.

"How badly compromised is the area?" Torran wondered.

Continuing to cautiously inch upward, Lindsey squatted to peer at the beginning of the damage. Torran and Franklin paused as Lindsey lifted her pad for a scan.

"The escalator took the brunt of the explosion and obviously the roof. The frame is intact, but there are some fractures along the flooring and walls." Lindsey stood and tucked her tablet away. Glancing over her shoulder, she flashed a smile as she shrugged. "In other words, let's hope it holds." With that comment, she started to gingerly find footing and hand holds amid the mound of debris and pulled herself up.

The wind blew through the exposed roof and buffeted the three soldiers as they climbed. Snow began to whirl about their heads and settle onto their helmets. Torran cautiously tested each spot before advancing. The sharp metal and glass made the climb precarious. Lindsey reached the apex of the mangled vestiges of the escalators and paused. Torran also hesitated when she glanced back at him.

"We have to jump across to the next landing," she said in a breathless voice.

Immediately, Torran's gut clenched into a tight knot. "Vanguard, let me move up and go first."

Beneath their bodies, the structure was creaking.

"No, MacDonald. Hold your position. This area is not very secure. It's a little over a meter jump. The problem is this shifting crap under me."

Struggling to not give into temptation and check to see how far they might fall, Torran searched for a different option. The metal creaked and the wind whistled loudly, making him even more afraid. He considered retreating to give himself more time to analyze their predicament. Maybe they could hold position at their location until they could discern a better way around the obstacle.

"We can't stay here," Franklin declared. It was as if she was reading his thoughts.

"Just long enough to figure a way past this mess," he replied.

"We can't," Franklin persisted. "They're inside."

Torran gave her a sharp look and recognized she was deadly serious. Torran increased the volume of his external mic and listened. What he'd first presumed to be the wind howling through the roof was actually something much more terrifying. It was the screech of the Scrags. Since the tube was soundproofed and they were too high to hear the herd at ground level, that meant they were inside the structure.

"Confirm they are inside," Lindsey ordered.

"They're inside," Torran grimly answered.

The noise was swelling, getting louder, or maybe he could hear it more clearly now that he was aware.

"Then we have no choice," Lindsey decided.

Torran turned about just in time to see her jump.

CHAPTER 28

When Lindsey leaped, she felt the wind tearing at her body and, for a frightening moment, was convinced that she'd be flung by the gust to the ground. Holding her breath, she sailed through the air over the gap between the wrecked escalator and the landing across from it. The river and the mass of Scrags in the road far below looked almost like a painting beneath her feet. If she fell, she would be dead the second she hit the water or the ground. Then the panorama was obscured by warped metal, dingy cement and broken tiles, and Lindsey crashed onto the landing. Momentum carried her forward and she rolled her body into a tight ball to keep from injury. Coming to a stop at the base of the next set of escalators, she raised her head to see Torran standing near the top of the rubble and staring at her in terror.

"I'm okay," she said quickly. "Just be careful when you jump. That pile is really unstable."

"Noted," Torran replied, and cautiously took a step forward.

Bits of cement, metal and glass rained down. With a resolute expression on his face, Torran launched himself forward. Lindsey scrambled to one side, giving him plenty of room to land. Being taller, longer, and stronger, he easily cleared the gap and landed on his feet. Stumbling forward, he caught himself on the wall and spun about to face her. His hand grasped hers for a split second, and she saw the fear in his eyes.

"Shit, they're almost here," Franklin shouted.

Lindsey immediately unhooked her weapon and aimed across the gap toward the spot behind Franklin. The other woman scrambled onto the rubble. The passage of Lindsey and Torran must have loosened the pile, because it visibly shifted beneath Franklin's feet. With a terrified cry, Franklin threw her body forward. Unable to kick off with her feet, she flailed through the air, hands stretching out to grab the platform. Torran dove forward, landing on his stomach, and miraculously managed to grab one of Franklin's wrists. He let out a grunt as he took the full brunt of her weight.

"I've got her. Cover us," Torran said through gritted teeth.

Lying across the landing, his arms over the edge, he struggled to pull Franklin onto the platform. It seemed odd that he was trying to help the woman who had abetted in the murder of the squad, but Lindsey knew Torran had his reasons. She was surprised and saddened by the coldness in her own heart toward Franklin. The soldier's urgent cries and terrified gasps of breath resounded in Lindsey's helmet, but she couldn't help but think of her squad thrashing in the water around her as they suffocated to death.

The first few of the pursuing Scrag horde scrambled onto the rubble heap. Screeching, their twisted faces almost appeared gleeful at the sight of the humans. Lindsey opened fire, aiming for their heads. The bodies of the Scrags toppled over the edge. More appeared, climbing without fear onto the noticeably rickety pile. Large chunks of the flooring gave way, spilling the escalator remains and other debris into the void below. Scrags tumbled through the widening opening, but more kept swarming onto the rubble in an attempt to reach the humans on the other side of the gap.

Torran finally managed to get a solid grip on Franklin's armor and started to drag her over the side. A Scrag hurtled itself off the disintegrating structure and slammed into Franklin, nearly wrenching her out of Torran's clutches. Torran shouted in pain and his body slid forward, toward the brink. Lindsey threw herself on top him, pinning him to the floor and stopping his slide.

The Scrag lost its grip on Franklin and fell.

The broken chains of the escalator on the other side gave way completely, spilling its innards. Stairs, glass, parts of the wall, luggage, long dead corpses and Scrags poured through the widening opening, and within seconds, the entire floor gave way with a thunderous crash. Through the smoke and debris cloud, Lindsey saw that the entire section they had just traversed was gone.

At last, Torran dragged Franklin onto the landing. No one spoke as they lay in a heap at the base of the next set of escalators. Lindsey aimed her weapon up the next expanse, but Scrags did not appear. Across the now much-wider divide, the Scrag rush continued unabated. Having no understanding of death, they attempted to hurtle themselves across the gap and plunged to a final death below. The torrent of bodies continued for more time than Lindsey cared to track. It seemed endless.

"We need to keep going," she said finally. Pushing her back against the wall, she slid upright. She was a bit wobbly from the adrenaline rush, but she found her footing and took a cautious step onto the next section.

"Thank you," Franklin said. "I thought I was going to die."

"We gotcha." Torran's comment was devoid of emotion and he brushed past Lindsey while unhooking his weapon to take point again. Was he angry at her for leaping? Angry at himself for saving Franklin? Or was he just scared?

The next few sections were absent of the discarded items they'd seen earlier. Lindsey speculated that everything had been left behind when the escaping people had barricaded the lower area. She noticed a lot more signs of a battle. Bullet holes were in the glass roof and shell casings were on the floor. Had a security team come down from the upper city to save those trapped inside the passage?

Over the arch of another escalator was a sign she was relieved to see. They'd finally reached the exit. Stepping into a room that matched the entrance on the ground, Lindsey was unnerved to observe that the doors were already open. She immediately pressed against the wall and motioned for Torran and Franklin to do so as well. Torran sidled up to her to get a view of the outside.

"There's a low number of Scrags out there," he said.

"Okay, now that we're up here, we need a new destination." Lindsey pulled out her pad and called up the grid of the city she'd downloaded before the excursion.

"Look for Rescue Hubs," Franklin suggested.

Rescue Hubs had been controversial in the days before the fall of humanity. They were constructed by a private company and people had to pay to have access during a Scrag outbreak. Situated strategically around the cities, the Rescue Hubs were basically lifeboats. The oval-shaped pod was built around a reinforced pole. Inside were supplies, a sleeping area, and a communication console. During an outbreak, people with passes could slip inside, activate the security protocols, and the pod would slide up the pole and remain elevated above the ground and out of the reach of the Scrag hordes. There was also a topside hatch so the inhabitants could be airlifted without ever being on the ground. There'd been protests among the general populace that the Rescue Hubs should be available to all citizens.

"They could all be locked," Torran pointed out.

"I can hack into one." Lindsey hated to admit it was a good idea to find one, but she also recognized that they were probably playing into Franklin's plans. Studying the maps, she sifted through all the data until she found a Rescue Hub located a few blocks away near a shopping district. A quick calculation revealed that they would just have enough time with the stealth activated to reach it as long as they didn't run into any trouble. Though she didn't like capitulating to Franklin, she knew they needed to find a secure place. With the snow falling and the storm building, nightfall wouldn't be their worst enemy. They would become visible to the Scrags if they were coated with snow.

"Okay, this is what we're going to do," she said, raising her head. She laid out her plan and there weren't any protests from Torran or Franklin. She supposed they were probably just as weary as she was and ready to be somewhere safe.

Activating the stealth on her suit, Lindsey darted through the opened doorway and exited into a wide courtyard with dense trees and foliage. Silent fountains were covered in mold, and statues and ornate columns showed signs of erosion from the elements.

"All the Scrags are dormant," Torran observed. "That's a good sign."

A few silent Scrags in torpor stood among the overgrown garden. Unmoving, they were waiting until prey was near. Most were women and upon further scrutiny, Lindsey ascertained they were clad in disintegrating nun habits. Glancing over the tangle of trees, she spotted the peaked roof of a cathedral made of glass and stone.

Leaving the courtyard, they stepped onto the sidewalk of a silent street. Since pod cars weren't allowed in the upper city, there was less debris scattered about. Most of the buildings were made from lightweight materials and were designed to reflect the sky. At one point, Lindsey was certain the upper city had been quite beautiful. Now most of the glass facades were broken and the decorative vegetation was overgrown with weeds. Monorail trains were stalled on tracks, and the remains of a tiltrotor were imbedded in a concert hall. Hurrying along the streets, the three soldiers were mindful of the hushed Scrags swaying back and forth in their blacked-out state.

"We're nearing the hub," Lindsey said while sprinting through an abandoned outdoor cafe.

She scooted around a corner and peered up the wide boulevard bordered by what used to be swanky shops. The upper city was always more costly to live in than the lower city in the two-tiered metropolitans, according to her research, and from the faded beauty that surrounded her, she believed that was most likely true. The locale still smacked of opulence. In the all-glass store in front of her, elegant eveningwear adorned mannequins that resembled Roman goddesses. Only the back of the store was made of a material other than glass, and that was probably the fitting rooms and storage. The glass walls were treated, so the sunlight hadn't bleached the dresses inside the shop. It almost looked ready to open for business.

"Just six meters up this road," Lindsey said.

"The long dead world," Torran breathed.

"Excess. Everywhere," Franklin said dismissively.

Scrags of all ages, races, and genders stood like sentinels in the street. It was quite a large group and Lindsey swallowed her fear. They had enough time left on their stealth suits to make it through the throng.

A transport vehicle sat at the far end of the street. Apparently, an airlift had been overrun. There wasn't any hope of using the transport to escape. The fuel in its tanks would have long gone stale and would need to be treated before use.

A short distance in front of the aircraft was the Rescue Pod. It had not been activated and still sat at street level.

"Be careful. This may get a little tricky. Keep close, but don't follow in a single line. I don't want us tripping over each other if we have to react quickly," Lindsey ordered.

She started along the road, mindful to keep her elbows tucked at her side and her weapon against her chest as she carefully advanced past the Scrags in the torpor state. Some were standing very close together, and she had to double back a few times to find a better path through the crowd. Torran and Franklin also carefully scooted around the Scrags, avoiding the more heavily populated parts of the streets. Lindsey climbed over a bench and walked along the seat to avoid a thick gathering of the undead before hopping down. The uncomfortably loud thump of her boots striking the ground reverberated through the air.

A few Scrags near Lindsey twitched, and she froze in place.

Nearby, Torran and Franklin also stopped and waited for the echo to fade.

Around the trio, the Scrags sluggishly stirred, eyes shifting about in their sockets seeking prey.

"Don't move," Lindsey ordered through the comm link.

Seconds ticked away as the soldiers waited for the Scrags to settle back into their lethargy.

Lindsey checked her timer and comprehended there wasn't any time to spare. They'd have to risk traveling through the crowd. She was the closest to the Rescue Hub, but wouldn't be able to activate the controls without the remote generator in Torran's pack. The Scrags continued to gradually rouse with no signs of returning to their torpor.

"We have to keep moving. We don't have a choice," she said. "MacDonald, as soon as we reach the hub, I need that remote generator activated. Franklin, cover us."

Gripping her weapon tightly, Lindsey surged forward, weaving through the Scrags as fast as she could without touching them. The rap of her boot heels against the ground was joined by those of Torran and Franklin. The noise clearly agitated the Scrags.

The Rescue Hub was a large oval-shaped structure tucked between two buildings. The fence surrounding it was already open and the decorative garden planted around the hub was long dead and full of weeds. Emerging from the center of the hub was a thick metal pole that rose high above the other buildings.

Directly outside the hub was a young male Scrag. He'd be the first to revive fully and the most dangerous. Lindsey rushed him, piecing her plan together as she ran. Once close enough, she swung her weapon, clipping his jaw, and sent him falling against the smooth, white exterior of the hub. Before he could fully awaken, she punched the butt of her rifle into his throat, destroying his larynx and stifling his screech. As he slid off the surface of the hub, one hand lashed toward her. She dodged it and struck again. The blow smashed in his skull, killing the Scrag.

A second later, Torran skidded to a halt beside her just as their armor shimmered and returned to normal. Whipping the pack off his back, he yanked out the remote generator and turned it on as Lindsey pressed her tablet against the wall next to the controls.

"They're definitely awake now," Franklin muttered.

Glancing over her shoulder, Lindsey saw the Scrags sluggishly starting to move. They'd be slow at first, which would give her a little time. "Cover me, but conserve as much ammo as you can."

As the Scrags nearest to the hub started in their direction, Torran and Franklin rapidly dispatched them, Torran using his weapon as a club and Franklin brandishing her knife. Lindsey tucked her firearm across her knees while working diligently on breaking the encryption on the lock.

"Rooney, you need to hurry. They're waking up faster," Torran said sharply.

"Working on it," Lindsey responded, concentrating on her task.

A second later, Franklin opened fire on the awakening Scrags.

"Franklin!" Torran shouted. "Don't!"

"They're already awake!"

The rising screech of the Scrags sent shivers down Lindsey's spine. The gunfire definitely was pulling the Scrags out of the blackout state even faster. Running footsteps sounded behind her, but Lindsey focused her attention on the panel in front of her. It was hard to concentrate as the weapons fired and the Scrags howled. Lindsey's fingers quivered while she worked. Finally, she was able to skirt around the security locks and uncover the manifest of the people who had bought passes into the hubs. Lifting the code of one of the approved clients, she entered in the string of numbers and letters and the hub door slid open.

Pushing the remote generator in, Lindsey ducked inside. The lights flicked on, illuminating the interior as Franklin jumped through the doorway and Torran retreated while still firing at the Scrags surging toward their position. Trusting Torran to keep the Scrags out, Lindsey rushed into the oval-shaped inner room and to the console. Activating the hub's internal generator with the flip of a switch, she quickly called up the main screen. The racket caused by the weapons firing abruptly ceased as Torran hit the door switch and it slammed shut.

"That could kill a person," he gasped, shocked at how swiftly the door had snapped close.

"It was meant to keep Scrags out," Franklin answered.

The surveillance camera feed clicked on, and Lindsey winced at the sight of the horde shoving their way into the area surrounding the hub.

"We need to go up!" Franklin snapped at Lindsey, slapping her hand against the wall near the panel.

"Back off," Lindsey retorted. "I'm working on it." The older programs were a little confusing to navigate, but she found what she needed and entered the directions.

A loud clacking noise was followed by a hum that vibrated through the shelter. A second later, Lindsey's stomach dropped as the pod shot upward. She steadied herself by grabbing the edge of the console, while Torran braced himself in the doorway. Franklin stumbled backward, then landed on her ass, much to Lindsey's amusement. A second later, the hub came to a jolting stop and there were several sharp clicking sounds as it locked into place.

"Your hub has been secured. Automatic notification of the activation of this hub is being sent to our security offices. Please remain calm. As soon as we can secure safe passage, you will be contacted with the details of your evacuation. Please sit tight and wait for rescue," a soothing female voice said over the loudspeakers.

"Betcha they won't show up," Torran said with a wink at Lindsey.

Now that they were safely away from the Scrags, Lindsey could afford a giggle. "Would be surprising if they did."

"Don't count on it," Franklin said grumpily.

Pulling out a chair from beneath the console, Lindsey waited for the back to flip up, then collapsed onto it. She stared at the readout on the screen as a preprogrammed diagnostic started on the hub. With still trembling hands, she popped the clasps on her helmet and tugged it off. The stale air inside the hub made her sneeze, but it was better than the helmet. Her blond braid flopped out, and she tossed it over her shoulder.

Torran leaned over and turned off the remote generator as Franklin climbed to her feet. Both removed their helmets and also sneezed a few times.

"The air isn't too pleasant," Torran noted.

"The air scrubbers are working. It'll be better soon," Lindsey answered. She was relieved to see all the internal systems in the hub were working.

Franklin tugged at the tabs on her armor and started to discard it. "We're safe. That's all that matters."

Lindsey bit her tongue. How safe were they really if Franklin was working against them and with an unknown group with an agenda to recover Maria? With a sigh, she started shimmying out of her own suit. Soon all three soldiers were down to the sleek black body suits they wore beneath the armor. Lindsey instantly felt incredibly lighter and stretched out her body while sweeping her eyes over their temporary haven. It was about seven meters in diameter, including the thick pole that took up the center of it. The hub featured a small kitchen area, bunk beds, and a sanitation station.

A weapons locker drew Torran's immediate attention, and he walked over to explore it. Meanwhile, Franklin started scrounging through the stores of food and water in the kitchen area. Lindsey remained at the console, too tired to move, and pressed her fingers to her throbbing temples. When Franklin handed her water, it took all her willpower to accept it with a smile.

"We made it," Franklin said, leaning against the wall.

"But the others are dead," Lindsey responded, then gulped some of the water. It tasted fresh. She was impressed.

Tilting her chin so she was looking away, Franklin was silent.

"Hobbes is gone," Lindsey added sorrowfully, watching Franklin out of the corner of her eye.

"I know." Franklin shoved off from the wall. "But I don't want to think about that."

"I thought you two were..." Lindsey watched the other woman's retreat. Maybe Franklin did feel remorse. Or was she just agitated?

"There will be time to mourn later. Right now I'm going to visit the sanitary station."

Brushing past Torran as he continued to take inventory of the small weapons locker, Franklin vanished inside the sanitation center and a small panel over the door read OCCUPIED.

Lindsey pivoted about on her seat as Torran took three sharp steps toward her and bent over her. Taking her face in his hands, his lips met hers in a tender kiss.

"What's happening?" Lindsey whispered, her eyes on the sign over the doorway.

"She's part of a group trying to find Maria. Solomon is part of it, too."

"Constabulary?" Lindsey's eyes widened at the thought. "Commandant Pierce?"

"I don't know. Just try to dial down the anger, and I'll try to get as much information out of her as possible. She has control of an aerial drone. I need the program she's using for it. When she comes out, make an excuse to go inside."

"I don't need an excuse. I need to piss a waterfall," Lindsey answered.

"Anyway, take some time so I can see what I can find out."

"Why did she tell you, Torran?" Lindsey took her eyes off the door panel and stared into his face.

"She thinks I'm a part of it. The cell must be a sleeper with the members not knowing each other except their primary contact," Torran replied.

"Solomon?"

"I think so."

"But why does she think you're part of it?" Lindsey stared into his dark eyes, fear nibbling at her nerves.

With a sardonic grin, Torran said, "Because I came to rescue you. She thinks it was part of the plan."

Checking the panel over the door again, Lindsey stood and kissed him lovingly. "Thank you for that."

"I'll always come back for you," Torran vowed, his Scottish brogue thickening.

"Same here."

The panel over the door went dark, and Lindsey flopped back into the chair as Torran pretended to study the screen in front of them.

Exiting, Franklin pulled several packs of ammo from the locker and walked over to the pile of her equipment. In silence, she started to reload her weapon.

CHAPTER 29

When Lindsey excused herself to use the sanitation facilities, Torran made a show of pulling a retracting chair out of the wall and collapsing into it. When the OCCUPIED sign flashed on over the door, Franklin sprang into motion.

"We need to hurry," she said, grabbing her helmet.

Torran sat up straight as Franklin picked up his helmet and set them side-by-side on the console. Accessing the side panels on both, she tugged out a connector and hooked them together. Using her wristlet to access her helmet computer remotely, Franklin started the program transfer.

"I checked the aerial drone while in the sanitary station," she said in a low voice. "The Scrags around the base are still riled up, but they're not a danger to us. They're the only active ones in the area. The drone also checked the stairwell. The mob following us up the escalators is gone. They all fell to their deaths." She smirked slightly. "Idiot creatures."

"You accessed your helmet through your wristlet I take it," Torran said, trying to sound casual.

Franklin stilled for a second, then said, "Yeah. So once the program is uploaded again on your helmet, you'll be up and running. It'll sync automatically with the ghost program in your wristlet."

"Right." Torran tried to look casual as he swept his hair back from his face and yawned. "Bloody exhausted."

"I'm going to go ahead and call in while she's in there. That way they'll know we're both on the job." Franklin activated her wristlet and started to swipe her way through the multiple layers of programs.

Tensing, Torran weighed his options. The second Franklin reported in, he'd be exposed. "Don't," he said before he could reconsider.

"Why not?"

"She might come out at any second."

"Or you might be afraid of what I might discover when I report in."

"And that, too," Torran confessed, not seeing the point in lying further. Franklin was on to him.

"So, you're *not* with us," Franklin said, continuing to work on her wristlet.

"Maybe I can be," Torran suggested.

Franklin smirked. "Right."

"Tell me what's going on."

"Why did you save Lindsey?" Franklin paused in her task.

"I love her," Torran answered simply.

The woman's full lips parted in an "O," then she laughed. "Of course. How did I miss that?" She resumed tapping on the screen of her wristlet.

"Seriously, stop." Torran stood up sharply. "I want to know why you want Maria Martinez."

Franklin paused again and raised her dangerously glinting eyes to regard him. "The virus in her veins, of course."

"Are you doing this for the president?"

"That idiot?" Her laugh was mocking.

"The Constabulary?"

"This is beyond mere politics and military branches," Franklin retorted, her expression turning sour. "This is about humanity."

"You want to save it?" Torran lifted his eyebrows. "Because if you do, you have a strange way of showing it by killing off your own squad."

"We want to save a *portion* of humanity. The part dedicated to the restoration of the planet and preservation of its ecosystem."

"You're Gaia Cult," Torran said, anger flaring to life. "I see."

"Gaia Liberation, not cult. Look at this monstrous city. It's arrogance. It's avarice! This is what happens when humanity only seeks to preserve itself." Franklin stared at him in defiance.

"So you find Maria and what? Give the virus she has to only those in the Gaia Cult?"

"There has to be a new Garden of Eden."

"I thought you wanted everyone *dead.*"

"We were purging the planet before. Removing the wasted mass of flesh that was choking the very life out of the earth. Now we'll start to rebuild outside of the walls. I can see from your expression that you're not impressed."

"Oh, no. I'm very, very impressed with your total lack of basic human empathy and kindness. Also, your arrogance is completely mind-blowing." Torran bestowed upon her his most intense Scottish glower.

Franklin dropped her hands as her body tensed. Her eyes flicked to her weapon and dagger just a short distance away.

"I'm expendable I take it?" Torran tilted his head as he watched her every move.

"You've blown our plans to get the information out of Lindsey without resorting to persuasive interrogation."

"Torture, you mean."

Franklin shrugged.

"Let's talk this out—"

The tall woman dove for her weapons, her sleek muscled body moving with predatory agility. Torran scrambled around the console. Just as Franklin lifted her weapon, Torran tackled her. They slid across the slick floor and into the far wall with a hard thump. With a hiss, Franklin attempted to punch Torran's face, but he struck her chin with a sharp blow of his elbow, stunning her briefly. Gritting his teeth, he concentrated on prying the firearm from her grip. Struggling ferociously, Franklin punched him in the ear and beat her feet against the floor. Torran managed to rip the weapon free from her grip just as Franklin wedged one leg between their bodies and shoved him off her.

Lashing out, she struck him in the side of the head, then crawled toward her dagger.

Torran flipped onto his back, aiming for Franklin when he saw Lindsey dart around the column in the center of the hub and kick the dagger away from Franklin's grasp. The blade spun across the floor and smacked into the wall. Seizing Lindsey's wrist, Franklin pivoted on her hip and dragged Lindsey down to the floor. Lindsey landed on her back with a loud thump, air whooshing out of her lungs. With startling speed, Franklin grabbed Lindsey's long braid and jerked her upright in front of her to use as a shield. Carefully, Franklin slid into a crouching position behind the stunned blond woman.

"Shoot," Franklin dared him.

"You can't win this," Torran replied, still lying on his side and aiming at the two women.

"We already have. You're cut off from The Bastion. There will be no rescue team except for the one we send. Someone *will* come in my place, and then you'll have much more to deal with than just me." Franklin grinned, her eyes gleaming with the fanaticism of a true believer. "I'm willing to die for what I believe in."

"Then you won't let her die," Torran replied. "And you won't kill her. You need Lindsey to get to Maria."

Fingers still gripping Lindsey's hair, Franklin clearly weighed her options.

Lindsey finally managed to drag a full breath. "Let go of me. We won't hurt you if you let me go."

"There's two of us and one of you," Torran said calmly, but his heart was beating so hard in his chest, he thought it would break his ribs. "We'll let you make the call to your people so they can come get us. We won't stop you." His only hope was that Franklin would see the sense of surrendering her hostage, so that Lindsey could lead the Gaia Cult to Maria.

"Give me the weapon then," Franklin ordered.

"Let go of her," Torran replied.

"Weapon first."

With a grunt, Torran slid the firearm across the floor. Franklin lunged for it as it whizzed past her, but missed. While she was looking away from him, Torran grabbed the dagger Lindsey had earlier kicked his way and tucked it into his waistband at the small of his back.

"Let go of her," Torran repeated.

With disgust, Franklin let go of Lindsey and moved to retrieve her weapon. "I'm calling for retrieval right now. I hope you'll cooperate, Lindsey. I would really hate to see you suffer, because in the end, you will help us one way or the other."

Torran cautiously climbed to his feet as Lindsey followed his lead, both with their hands raised.

"I don't care much for torture," Lindsey retorted.

"Then you'll help us right away, won't you?" Bending over, Franklin retrieved her weapon. "As for you, Torran, you're really not necessary." She swung the weapon around to fire.

Torran grabbed the dagger from his belt and flung it at Franklin. "I figured you say that."

Seeing the blade slashing through the air toward her, Franklin dodged. Lindsey pivoted about and administered a roundhouse kick that met Franklin's head with a meaty thwack. Stunned, Franklin dropped her firearm and it clattered to the floor. Lindsey hit her again with a knee to the stomach, doubling Franklin over.

Torran wasn't sure if they were going to be able to restrain the other woman. When Franklin lunged at Lindsey and managed to get her fingers around her throat, he recognized they were locked in a battle to the death. There was no way the cultist was going to capitulate.

The two women grappled with one another, Franklin intent on reaching one of her two weapons, while Lindsey fought to stop her. Torran rushed to help Lindsey, but Franklin saw him coming and managed to shove her opponent into him. Torran caught Lindsey as Franklin lunged for her firearm. Again, Lindsey rolled forward and kicked out, striking Franklin's knee and knocking the other woman aside.

Torran spurted forward and grabbed the firearm. Meanwhile, Franklin picked up her dagger and slashed at Torran. Pain streaked through him as she caught his bicep.

"No!" Lindsey tackled the other woman and they wrestled for control of the bloodied knife.

Unable to shoot, Torran attempted to get close enough to strike Franklin. The taller, stronger woman saw him coming and thwarted him by using Lindsey to block him again. Dragging Lindsey about, Franklin used her former friend as a shield. Ignoring the pain in his arm, Torran stalked after them with the weapon raised, waiting for a chance to shoot.

Lindsey planted her feet on the floor and drove Franklin backward. Propelling them both across the hub and into the entrance, Lindsey scrabbled at the hand clutching the dagger. Franklin seized Lindsey's long braided hair with her other hand and wrenched her head to one side.

Torran finally had a shot, and fired. The bullet ripped through Franklin's shoulder, stunning her. A second later, Lindsey hit the controls and the door Franklin was sagging against snapped open. Her own weight carried her out of the entrance, but the fingers wrapped around Lindsey's hair dragged the blond woman after her. Torran shouted in terror.

Lindsey's fingers hit the controls, and the door banged shut as rapidly as it had opened. With a painful sounding thud, Lindsey smacked into it. Caught by her braid, Lindsey slumped against the doorjamb.

"Ouch," she said in a very deadpan voice.

Torran almost laughed, but the seriousness of the situation stole the inclination away. Setting the weapon aside, he hurried over to help her. The golden braid was partially severed by the door and unfurling down along her neck.

"Your hair is still caught," he said.

"Well, don't open the door. Just find something to cut it off with." Lindsey sighed and wiped a tear away. "Fuck."

Torran searched the kitchen area first and found a pair of scissors in a utility drawer. Rushing back, he saw the agony in Lindsey's eyes.

"I'm sorry about Franklin," he said, then carefully snipped through her braid.

"Fuck her. Fuck all of them. I won't lead them to Maria."

The thick blond braid unraveled in a ragged wave across her shoulders, leaving the rest in the door. As she straightened, Lindsey raised her hands to her hair. Huge tears formed in her eyes, but she obviously tried to fight them. Feeling awkward, Torran handed her the scissors.

"I swore I would never cut it," she said with a break in her voice. "I promised my father when he died I wouldn't cut it. I know it was dumb, but..."

"He'd understand, Lindsey." Torran rested his hand on her slumped shoulder and squeezed.

"Is she dead?" Lindsey looked toward the console and the security feed. She obviously wanted to change the subject.

Torran reluctantly left her side to check the external security cameras. The outside entrance was empty. Only the tip of Lindsey's braid was sticking out of the door.

"She fell. That's a long fall. If she didn't die on impact..."

"She's a Scrag."

"Yeah."

Nodding with satisfaction, Lindsey opened the door to the sanitation unit and stepped inside. She didn't shut the door, so Torran had the heart-rending view of her cutting her hair until it was even. It now fell to her chin, but the shorter cut didn't detract from her beauty. Sweeping her shortened locks behind her ears, Lindsey stood, staring at her reflection.

Torran leaned in the doorway and tilted his head to gaze at the mirror. "It looks lovely."

With a bitter laugh, Lindsey finally looked at him. "You're a flatterer."

"That's why you like me," he answered with a faint smile.

Returning her gaze to the new hairdo, Lindsey shrugged. "My father probably would've liked it."

"Probably." Torran tugged at his own spikes along the front of his hairline. "So, here is my hair secret. My mum loves my cowlick. Loves it. My whole life she always ruffles it whenever she sees me. She hated it when I had my hair all buzzed down when I was in the Constabulary. So when I enlisted with the SWD, I let it return to its unruly ways. So that's why I have horrible non-regulation hair."

The smile on her lips made the heaviness inside his heart more bearable.

"The things we do for the ones we love, huh, Torran?"

"I would do anything for you," Torran said, meaning every word.

"Including leaping out of a tiltrotor into a Scrag infested river."

"And I would do it again."

Lindsey flung her arms around his neck and dragged him down to her eye level so she could stare into his eyes. "Thank you," she said, her lips soft against his.

Torran clutched her slim body close to his, relishing the strength of her grip. "Like I said... I'll always come for you."

" So Gaia Cult, huh?"

"You heard?"

"I sneaked out to spy."

"I noticed. Thankfully. She might've gotten me otherwise."

"I'll always come to your rescue."

Torran tenderly slid his fingers along her cheek. "I know."

"So... the Gaia Cult is still around."

Torran exhaled slowly. "Yeah. And Solomon is part of it, too. And probably someone else on the tiltrotor that didn't survive. And at least one mechanic at the SWD who helped sabotage the ship."

"What are we going to do?" Lindsey asked. "We're stuck out here. We can't get home. What do we do?"

Settling his hands on her waist, Torran bent down to press his forehead against hers. "Eat, sleep, and worry about it later."

"That easy?" she asked.

"Yeah. That easy."

As always, her kiss was sweet, and her trust in him sweeter. "Okay."

The bunk beds weren't very comfortable with two people squeezed onto one, but neither one of them wanted to be alone. Lindsey managed to sleep for a few hours, but was roused by the many questions floating through her mind.

After showering and eating, they'd had a long discussion about their knowledge about the supposed SWD mission to bring back Dwayne and Maria, but it had created more questions than she liked. Lindsey was still a little peeved that Torran had admitted he had been dedicated to the mission in order to save her and the rest of humanity, but at the same time she couldn't blame his reasoning. The idea of being able to walk among the Scrags without fear was very tempting.

Dressed in her dark gray undershirt and panties, she slid onto the chair at the console and started perusing the files she'd found on the hard drive cache. It was mostly security reports from the Rescue Hub command center, but there were also other tidbits of information from various news sources. There had to be a way out of the Rescue Hub other than an airlift. Dragging Franklin's helmet onto her lap, she connected it to the console and started searching through the hidden program. She hoped to duplicate it and download it to her wristlet so she could contact the aerial drone and keep tabs of the Scrags around the location. Maybe she could even find a way to drag the active Scrags around the Rescue Hub away from their location.

Though Lindsey had initially riled up the Scrags by jumping off the bench, she now wondered if Franklin had deliberately roused the rest by firing her weapon so the three of them would be trapped. Torran had said that the plan had been to force Lindsey to contact Maria once a rescue team didn't arrive. Lindsey hated to admit that it may have worked if the situation had been dire enough and she believed they were the only hope of rescue. She would've sent word to Maria and Dwayne that she was stranded using the floating cloud she'd constructed to keep them updated.

With a frown, Lindsey pulled up the copy of the program that had attempted to hack into Maria and Dwayne's wristlets during the pulses to Beta City. It had forced the couple to go offline completely. She'd never been able to trace it back to its point of origin, and had set it aside. Now, she compared it to the one imbedded in Franklin's helmet. Examining both programs, she saw similar patterns.

"Same programmer," she whispered.

The Gaia Cult had been searching for her friend from the beginning. Dr. Curran had urged Lindsey to seek answers, but now that they were right in front of her, Lindsey was cut off from sharing what she'd uncovered. Without a pulse to connect The Bastion grid, there wasn't a way for her to transmit the information.

"Why aren't you sleeping?" Torran asked, pulling a chair out from beneath the console. The back flipped up and he sat down next to her.

"I figured a few things out." She reached up to tug on her braid and realized it wasn't there. Instead, she tucked her shorter hair behind her ears. It was time for new habits, she supposed. "Gaia Cult is working within both the SWD and Constabulary. You said that you and Dr. Curran were supposed to find Maria and Dwayne, but nothing really came about after that meeting."

"Nah. Not at all. I thought it was weird," Torran confessed.

"I think it was bait."

"Eh?"

"Well, Dr. Curran worked with Commandant Pierce and Dwayne to bring down Admiral Kirkpatrick. So I think the Gaia Cult thought maybe she was in contact with Dwayne and Maria."

"Okay, I can see that reasoning, but why me?"

"We'd already been seen together," Lindsey said, shrugging.

"Oh."

"We weren't all that careful before the mission. If the Gaia Cult was watching me because I'm Maria's best friend, then they would have seen that you were spending the night with me."

"So, they call me into a meeting, tell me about the mission, and I tell you—"

"But you didn't tell me." She stuck out her tongue.

"Eh, I'm loyal. To a fault. I admit it." He winced and had the decency to look chagrined.

"So when I don't reach out to Dwayne and Maria in a way they can trace—"

"They decide on another tactic. It makes sense." Torran scrubbed his hand over his hair and sighed. "Okay, so Commandant Pierce wanted you to thwart the SWD plans. So she's not a part of it. But Trevino and Martel are behind my assignment and Dr. Curran's. They clearly want Maria."

"One or both of them are Gaia Cult. Also, Solomon picked the Beta City depot for a reason. Dr. Curran couldn't figure out why, or maybe she was just trying to get me to come to a conclusion. Who knows with her?"

"So what *is* your conclusion?"

"Solomon knew the Beta City depot was sabotaged by Gaia Cult because she's one of them. She knew we'd run into some trouble. And because we did have problems, she received a much bigger squad, more equipment, more aircraft, more drones..."

"Yeah, yeah, yeah. In other words, she probably got more Cultists on the squad and basically was given the equipment she needed to find Dwayne and Maria."

"Including Dr. Curran. The Gaia Cult will probably need her to handle the virus." Lindsey pressed the heels of her hands to her eyes and let out a growl. "Shit... shit... shit..."

"The food shortages worsened because of failures in storage." Torran's voice was very thoughtful.

"Infrastructure breakdowns. The mechanical failures."

"The gate being opened." Torran slumped down in his chair. "Gaia Cult. All of it, or most of it."

"Probably the only reason they didn't release the ISPV inside The Bastion is because they didn't have access to it. Everyone always made fun of the wall patrols, but that's probably what kept them from doing something like hooking a Scrag and dragging it over the wall."

"Or maybe there weren't that many Cultists for a while. Maybe Gaia Cult is resurging." Torran shrugged. "Hard to say with radicals."

"I should have put it together about Franklin. Remember what she said about humans outliving their extinction event, or something like that?"

"She slipped. Just a wee bit, eh?"

"Yeah..." Lindsey didn't want to think about Franklin, or Hobbes. At least Giacomi was still alive in The Bastion, but what if she couldn't be trusted either? What if Hobbes was the other Gaia Cultist, but had unexpectedly died in the crash? The thought made her heart hurt.

"We need to get the hell out of here," Torran declared. "We're right where they want us."

"Torran, we can't survive in this city for long," Lindsey said, the thought making her heart beat so much harder.

"We'll find another Rescue Hub."

"You don't think they'll search each one until they find us?"

"Fuck."

"This isn't just about us anymore, you know." Lindsey pressed the knuckles of one hand against her lips. The weight of responsibility crushed down on her. It made her feel like she was suffocating. How had Maria dealt with it during the special ops mission?

"Yeah, I know. It's about The Bastion and everyone living in it."

"If the Gaia Cult manages to get a hold of the virus that's in Maria, they'll infect their own people and then what? Leave everyone else to rot in The Bastion?" Lindsey blinked the tears forming in her eyes.

Folding his arms over his chest, Torran wagged his head somberly. "No, they'll find a way to kill them. Finish what they started when they opened the gate and let the Scrags into the valley."

"We're so screwed."

Torran took hold of her hand and dragged it away from her face. Bending over their entwined fingers, he kissed the back of her hand. "I don't want to lose you, but we can't ignore what's happening. We can't just save ourselves."

Enfolding him in her arms, she kissed the top of his head and rubbed her fingers over the muscles in his back. "We have to try to reach The Bastion. If we can't do it physically, we have to try to communicate with them. We have to reach Commandant Pierce."

"And if that doesn't work?"

"Maybe I will have to call Maria to come rescue us. Maybe she can get us closer to the city."

"We shouldn't risk it," Torran raised his head as she leaned back in her chair.

"I know, but that's our fallback plan only."

"So you have a different plan?"

"Yeah." Lindsey pulled away from him and reached for the console. "I have an idea. There is a communication tower on the west side of this platform. It's on top of the newscast building. Now, according to the reports I gleaned off this computer, this platform was one of the first to be evacuated. So that might be a good thing. Less Scrags. Also, there is a monorail track that goes right up to a station next to the building with the tower. It's a long-range tower. We might be able to reach The Bastion if it still has an operational emergency generator."

"But how do we get there with a crowd of rabid Scrags waiting for us below? Because I don't think they'll be calming down anytime soon. They saw us come in here."

Pursing her lips, Lindsey's mind sifted through all the possibilities. Gradually, a wide smile slid onto her face.

"That's a truly frightening smile," Torran decided.

"Well, first I have to get nice and cozy with the aerial drone once I hack and rewrite this program, but I definitely think I have an idea."

"Is this the point where I go make you a pot of coffee?"

"Yes." She leaned toward him for a kiss.

"I'm on it," he replied, and left her to her work.

CHAPTER 30

The aerial drone dropped through the hatch into the hub. Its long legs extended toward Lindsey as it adjusted the rotors like bizarre antenna to keep it aloft. Torran was unnerved by the aerial drones. He considered them to be intrusive buggers even though they were helpful on the squad's excursions. The Bastion government had grown far too dependent on the insect-like robots of late.

"Hey, Baby," Lindsey said in greeting.

Torran raised one eyebrow.

"Hello Mother," the drone answered.

"You programmed it to answer you?" Torran shook his head with amusement. He'd left Lindsey to her own devices while he'd done maintenance on their armor and filled two backpacks with supplies. Obviously, Lindsey had done more than just gain control over the aerial drone.

"Well, they're all programmed to speak, but usually just pre-recorded threats. I gave this little guy a little boost with an A.I. program I've been toying with, so he can answer rudimentary questions and carry on short conversations."

"I am smart," the aerial drone informed Torran.

Lindsey flashed a proud smile. "Isn't it cute?"

Torran winced. The electronic hum of the drone's voice was disconcerting. "Oh yeah, the giant mechanical bug is adorable."

Picking up Franklin's helmet, Lindsey handed it to the hovering drone. "You know what to do."

"Yes, Mother." The drone's many claw-like hands gripped it tightly.

"What do you do when you're done?"

"Return to you in victory."

"Does it have to be a smart ass like you, Linds?"

"Yes, Father," the drone replied.

"Hey! None of that!"

"Call him Mr. MacDonald. He's obviously not very friendly." Lindsey patted the drone's metal carapace.

"Give it another name other than 'Baby', okay?" Torran gave them both a disapproving look. He was convinced the drone's many small cameras at the end of tentacle-like stalks all swiveled toward him to glower.

"Like what?"

"Uh... hell if I know."

Lindsey stared up at the aerial drone thoughtfully. "Teeny, that's your name."

"Yes, Mother."

"I'd really rather it didn't call *you* that," Torran grumbled.

"You're just jealous that I have a new thing to love," Lindsey teased. She waved her hand at the drone. "Off you go. Do your job, Teeny."

"Yes, Mother."

The aerial drone shifted its rotors and lifted out of the hub. The overhead hatch clanged shut.

"You're so strange sometimes," Torran decided, but he was amused by her interaction with the drone. Lindsey almost glowed with delight whenever she was indulging in her passion for tech.

"And things are about to get stranger." Sliding her arms around his waist, she gazed up at him, her expression altering to a more somber one. "One last kiss before we go?"

"Not a last kiss. Just one to hold us over until the next," Torran answered. Clutching her close, he tucked his lips over hers and kissed her until they were both nearly breathless.

With great reluctance, Lindsey slid from his arms, her hand clutching his for a few more seconds.

"We'll be okay," Torran said, though he knew they probably wouldn't be unless fate was very kind.

With a small smile, Lindsey picked up his helmet and tossed it to him before donning her own. "I'll hold you to that."

Clad in their armor, they were ready for their departure. Both wore backpacks and carried multiple weapons. Torran had decided to carry the remote generator even though it was low on power and it added extra weight to his pack. Lindsey's was filled with food, water, and additional ammunition.

A few seconds after Torran connected his helmet to his armor, the feed sputtered on. It was truncated as it was only scrolling information from his armor, Lindsey's suit, and Teeny. Since the drone had more than one camera, it was broadcasting multiple feeds at once.

It was a little dizzying to watch Teeny skimming over the Scrags and being completely ignored.

The Scrags were definitely still obsessed with the Rescue Hub and the prey within.

According to old reports, once the Scrags knew the location of humans, they did not leave the area unless distracted by new prey. Even if Lindsey and Torran waited until the Scrags fell into torpor, once the Rescue Hub returned to its station, the vicious beings would waken and become an instant threat. Therefore, a plan to lure them away had been concocted.

Torran and Lindsey walked somberly to the exit and leaned against the wall while watching the drone's feed. Teeny finished surfing over the herd and dropped to street level to hover just outside the doorway of a glass-walled dress shop. A thick blanket of fresh snow adorned the building's roof. Extending several of its arms, the drone pried the doors open and slipped inside.

"If this works..." Torran said to Lindsey.

"It will work." She pouted. "Don't doubt me."

"I don't. It's just such a long shot."

"Maybe, but we have to try."

Teeny whirred over to a mannequin that was sporting a bright red evening gown.

"I told it to find a bright color," Lindsey explained.

The drone deftly set the helmet on the mannequin's head. Its pincher-like fingers slid under the helmet and activated the stealth. On the feed it looked the head of the mannequin vanished.

Lindsey twisted her lips to one side while watching the feed on her faceplate. It was an endearing habit that Torran hoped he'd continue to observe for a very long time.

"Okay, Teeny, activate the secondary program."

"Yes, Mother."

Again the drone made adjustments. It was disconcerting to see a recorded projection of Lindsey's head appear on the helmet.

"I guess my new hairdo does look okay," Lindsey observed. "Teeny, go get the baddies now."

"Yes, Mother."

The drone picked up the mannequin by its torso, rapidly flew out of the shop, and along the street toward the Scrags. It was a little nausea-inducing to observe how fast it flew. One of the cameras was aimed down and showed the mannequin with Lindsey's face superimposed over its head dangling from the drone's clutches.

"Teeny, activate audio," Lindsey ordered.

Instantly, the drone played Lindsey's voice screaming for help. It was amplified to catch the attention of all the Scrags. At first the creatures were making such a ruckus, they didn't hear the recording, but the drone increased the volume. Sluggishly, the Scrags twisted about to face the mannequin suspended above the ground.

"They're interested at least," Torran remarked.

"It's going to work," Lindsey said confidently. "Watch and see."

As always, it took only one Scrag giving chase to unleash a horde. Within seconds after the first Scrag lurched toward the bait, the herd rushed the mannequin.

"Go Teeny!" Lindsey cried out.

The aerial drone whirled about and flew away clutching the facsimile of Lindsey screaming for help. The Scrags raced after it.

Lindsey gave Torran a triumphant look. "See?"

"Extraordinary," Torran admitted.

"I'm amazing!"

On the feed, the aerial drone sped around a corner, leading the herd to the tube the soldiers had taken the day before. If all went according to plan, the Scrags would pursue Teeny down the stairwell and fall through the gap.

Lindsey opened the door, and they both peered out. Every Scrag that had been gathered under the Rescue Hub was gone.

"Well done," Torran said with admiration, then pulled the emergency exit lever near the door. "Now let's get out of here."

A ladder unfurled from a hidden compartment beneath the door. The metal pieces locked together, forming a stable exit out of the hub. Torran climbed down first, holding his weapon in one hand just in case any were lurking in the shadows. The clank of his boots against the rungs was a little louder than he'd like, and Torran kept his external mic on high to pick up any telltale shrieks. Once he hit the ground, he crept forward to check on the street again. The thin layer of snow crunched beneath his feet.

Dropping down, Lindsey immediately lifted her weapon and joined him. "Status?"

"Clear for now."

"Then let's go."

Keeping their weapons at the ready, they activated the stealth on their suits and scurried along the snow-flecked street. The grips of their boots would keep them upright if they stepped on black ice. While Torran watched the left side of the street, Lindsey monitored the right. Their objective was the monorail station a few blocks away. Teeny had swept through the area earlier, and there was minimal activity in the district. Without the clutter of street vehicles, it was easier to spot any potential dangers.

Torran shifted his view to the drone's cameras again. The Scrags were still following it through the stairwells. At least this part of the plan was working well. He was still unsure of Lindsey's designs to reach the communication tower, but he didn't see where they had any other choice. They had to warn The Bastion about what they knew of the Gaia Cult's persuasive presence in the city and its terrifying stratagem.

Sprinting along the boulevard, the feeling of vulnerability Torran experienced made it a little difficult to breathe. Even though his suit was in stealth mode, it was difficult to be out in the open. In The Bastion, the high walls were always in sight, but here, there was no sense of security. Tall, glass buildings and a vast, gray sky made him feel small and exposed.

They were almost to the monorail station when the stealth deactivated sooner than expected.

"What the hell?" Torran muttered.

"The tech is built with old parts. They're crapping out." Lindsey pointed ahead. "But we're almost there!" She dashed through yet another courtyard toward the monorail station.

"Be careful!" Torran warned.

Lindsey dropped to a quick walk, sweeping through the area with a little more care. The monorail station consisted of several white concrete canopies over a glass-enclosed waiting area. There were a few Scrags inside, but Torran and Lindsey planned to bypass the passenger area and head onto the tracks. As they drew closer, the undead started to stir.

"Should we kill them?" Lindsey asked.

"There's not enough of them to break the glass, so I say we just let them be." Torran again checked the aerial drone's feed. It now hovered over the gap in the escalators observing the Scrags falling to their final death. "Looks like your little buddy did his job."

Scooting past a thick gnarl of trees overgrown with vines, Lindsey looked pleased with herself. "I should name it Buddy!"

"No, you shouldn't."

"You're not very fun sometimes."

"I'm very fun most of the time."

"And I'm brilliant. We make a good team." Though her tone was purposefully playful, she cautiously checked a darkened area for Scrags before continuing toward the station.

The seriousness of their situation was crushing in its intensity, but Torran was determined not to let Lindsey see his fear and worry. He knew her well enough to see that she was thrilled with her triumph with the aerial drone but also very scared.

Torran trailed behind her, keeping a sharp eye on their surroundings. The aerial drone had been right about the low infestation level, but Torran was well aware that a shriek from a Scrag would awaken all the others in range. Then again, Franklin's terrorist cell had purposefully chosen a platform of the upper city with a low infestation level, but he refused to be grateful. Though Lindsey hadn't said anything, Torran noted that Franklin's body had been missing. Which meant she'd become a Scrag. To Torran, it seemed like a fitting fate.

The Scrags inside the monorail waiting area stumbled toward the glass walls. They were in much better condition than those wandering outside in the elements. Though the creatures were obviously shrieking, the soundproof construction muted the terrible sound.

Darting onto the tracks, Lindsey sighed with relief. "We made it."

Torran gestured toward the communication tower in the distance. "We have a ways to go."

"Yeah, but that was the harder part, right?" Lindsey waited for him to join her, then together, they started along the elevated track. "We need Teeny to join us. I'm calling him back."

Torran nodded, rotating about to make sure the Scrags were still trapped in the station. They were. On the feed, Teeny ditched Franklin's helmet and the mannequin before swooping out over the river and rising toward the platform. Its job was done.

Though Lindsey had devised a way to hide their wristlet signal from the Gaia Cult, the one she'd created for Teeny allowed the drone to track her. Of course, walking along the monorail line was a risk. Both the Scrags and the Cultists could spot them on the elevated track. Hopefully, they would make it to the communication tower before that happened.

"So, we escaped the Rescue Hub, made it to the monorail track, and our aerial drone killed a good chunk of the Scrags," Lindsey said. "That's not bad for an early morning start."

"We just have to reach the communication tower, somehow start up the generator, transmit a top secret message to the commandant, and save what's left of humanity."

"Sounds like a full day's work," Lindsey decided.

"Just the same old, same old. Save the day. Go home. Make love to the girlfriend."

"Girlfriend? Is that what I am? We actually never agreed to titles."

Though they were both obviously nervous, alert, and always checking behind and ahead of them, Torran loved every moment he could spend with her. It made life worth living.

"Well, girlfriend does have a nice sound to it, don't you think?" Torran peered over the edge of the track at the road below. There were no Scrags in sight for the moment.

"Most definitely better than significant other. That sounds far too formal."

"Lover," Torran said, rolling the word off his tongue. "Lover sounds..."

"Sounds a bit dirty."

"Does it?"

"Definitely."

"So not lover."

"Well, unless we're naked and in bed. Then you can be my *lover*." Lindsey dragged the word out provocatively.

Torran started to answer, but the track beneath his feet started to tremble. Lindsey crouched and grabbed onto the rail with one hand as the quaking intensified. A second later, Torran's helmet lit up with an array of information streaming in from a nearby source, then was abruptly cut off. The air vibrated and a familiar sensation swept over him.

At the same time, Lindsey and Torran stood to face the squad tiltrotor cresting over the buildings of the upper city. Aerial drones flew at the two soldiers in a tight formation.

"Shit," Torran breathed, realizing there was nowhere for them to go.

Lindsey turned toward him, a look of fright on her face.

Then they were peppered with electroshock discs and the world went black.

CHAPTER 31

Lindsey's head pulsed painfully as she opened her eyes. At first, the world was blurry and surreal, then her vision adjusted. She was lying on a medbed and only clad in her black jumpsuit. Her armor, helmet and pack were gone. Swiping her wristlet, she saw it was locked down.

Across from her, Torran was still unconscious on another medbed. The room was white, sparse, and had three medbeds. The third was empty and it took her a second to realize they were not alone.

"MacDonald was hit a few more times than you were," Dr. Curran said, stepping into the room from a small sanitation station in one corner. "He'll take a little more time to recover."

"Where are we?" Lindsey sat up sluggishly, her head swimming.

"It's called the Louvre Rescue Center. We're on the top floor. It's secure. The Scrags can't get through the bulkhead doors. We have roof access, which is how we got in." Dr. Curran was still dressed in her Sci-tech uniform, and the bun on the back of her head looked a little ragged. Dark circles were under her eyes and there was a nasty bruise on her jaw.

Lindsey tried to drop her legs over the edge of the bed, but realized they were shackled to the frame. "Oh, nice." She tugged at the heavy restraints, but comprehended quickly that there was no way she'd pry them off without tools.

"They're not certain how you'll react, so they're taking precautions," Dr. Curran explained.

Motioning at the scientists face, she said, "Is that what that is? A precaution?"

The older woman gingerly touched the bruise. "There was some conflict earlier, yes. Vanguard Rooney, do you know who's holding us?"

"Us?" Lindsey stared at the scientist distrustfully.

Dr. Curran pulled up a chair and sat down between the two beds where Lindsey and Torran were restrained. "Yes, us."

"You're not shackled."

"I'm not a potential troublemaker." Dr. Curran sighed, clenched her hands together, and set them on her lap.

"That's what the bruise is from? Them making sure you weren't a troublemaker?"

"I admit I had a bit of a temper tantrum. Considering that I attempted to kill one of Solomon's people, I got off a bit easy."

"And they need you."

Dr. Curran bitterly laughed. "You've figured some of it out, haven't you?"

"They want the virus, so they're going to need someone who knows how to work with it to ensure it's properly handled. They'll also need someone who can create the vaccines, administer it in proper dosages, and all that shit." Lindsey flopped back onto the flat pillow beneath her head. She didn't see the point of trying to sit up with her legs bound. "Plus, you created Maria."

"They hoped I knew where she's hiding. They were under the false impression I helped save her. They didn't know I encouraged the castellan to kill her to protect The Bastion. They were surprised when I told them."

"You're a fuckin' bitch," Lindsey snarled.

Dr. Curran shrugged. "Perhaps."

"All of this is your fault."

Eyes flashing with fury, Dr. Curran leaned toward Lindsey. "If not for me, humanity would not have a chance at survival right now."

"Sorry to burst your bubble, but you created a weapon against humanity that the Gaia Cult is going to use to wipe us out!" Lindsey crossed her arms over her chest and glared at the ceiling, not wanting to even look at the scientist.

"Of course, the Gaia Cult doesn't see it quite that way. They feel they're saving the best of humanity by starting a new world with like-minded people that will do away with all tech, return to the basics, and start again. They'll leave places like this to rot away until it's nothing more than a memory."

"And to do that they need immunity like Maria's." Lindsey snorted with contempt.

"Exactly."

"So they kidnapped you, too."

"Yes, they did."

"When?"

Dr. Curran stood and leaned over Lindsey so she was forced to look her in the eye. "I know you're angry, but you're not the only one suffering right now. Yesterday, no one returned to The Bastion. Solomon's tiltrotor fired on the transports and destroyed them before they reached the mountain range."

"They destroyed the food?" Lindsey stared at Dr. Curran in shock. "Killed the transport crews? Why?"

"Malice? Vengeance? Who knows?"

"But the transports must have sent out a mayday."

"Carter rigged a communication suppression system that didn't allow the transports to call for help."

"Carter?" Lindsey tried to wrap her mind around the idea of Carter, with his massive build and goofy grin, being a mastermind behind a suppression system.

"Yes, Carter."

"Of course, your tiltrotor was sabotaged so it would crash into the river. That had been carefully planned out. There was a violent takeover on the remaining tiltrotor. Anyone not Gaia Cult or deemed essential to their plans was killed. There was a scuffle. I tried to kill Yates and Solomon hit me. When I awakened, we had already arrived here. I was interrogated for hours. Finally, they concluded I really don't know where Maria is located. So then they settled in to wait for

Franklin to check in. She never did. So this morning they went looking for you and happened across you on the monorail tracks."

"So I suppose they want me to lead them to Maria."

"They do."

"I have no idea where she is," Lindsey answered truthfully.

Dr. Curran pressed her lips together in a grim line, slightly shaking her head.

The room was probably being monitored. Was this her interrogation? Did she just doom herself? "I know where she was weeks ago," Lindsey added, uncertainty filling her. Glancing at Torran fearfully, Lindsey's heart sped up.

Noticing where Lindsey was looking, Dr. Curran said, "As for Master Seeker MacDonald, they have high hopes he'll be joining them. His psych test reveals a man who's very unhappy with the status quo of the city."

"And you've joined them?"

"I don't have a choice, do I?" Dr. Curran gave her a bitter smile.

Swallowing the hard lump of dread in her throat, Lindsey said, "We all have choices. They just might be hard to live with."

"Especially if those choices make you very dead."

"You suspected Solomon of being Gaia Cult, didn't you?"

"Yes, but I also thought I had more time to put the pieces together." Dr. Curran sighed, her fingers pinching the bridge of her nose. "Of course, I shared my suspicions with the one person I trusted more than any other, but she assured me I was being overly imaginative."

"Martel." Lindsey remembered the dinner reservation she'd uncovered while snooping. "She's your..." Lindsey hesitated, remembering her conversation with Torran about relationship titles. The memory caused more pain than she'd ever dreamed. They'd never even agreed on what to call each other.

"She's my girlfriend. Or I thought she was. And she's in the Gaia Cult."

"You had no idea, did you?"

Dr. Curran shook her head sorrowfully. "No, I didn't. But upon reflection, I can see now how she seduced me. I always loved her, but she was always romantically entangled with men and didn't show any inclination toward returning my affections. Then, soon after the liberation of the valley, she reached out to me and suggested we get reacquainted over dinner. At first, I thought maybe it was my newfound celebrity that attracted her, but she convinced me it was love. That she'd been in denial."

Lindsey rubbed her lips together, not really wanting to feel bad for the scientist, but she actually did. "That's really fuckin' awful."

"Yes, well, we're all fools for love at some point. Look at what the castellan did for Maria. I never dreamed he loved her so much." Dr. Curran wistfully sighed, then returned to her chair.

"What happens next?"

"They'll talk to you. Hope you see the error of your ways and embrace the future by helping them find Maria. Which you should do if you want to live." Dr. Curran's voice was somber and devoid of warmth.

"Is that a threat?" Again, Lindsey wondered if this was the interrogation. Was Dr. Curran lying to her? Creating false sympathy? Or was there something more at play?

"No, Vanguard Rooney, it's just reality."

"Then reality can shove it up its asshole,"

Anger was keeping Lindsey from despair. There had to be a way out of the situation. She'd never allow Gaia Cult to find Maria. That would doom everyone in the city. The idea of tricking them came to mind. She could maybe use the remote communication cloud to divert the Gaia Cult to a wrong location, but Carter was a concern. He'd probably be watching her every little move if they allowed her near the equipment to transmit messages to Maria, and it was uncertain if his skills matched her own. Maybe it was arrogance, but she doubted he could best her.

"Listen to what they have to say," Dr. Curran urged. Tilting her head down, the scientist moved her lips, but didn't say actual words. It took Lindsey a few seconds to finally figure out what she was mouthing.

I have a plan.

The three prisoners were being escorted down a long corridor and Torran was still struggling to wake up completely. It had been disorienting and infuriating to return to consciousness strapped to a bed. He'd been relieved to see Lindsey was all right, but unnerved by the presence of Dr. Curran.

"Bloody hell," Torran growled, rubbing the top of his head vigorously with his bound hands. "How many of those damn things did they hit us with?"

"Enough," Dr. Curran replied.

When he dropped his hands, Lindsey shifted her bound wrists so she could intertwine her fingers with his. There was no point in denying their relationship in front of the people who'd seen him leap into a river to save her. There was also a strong possibility they'd been watched before the food retrieval mission had even become a reality.

"No touching," Carter ordered.

Lindsey gave the man a dark look, but let go of Torran.

"It'll be okay," Torran said to Lindsey.

"If you cooperate," Yates interjected. Her short blond hair was slicked back from her face making her appear even more imposing.

The two women had been filling him in on their circumstances when his former squad members had come to claim them. Carter,

Yates, and Ramirez had stripped their armor of their insignias and now wore Gaia Cult armbands. All three had remained unresponsive to every question hurled at them while they were releasing Lindsey and Torran from the bed restraints. The Cultists had then shackled their prisoners' wrists and ankles, making it difficult to walk. Dr. Curran, apparently having gained some of the trust of the Cultist, was left unrestrained.

Now Torran stumbled beside Lindsey through the new headquarters of the Gaia Cult. Since there wasn't power in the facility, remote generators were tucked near doorways to give power only to certain areas. It left most of the floor in the dark, which was disconcerting. Torran found it amusing that a group so adamantly against tech were dependent on its use.

The prisoners were escorted into a large room that had once been the primary hub of the rescue center. There was a lot of damage to the room, and upon closer inspection, Torran saw it was probably from the evacuation. Entire consoles had been yanked out of the walls. A few of the old screens were operational, and Torran saw more of his former squad members working to restore others.

Meanwhile, Chief Defender Solomon sat in the command chair, observing their approach. As they stepped into the room, she gave them a disquieting smirk. "Welcome."

"You have a strange way of making people feel *welcomed,*" Torran said, holding up his bound wrists.

"And this place doesn't really feel all that welcoming," Lindsey added, looking about the room. "Not very safe either."

"I beg to differ, Vanguard Rooney," Solomon said. "When this facility was built, it was claimed that no Scrag could ever breach the doors. It was created to survive in the worst outbreak. This declaration was actually correct. The Scrags didn't breach the doors. Gaia Liberation opened them. One floor after the other. Except for the one at the far end of the hall. We kept that one closed so we could return for needed equipment after the facility was abandoned." Solomon pointed at one of the screens that revealed a stairwell packed with Scrags. "So if you're worried about security, I can assure you: we're safe."

"How many rescue centers failed because of the Gaia Cult?" Lindsey asked, her gaze openly hostile.

Solomon settled back in her chair and crossed her legs. "Most of them."

"It's the hidden history of the outbreak," Dr. Curran said somberly.

With a shrug, the former chief defender said, "We didn't have to work too hard to topple countries and governments. The strife already ripping apart the world helped with the downfall of civilization. Once ISPV appeared, it became the weapon of choice against one's enemies. That's why humanity learned to build walls and lived behind them for nearly a century before the fall. When it became evident that this was our extinction event, Gaia Liberation just helped Mother Nature along."

Torran shook his head in disbelief. "Why? Why do that? We're all humans!"

"There is a natural ebb and flow to life. Life evolves. Life goes extinct. Look at the history of the planet. It was our turn. ISPV evolved to rid the planet of *us*. Global warming, wars, overpopulation, the stripping of natural resources, the out-of-control building of mega-cities..." Solomon shook her head in disgust. "Just look at the history vids. It was our time. Or so the founders of the Gaia Liberation believed."

Dr. Curran was unrestrained, so she made her way to an empty chair in front of a gutted console and sat down. "Your fairytale amuses me."

"Fairytale?" Solomon shot the scientist a fierce look. "Look at history. Look at science."

"You said the founders believed it was our extinction event," Lindsey interrupted, "but you give the impression that's not what *you* believe."

"When the existence of the Inferi Boon came to light, it became evident to the leadership that maybe Mother Nature didn't want all of us dead. This was confirmed when Dr. Curran admitted in a personal conversation—"

"With someone who was sent to spy on me," Dr. Curran snapped.

"—that she didn't actually create the Inferi Boon virus. She discovered it among samples from other labs. Mother Nature created a virus to destroy humanity, but also one to save us."

"You talk like Mother Nature is real," Torran said skeptically. Though Solomon had valid points about certain aspects of history, he couldn't understand how it warranted the destruction of human civilization.

"Isn't she? The planet is an organism that we're just a part of. We made the planet sick and it responded. Call it Gaia, Mother Nature, Terra, Earth, whatever...it's still the same thing." Solomon gave them a sad, weary smile. It was obvious she thought they were ignorant. "When we started to spread our disease outside our biosphere, that is when the ISPV appeared. Coincidence?"

"You're talking about Luna Colony and Mars Outpost," Lindsey said, her voice accusing. "Gaia Cult wiped them out?"

"That was our first major operation. It took years of preparation."

"It was one of the greatest acts of terrorism in the history of mankind. Thousands died!" Torran stared at her in horror.

In school, all children learned of the destruction of the two Earth colonies. At the time, no one had claimed responsibility. Wars had broken out among countries that had accused each other of the terrorist act. Conspiracy theorists had blamed aliens. Then the Scourge had started to spread across the globe and the world had fallen apart.

"Oh my God," Lindsey whispered in shock. "You're so wrong."

"You're clearly close-minded," Solomon retorted.

"No, you're wrong because Mother Nature had nothing to do with the virus."

"Rooney! No!" Dr. Curran snapped.

Torran swiveled toward Lindsey. "What are you talking about?"

"Nothing else like ISPV exists in nature. It's perfect and unique," Solomon said in a sharp tone. "Nothing. It wasn't created by humanity. It was created by Gaia to purge herself of us."

"No, it was created by an alien race as a gift to us," Lindsey snapped back. "We just screwed it up by altering it."

Solomon broke into wild peals of laughter as did the others gathered in the room. "Really? Is that what you believe?"

"Think about it. The virus appeared after we started making our forays out into the solar system and sending more advanced probes into deep space," Lindsey answered, but she sounded a little meek in the face of the Cultist derision.

From the look on Dr. Curran's face, Torran suspected Lindsey was telling the truth, and the scientist was relieved that no one believed her.

"We're wasting time," Solomon said, dismissing the whole conversation with the sweep of her hand. "We need your help, Rooney, to find Maria Martinez. We won't hurt her. We just need a sample of her blood so Dr. Curran can extract the modified virus and begin replicating it."

"I don't know where she is," Lindsey replied, her eyes downcast.

Torran shifted his weight so his arm pressed against her shoulder. Though he knew her refusal would have dire repercussions, he stood by her choice and supported it. But that didn't mean he wouldn't try to save them. "It's the truth. She doesn't. I tried to get the information out of her for the SWD."

"So you *were* conscripted to recover Maria. Dr. Curran wasn't lying about that," Solomon said, and this obviously pleased her. "She also said you might be sympathetic to our cause."

"I don't agree in the mindless destruction of civilian populations, but I'm not opposed to the Gaia Cultist starting their own colony elsewhere in the world. I will help you if you agree to let The Bastion continue to exist while your people start over." In his periphery, Lindsey gave him a sharp look. "I have information I'm willing to share if you'll come to an agreement with me."

Solomon's eyes narrowed, her fingers tapping on the armrest. "Why do you think the Gaia Cult would destroy The Bastion?"

"Because it fits with your belief system. You believe Gaia has provided a path to a new Eden with the virus Maria has in her veins," Torran said, shrugging. "Let's say that Dwayne and Maria are the new Adam and Eve out there in the world. Now, you and your people want to join them. I totally understand that desire. But Gaia Cult has actively tried to destroy people who don't agree with their philosophy in the past. What I'm asking you to do is let nature take its course. If I help you, then you must allow the last vestiges of humanity to have a shot at surviving."

Yates stepped forward. "They'll come for us, Solomon."

"They don't know you're alive," Lindsey said. "And if you let us go, we won't tell them."

"This world is vast. It's huge. You can pick any spot in the world and start over." Torran knew that any promise Solomon gave him would most likely be broken, but he needed more time for a solid escape plan.

"If The Bastion survives, we fail," Yates insisted.

"If the citizens of The Bastion survive, they're trapped," Dr. Curran pointed out. "They can't leave their valley. The Inferi Scourge will forever keep them trapped while you take over the world."

Solomon patted the armrests of her chair with the palms of her hands a few times, then stood up sharply. "All right, Torran. Let's talk terms."

"First, you give up the search for Maria Martinez."

"We need the virus!"

"There is another way to get it," Torran said boldly.

Dr. Curran swiveled about to stare at him with widened eyes filled with uncertainty. Lindsey cocked her head while staring at him with interest.

Solomon set her hands on her hips. "If you can find another source of the virus, we will let you and Rooney go."

"Dr. Curran, too," Torran added.

"No. Not her. We need her. We need her to administer the virus in the proper dosages and to oversee the process." Solomon shook her head adamantly. "We can't let her go."

"I'm fine with that," Dr. Curran said, her voice hollow. "I have nothing to return to."

"And you can't just turn us out into the world," Lindsey said firmly. "We have to be provided with safe passage back to secure a location where we can contact The Bastion for retrieval."

"Good point." Torran gave Lindsey an appreciative smile. Solomon might just decide that plopping them down in an infested city was sufficient in keeping her side of the bargain.

"Fine. Agreed." Solomon cocked her head and gazed at Torran. "Are we done negotiating now?"

"Yes. So..." Torran took a deep breath and stared directly into Solomon's eyes. He had to sell this lie and buy them time. He hoped he could keep the lie simple. The more elaborate the falsehood, the more likely he'd be discovered. "The SWD has knowledge of another sample of the virus in the dead world. I was told to either retrieve Maria Martinez or return with the sample."

"I see," Solomon said warily. "Where is it?"

Searching his memories for a plausible location, Torran hesitated. His lie seemed to have Solomon on the hook, but he was piecing everything together as he talked. Wherever he chose had to make sense.

"I know where it is," Dr. Curran muttered.

Torran gave her a sharp look.

"It's in an offsite lab attached to the Saint Marie Center for Disease Control in the upper city of the Notre Dame Metroplex," Dr. Curran continued. She looked very tired and was as pale as her uniform. "Though the primary lab was destroyed, the offsite wasn't. Right before the fall of the city, some of the modified virus samples were moved to the offsite location. I don't know how the SWD found out about the samples. I scrubbed all the information from the databases after the disaster with the Inferi Boon."

"Why didn't you reveal this information yesterday?" Solomon demanded.

Dr. Curran shrugged. "I just wanted all of this to be over. For it to end. I didn't realize the SWD knew the truth."

Torran and Lindsey exchanged apprehensive looks. They hadn't expected this development.

"You had best not be lying," Solomon said to the scientist.

"I'm not," Dr. Curran replied, lifting her bruised chin defiantly. "But now that you know, you'll let them go, correct?"

"Not until the virus is secured," Solomon answered. "Take them back to their room. Tomorrow morning, we retrieve the virus."

CHAPTER 32

"Can we talk?" Lindsey asked in a lowered voice once they were returned to their room.

Torran stood with his head tilted to gaze through the small observation window tucked in the locked door. He held up a hand, indicating for them to wait.

The lights that had been on earlier were now off, and the only light source was the glow under the door emanating from the hallway. The gloom infesting the rest of the floor had already helped her vision adjust to the dim lighting. Dr. Curran was the first to activate her wristlet to cast more light in the room, and Torran and Lindsey followed suit. The starting menu popped up, but access was being denied due to the suppression program Carter and created.

In the dim illumination, the man she loved looked much more composed than she felt, but then again, he was very good at hiding his emotions.

Setting her hands on her hips, Lindsey waited while watching Dr. Curran closely. She definitely didn't trust the scientist.

After a few minutes, Torran relaxed. "They left. Is there a camera in here?"

Dr. Curran shook her head. "They don't have enough remote generators to activate security."

Lindsey exhaled and sat on the edge of one of the beds. "So now what do we do?"

"Well, I'm not really counting on them to keep their end of the bargain," Torran admitted. "So I'm trying to sort out how to escape."

Looking around the room, Lindsey yearned for the comfort of her old flat. "If we escape, how do we get out of the building?"

"We'd have to steal the tiltrotor," Torran answered.

"And there is how many of left of the squad?"

"Twelve." Dr. Curran settled onto a chair, crossed her arms, and stared at Torran thoughtfully. "Tell me, MacDonald: how did the SWD know about the virus?"

Torran's smirk was barely visible as he turned to look at the scientist. "They don't. I lied to give us more time to come up with a way of getting out of here safely."

Dr. Curran stared at Torran in surprise, then started to laugh. "I see."

"How did *you* know about the virus samples in the offsite lab when no one else in the SWD did?" Lindsey asked.

"During my initial research for the Inferi Boon project, I discovered a manifest from the primary lab to the offsite lab misfiled in the historical database. It didn't seem important at the time, but when everything went to hell with the Inferi Boon special ops team, I destroyed it to prevent the SWD from acquiring it."

"But you wanted samples from Dwayne and Marla," Lindsey said.

"Yes, but I would have hidden that fact from my superiors. I want to find a way to inoculate *everyone* without risk of Anomalies or Aberrations developing. The SWD would just use it to acquire more power," Dr. Curran answered tersely.

"And you wouldn't?" Lindsey gazed at the woman distrustfully.

"Believe what you like."

"Fine, but back to the matter at hand. You said *you* had a plan," Lindsey said sharply to Dr. Curran. "What is it?"

"Just trust me." The scientist's shadowy smile made Lindsey feel unsettled and not comforted.

"That doesn't sound like much of a plan," Lindsey replied sourly. "Especially because I *don't* trust you."

"Why don't you tell us what you have planned so far as a show of good faith?" Torran curtly suggested.

"I'm still working on the details," Dr. Curran answered, shrugging slightly.

Lindsey scoffed. "You can't just leave us in the dark. And that wasn't meant as a joke."

Dr. Curran narrowed her eyes, looking a tad peeved in the pale illumination from her wristlet. "Yes, I can."

Torran sat on the bed next to Lindsey and gave Dr. Curran his best glower. "You're not being helpful."

Lindsey wrapped her arm around his and leaned her head against his shoulder. The dreadful idea of never being able to hold him again was making a mess of her nerves. "Come on, Curran, out with it. We're all in this together."

"If you're lucky, they'll let you go. If you're not lucky, I have a plan. That really should be enough for you to know," Dr. Curran sniffed.

"That's not acceptable," Lindsey snapped.

Though she hoped Torran and she would both make it out alive, she had enough doubts to make her short tempered. It was hard to cling to her last shred of hope.

Dr. Curran shrugged, slid off her chair, and entered the sanitation station. The door shut, leaving the couple alone.

"I hate her," Lindsey grumbled.

"So do I." Torran slid an arm around Lindsey's shoulders and kissed her temple. "I would do anything to be anywhere but here right now."

"Same here, but at least we're together," Lindsey replied.

If he hadn't rescued her, she'd still be in Franklin's clutches. What would've followed was torture and a lonely death. She was certain of that fact, so it was hard to ignore the feeling of living on borrowed time. "Everything is better when we're together. Even when it's bad.

Torran's lips spread into a charming smile and he stared at her adoringly. "Well said, and true."

Melting under his admiration, she tilted her head upward for a kiss.

Torran adorned her lips with several short pecks, then a longer smoldering one. "We'll be okay," he said again.

Lindsey almost believed him. "I have faith you'll do everything in your power to get us out of here."

"But you don't think we'll make it, do you?"

Snuggling into his side, she tucked her head under his chin. "No, no, I don't, but that doesn't mean I'm going to just give up."

"Neither am I."

Lindsey was lost without her pad, active wristlet, and computers, but her brain was still spinning out possibilities for survival. None of them were feasible.

When Dr. Curran stepped out of the sanitation station, her face and hair were a little damp. Maybe she was feeling overwhelmed, too. Lindsey still didn't want to feel sympathy for her. Pointedly ignoring the couple, Curran lay on the bed furthest from them and faced the wall. The light on her wristlet turned off.

Lindsey and Torran followed suit and the room was filled with darkness.

Since apparently they weren't going to be secured to the bedframes again, Lindsey and Torran stretched out on one of the medbeds. It was cold inside the building without any heat, and their black jumpers didn't provide the warmth their armor would have. Burrowing under the covers, the couple snuggled together for warmth.

"Much better," Torran whispered against her ear.

Resting her hands on his arm wrapped about her, she couldn't help but smile just a little. "I agree."

"I have a confession to make," Torran said in a low voice.

"Oh?"

"I can understand the allure of the modified virus. We wouldn't have to be trapped here, and we could venture out and see the world."

"Where would you choose to go?"

"Scotland. Back to my family's homestead. I've seen photos and heard stories about it all my life. You?"

Lindsey pondered the question. "I'd go there. With you. You're my home, Torran." Rolling her head to the side, she kissed the tip of his nose.

"You're the only thing I believe in anymore," Torran confessed.

"Then I'll do my best to not let you down."

"You never could," Torran assured her. "Ever."

Hours later, Lindsey was dragged out of a nightmare by the sound of the tiltrotor lifting off. The entire room trembled around her. It took several seconds to realize she was no longer curled up next to Torran, but strapped to a bed. Both her hands and feet were secured and she couldn't move.

"Torran," she rasped.

"Bloody hell," he grunted. "Did they hit us with the electroshock rifles again while we were sleeping?"

Trying to lift her head, Lindsey grunted. "Ugh! It feels like it."

"Shit," Torran muttered.

"I really hate them. So much." Tilting her head to one side, she saw the third bed was empty and the sanitation station was open. "They took Curran."

"They're getting the virus."

"Yeah." Lindsey jerked her hands, trying to wrestle them free of the restraints. "We need to get free of these damn beds and attack them when they come to get us."

"Agreed."

It was nearly two hours later when the tiltrotor returned, and neither of them had even managed to free one limb. Solomon entered the room with Yates and Carter soon after. The former commanding officer noted Lindsey and Torran's raw wrists from their escape attempts and smiled with amusement.

"Not trusting our agreement?" she asked.

"I have this great aversion to being tied up," Torran answered.

"Unless it's by me," Lindsey added.

"True," Torran said with a grin.

"Charming." Solomon motioned for her prisoners to be released. "Our mission was a success. Carter was able to disable the security and we retrieved all the samples."

Lindsey raised her eyes to stare at Carter. His beefy body and vacant look had deceived her. She never would have pegged him as a hacker. It made her a little angry that she'd been fooled by so many.

Yates dragged Lindsey to her feet while Carter did the same with Torran. This time they left their ankles unshackled, but bound their wrists.

"Dr. Curran is looking over the samples we retrieved. She should be able to confirm whether or not we have the modified virus or not," Solomon said.

"You didn't take her with you?" Lindsey was a little surprised by this revelation.

"She was overseeing the setup of her new lab," Solomon answered. "She's earned a certain degree of our trust."

"So once the virus is confirmed, you'll see about returning us, right?" Torran queried.

"Of course," Solomon answered.

And Lindsey knew she was lying.

Without a doubt Torran knew they were about to die. It was a feeling unlike any he'd had before. Whenever facing the Scrags, there had been the hope of survival. But not now. Looking into the hardened faces of the Cultists escorting him and Lindsey through the dimly-lit corridor, Torran was certain that each one of them was more than willing to kill him and Lindsey. Meeting Lindsey's gaze, he saw that she'd come to the same conclusion as well. He supposed it was a solace that they'd had one more night sleeping in each other's arms. Anger and sorrow filled him when he considered the loss of a future together. A small, encouraging smile flitted across Lindsey's lips and he tried to return it, but it was hard.

Most of Solomon's people appeared out of various doorways clad in their black jumpsuits. Seeming curious, they joined the escort to the lab, and Torran was very troubled by that fact. Any attempt to escape now would only speed up their deaths. The only reason they were still alive was as insurance. If the virus was in the Cultists' hands, they would be dead in minutes. If the virus hadn't been retrieved, then at least Solomon would have chance at finding Maria through Lindsey. Torran was fairly certain he was alive because he'd be tortured to convince Lindsey to talk.

Yet, reflecting on the last few months, Torran realized his death was actually coming at one of the happiest times of his life.

"I'm glad we took that walk that day," Torran said abruptly.

"Me too," Lindsey answered, grinning.

"Both of you shut up," Yates ordered.

"I'd rather not be taking this walk though," Torran added.

"Yeah, the company leaves something to be desired." Lindsey glowered at Yates.

The building was very cold, and the air tasted and smelled stale. Instead of proceeding to the command center, they were directed down another hallway. Several remote generators were set up at the far end and the open doorway glowed with bright light.

"Why not torches?" Torran asked. "I mean, you hate tech, so why not shuck off the generators and go for good old fashioned fire?"

"Why don't you shut up?" Yates responded, aggressively pushing her weapon into his back.

"Aren't you going to miss it, Carter? No more hacking?" Lindsey squinted at the big man, but he only scowled in return. "As a fellow hacker I know that high that comes from being able to unlock all the hidden secrets of those in power. The pleasure of the tech bending to your will. It's like it becomes a part of you."

Torran witnessed the slightest twitch in Carter's grip on his weapon and he immediately stepped between Lindsey and the big man. "She's just curious. No need to get agitated."

"Keep moving," Solomon ordered from behind them. "Stop aggravating my people."

Lindsey gave Torran a triumphant look. Maybe she was enjoying needling their soon-to-be executioners, but he wanted to enjoy what little time he had left with her, not squabbling with the Cultists.

Carter gruffly pushed Torran and Lindsey inside the lab when they reached their destination. Dr. Curran stood behind a wide counter loaded with lab equipment with her attention focused on a microscope. Ramirez stood at the scientist's side, watching her every move. Some of the screens along one wall were active, scrolling data from Dr. Curran's examination. A containment chamber with thick glass walls sat in one corner and the sight of it made Torran uneasy. Why did he suddenly feel like a lab rat?

Carter pushed Torran and Lindsey deeper into the room, while Yates trailed behind, followed by Solomon and the rest of her people.

Dr. Curran finally looked up from the large, high-powered microscope and regarded them with a blank expression.

"Did we get the virus?" Dr. Solomon asked.

Torran's heart sped up and he stepped closer to Lindsey. All the Cultists gathered in the room stared at the blond scientist expectedly. Had they been successful, or not?

"Let me show you my results so far," Dr. Curran said, picking up a pad and turning toward Ramirez. "Would you mind giving this to Solomon?

Ramirez reached toward it, but Dr. Curran accidently dropped it.

"Oh, sorry, let me just get that," she said, bending over.

There was a sharp bark and a fount of blood erupted from just under Ramirez's chin.

Carter shoved both Lindsey and Torran to one side, and it registered in Torran's confused mind that the big man had shot Ramirez.

Torran drew in one sharp breath.

Carter fired again, this time striking Solomon in the shoulder, knocking her back through the doorway.

Pandemonium erupted.

Most of the squad was already out of their armor, but Carter and a few others were not. Yates returned fire, but in her panic, hit Carter's armor and missed any killing shots. Meanwhile, Carter aimed for her head, bullets punching into the wall near her as she scuttled for cover.

Lindsey ducked and scrambled toward the counter Dr. Curran was hiding behind. Torran scurried behind her. Gunfire destroyed the equipment beside him, sending Torran sprawling onto the floor. Raising his head, he saw Lindsey lying on her side, clutching her stomach.

"No!' Torran exclaimed, realizing she'd been shot.

He attempted to go to the woman he loved, but Carter grabbed him by the collar and flung him behind a bank of computers. Torran crashed into the wall with a loud thud. Twisting about, he searched for Lindsey and spotted Dr. Curran dragging her to safety. Blood was pulsing between Lindsey's fingers and her expression was one of shock.

The thunder of battle raged on.

To reach Lindsey, he'd have to cross an open area, but he was willing to take the risk. It was difficult getting to his feet with his hands still secured, but he managed. Peering out around the equipment that was providing shelter, he spotted Carter exchanging fire with Yates and the remains of the squad taking cover in the hallway.

Desperate to get to Lindsey, Torran fought the wild staccato of his heartbeat and dashed toward her location. Carter shouted at him, but Torran wove through the room, avoiding fire. The big man lunged out from behind cover, grabbed Torran about the arm, and hurled him back to where he'd been before. Torran slammed into the wall, smacking his head so hard his vision blurred.

A second later, Carter grunted as Yates took advantage of him being distracted, and there was a heavy crash as the man hit the floor.

"He's down!" Yates shouted.

Guilt ate at Torran, knowing he'd inadvertently caused Carter's death, but he was frantic to get to Lindsey. Torran crawled across the floor in the direction of the counter. Carter lay dead nearby, his head split open. Other members of the squad lay in heaps, blood pooling on the floor. Torran reached the end of the counter and pulled himself around just as he was seized from behind. A still-hot weapon was pushed into his back.

"Room is secure," Yates announced. "I've got the prisoner."

Torran ignored the weapon pressing into him and jerked himself free of Yates' grip. All he cared about was the scene in front of him. Dr. Curran sat on the floor, holding Lindsey's hand. Blood covered her white Sci-Tech suit and Lindsey's face was far too pale. It took Torran a second to realize she wasn't breathing.

"She just passed," Dr. Curran said in a flat tone. "The bullets hit her vital organs and an artery."

"No," Torran gasped. Though he felt as though all his strength had been sapped out of him at Dr. Curran's words, he crawled to Lindsey's still form. "Linds, Linds..." He didn't even realize he was crying until his tears fell onto her lips.

"Get him up," Solomon ordered.

"No!" Torran gasped. "No! Someone needs to help her!"

Yates jerked him off Lindsey and dragged him toward the containment chamber.

Torran couldn't tear his gaze from Lindsey's still form. Dr. Curran set Lindsey's hand down over her stilled heart and shakily stood.

Yates shoved him into the containment cell, and shut the door. The blond woman's stern face was without remorse. "I guess you're the only lab rat now," Yates sneered.

"I'm going to kill you," Torran hissed.

"No. No you're not." Yates grinned and turned her back on him.

In a fury, Solomon confronted the scientist, "I hope you had nothing to do with this." The Cultist pressed her hand against her wounded shoulder, trembling from the pain.

"Do you think I'd risk the samples? You're responsible for your people. You should have known your hacker was a spy," Dr. Curran retorted. "Why would a hacker turn on tech?"

"How do I know *you* weren't working with him? It was convenient how he opened fire when you were in cover!"

"Maybe he was taking advantage of a clear shot of Ramirez. This is your mess, Solomon. Not mine."

Slapping her hand on the counter, Solomon leaned toward Curran. "Don't push me."

"I can push you all I want because you need me." Dr. Curran smirked, her eyes gleaming. "And you know it."

Solomon hissed through her teeth with frustration, anger, and, Torran hoped, a lot of pain. "Did we get the virus?"

Dr. Curran waved her hand at the broken equipment. "We're lucky ISPV is not airborne, or we'd all be infected and our dead would be Scrags! So far, the samples have all been the regular virus. I have six more to check, but the equipment..." Curran shoved the broken microscope off the table. "Find me another one and I'll tell you if the remaining samples are the modified virus or not!"

"I just lost six people and the woman who could lead us to Martinez!"

"That's not my problem!"

Solomon's face flushed with anger. "Yates, dump the bodies, then prepare to return to the offsite lab to recover another microscope."

"Yes, sir," Yates said.

"Solomon, let me out," Torran shouted, banging on the glass wall. He wanted to hold Lindsey one last time.

Evins, one of the bigger soldiers still clad in armor, moved to claim Lindsey's body. Pressing his palms flat against the glass, Torran watched with a breaking heart as Lindsey was unceremoniously dragged across the floor to be piled with the other dead.

He'd been convinced they'd die together, and that thought had terrified him.

Now Torran knew what was worse.

To survive when Lindsey was dead.

CHAPTER 33

Ever since Lindsey had enlisted in the Constabulary, she'd wondered what it would feel like to know she was about to die. During the failed final push against the Scrags outside the Bastion, she didn't have a chance to ponder her fate when she'd been rendered unconscious by a grenade. Now that she actually knew the countdown on her life was underway, she was surprised to not feel terror, but rebellion. If she was going to die in a few minutes, she wasn't going to give her executioners the satisfaction of seeing her afraid.

Catching Torran's eye, she gave him an encouraging smile. At least they'd be together in the end. It was very difficult for the man she loved to alter his scowl into anything resembling a smile, but he tried. She loved him all the more for it.

"I'm glad we took that walk that day," Torran said to her.

"Me too," Lindsey replied, meaning it with all her heart. At least the final season of her life had been filled with love and companionship.

Yates poked the barrel of her weapon into Lindsey's back. "Both of you shut up."

"I'd rather not be taking this walk though," Torran continued, ignoring Yates.

"Yeah, the company leaves something to be desired." Lindsey tossed a venomous look over her shoulder at Yates.

Yates' eyes were cold and angry. She jabbed Lindsey again in the ribs.

"Why not torches?" Torran gestured with his bound hands at the room at the end of the hallway clearly illuminated by the remote generators. "I mean, you hate tech, so why not shuck off the generators and go for good old fashioned fire?"

"Why don't you shut up?" This time Yates rammed Torran with her weapon.

Picking up Torran's train of thought, Lindsey glanced at the big silent man behind Torran. "Aren't you going to miss it, Carter? No more hacking? As a fellow hacker I know that high that comes from being able to unlock all the hidden secrets of those in power. The pleasure of the tech bending to your will. It's like it becomes a part of you."

Carter narrowed his eyes at Lindsey, and something about the look deeply unsettled her.

Torran protectively moved in front of Lindsey. "She's just curious. No need to get agitated."

"Keep moving," Solomon said briskly "Stop aggravating my people."

Satisfied, Lindsey flashed a wide grin at Torran. He gave her a troubled look. The storm clouds of bitter emotions filling his dark eyes were understandable. She wasn't too thrilled about them facing death either, but Torran had a protective streak that both touched her and made her just a bit annoyed. They didn't have any hope of getting out of the situation alive, but he'd never accept that truth. Sadly, she did, but was determined to meet her fate without fear or regret.

Lindsey was just reaching for Torran's arm when Carter shoved them both into the room. Shooting the big man an angry look, Lindsey wobbled on her feet. Yates grabbed her shoulder roughly and set her upright. Yanking out of Yates' grip, Lindsey wondered if she could somehow manage to punch the woman in the face even with both her hands bound. Yates stepped back as Carter yet again pushed his prisoners forward.

Directing her focus at Torran, Lindsey saw he was grimly studying the room, probably searching for a way out. His hair was disheveled and his jawline was scruffy and in need of a shave, but he was absolutely the most handsome man she'd ever seen in her life. She loved him completely, and it saddened her that their final act together would be to die at each other's side. The conversation around her didn't mean anything anymore. Torran and she weren't going to be released. The Gaia Cult would claim the virus and humanity would come to a terrible end. The thought of the Cultists winning infuriated her, but someone else would have to stop them now.

Lindsey returned her attention to the scene before her just as Dr. Curran bent over to retrieve something she dropped. Out of the corner of her eye, Lindsey saw Carter raise his weapon and fire. Lindsey froze in terror, then realized it wasn't Torran Carter had shot, but Ramirez. Swiveling about, Carter fired at the doorway.

Immediately, Lindsey lunged toward the counter where Dr. Curran had stood seconds before. With relief, she heard Torran's footsteps behind her. Gunfire exploded and bullets ripped through the air. Nearby, Yates aimed at her and Lindsey attempted to dodge. Something hard punched into her torso three times, stealing her breath and knocking her off her feet. Falling onto her side, Lindsey rasped for oxygen and pressed a hand to her stomach. Blood surged over her fingers. Shock and confusion shorted out her brain. What was she supposed to do now?

"No!" Torran shouted.

Lifting her eyes, she sought out Torran. He was staring in terror at her from where he'd fallen while trying to avoid the barrage. She wanted to say something comforting to him, but it was hard to breathe. The Scotsman scrambled toward her on hands and knees, but Carter grabbed Torran about the waist and effortlessly tossed him behind some equipment.

Trying to say his name, but unable to, Lindsey realized she needed to get out of the open. She shoved the heels of her boots against the floor in an attempt to scoot herself around the counter. To her surprise, Dr. Curran crawled into view and hooked her hand under Lindsey's arm. One mighty tug pulled Lindsey into cover, but sent waves of agony washing over her. Dr. Curran continued to drag Lindsey around the counter until they were both in relative safety. Lindsey couldn't see Torran anymore, and she hoped he was safe.

"Fuck," Lindsey finally wheezed. She was going to die and not be able to say goodbye to Torran. Tears of regret filled her eyes and spilled along her cheeks.

Dr. Curran plucked Lindsey's blood-covered hand from the wounds and performed a quick cursory examination as the sound of the battle continued. "Well, you're going to die."

"Yeah..." Lindsey struggled just to get that one word out.

Bending over Lindsey, the scientist's eyes were so dilated they looked black. "Do you want to live?"

Unable to speak anymore, Lindsey nodded, but also wanted to laugh. The question was ridiculous.

"Excellent."

A sharp prick against her palm followed, and hot lava filled Lindsey's veins. With a gasp, she understood what the scientist had done. Fear, anger, relief, and despair filled Lindsey as the other woman clenched her hand tight.

"I'll be waiting for your rescue," Dr. Curran whispered.

In her imagination, she'd pictured dying with Torran pledging his love and holding her close. Instead, Lindsey saw the world fade as Dr. Curran's thin lips turned upward in a triumphant smile.

Lindsey's final thoughts were

Oh shit.

"Mother?" an electronic voice queried. "Mother, are you awake?"

Lindsey groaned.

"Mother? You have sustained dire injuries. Shall I call for assistance?"

Peeling her eyes open, Lindsey gazed up at the aerial drone hovering over her. Beyond the insect-like robot was a gray sky and tall buildings. Her body ached and there was a strange humming in her ears. Whatever she was lying on was vastly uncomfortable. What was even more annoying was something very heavy pinning her legs. Shoving herself up on one elbow, she observed she was in a long, narrow alley that ended on both sides with tall barricades. Also, she was lying on bodies piled at the bottom of a long garbage chute. Without a dumpster in place, the corpses of the dead squad members and broken equipment littered the ground.

It was Carter's corpse lying across her legs. With a grunt, she pushed him off with her hands. He'd tried to stop the Gaia Cult and failed. Now she regretted all her angry thoughts directed at him. Had he been part of Dr. Curran's plans all along? Or had he acted on impulse? Had Lindsey's taunt maybe compelled him to action? It was hard to know, since the big man was dead.

"Teeny?"

"Yes, Mother?"

"I need a date and time."

The aerial drone responded and Lindsey swore.

"Fuck. I've been dead for a day."

"Though your vital signs are cause for concern, you're not dead," the aerial drone assured her.

"Yeah. Not now. But I was."

Lindsey touched her chest. Dried blood covered the black jumpsuit and the ragged holes showed where the bullets had pierced her. Poking the tip of her finger through the fabric, Lindsey touched the healing wounds beneath. They hurt, but not nearly as much as when she'd received them. As she scooted off the heap of corpses, bullets skidded off the black fabric of her clothing. Apparently her healing body had discarded them.

She was Inferi Boon.

Lindsey giggled at the ridiculousness of her new state. Was this how Maria had felt? Raking her hands through her short hair, Lindsey stood over the deceased and felt like laughing again. She should be dead just like the rest of them, but instead, she was alive because of Dr. Curran's meddling. Guilt, fear, and relief fought for dominance of her emotions. Instead, she ignored them all and concentrated on what she had to do.

"How'd you find me, Teeny?"

"Your wristlet reactivated."

Swiping her screen, Lindsey was relieved to see it was functional again. Maybe dying had reset it and removed the suppression program Carter had written. All the corpses had their armor and weapons removed, but Lindsey decided to check them for anything she might be able to use. When her search turned up empty, she set her hands on her hips and peered down the alley. She had plans to make, but first she needed some information and supplies.

Lindsey picked a direction and started walking. Though slightly disoriented and sore, her mind was already spinning out possible courses of action.

The aerial drone dropped to the ground and padded along behind her on its long legs.

"Why are you walking, Teeny?"

"I require refueling for flight. I've been preserving my reserves while searching for you."

"We'll take care of that soon," Lindsey promised.

The clacking noise of the drone trailing her was a little distracting, but she was actually glad for its company. Reaching the end of the alley, she climbed onto the barricade and peered over to see a thick mass of Scrags gathered near the shattered entrance of the rescue center. The tiltrotor had probably dragged them to the area.

Even though some of the creatures were within five feet of her, none of them paid her any heed. Lindsey pulled herself on to the top of the cement wall, careful to avoid the rusted razor wire. Fear chewed on her nerves, yet she had to know if she was truly Inferi Boon. Teeny crawled up next to her and perched at her side.

"Prepare to open fire, okay?" Lindsey said.

"Yes, Mother."

"Hey, fuckers!" Lindsey shouted.

A few Scrags looked up sharply, but didn't appear to register her appearance.

"Okay, so I'm either a ghost or Inferi Boon."

"You are Mother," Teeny informed her.

Lindsey grinned at the drone. "Yeah, I am. Let's try this again." Lindsey picked up a small chunk of the crumbling cement barricade and threw it at a female Scrag. "Asshole!"

The Scrag spun about, eyes searching for prey, but dismissed Lindsey's presence.

"They don't see me as human, do they?"

"No, Mother. They're ignoring you."

"Well, that answers that," Lindsey said, grinning with satisfaction. With a delighted smile, she jumped off the wall and into the horde.

Teeny followed.

"How long?" Solomon demanded.

"Do you want it done right, or quickly?" Dr. Curran replied.

Torran looked up from his corner of the confinement chamber. He'd been sitting with his eyes closed and hadn't seen the former chief defender enter the lab. The short woman's shoulder was heavily bandaged and she had dark circles under her eyes. Yates stood behind her in full armor. Evins, dark hair standing on end and looking very bleary-eyed, sat in the corner, watching Curran with his weapon leveled at her. With half the Cultists dead, the survivors were stressed and weary.

Torran was glad to see it.

It was agonizing, sitting in the small chamber. They'd fed him once and let him use the sanitary facilities twice. No one spoke to him anymore except Yates. She didn't call him by his name anymore, but by "lab rat." The sharp-featured woman with the fair hair took obvious delight in his suffering. He'd never had a negative interaction with her, so he wasn't sure why she was so cruel. Maybe it was her nature.

Though it was difficult to look at the spot where Lindsey had died, Torran cocked his head to watch the two women arguing.

"Is this the same virus you gave Maria Martinez or not?" Solomon was shouting.

"It's a very close variation," Dr. Curran answered. "It should grant the exact same immunity as the one I gave her."

"Without the Anomaly or Aberration side effects?" Solomon pointed a finger in the scientist's face. "I want answers, Curran. The only person who could lead us to Martinez is dead thanks to you and Carter!"

Rage filled Torran, and he clenched his hands into fists. Lindsey had been so much more than a mere pawn, but the people standing on the other side of the glass would never comprehend that truth.

"Give it to the lab rat," Yates suggested.

"I have to make sure the dosage is correct to avoid side effects," Dr. Curran snapped. "There are many factors that I have to take into consideration."

"Then take them into consideration and try it on him. I want to know if it works or not." Solomon was obviously close to losing her temper. Her face was aflame with anger.

"We should have just given it to one of the dead bodies," Yates uttered while giving the scientist a distrustful look.

Dr. Curran leaned toward Yates, her expression virulent. "Then you'd have an Abscrag on your hands. This virus has to be given to the living to take full effect and avoid creating a creature that's smart enough to hunt us for our flesh. Abscrags *eat* us."

"She's not lying. They do. I saw it with my own eyes," Torran said. "And though the idea of ripping your throat out is highly appealing, Yates, I don't enjoy the thought of becoming a cannibal."

Yates sneered at him.

"But didn't Maria return to life?" Solomon asked.

"Yes, but she's the only one. The others went feral," Dr. Solomon replied. "That's why the dosage is so important."

It was then Torran realized she was lying. The SWD had only divulged certain details to the public and Constabulary, but Lindsey had told him everything Dr. Curran had disclosed. Maria Martinez had received a different virus from the rest of the Inferi Boon and that was the reason for her unique return to life. Dr. Curran was buying time, but for what reason? Torran was imprisoned, and she was under constant watch.

Torran's heart thumped a little harder as he replayed Lindsey's death. Running his hands through his hair, he almost hyperventilated when a wonderful, yet terrible revelation struck. Dr. Curran had been holding Lindsey's hand. The woman was cold, aloof, and had a terrible bedside manner. That she would give Lindsey an iota of sympathy even at her passing seemed odd for the scientist. So what if she'd been holding Lindsey's hand for another purpose?

It was madness to even entertain the idea, yet Torran couldn't help his broken heart from wildly latching onto the possibility that Dr. Curran had given Lindsey the virus.

Which meant what?

The rest of the argument was lost to him as Torran sat in his cell, daring to hope on the impossible.

CHAPTER 34

Huddled in the Rescue Hub, Lindsey gnawed on a protein bar while observing the vid screens. It felt odd, returning to the location after escaping so dramatically two days before. Climbing up the ladder, she'd wished with all her heart that Torran was with her. In his place was the altered aerial drone. Hopefully together, their unlikely team could rescue the man she loved and humanity at the same time.

On the other side of the hub a mini-fuel revitalizer chugged away. She'd discovered it at a security depot and, with Teeny's help, dragged it to the Rescue Hub. After raiding several more city security posts, she'd sent Teeny to deposit cameras and scanners around the rescue center where the Gaia Cult had taken refuge.

Swallowing the vanilla-flavored protein mush in her mouth, Lindsey was relieved she wasn't craving anything red and fleshy. Her appetite seemed to be exactly same. After staring into the mirror in the sanitation station for ten minutes, she was certain her eyes were not tinged with red. She was definitely Inferi Boon, and not an Abscrag.

The door to the hub opened, and Teeny stomped through the entrance, clutching a helmet in its pinchers. At least she thought it might be stomping.

Lindsey eyed the drone thoughtfully. "Teeny?"

"Yes, Mother?"

"Are you having a temper tantrum?"

"I had to climb down to the lower city and recover the helmet from the *river*," came the response. "Without fuel, I was unable to fly. It took a very *long* time."

Leaning over, Lindsey eyed the little drone. "You mad?"

Tapping a claw against the floor, the drone's camera-tipped stalks turned away from her.

It was definitely not happy with her.

"Heh, what do you know? That A.I. proggie is working. You're developing a nice little personality. Just don't turn on me and try to kill me in my sleep." Lindsey straightened and took another bite of her protein bar. Spotting an issue in her code, she quickly typed a new string of text.

Carrying the helmet over to Franklin's armor, Teeny connected it and turned it on. "The helmet is operational."

"Yay! Especially since you had to go *all* that way to retrieve it."

"You are sarcastic, Mother."

"Yeah, I know."

Teeny clattered over to her side and crawled onto the chair next to her. It was the same chair Torran had sat on earlier in the week, and Lindsey fought back a fresh batch of tears. Though she could walk among the Scrags, survive death, and endure a substantial amount of damage, she still felt like the same woman she'd been before her transformation. Which meant she was worried sick about Torran, determined to save him, and anxious to destroy the Gaia Cult.

Directing its cameras toward the vid screens, Teeny hunched down. "The program is nearly finished?"

"Yeah. It's almost ready. I still have my touch." Switching to the camera and scanner feeds, Lindsey took a sip of her water. The scanners clearly showed human bodies moving about on the top floor of the rescue center. "The six remaining Cultists are all on the top floor. I've determined that four are always on shift, with two sleeping in this room here." Lindsey pointed to the screen. "At least three are usually in the command center, and one in the lab with Dr. Curran and Torran."

"Father is still alive," Teeny said.

"Call him Mr. MacDonald. He's sensitive," Lindsey corrected.

"Yes, Mother."

"So what we need to do is break into the building, go up the stairs, get through the security doors on the top floor, kill all the bad guys, and rescue Torran. Easy, right?"

"Actually, it sounds hard, Mother," Teeny answered.

"Remind me to teach you to lie," Lindsey grumbled.

"Yes, Mother."

※

Lindsey chose the period right after sunset for her attack with hopes that darkness would disorient her enemies. The night would also provide cover for her and Teeny. She knew for certain that the Gaia Cultist did not have adequate equipment and would not be able to detect her and the aerial drone until they infiltrated the building.

An hour before the designated time, Lindsey suited up. Franklin's armor was a bit big on her, but Lindsey had managed to adjust the straps on the arms and legs for a better fit. It was odd, wearing the dead woman's stealth suit, but Lindsey didn't want to risk further injury. Her wounds were fully healed and she felt fine, but she didn't want to test the limits of her altered body.

After the fuel reviver finished its process, Lindsey re-filled Teeny. The little drone twirled around the Rescue Hub a few times, clearly relieved to be airborne again. She then made sure the drone's guns were fully loaded before claiming a few firearms for herself from the weapons locker. The pack on her back carried ammunition, water and food, and a pad filled with information on the Gaia Cult. Another pad was tucked into one of the pouches in her armor. That one held the program she'd been working on all day.

When she finally started out toward the rescue center where the Gaia Cult was holed up, Teeny followed, clutching a remote generator. It was odd, being able to walk past Scrags without fear, but Lindsey was quickly adapting. Noting the helmet appeared to rile the creatures, she took it off and walked with it tucked under one arm.

Several blocks from the rescue center, she arrived at the edge of the massive crowd of Scrags gathered around the building. Most on the outer edges were in a stagnant state, but those closer to the building were in an uproar. The comings and goings of the tiltrotor over the last couple of days had kept those Scrags sufficiently riled.

As Teeny sailed over the Scrags, Lindsey pushed her way into the throng. The Scrags smelled incredibly awful, and she almost retched. Unwashed bodies pressed in around her from all sides. The reek of death was on their breath and their empty white eyes were chilling. Being up close to the creatures was disconcerting, but she swallowed her fear and advanced toward the building.

As she continued her passage through the horde, a Scrag screeched as she brushed past it. She immediately came to an abrupt stop and swiveled about to face it. Teeny swung back around overhead, extending the barrels of its weapons. The undead being stared Lindsey, and the soldier waited, holding her breath. Finally, the Scrag let out a querying cry, confused when it was unable to find prey.

Exhaling with relief, Lindsey resumed shoving her way through the increasingly compact crowd. In due course, she was forced to squeeze between the walking corpses. Near the front doors to the rescue center, she finally had to give up. It was impossible to pass through the crush of bodies anymore.

"Teeny, I need your help," she called out.

Aware of the drone's weight limitations, she handed Teeny her pack and ordered it to take it inside the building and leave it in the stairwell along with the remote generator.

For the next few minutes, she waited as the agitated dead flailed against the walls of the building and fought each other to get closer. The bottom of the building was smeared with blood and viscera from the Scrags constantly battering themselves against it.

Teeny whirred overhead and extended its long legs. Lindsey clutched the helmet to her chest as the drone lifted her off the ground and carried her over the heads of the Scrags. Warning lights popped on its underside and the drone's tiltrotors increased speed to keep them aloft. Tucking her legs up under her bottom, Lindsey tried not to snag her armor on the Scrags just inches below. Teeny dipped to get her through the front entrance and Lindsey found herself being dragged across the heads of the Scrags. The already agitated creatures swiped at her, and she clambered over them on her hands and knees until Teeny was able to lift her again.

The main floor of the building was so completely packed with the undead, Lindsey wondered how the building didn't burst at the seams. Teeny hoisted her through several large rooms until it reached the stairwell leading up. The drone dropped her onto the wide, cement railing that edged the stairs, where her pack and the remote generator waited for her. Hooking the helmet onto the armor, Lindsey shrugged on the pack and slung the remote generator over one shoulder.

The Scrags filling the stairs constantly shifted about, clawing at the walls and each other. Lindsey managed to edge up as Teeny flew just ahead of her. The bodies crammed into the stairwell actually helped her keep her balance as she scooted up the handrail.

At every floor, she found the massive metal doors on the landing standing open with Scrags crowded inside, and she remembered how Solomon had said the Gaia Cult had helped the Scrags overrun the rescue center.

When she neared the top floor, Lindsey set down the remote generator and activated it. Instantly, the controls next to the massive security door lit up. She pulled her pad out of the pouch in her armor and activated it. "Teeny, remember to shoot anyone who is not Dr. Curran or Torran."

"Or you, Mother?"

Lindsey eyed the aerial drone. Was it joking? "Yes, *don't* shoot me."

Unable to drop to the floor, Lindsey instead crawled on top of the Scrags to the door controls and pressed her pad against the wall. Within seconds she had the door hacked and unlocked. Activating it, she scrambled back over the Scrags and ducked down.

The massive door let out a warning beep as it started to yawn open.

Disengaging her weapon from her armor, Lindsey aimed over the heads of the increasingly excited Scrags. As the long hallway came into view, she caught sight of a soldier rushing toward the door, holding their weapon aloft.

The Scrags also spotted the human.

Screeching, the undead pushed their way through the entrance. Teeny sped past toward Dr. Curran's lab. Lindsey leaped down as soon as she saw a bit of the floor and was swept along with them. Shouts of fear rose over the shrieks of the dead. Gunfire erupted, a sound that sent shivers down Lindsey's spine. The front edge of the horde fell under the barrage of bullets. Lindsey attempted to cautiously circumvent the limbs of the fallen, but the crowd pressed forward, carrying her with them.

Up ahead, a blast door started to descend. Teeny dodged under it, but Lindsey grasped that to get through it before it closed, she'd have to break free of the Scrags and risk being shot by the Cultists.

Shooting the Scrags in front of her, she cleared a path for herself and ran toward the descending door. Someone on the other side saw her coming and stooped to spray the corridor with bullets in an attempt to cut her down. Several hard thumps against her armor caused her to stumble, but she dove under the barrier and rolled. She was almost on the other side, when the strap on her weapon caught on the body of a Scrag. Bullets ricocheted around her and Lindsey tugged on her firearm one more time, but it didn't shake loose. With a cry of frustration, she released the strap and abandoned the weapon as she scrambled away.

Another shot hit her side, but the armor held. The sting slowed her down, but she aimed for a doorway to take shelter. The soldier at the end of the hallway continued to shoot, determined to kill her. Fear spurring her on, Lindsey rushed toward safety. Another bullet slammed into her arm, bounced off, and hit the wall.

There was a sharp cry then the person firing at Lindsey slumped to the floor.

Teeny spun about in the air over the fallen soldier and a smoldering remote generator. "I got her, Mother! And the generator!"

The screech of the Scrags grew louder behind Lindsey.

Looking over her shoulder, Lindsey realized the barricade had stopped descending. Without the remote generator powering its controls, the blast door had stopped.

"Uh, hitting the generator was bad, Teeny."

"Oh. Sorry, Mother."

Scrags scrambled under the barrier, their predatory screams filling the air.

"Teeny, get to the lab and protect Torran and Dr. Curran," Lindsey screamed.

A second later, Yates stepped into the hallway from the command center, followed by aerial drones.

Lindsey ducked into a room as they opened fire.

Torran instantly woke the second he heard gunfire. Rising to his feet, he looked sharply toward Dr. Curran. The scientist froze at her workstation, her expression hopeful, yet frightened. Evins immediately pushed off the wall he'd been resting against and hurried to the doorway.

"What the fuck is going on?" Evins shouted.

A second later, Torran heard the shrieks of the Scrags.

"We have a breach," Solomon said over Evin's wristlet, her voice small and tinny. "I'm heading to the lab. Wait for me, Evins!"

"I need to lock the door!" Evins protested.

"Wait!" Solomon ordered, sounding much louder over the wristlet speaker. And maybe a lot more desperate.

Torran pressed his hands against the glass while straining to see into the corridor past the open doorway. How had the Scrags infiltrated the upper floor? Was someone else sabotaging the plans of the Gaia Cult, or was it something much more fantastic?

"Close the door," Dr. Curran shouted at Evins.

"I have to wait for Solomon," he snapped.

"Close it or we'll die! The Scrags are inside!"

Dr. Curran lunged toward the door, but Evins turned his weapon toward her.

"We're waiting for Solomon!"

"You won't shoot me," Dr. Curran said, raising her chin and taking a step forward.

"Yes, yes, I will," Evins promised, and aimed at her shin. "I'll put a bullet in your leg."

That stopped Dr. Curran. She literally growled at the man, raising her fists in frustration. "You idiot man!"

Nerves frayed, his stomach in knots, Torran listened the cries of the Scrags and the bark of weaponry. Frustrated at being trapped, he paced back and forth, staring at the open doorway.

A shadow fell across the threshold and Dr. Curran recoiled. Evins swung about and almost fired he was so jittery. Solomon was faster. She batted the weapon out of her face, closed the door, and activated the locks.

"We've been infiltrated. Yates and the drones are on it. We saw at least one person among the Scrags." Solomon surged toward Dr. Curran and grabbed her by the throat with one hand. "There was a soldier, firing at us, among the Scrags! What did you do?"

Dr. Curran looked positively reptilian as she smiled. Torran wouldn't have been surprised if a forked tongue had slithered out from between her lips.

"It's Lindsey, isn't it?" Torran called out to the scientist. "You saved her, didn't you?"

Dr. Curran didn't look his way, but she didn't deny it.

"You gave her the virus!" Solomon shouted in a rage. "You betrayed us!" Solomon dropped her hand to her waist, jerked out a dagger, and before Dr. Curran could dodge away, slashed the scientist's throat.

Outside the doorway, Scrags danced under the hail of gunfire, their bodies shredded. Blood and guts poured out onto the floor. Yates and the aerial drones continued to pulverize every Scrag crawling under the barricade. In a very short time, the gap would be clogged with bodies, making it harder for the undead to enter the hallway. That's when Lindsey knew Yates would come for her, and Lindsey was unarmed.

Lindsey pressed her back to the wall just inside the door and activated her wristlet. When Teeny responded to her hail, relief washed over her. The drone had managed to reach the outside of the lab only to find it closed. It wouldn't be able to fight Yates and the other drones by itself either. Biting her bottom lip, Lindsey sorted through all the ideas flooding her mind and finally decided on an option. After transmitting directions to Teeny, she started to shove the furniture room together. When it looked like sufficient cover, she checked outside the door. There were pauses in the deafening salvo as Yates and the drones reloaded, but now the barricade of bodies was holding back the onslaught of the undead, for the time being.

Ducking into cover, Lindsey waited for Yates.

Short bursts of gunfire continued, but Lindsey also heard approaching footsteps. The cries of the Scrags were muffled by the combination of the blast door and pile of corpses blocking their way. Daring to peek, Lindsey saw the aerial drones fly to the jammed blast door, aiming their weapons down to kill any Scrag pushing through the tangle of dead bodies.

A second later, Yates slipped into the darkened room.

"Rooney," Yates breathed. "I saw your weapon outside. Oops. Did you drop something?"

Lindsey remained silent.

"Rooney...answer me, Rooney. I saw your face. I know it's you."

Staying very still, Lindsey pressed her lips together.

"I guess Curran betrayed us. I'll enjoy killing her once her purpose is done. Once I'm like you."

Yates fired a single shot into the furniture, making Lindsey jump.

"So, Rooney, did you come to save Dr. Curran, or your boyfriend lab rat? It's really a shame he changed into an Anomaly. I think he would have eventually come around to our way of thinking."

This time, Lindsey drove her teeth into her bottom lip to keep from responding. Torran had to be alive.

Yates pulled the trigger again. The burst again made Lindsey start.

"I need you to come out so I can figure out this Inferi Boon thing. How much damage will I be able to take before dying? And will I actually die? Will I come back if I take a shot to the head? I really want to know. For future reference, you see."

Yates kicked over the furniture. When she realized Lindsey wasn't behind it, she swung her weapon about as she searched the dark for her prey.

"Why are you hiding, Rooney?"

"You know, Yates, being Inferi Boon is a lot of fun. You can walk among the Scrags and not worry one little bit about them trying to take a chunk out of you. But they're not what you really need to worry about."

"Oh? What do I need to worry about? I'm not the one who's unarmed."

"You should be worried about the fact I was waiting for the drones to finish downloading my program."

Lindsey saw Yates freeze in place.

"Fire," Lindsey ordered.

The drones clustered in the doorway obeyed.

From Lindsey's hiding place in the sanitation station, she watched Yates's body dance in the bombardment, then fall to the ground.

"Mother, she's dead," Teeny announced, sounding a little proud.

Pushing the agape door to the sanitation station all the way open, Lindsey stepped into the room and claimed Yates weapon. "Teeny, instruct half the drones to secure the command station. Leave the other half protecting the barricade. You're coming with me."

"Yes, Mother."

It was time to get Torran.

CHAPTER 35

Staggering away from Solomon in shock, Dr. Curran pressed her hands to her sliced throat. Solomon stalked after her, the bloody knife clutched in one hand.

"Evins, no one comes in this room," Solomon ordered. "Eyes on that door!"

"Yes sir!" Evins swiveled about, set his feet apart, and aimed at the door.

Dr. Curran reached her workstation and her red-stained fingers fumbled across the top as she appeared to search desperately for the vials she'd been meticulously working with all day.

"Save yourself, Beverly. Administer the virus." Solomon slashed Curran again, this time the dagger slicing into her arm.

"Leave her be!" Torran shouted. Frustrated with his inability to help, Torran pounded on the glass with his fists.

Pointing the bloody blade at him, Solomon said, "You're as good as dead, so I suggest you shut up unless you want to die now."

Dr. Curran plucked a vial from the workstation and shoved it into an injector. The cut in her throat was deep, but hadn't hit the carotid. Nonetheless, she would be dead soon from blood loss. Holding the injector in a trembling hand, she shrank away from Solomon and moved to press it to her arm.

Solomon snatched the injector out of the dying woman's hand. With a triumphant look, the former chief defender shoved it against her own palm. "Thank you, Dr. Curran. You can die now."

Unable to speak, Dr. Curran bestowed a hideous, bloody smile at Solomon while pointing at the used injector.

Solomon narrowed her eyes, her gaze flicking between the injector and Curran's gloating face. Letting out a hiss of pain, Solomon doubled over. Rage flooding her features, she slashed at Dr. Curran, but the scientist shrank into the corner. Tugging another injector out of her pocket, Dr. Curran pressed it against her neck right beside the terrible, gaping wound.

"Evins, you idiot! Solomon is infected," Torran shouted at the oblivious soldier. "Kill her!

Turning about, Evins stared at the bloody display in front of him, then noticed Solomon was in distress. "Sir?"

Solomon smashed into the counter, her body violently shaking.

Dr. Curran slid along the wall, away from the transforming woman.

With a cry of agony, Solomon started to flail about, knocking over equipment and vials. Befuddled by the events unfolding, Evins hurried over to Solomon.

"What did you do, bitch?" he shouted at Curran.

Unable to answer, Curran shrank away from the armed man.

Solomon raised her head, and snarled, "Kill her!"

Evins lifted his weapon and aimed at Dr. Curran.

Curran froze in place.

"Not her!" Torran shouted at Evins. "Don't shoot Curran! Kill Solomon! She's changing into a Scrag!"

Confusion dominated Evins' face. "What the fuck is going on?"

Solomon tossed back her head and screamed.

"She's almost turned!" Torran slapped his hands against the door. "Kill her!"

Evins shifted his gaze from Torran, to Curran, and finally back to Solomon. Hunched over the workstation, Solomon was violently shaking. Then, in a viper-fast movement, she whipped about and screeched.

Raising his weapon, Evins fired at Solomon, but struck her neck. The Scrag surged toward him, knocking his weapon out of his hands as it tried to grab him. The firearm fell to Evins' side, dangling by the strap. Evins shouted, skidding backward as he tried to evade Solomon's reach. The weapon caught on the rungs of the chair. Evins dragged it along with him as he yanked on the strap, trying to reclaim his weapon. Solomon was right on him, ripping at his armor with her hands, howling and snapping her teeth at his face. The chair thudded along the floor after them.

"No, no!" Torran exclaimed when he realized where Evins was headed. Not toward the door out of the room, but the containment chamber.

Evins grabbed the door lock, twisted it, and pulled it open as he tried to get inside with Torran. The chair lugging along after him banged loudly into the door, then wedged into the gap.

"Shit! Shit! Shit!" Evins howled.

Solomon clambered over it and launched herself at Evins.

"You idiot!" Torran lunged forward, grabbed the tab on the strap on Evins' armor and yanked it free.

Holding Solomon at arm's length, Evin shouted in fright as the Scrag continued to attack.

Jerking on the strap, Torran tried to get the weapon free of the chair rungs. Realizing it wasn't going to work, he shoved the chair out of his way and stumbled out into the room. The door to the chamber hissed shut behind him just as Solomon finally sank her teeth into Evins' face.

A second later, the door to the laboratory flew open. Lindsey rushed into the room trailed by her pet drone. In the hallway behind her was a crowd of Scrags. Kicking the door shut behind her, Lindsey took in the chaos in the room.

"Oh shit," she muttered.

"Good to see you too," Torran said, barely able to breathe at the sight of her. Though he had hoped she was somehow alive, the sight of her left him nearly breathless.

"What happened to Dr. Curran?" Lindsey asked, eyeing the bloodied woman.

"Solomon slit her throat," Torran replied. "But she won't die. She infected herself with the same virus as you."

The sadness filling Lindsey's eyes nearly wrenched Torran's heart out of his chest. Unhooking the helmet from her armor, she slid it over her head. "I see...I would kiss you hello, but..."

"If you do, we can both get out of here alive with no problem," he said, and his heart beat so hard in his chest he was convinced it would break his ribs. He was willing to do anything to be with her.

The lights in the helmet flicked on, and when he saw Lindsey's expression, he knew immediately she would refuse him. Since he was not infected with the modified virus, he alone could return to warn The Bastion. Dismay filled him at the realization, but he refused to believe there wasn't another way.

"You need to save the world," she said. "But first, let's save you."

In the moment when Torran told her about Dr. Curran being infected, Lindsey sadly accepted that life had become a little more complicated. It took all her willpower to tug on the helmet, creating a barrier between her and Torran. She wanted nothing more than to kiss him and hold him close, but that desire had to be denied if they were to save the rest of humanity from the plans of the Gaia Cult.

"You need to save the world," she said. "But first, let's save you."

"I see," Torran said, and the hurt in his voice was profound, yet there was understanding in his gaze.

Behind her, the door to the laboratory shuddered under the assault of the Scrags. She didn't have much time before they burst through. The makeshift lab was not a high security room. The door would be breached.

Peering into the containment chamber, Lindsey regarded the two freshly turned Scrags with disdain. "And how did they end up Scrags?"

"I fooled Solomon," Dr. Curran rasped. Dropping her hands, she revealed an ugly slash across her neck. "She cut my throat hoping I'd try to save myself. So I pretended that a vial with ISPV was the modified virus and she fell for it."

"And she took it to save herself." Lindsey watched in amazement as the skin on the scientist's neck knitted itself back together.

"Yes."

"And then you took the real virus?"

Dr. Curran nodded.

"Torran, step away," Lindsey ordered. "Teeny, cover the door in case the Scrags break through it."

"Yes Mother."

Opening the containment chamber, Lindsey fired two shots, killing both Scrags. Dr. Curran had the decency to help her drag the bodies out, then sanitize the chamber. The entire time, she felt Torran watching her and longed to rush into his arms. But with the Scrags pounding on the lab door and possibly about to breach it, she needed him to be safe.

"Torran, get inside," she ordered.

"I'd really rather not," Torran grunted, folding his arms over his chest.

"The Scrags are going to bust down that door, and if you're not in there, you'll end up one of them."

"Make me one of you," Torran replied with a stubborn set to his jaw and his eyes flashing with anger.

"You need to go back to The Bastion and let them know what Gaia Cult is planning, Torran. You need to convince them of the truth. I was hoping Dr. Curran would do it, but..."

"I understand that, Linds. But let's find *another* way."

"Torran, please listen to reason." She'd known Torran would choose to be with her in the dead world, and she'd hoped to send Dr. Curran back with all the evidence she'd compiled, but that option was gone. "We can't let anyone with the modified virus return to The Bastion. You know what would happen."

"Fuck my life," Torran swore fiercely.

"I'm sorry. I am," Lindsey replied.

The wall around the doorway to the lab was starting to display stress cracks.

"I want to be with you." Torran stalked over to her and gripped her arms tightly. Staring at her through the faceplate, his dark eyes were volatile with his unchecked passions. Anger and love poured out of his soul and filled her with remorse.

"She's right, Torran," Dr. Curran croaked out of her healing throat.

"You're not a part of this!" he snapped.

"But she *is,* Torran. She's what I am, and we can't go back to The Bastion." Lindsey sighed and placed her gloved hands on his waist. "Stop being a bullheaded Scot and get in the damn chamber."

"Mother, the Scrags are about to breach our perimeter." The drone sounded worried.

With a gentle push, Lindsey directed Torran into the chamber. He backed into it reluctantly, his hands clinging to her arms. When she tried to draw away, he bent his head to kiss the top of her facemask. His lips left a faint imprint.

"I love you," he said.

The words filled her with both joy and sorrow. "And I love you."

Lindsey shut the containment chamber just as the wall and doorway collapsed under the assault of the Scrags. With grim resolve, she lifted her weapon and started to kill.

Sitting in the containment chamber, Torran waited for Lindsey to return. The gunfire continued for hours as Lindsey and her swarm of drones pushed back the Scrags that had invaded the top floor. Dr. Curran packed her equipment, and when done, sat quietly in a chair, listening to the battle. They didn't speak, which suited Torran just fine.

At last Lindsey returned, and her faithful aerial drone followed in her wake, carrying Torran's stealth suit, helmet, weapon and pack. Lindsey's suit gleamed in the light, and he realized she'd made sure to scrub it down before returning to his side to avoid infecting him.

"Is it clear?" Dr. Curran's throat was nearly completely healed.

"We killed all the ones on the floor, shut the blast door, and did a second sweep. They're all dead."

"And Solomon's people?" Torran asked, glancing at the bodies hidden under a cover in the corner of the lab.

"Dead."

"Good," Dr. Curran said.

Rising to his feet, Torran watched as Lindsey tugged open the door to the containment chamber and handed him the accoutrements of the life he was ready to abandon for her. He reluctantly took the items and started to suit up inside the chamber. While he strapped on his armor, Lindsey transferred items from her pack to his.

"This is all the evidence I compiled, along with some suggestions for further investigation. I also transferred over all the logs from the squads' armor, aerial drones, and Solomon's wristlet."

"So you just weren't killing Scrags for the last few hours," Torran observed.

"No, I wasn't." Lindsey raised her eyes to gaze at him, and he knew it was petty that he was glad she was suffering as much as he was in the face of their separation.

Torran finished suiting up and dangled the helmet from his fingers. "We could just transmit the information. Get close enough to send it to them."

"No." Dr. Curran said sharply. "You need to go back and convince them. Leave no doubt in their minds."

"And we need to be dead. They can't know that we're infected with the same virus as Maria," Lindsey added. "If we were to send a message, then disappear abruptly, it would be too coincidental. It would cause suspicion and they'd search for us."

"They'd suspect we took the virus ourselves and ran away." Dr. Curran adamantly wagged her head. "We need you to be the sole survivor."

Torran winced at the words, and Lindsey rested her gloved hand against his cheek.

"Torran, you need to make sure they believe you. That they will start an investigation."

"Commandant Pierce will listen," Torran replied.

"But she's not the only one that needs to believe," Lindsey said, and he knew she was right.

Kissing the palm of her hand, he wished he could feel flesh and not the glove. "I know." Dragging her into his arms, he rested his head against her helmet. She clung to him in silence and he knew she was crying. At last he pulled away and pressed his hand to her faceplate. She blew a kiss and smiled through her tears.

"Walk me out?" he asked, though he knew already she would.

"Absolutely. I always like our walks. Except the ones where we're being held hostage."

Torran donned his helmet, grabbed his pack and its valuable cargo, and attached his weapon to his armor. As she escorted him to the tiltrotor parked on the pad on the roof, he was stunned to see the many Scrag bodies lying about. He hadn't imagined so many had infiltrated the upper floor and saw the wisdom of her securing him in the containment chamber. Walls and doors were completely demolished under the onslaught of the dead. How easily a horde in The Bastion would destroy the flimsy homes of the citizens. That truth didn't alleviate his dismay at being parted from Lindsey, yet it fortified his determination to fulfill his new mission.

Once they arrived on the roof, Torran gazed up through the gentle snowfall at a sky so black and full of stars, it took his breath away. Clouds sailed over the dark expanse and occasionally obscured the half-smile of the moon. Looking over at Lindsey, he saw she was staring upward, too.

"Beautiful, isn't it?"

"It's different out here," she admitted. "No city lights to muck it up."

"They used to call this the city of love. It was famous for lights and some massive metal sculpture that was blown up by terrorists long, long ago."

"That's a bit lovely and sad at the same time," Lindsey decided, frowning. "But I guess the whole world is that way."

"You'll experience the world alone," he lamented. "Well, I guess not exactly alone. You'll be with *her*."

"No." Lindsey shook her head. "Not with her. I'll find her a nice lab somewhere, reprogram a few drones, and leave her to her work on an inoculation against the Scrags. I can't stand the sight of her."

"So you'll be alone." Torran didn't like the thought of that. "Or will you look for Dwayne and Maria?"

"No," Lindsey said. "Let them find their own way. I'm going home."

"And where's that?"

With a very wide smile, Lindsey answered, "Where you'll be."

The heaviness crushing his heart alleviated in that moment, and raising his eyes to the heavens, said, "Then I'm ready to go."

Through the cottage window, Lindsey gazed toward the greenhouse where Teeny was enthusiastically tending the plants. The little drone was much better at the task than she was and she enjoyed watching it zip around inside the glass structure.

On the horizon, rain was on its way, but it seemed to always be damp in Scotland. Stepping away from the window, she took another long sip of her black coffee. It helped keep the chill out of her bones. Though she was still repairing the cottage, the main area was nice and snug. With flames dancing in the fireplace, it felt cozy even when the wind howled and the rain beat on the windows.

Setting her coffee aside, Lindsey made one more sweep through the downstairs, making sure everything was in its proper place. The combination of restored MacDonald family furnishings and the furniture she'd salvaged from other locations was a little eclectic, but she rather liked it. She had started a new mural of photos from magazines she'd found stored in an old library. She missed the collage of images her father had helped her collect, but her life in The Bastion was over.

She knew Torran had wondered about her collage, but she hadn't been ready to share the story she and her father had constructed over the years of an alternate-world free of Scrags using photos they'd gleaned from The Bastion archives. It had all started on a rainy day when Lindsey had been very ill during a flu outbreak and her father had searched for a way to entertain her. Her father had somehow secured a stack of paper and an old printer and they'd spent hours creating all sorts of adventures of the alternate-world Lindsey, wearing fancy clothes and visiting exotic locales.

"In another world you're wearing a fancy hat," her father had said when he'd pinned the first image of a model in a wide brimmed hat on her childhood wall. "And the streets are lined with trees," he continued, adding another image of a little girl skipping down a sidewalk.

The new collage only had a few images. Touching each image in the new patchwork of photos, Lindsey whispered, "Real-world Lindsey lives in a cottage on the Scottish moors with her faithful dog, who happens to be a drone, and she wears a long leather coat along with bright red rain boots." The last image brought tears to her eyes. It was a printout of an image she'd downloaded from her wristlet. It was of Torran. "And real-world Lindsey won't be alone anymore."

Wiping away a tear, she hurried over to a mirror to check her side swept bangs and short braids. Her hair was growing, which made her feel a bit more human. The braids weren't too ragged, so Lindsey donned a floppy wool hat, her leather jacket and heavy boots. Excitement was bubbling inside her and she could barely contain it.

Exiting the house, she walked along the path that meandered to the wall separating the cottage from the wild moors. Once she reached it, she climbed up, sat on the uneven stones, and gazed toward the mountains. Though the scene was idyllic, her mind was buzzing with concepts, ideas, and plans.

Beverly Curran had finally sent her latest report that morning. The scientist tended to be so engrossed in her work that she'd forgot to send messages through their secure channels, and Lindsey had to hound her for updates. Sometimes Lindsey thought the scientist saw her as nothing more than a specimen. Every week Lindsey had to send a full bio-scan for Dr. Curran's records. The truth was that they still didn't know the full effects of the modified virus or if it would continue to mutate. At first, Lindsey had worried about turning into an Abscrag and occasionally had nightmares about it, but she finally accepted there was nothing she could do but wait and see. When Lindsey had asked Dr. Curran if she really thought she could create an inoculation against the Scrags, Dr. Curran's response was that she had all the time in the world to try. Of course, humanity did not have that much time.

Maria's latest message left on the remote cloud simply stated she and Dwayne were safe. Though Lindsey had entertained the idea revealing her new nature as an Inferi Boon and trying to meet up with them, she decided not to. It was best to keep the Inferi Boon scattered and not all in one place for all their safety.

The powers ruling The Bastion were still dangerous.

Lindsey received regular updates from Commandant Pierce via her remote cloud. Despite all of Torran's hard work, only Legatus Martel had been arrested as part of the Gaia Cult conspiracy.

The Gaia Cult had probably gone underground for the time being and was still a threat.

The Bastion had stopped all excursions into the outside world in the aftermath of the Notre Dame Depot disaster. Elections were soon, and President Cabot didn't want to take any more risks.

Lindsey would do her best to help from afar. Though she now stood outside humanity, she was dedicated to its survival.

Meanwhile, it was time for her to fully embrace her new life.

At first, she didn't see the small aircraft. It resembled a bird coasting the air currents, but then it grew steadily larger. If it had been any other day, she would've scrambled for cover, but today, she stood and waved.

The silver-black aircraft set down not too far from her location, and Lindsey eagerly skipped toward it. The canopy popped open and Torran scrambled out. The sight of him with his long black coat flapping around his lean body, his cowlick springing upward in the wind, and his joyous grin elicited a gleeful laugh from her lips.

At last, he was home.

"I heard you're dead!" she shouted at him as he raced down the path toward her.

"I know! It was tragic! Pneumonia. Of all things!"

"Poor Commandant Pierce having to report such a terrible loss to the public!"

"She seemed really choked up about it! Then there was a blackout and one of the aircraft vanished from the inventory lists. Imagine the incompetence!" Torran ran toward her, his long coat resembling wings.

Lindsey giggled. "Nice escape plan!"

"It was rather fun and exciting."

Lindsey launched herself into Torran's arms and he swung her about.

When Torran set her down, his smile could barely contain his elation. "God, you're beautiful."

Wrapping her arms around his neck, Lindsey clung to him, relishing the smell of his hair and skin, and the feel of him against her body. "I've never been so happy to see a death announcement in my communiques."

Torran set her on her feet and pressed his forehead to hers. "Never been so glad to be dead."

Pressing her hands against his cheeks, she stared into his dark eyes. "I knew you'd come."

"Was there ever any doubt?"

"Never."

Torran's kiss was sweet and passionate. Lindsey relished every caress of his lips and touch of his tongue. When their mouths finally parted, she was flushed and even cheerier than before.

"God, I've been dreaming of that kiss," she admitted.

"I've been dying for it. I feel a little burn in my veins," Torran said, smacking his lips. "Think I'm infected yet? Should we give that another go?"

Grabbing his hand, Lindsey tugged him toward the cottage. "We definitely need another go. But in bed and naked."

"You realize we now need an official name for this thing we have between us," he said with a wicked gleam in his eye as he strolled alongside her.

"We'll think of something eventually," Lindsey assured him. "After all, we have forever."

ABOUT THE AUTHOR

Rhiannon Frater is the award-winning author of over a dozen books, including the As the World Dies zombie trilogy (Tor), as well as independent works such as The Last Bastion of the Living (declared the #1 Zombie Release of 2012 by Explorations Fantasy Blog and the #1 Zombie Novel of the Decade by B&N Book Blog), and other horror novels. She was born and raised a Texan and presently lives in Austin, Texas with her husband and furry children (a.k.a pets). She loves scary movies, sci-fi and horror shows, playing video games, cooking, dyeing her hair weird colors, and shopping for Betsey Johnson purses and shoes.

You can find her online at rhiannonfrater.com
Subscribe to her mailing list at tinyletter.com/RhiannonFrater

A SPECIAL THANKS
TO MY PATRONS:

Erin Hayes
Amy Fournier
Jen Runkle
Susie McHenry
Melissa Keaton
Heather Harrigan
Zack Adamson
Steve Tidd

Lena
Valory P Zeck
Meghan Helmich
Karen & David Fisher
Traci Loya
Christoffer Lernö
Tres Davis

Become a patron of Rhiannon Frater
and gain special incentives at
www.patreon.com/rhiannonfrater

9859609R00163

Printed in Great Britain
by Amazon.co.uk, Ltd.,
Marston Gate.